PENGUIN BOOKS

BRAZZAVILLE BEACH

'[Boyd's] splendid new book . . . Distinctive, unusual
and absorbing'
– Anthony Quinn in the *Independent*

'Boyd's heroine Hope Clearwater sits on
Brazzaville Beach, somewhere in post-colonial
Africa and ponders her own past lives, one fairly
recent, and one more distant . . . Boyd juggles the
three time-zones brilliantly, maintaining the
suspense in each with such skill that this novel, as
intelligent as anything you're likely to read this
year, slips by like a thriller'
– John Morrish in *Time Out*

'An unmistakable supernova with every conceivable
virtue: it is beautifully written, evocative,
compelling, full of humour and, at the same time,
an intricate work of intellectual argument'
– Celia Brayfield in *She*

'The real Africa seeps through these pages, in its
garishness, in its physicality, in the half-sad, half-
comic dereliction of its European technology
wilting in the primeval heat'
– Christopher Hudson in the *Evening Standard*

'Serious, provocative and intelligent, Boyd's writing
is endlessly receptive to ideas and always prepared
to risk emotion'
– Richard Rayner in the *Daily Telegraph*

BRAZZAVILLE BEACH

A NOVEL

—

WILLIAM BOYD

PENGUIN BOOKS
IN ASSOCIATION WITH SINCLAIR-STEVENSON LTD

PENGUIN BOOKS

Published by the Penguin Group
Penguin Books Ltd, 27 Wrights Lane, London W8 5TZ, England
Penguin Books USA Inc., 375 Hudson Street, New York, New York 10014, USA
Penguin Books Australia Ltd, Ringwood, Victoria, Australia
Penguin Books Canada Ltd, 10 Alcorn Avenue, Toronto, Ontario, Canada M4V 3B2
Penguin Books (NZ) Ltd, 182–190 Wairau Road, Auckland 10, New Zealand

Penguin Books Ltd, Registered Offices: Harmondsworth, Middlesex, England

First published in Great Britain by Sinclair-Stevenson Ltd 1990
Published in Penguin Books in association with Sinclair-Stevenson Ltd 1991
13 15 17 19 20 18 16 14

Printed in England by Clays Ltd, St Ives plc
Set in 10/13 pt Monophoto Times

For Susan

'The unexamined life is not worth living.'

SOCRATES

PROLOGUE

I live on Brazzaville Beach. Brazzaville Beach on the edge of Africa. This is where I have washed up, you might say, deposited myself like a spar of driftwood, lodged and fixed in the warm sand for a while, just above the high tide mark.

The beach never had a name until last April. Then they christened it in honour of the famous *Conferençia dos Quadros* that was held a few years ago in Congo Brazzaville in 1964. No one can explain why but, one day, over the laterite road that leads down to the shore, some workmen erected this sign: 'Brazzaville Beach', and written below that, *Conferençia dos Quadros, Brazzaville, 1964*.

It is an indication, some people say, that the government is becoming more moderate, trying to heal the wounds of our own civil war by acknowledging a historic moment in another country's liberation struggle. Who can say? Who ever knows the answers to these questions? But I like the name, and so does everyone else who lives around here. Within a week we were all using it unselfconsciously. Where do you live? On Brazzaville Beach. It seemed entirely natural.

I live on the beach in a refurbished beach house. I have a large cool sitting-room with a front wall of sliding meshed doors that give directly on to a wide sun-deck. There is also a bedroom, a generous bathroom with bath and shower, and a tiny dim kitchen, built on to the back. Behind the house is my garden: sandy, patchy grass, some prosaic shrubs, a vegetable plot and a hibiscus hedge, thick with brilliant flowers.

The beach has seen better days, true, but I feel its years of decline are over. I have neighbours now: the German manager of the bauxite mines – my boss, I suppose – and on the other side a droll, beefy Syrian who runs an import–export business and a couple of Chinese restaurants in the town.

They are only here at weekends, so during the week I have the place more or less to myself. Though I am never alone. There is always someone on the beach: fishermen, volleyball players, itinerants, scavengers. European families come too. The French and the Portuguese, the Germans and the Italians. No men, just wives, many of them pregnant, and noisy young children. The children play, the wives sit and chatter, smoke and sunbathe and scold their kids. If the beach is quiet they will sometimes slyly remove their bikini tops and expose their soft, pallid breasts to the African sun.

Behind my house, beyond the palm grove, is the village – an attenuated shanty town of mud huts and lean-tos, occupying the scrubby strip of ground between the shore and its treeline and the main road to the airport. I live alone – which suits me fine – but there is enough life around to prevent me from ever being lonely.

I even have a boyfriend, now, after a fashion. I suppose you could call him that, although nothing remotely carnal has ever happened between us. We dine together once or twice a week at the Airport Hotel. His

4

name is Gunther Neuffer; he's a shy, morose, lanky man in his mid-thirties with a hearing aid. He is a sales director at the bauxite mines. He has only been here six months but he seems already haggard and tired of Africa, of its rabid energy and bustle, its brutal frustrations and remorseless physicality. He pines for cool, ordered Göttingen, his home town. I remind him of his younger sister, Ulricke, he says. Sometimes I suspect that is the only reason he goes out with me: I am a spectral link with his old life, the ghost of Europe sitting opposite him.

But I mustn't digress: Gunther has no significant part to play in this story. I introduce him only to explain my present circumstances. Gunther gives me work. I earn most of my living working for him as a part-time commercial translator, for which he pays me far too well. Indeed, if it wasn't for Gunther's job I couldn't live on Brazzaville Beach. What I will do when he goes, I have no idea. In the meantime a melancholy meal in the Airport Hotel is no penance.

I love the beach, but sometimes I ask myself, what am I doing here? I'm young, I'm single, I have family in England, I possess all manner of impressive academic qualifications. So why has the beach become my home . . .?

How can I explain it to you? I am here because two sets of strange and extraordinary events happened to me, and I needed some time to weigh them up, evaluate them. I have to make sense of what has taken place, before I can restart my life in the world, as it were. Do you know that feeling? That urge to call a temporary halt, to say: enough, slow down, give me a break.

Two sequences of events, then. One in England, first,

and then one in Africa. Two stories to tell. I fled to Africa to escape what happened in England and then, as the continent will, it embroiled me further.

But that's not the way to start.

Another problem: how do I begin? How do I tell you what happened to me?

My name is Hope Clearwater ... Or, 'Hope Clearwater is that tall young woman who lives on Brazzaville Beach.' It's not so easy. Which voice do I use? I was different then; and I'm different now.

I am Hope Clearwater. She is Hope Clearwater. Everything is me, really. Try to remember that, though it might be a little confusing at first.

Where shall I begin? In Africa, I think, yes, but far from Brazzaville Beach.

A final note: the important factor in all this is honesty, otherwise there would be no point in beginning.

So: let's start with that day I was with Clovis. Just the two of us. Yes, that's a good place ...

BRAZZAVILLE BEACH

I never really warmed to Clovis, he was far too stupid to inspire real affection, but he always claimed a corner of my heart, largely – I suppose – because of the way he instinctively and unconsciously cupped his genitals whenever he was alarmed or nervous. It was rather endearing, I thought, and it showed a natural vulnerability, in strong contrast to his usual moods: raffish arrogance or total and single-minded self-absorption. In fact, he was self-absorbed now as he sat grandly at ease, frowning, pursing and unpursing his lips – completely ignoring me – and from time to time sniffing absent-mindedly at the tip of a forefinger. He had been similarly occupied for upwards of an hour now and whatever he had stuck his finger into earlier that day had obviously been fairly potent, not to say narcotic and ineradicable. Knowing Clovis as I did, I suspected he could maintain this inertia for ages. I looked at my watch. If I went back now it might mean talking to that little swine Hauser ... I debated the pros and cons: spend the remaining hour I had left to me here with Clovis or risk enduring Hauser's cynical gossip, all silky insinuation and covert bitchery?

Should I tell you about Hauser now, I wonder? No, perhaps not; Hauser and the others will engage us as we meet them. They can wait awhile; let us return to Clovis.

I changed my position, uncrossed my legs and stretched them out in front of me. A small ant seemed to have trapped itself under the strap of my brassière and I spent a few awkward minutes trying vainly to locate it. Clovis impassively watched me remove first my shirt and then my bra. I found no insect but discovered its traces – a neat cluster of pink bites under my left armpit. I rubbed spit on them and replaced my clothes. As I did up the top button on my shirt, Clovis seemed to lose interest in me. He slapped his shoulder once, brusquely, and clambered into the mulemba tree beneath which he had been sitting and with powerful easy movements he swung through the branches, leapt on to an adjacent tree and was away, lost to sight, heading north-east towards the hills of the escarpment.

I looked at my watch again and noted the time of his departure. Perhaps now he was going to rejoin the other members of his group? It was not unheard of for Clovis to spend a day on his own but it was out of the ordinary – he was gregarious, even by chimpanzee standards. I had been watching him for three hours, during which time he had done almost nothing singular or unusual – but then that too was worth recording, of course. I stood up and stretched and walked to the mulemba tree to examine Clovis's faeces. I took out a little specimen bottle from my bag and, with a twig, collected some. That would be my present for Hauser.

I walked back down the path that led me in the general direction of the camp. A large proportion of the trails in this part of the forest had been recently cleared and the going was easy. I had had markers and direction arrows nailed to trees at important intersections to help me find my way about. This portion of the reserve, south of the big stream, was far less familiar than the main research area to the north.

I walked at a steady even pace – I was in no particular hurry to get back, and in any event was reasonably tired. The real force of the afternoon's heat had passed; I could see the sun on the topmost branches of the trees but down here on the forest floor all was dim shadow. I enjoyed these walks home at the end of the day and I preferred the confined vistas of the forest to more impressive panoramas – I liked being hemmed in, rather than exposed. I liked the vegetation close to me, bushes and branches brushing my sides, the frowsty smell of decaying leaves and the filtered, screened neutrality of the light.

As I walked I took out a cigarette. It was a Tusker, a local brand, strong and sweet. As I lit it and drew in the smoke I thought of my ex-husband, John Clearwater. This was the most obvious legacy of our short marriage – a bad habit. There were others, of course, other legacies, but they were not visible to the naked eye.

João was waiting for me, about a mile from camp. He sat on a log picking at an old scab on his knee. He looked tired and not very well. João was very black, his skin almost a dark violet colour. He had a long top lip that made him look permanently sad and serious. He rose to his feet as I approached. We greeted each other and I offered him a cigarette which he accepted and carefully stored in his canvas bag.

'Any luck?' I asked.

'I think, I think I see Lena,' he said. 'She very big now.' He held out his hands, shaping a pregnant belly. 'She come very soon now. But then she run from me.'

He gave me his field notes and I told him about my

uneventful day with Clovis as we strolled back to camp. João was my full-time assistant. He was in his forties, a thin, wiry man, diligent and loyal. We were training his second son, Alda, as an observer, but he was away today in the city, trying to sort out some problem to do with his military service. I asked how Alda was progressing.

'I think he will return tomorrow,' João said. 'They say the war is finish soon, so no more soldiers are required.'

'Let's hope so.'

We talked a little about our plans for the next day. Soon we reached the small river that Mallabar – I think – had whimsically named 'the Danube'. It was fed from the damp grasslands high on the plateau to the east, and descended in a series of pools and falls in a long deepish valley through our portion of the Semirance Forest, and then moved on, more sedately and ever broadening, until it met the great Cabule River a hundred and fifty miles away on the edge of the coastal plain.

Beyond the Danube, to the north, the forest thinned out and the walk to the camp cut through what is known in this part of Africa as orchard bush: grass and scrubland, badged with occasional copses of trees and small groves of palms. The camp itself had been on this site for over two decades and, as it had become established, most of its buildings had been reconstructed in more permanent form. Canvas had given way to wood and corrugated iron, which was in turn being replaced by concrete bricks. The various sheds and dwelling-places were set generously far apart and were situated on either side of a dirt road that was known as Main

Street. However, the first sign of human habitation you came across, as you approached the camp from the direction of the Danube, was a wide cleared area, about the size of three tennis courts, in the middle of which was a low concrete structure – hip-high – with four small wooden doors set in one side. It looked like some sort of cage or, I used to think, something to do with sewerage or septic tanks, but in fact it was the research project's pride and joy: the Artificial Feeding Area. It was deserted now, as João and I passed it, but I thought I saw someone sitting in one of the palm frond hides at the perimeter – Mallabar himself, possibly. We kept on going.

The camp proper began at the junction of the forest path (that led south to the Danube) with Main Street, which was itself just an extension of the road from Sangui, the nearest village, and where João and most of the project's assistants and observers lived. We stopped here, arranged to meet at 6.00 a.m. the next day and said goodbye. João said he would bring Alda if he had returned from the city in time. We went our separate ways.

I sauntered through the camp towards my hut. On my left, scattered amongst nim and palm trees and big clumps of hibiscus hedge, were the most important buildings in the camp complex – the garage and work-shops, Mallabar's bungalow, the canteen, the kitchen and storage sheds, and beyond them the now abandoned dormitory of the census workers. Beyond that, over to the right, I could just see, through a screen of plumbago hedge, the round thatched roofs of the cooks' and small boys' quarters.

I continued past the huge hagania tree that dominated

the centre of the camp and which had given it its name: grosso arvore. The Grosso Arvore Research Centre.

On the other side of the track, opposite the canteen, was Hauser's laboratory and behind that was the tin cabin he shared with Toshiro. Thirty yards along from the lab was the Vails' bungalow, not as big as *chez* Mallabar but prettier, freighted with jasmine and bougainvillaea. And then, finally, at the camp's northern extremity, was my hut. In fact 'hut' was a misnomer: I lived in a cross between a tent and a tin shack, a curious dwelling with canvas sides and a corrugated iron roof. I suppose it was fitting that it should go to me, on the principle that the newest arrival should occupy the least permanent building, but I was not displeased with it and was indifferent to what it might say about my status. In fact Mallabar had offered me the census hut but I had declined; I preferred my odd, hybrid tent and its position out on the perimeter.

I reached it and went inside. Liceu, the boy who looked after me, had tidied up in my absence. From the oil drum of water in a corner I poured a few jugfuls into a tin basin set upon a stand, took off my shirt and bra, and washed my sweaty, dirty torso with a flannel. I dried myself down and pulled on a T-shirt. I contemplated a visit to the long-drop latrine outside, housed in a structure that looked like a sentry box woven from palm fronds, but decided it could wait.

I lay down on my camp bed, closed my eyes and, as always when I returned home at the end of the day, tried not to let my feelings overwhelm me. I arranged my day and my routine in such a manner as not to leave myself with much time alone and little to do, but this moment of the early evening, the light milky and orange, with the first bats jinking and swooping between the trees, and the tentative *creek-creek* of the crickets announcing the onset of dusk, always brought in its train a familiar melancholy and *cafard* and, in my particular case, an awful self-pity. I forced myself to sit up, took some deep breaths, inveighed powerfully against the name of John Clearwater, and went to sit at the little trestle desk where I worked. There, I poured myself a glass of scotch whisky and wrote up my field notes.

My desk was set in front of a netting window in the canvas side wall which I rolled up to let in as much breeze as possible. Through it I had a view of the back of Hauser and Toshiro's cabin, some eighty yards away, the matting sentry box of his latrine and the wooden shower stall that Hauser had personally constructed beneath a frangipani tree. The shower was an elementary contraption: the shower rose was fed from an oil drum set higher in the tree, the flow controlled by a spigot. The only onerous task was the filling of the oil drum, buckets of water had to be lugged up to it by ladder, but that was a job Hauser was happy to leave to his houseboy, Fidel.

As I watched, the door in the shower stall opened and Hauser himself appeared, naked and glossy. Clearly, he had forgotten to bring a towel. I watched him tread carefully across the prickly grass to his back door. The tight dome of his big belly gleamed and the little white stub of his penis waggled comically as he flinched his way to safety. Hauser did this quite often – that is, wandered naked to and fro from shower stall to cabin. He had a full view of my tent with its windowed sides. It had crossed my mind several times that he might be deliberately exposing himself.

The sight of Hauser's little penis and the taste of the scotch combined to cheer me up and it was with restored confidence that an hour later I walked down Main Street towards the canteen, now lit with the blurry glow of hurricane lamps. As I passed his cabin, Hauser emerged.

'Ah, Mrs Clearwater. Such timing.'

Hauser was bald and thickset – a strong fat man – and his eyes were dull and slightly hooded. In the months I had been at Grosso Arvore our relations had never advanced beyond mutual guardedness. I suspected that he didn't like me. Certainly, I didn't warm to him at all. As we walked together to the canteen I gave him the specimen bottle full of Clovis's faecal matter.

'Could you find out what this one's eating?' I asked him. 'I think he might have been ill.'

'An *amuse-gueule*.' He inspected the bottle. 'Chimp shit, my favourite.'

'You don't have to if you don't want to.'

'But this is what I'm here for, my dear young lady: handsomely paid haruspication.'

This was exactly the sort of fake-donnish banter I couldn't stand. I gave Hauser a look of what I hoped was candid pity and pointedly turned away from him as we entered the canteen. I collected my tray and knife and fork and the cook served me up with a plateful of boiled chicken and sweet potato. I went to the end of the long table and sat down beside Toshiro, who nodded hello. We were free to return to our own quarters with our food if we wished, but I invariably ate in the canteen because of the length of the journey back. One blessing was that there was no requirement, official or unofficial, to make conversation. With the members of

16

the project so reduced it would have provoked unbearable tensions if we had felt obliged to indulge in small talk every time we met. Toshiro, taciturn at the best of times, munched on pragmatically. Hauser was arguing with the cook. No one else had arrived. I started my bland chicken with little enthusiasm.

In due course the other members of the project drifted in. First came Ian Vail and his wife Roberta. They said hello and then took their trays back to their cottage. Then Eugene Mallabar himself entered, collected his food and sat down opposite me.

Even his most embittered enemy would have to concede that Mallabar was a handsome man. He was in his late forties, tall and lean, with a kind, regular-featured face that seemed naturally to emanate all manner of potent abstract nouns: sincerity, integrity, single-mindedness. For some reason his too neatly trimmed warlock's beard, and its associations of substantial personal vanity, did not detract from this dauntingly positive air he possessed. Tonight he wore a faded blue polka-dot cravat at his throat which set off his tan admirably.

'Where's Ginga?' I asked, trying not to stare at him. Ginga was his wife, whom I quite liked, despite her stupid name.

'Not hungry, she says. Touch of flu - perhaps.' He shrugged and forked chicken generously into his mouth. He chewed lazily, almost side to side, as if he were eating cud. He used his tongue a lot, pushing his food against his palate, searching for morsels around his molars. I knew this because I could see it: Mallabar ate without closing his mouth properly.

'How was your day?' I asked, looking down at my plate.

'Excellent, excellent . . .' I heard him drinking water and wondered when it would be safe to look up. 'Mmmm,' he went on, 'we had five in the Feeding Area. Four males and a female in oestrus. Fascinating series of copulations.'

'Just my luck.' I snapped my fingers in parody disappointment.

'What d'you mean?'

'Ah.' I felt an immediate and intense weariness descend on me. 'You know: I'm in the south. All that fun going on here.'

He frowned, puzzled, still not with me.

'It's not important,' I said. 'Forget it. So Ginga's got flu?'

'We have it on film.'

'What?'

'Today. At the feeding area.'

'No, Eugene. Please. It doesn't matter.'

He smiled slyly, nodding. 'All right. Got it. You were teasing me.'

'Look, Eugene . . . Oh God.'

He was snapping his fingers. 'Just your luck. Got it.'

I felt my neck muscles knot. Jesus Christ.

He forced out a long chuckle and ate on, hugely.

'How was your day?' he said after a while.

'Oh . . . Clovis smelt his finger for a couple of hours.'

'Clovis?' He shook his fork at me.

'XNM1. Sorry.'

Mallabar smiled benignly at my error, stood up and went to refill his plate. Mallabar was one of those people who could eat as much as they liked and remain thin. As he moved to the buffet he passed Ian Vail who was returning with his tray for the pudding of sliced mangoes and condensed milk. Vail smiled at me. It was a nice smile. The adjective was exact. He had a nice face too, only a little plump, with pale eyelashes and fine blond hair. He put his tray down, came over and squatted close by me.

'Can I come and see you?' he said, softly, so Toshiro wouldn't hear. 'Later. Please? Just to talk.'

'No. Go away.'

He looked at me: his eyes were full of rebuke for my coldness. I stared back. He stood up and left. Mallabar returned with a heaped plate. He watched Vail leave before sitting down.

'Are you going with Ian tomorrow?' he asked.

'NO,' I said, too abruptly. 'No, I'm back in the south.'

'I thought he was planning to invite you.' Mallabar was eating vigorously again. I watched him with genuine fascination. Why had no one ever told him, I wondered, that he ate with his mouth open? I supposed it was too late to change, now.

'I don't know,' I said.

'What was he saying to you, then? It was very brief.'

'Who?' I said ingenuously. Mallabar was notoriously curious about his colleagues.

'Ian. Just then.'

'Oh . . . That he was passionately in love with me.'

Mallabar's mobile face stopped.

I looked at him: head cocked, open-faced, eyebrows raised.

He smiled with relief.

'Good one,' he said. 'Excellent.'

He laughed hard, showing me more of the contents of his mouth. He drank water, coughed, drank some more.

Hauser stared curiously at me from the other end of the table.

'Ah, my dear Hope,' Mallabar said and touched my hand. 'You're incorrigible.' He raised his glass to me. 'To Hope, our very own tonic.'

WHAT I LIKE TO DO

What I like to do with him is this. We are lying in bed, it doesn't matter when, at night or in the morning, but he is warm and drowsy, half asleep and I am awake. I lie close to him, my breasts flattened against his back, his buttocks press against my thighs, my knees fitting his knee backs, his heels on my insteps.

Without much ado I slide my hand over his hip and hold him, very gently. His penis is soft and flaccid. So light in my palm. Light as a coin – a weight, a presence merely, but that is all. For a while nothing happens. Then the warmth of my cradling fingers slowly makes him grow. That fleshy inflation, the warmth now transferring back to me with the exothermic flush of blood irrigating the muscle tissue. This power I have, this magic transformation that my touch effects, never fails to excite me. Engorged, thickening, veined like a leaf, it slowly pushes through the loose cage of my fingers, and he turns to face me.

Hope Dunbar had heard people talking about John Clearwater in college for some time before she met him.

Clearwater.

The name stuck in her head. Clearwater ... She

recognized its reoccurrence in conversations several times without taking in its context.

'Who is this Clearwater everyone's talking about?' she asked her supervisor, Professor Hobbes.

'John Clearwater?'

'I don't know. I just keep hearing the name.'

'He's the new research fellow, isn't he? I think that's the one.'

'I don't know.'

'Incredibly brilliant man, that sort of thing. Or so they say. But then they always say that. I'm sure we've all been "incredibly brilliant" in our time.' He paused. 'What about him?'

'Nothing. Just curious about the name.'

John Clearwater.

A few days later she saw a man in her street with a folded newspaper in his hand looking up at the houses. He wore a gaberdine raincoat and a red baseball hat. He looked up at the façades of the terraced houses curiously, as if he were thinking of buying them, then he turned away.

Hope had rounded the corner off the Old Brompton Road and he was headed in the opposite direction, so she never managed a proper look at him. It was the conjunction of the raincoat and the baseball hat that made him singular in some way. The thought came to her, unbidden, that this man might have been John Clearwater.

Two days after this encounter she was walking along an unfamiliar corridor in the college (she had been up to the computing department to collect a print-out for Professor Hobbes) when she passed a door that was open by about six inches. The name on it was 'DR J. L.

CLEARWATER'. She stopped and peered in. From where she was standing she could see a corner of vermilion college-issue carpet and a bare wall with Sellotape scars.

For some reason, and with untypical presumption, she took a step forward and pushed the door wide.

The room was empty. Clouds in the sky shifted and the spring sunshine suddenly painted a yellow window on the wall. Dust motes still moved, unsettled recently.

On the floor were a dozen cardboard boxes filled with books. The desk was clear. She went round it and opened two drawers. A chain of paper clips. An olive-green paper puncher. Three boiled sweets. She searched the other drawers. Empty. A tension and baffled excitement was beginning to quicken inside her. What was she doing in this man's room? What was she playing at?

On the soft chair in the corner was a coat. A woollen coat, charcoal-grey herringbone. Then on the mantelpiece above the gas fire she saw a mug of coffee.

Steaming.

She touched it. Hot.

Her mouth was dry now as she picked up the coat and went through the pockets. A pair of sheepskin gloves. A small plastic bottle of pills marked *Tylenol*. Some change.

There was a noise at the door.

She turned. Nothing. No one. It swung mysteriously on its hinges, an inch or two, shifted by some nomadic breeze roaming the building.

She laid the coat back on the chair. *John Clearwater*, she heard teasingly in her head, *John Clearwater, where aaaaare you?* Her eyes flicked around the room looking for something – she wasn't entirely sure what. She wasn't entirely sure what weird motives were making her behave in this way.

She picked up the mug of coffee and sipped it. Strong and sweet. Three spoonfuls of sugar, she would guess. She put it back down. The pink lipstick crescent of her lower lip was printed on the rim.

She turned the mug so her trace was unmissable, and left.

There was another sighting, she thought. Again, she could not say why her instinct was so emphatic, but she was sure that this was her man. She deliberately did not seek him out, but she found that as she wandered through the precincts of the college, going about her business, she was evaluating, unconsciously, every strange male face she encountered. She had an absolute confidence that she would recognize him.

Then, one evening, she was at an off-licence buying a bottle of wine, *en route* for a friend's dinner party. The place was busy and there was a queue at both tills. Her bottle was wrapped in tissue, but when she presented her ten pound note it was discovered that there wasn't sufficient change. While the attendant burrowed in the adjacent till for a fresh supply of coins her attention was suddenly attracted by a man leaving the shop.

He was at the door, on his way out, when she turned. He was bareheaded, dark-haired and wearing a biscuit-coloured tweed jacket. From each pocket protruded a bottle of red wine. Under his right arm he carried an untidy bundle of books and papers. The weight of the bottles stretched the material of his jacket across his broad shoulders. She thought, first: that's one way to ruin a jacket. And then, almost immediately: that's John Clearwater. He left the shop and moved out of sight.

The sales assistant laboriously counted out her change. By the time Hope was outside there was no sign of him. She felt no frustration; she knew it had been him. And she felt quietly sure that she would meet him, eventually. There was time enough.

And she was right. It took a little longer than she had calculated, but their respective trajectories finally touched at a faculty party. She saw him standing by the drinks table and knew at once it was him. She was almost drunk, but it was not alcohol that gave her the confidence to push through the room and introduce herself. The time had come, it was as simple as that.

THE MOCKMAN

Pan troglodytes. *Chimpanzee. The name was first used in 1738 in the* London Magazine. *'... A most surprising creature was brought over that was taken in a wood in Guinea. She is the female of the creature which the Angolans call "Chimpanzee", or the Mockman.'*

The Mockman.

Chimpanzees can, without encouragement, develop a taste for alcohol. When Washoe – a chimp reared with a human family and taught deaf and dumb sign language – was first introduced to live chimpanzees, and was asked what they were, he signed, 'Black Bugs.' Chimpanzees use tools and can teach other chimpanzees how to use them. Chimpanzees have pined away and died from broken hearts ...

Genetically, chimpanzees are the closest living relatives to human beings. When genetic matches were made of chimp and human DNA it was found that they differed *only by a factor of $1\frac{1}{2}$ to 2 per cent. In the world of taxonomy this means that chimpanzees and human beings are species siblings and, strictly speaking, the classification should really be changed. We belong to the same genus – Homo. Not Pan troglodytes, then, but Homo troglodytes and Homo sapiens. The Mockmen.*

I was eating my breakfast – a mug of milky tea and a drab slice of bread and margarine – when João arrived, Alda accompanying him. Alda was slim, like his father, eighteen years old and, oddly, with much lighter-toned skin, almost caramel-coloured. He had a big, open face and an attentive air, as if he were curious about everything he saw. He was not particularly bright, but he was very keen. I asked him what had happened about his military service.

'No, no,' he said with a relieved grin. 'Too many soldiers now. War he finish soon.'

'Oh yes?' This was news to me. 'What do you think?' I asked João.

He was less sanguine. 'I don' know.' He shrugged. 'They say UNAMO is finish . . . But you still remain with FIDE and EMLA.'

'UNAMO *is* finish,' Alda said with some emphasis. 'They catch them at Luso, near the railway. Kill plenty plenty.'

'Who caught them?'

'The Federals . . . and FIDE.' He made diving sounds, his caramel hands swooping. 'Gasoline bombs.'

I reflected on this. 'I thought FIDE was against the Federals.'

'Yes, they are,' Alda said patiently, 'but they both don't like UNAMO.'

'I give up,' I said. 'Let's go.'

It was cool this early in the morning, sometimes I thought I saw my breath condense, just for an instant. The sky was white and opaque with misty cloud, the light even and shadowless. A heavy dew on the grass turned my dun leather boots chocolate in seconds. We walked through the silent camp, heading south.

As we passed Hauser's cabin I heard my name called. I turned. Hauser stood in the doorway wearing an unattractively short, towelling dressing-gown.

'Glad I caught you,' he said. He handed me back my specimen bottle, clean and empty. 'Most amusing. Did you think it up by yourself or did that genius Vail help you?'

'What're you talking about?' I said coldly. I can be as frosty as the best of them.

'Your feeble joke.' He pointed at the specimen bottle. 'For your information, the last meal your chimp enjoyed appeared to be a chimpburger.' His thin false smile disappeared. 'Don't waste my time, Dr Clearwater.'

He went back into his cabin, haughtily. João and Alda looked at me with eager surprise: they rarely witnessed our arguments in the camp. I raised my shoulders, spread my palms and looked baffled. This needed further thought. We set off once more.

Eugene Mallabar had started the Grosso Arvore Research Project in 1953. It began modestly, as a field study to flesh out some chapters in his doctoral thesis. But the work fascinated him and he stayed on. He was joined two years later by his wife, Ginga. Between them their investigations into the society of wild chimpanzees, and their scrupulous and original field studies, soon brought scientific acclaim and increasing public renown. This became genuine celebrityhood, on Mallabar's part, when he published his first book, *The Peaceful Primate*, in 1960. Television films and documentaries followed and Grosso Arvore, along with its telegenic founder, thrived and grew. Research grants multiplied, eager PhD students offered their services and government influence broke through the hitherto impenetrable barriers of red tape that had stood in the way of real expansion. Soon Grosso Arvore became a pioneering national park and game reserve, amongst the first in Africa. Then came the international success of Mallabar's next book, *Primate's Progress*. Invitations, citations and honours followed; Mallabar became the recipient of a baker's dozen of honorary doctorates; there was a biennial cycle of lucrative lecture tours in America and Europe; Mallabar chairs in Primatology were established in Berlin, Florida and New Mexico. Eugene Mallabar's place in the annals of science and ethology was secure.

The essence of the Mallabar approach to the study of chimpanzee society was painstaking and time-consuming. Its first and key requirement was that the observer habituate himself with the apes he was studying so that they accepted his presence in their world without fear or inhibition. Once that had been achieved (it had taken Mallabar almost two years) then the next stage was to observe and record. Over the years of the project this process had evolved into something highly organized and systematic and vast amounts of data were gathered and analysed. All observations were logged in a uniform way; chimps were identified, followed, and their biographies were steadily compiled and annotated over the years. The result was that, over two decades on from Mallabar's initial studies, the Grosso Arvore project now represented the most exhaustive and thorough study of *any* animal society in the history of scientific investigation.

Mallabar was not alone, of course: there were other celebrated primate studies going on as well in Africa – at Gombe Stream, at Mahale National Park, at Bossou in Guinea – but there was no doubt that Mallabar, and Grosso Arvore, had the highest profile and attracted, thanks to the allure and skill of its founder, a reputation that could only be described as glamorous.

In this long catalogue of success and glory Mallabar had made one important error – but it was one he could not have foreseen, to do him justice. He had chosen the wrong country. The civil war which began in 1968 brought massive problems, not to say occasional danger. Happily, the fighting that took place was always at a safe distance, but there remained always the threat of sudden upheavals and breakouts from enclaves. The crude violence employed by the four armies contesting power, and the unpredictable nature of their fortunes, meant that the old days of glossy magazine stories, cover features and TV documentaries were over. The census of the chimpanzee population of the Semirance Forest (a very expensive and ambitious undertaking) was the first casualty of the unrest once the supply of PhD students dried up. Work permits and visas for the remaining scientists became far harder to come by, and all manner of provisions became unobtainable as international opinion and superpower muscle-flexing imposed official or unofficial economic sanctions. Worse

28

still, the uncompromising savagery of the Federal Government's attempts to crush the competing guerrilla factions drew mounting condemnation and opprobrium from the West. The supply of grants and awards – the fuel upon which Grosso Arvore ran – began to dwindle alarmingly. Eugene Mallabar and Grosso Arvore found themselves attached, by association, to a bankrupt regime with an unsavoury international reputation. Mallabar, needless to say, protested everywhere that the interests of scientific research had nothing to do with politics, but to little avail.

But good times, he said in his inimitable fashion, were just over the next hill. Lately, a UN resolution had been ratified and widely supported. The most radical of the guerrilla armies, UNAMO, appeared to be terminally underaided and the other two – FIDE and EMLA – began to talk vaguely of reconciliation. Thus prompted, the Federal Government started to make noises of appeasement and hatchet-burying. Suddenly there was a little new money available, but still – despite all the peace-mongering in the air – nobody was prepared to take up the short-term job it was meant to fund. Until, that is, I came along. What made me do it? I shall tell you about that in due course.

Mallabar had a new book almost completed, a summation of his life's work. It was destined to be his *chef d'oeuvre*, the last word on chimpanzee society and what the years of work at the Grosso Arvore project had taught mankind about his closest biological cousin. It was also designed as the crowning celebration of Grosso Arvore's silver jubilee: we were securely placed on the scientific map, but the new book was designed to etch Grosso Arvore's name in stone.

But as the book was in its final stages there had been a mystifying schism in the chimpanzee tribe that Mallabar had documented so thoroughly. For some unknown reason, a small group of chimpanzees had broken away from the main unit, had migrated south out of the Grosso Arvore park and had established themselves in an area of the forest not hitherto covered by the research project. Why had they left? Was this important? Did it signify something crucial and unrecognized in the evolution of chimpanzee society? A new job was funded to try and answer these questions. It fell to me to observe this small breakaway group – the southerners, as they were known – and continue the documentation of their daily lives until the book was ready, and to see if there was any explanation forthcoming for their untimely departure. 'And besides,' Mallabar had said in – for him – a rare moment of anthropomorphism, 'they are family. We would like to know why they left us and how they are getting on.'

João left me and Alda and set off in the rough direction Clovis had taken the day before. Alda and I planned to go to a large fig tree where the southern group often fed. We followed a winding path through the humid undergrowth. The seasonal rains were expected soon and the air was heavy with moisture, warm and stagnant. We walked at an easy pace, but I was soon sweating, and waving futilely at the platoons of flies that escorted us. Alda walked in front of me, the dark triangle of perspiration on his pink T-shirt pointing the way.

The fig tree proved to be empty apart from a small

troupe of colobus monkeys. But in the distance, not too far off, I could hear the sound of the excited hooting and screaming of chimpanzees. Another fig tree grew in an outcrop of rocks about half a mile away. From the noise that was being generated it sounded as if the whole southern group might be there.

It took us half an hour to reach it. Alda and I approached with our usual caution; I led the way. I sank to my haunches about forty yards from the tree and took out my binoculars. I saw: Clovis, Mr Jeb, Rita-Mae with her baby Lester, Muffin and Rita-Lu ... Alda ticked their names off on the daily analysis sheet as I recited them. No sign of Conrad. No sign of pregnant Lena.

They were sitting high in the branches of the fig tree, a partially leafless *Ficus mucosae* that at some juncture, I guessed, had been hit by lightning. Half of the tree was dead, stuck in a permanent winter, while the other half, as if in compensation, flourished vigorously. The chimps foraged idly on the ripe red fruit. They seemed content and unconcerned. I wondered what had made them scream.

Alda and I settled down for a long period of observation, our analysis sheets ready, our field journals open. The chimps glanced at us from time to time but otherwise ignored us – they were thoroughly habituated to observers. Through my binoculars I studied them all individually. I knew them and their personalities, I felt, as well as I knew my family. There was Clovis, the alpha male of the group, with his unusually thick, dense fur. Mr Jeb, an old male, bald-headed with a grey goatee and a withered arm. Rita-Mae, a strong mature female, with patchy brown hair. Rita-Lu, her daughter, an almost mature adolescent. Rita-Mae's son was Muffin, an adolescent, a nervous, neurotic chimp who was only happy in his mother's presence and who had been deeply upset by the arrival of her new baby, Lester. The two members of the group who were missing were Conrad and Lena. Conrad was an adult male, whose eyeballs around the iris were white, not brown, a feature that gave him a disconcertingly human gaze. Lena was heavily pregnant, by whom I had no idea. She was a lone female who had attached herself to this southern group. Sometimes she travelled with them for a few days but she always left of her own accord after a while, to reappear up to a week or so later. She kept herself somewhat aloof, on the fringes of the group, but they seemed to accept her comings and goings without fuss.

We watched the chimps for over two hours. Muffin groomed Rita-Mae. Rita-Lu left the tree for twenty minutes and returned. The troop of colobus monkeys – from the first fig tree, I supposed – passed nearby. The chimps barked at them. Clovis displayed aggressively, shaking branches, the hair on his body erect. Later Mr Jeb tried, half-heartedly, to copulate with Rita-Lu, who was partially in oestrus, but she drove him away. Lester played with his mother and brother. And so the time wore on, an average chimp day: feeding, grooming, relaxing, with a certain amount of aggression and sex.

And then they seemed to have eaten their fill. Rita-Mae picked up Lester, slung him on her back and slid down one of the huge buttressing roots of the fig tree to the ground. Slowly the others followed. They prowled around the foot of the tree for a while, munching on some fallen figs. Then baby Lester slipped off his mother's back and ran off to tug and pull at what looked like a tangle of rotting vegetation. Rita-Lu scampered after him, snatched the bundle away and flailed it violently up and down, making loud waa-bark noises as she did so. Through my binoculars I could see that the object she was flinging about was limp, but solid, like a very oily rag, say, or a dead fish.

She soon lost interest, however, as she saw the other members of the group moving out of the fig tree clearing, and threw the bundle away as she ran to follow them.

'We go?' Alda said. Normally we would spend the rest of the day trailing the group.

'No. Wait,' I said. Something about that bundle intrigued me. We picked our way over the rocks to where Rita-Lu had flung it. Alda crouched down and prodded it with a twig.

'Baboon,' he said. 'Baby baboon.'

The tiny carcass was half eaten. Most of the head was gone, as was the chest and stomach. Two legs and an arm remained. A gleam of thin white ribs, like the teeth of a comb, shone through blackening membrane. The pale body, a bloodless bluey grey, was covered in the finest down. It looked distressingly human.

A dead baby baboon, eaten by chimpanzees, was not extraordinary. Chimps would eat baby monkeys, duiker, bush pigs, anything they could catch . . . But I knew this wasn't a baby baboon. This was the corpse of an infant chimpanzee, a few days old.

We have been aware for a long time now that chimpanzees are not pure vegetarians, like gorillas. In London Zoo, in 1883, a chimp called Sally was observed to catch and eat a pigeon that had flown into her cage, and she continued to feast on any curious bird that hopped in looking for pickings. Indeed, Mallabar's own work here at Grosso Arvore had done much to establish the different types of meat that chimps consumed, and revealed for the first time their predatory nature. Mallabar was the first person ever to observe and photograph chimpanzees hunting monkeys. In a memorable film he shot, the world saw a group of adult chimpanzees organize themselves into a hunting party, chase, capture and consume a baby bush pig. Chimpanzees liked eating meat – people were very surprised to learn – and chimps hunted and killed in order to get it. It made them less lovable, less gentle, perhaps, but more human.

I walked around the rocks and the blasted fig tree and I thought of the way Rita-Lu had thrashed the ground with the tattered remains of this baby. I wondered what Eugene Mallabar would make of this. Alda waited patiently for me.

After a minute or two I told him to put the corpse in a plastic bag and seal it. As he did so, I examined the ground beneath the fig tree and collected samples of faeces in my specimen bottles. As I labelled them I tried to keep my thoughts calm and rational. What I had here was some very interesting evidence, but the case it made was highly circumstantial . . . First, there was the meat in Clovis's faeces. Second, the half-eaten corpse of a baby chimp, two or three days old. Third, the gleeful aggression Rita-Lu had displayed towards the corpse. And fourth? Fourth, the possibility of more meat traces in the faecal matter just collected. What did that add up to? I checked my natural excitement: softly, softly, I thought.

Then there was the baby. Whose baby? Lena's? It was possible, she was due to give birth any day. But if so, how did the baby die? And what had eaten it? And why? And why had Rita-Lu behaved in such a way? I stopped myself from further unprofitable speculation. We needed more facts, more data. I sent Alda off to find João and said that both of them should try to locate Lena, find out if she had given birth and if her infant was with her. I picked up the plastic bag with the dead baby in it – so light – and headed back to Grosso Arvore.

I stood in Hauser's lab. The simple building, a rectangular, corrugated iron shack, contained a small but surprisingly efficient and well-equipped laboratory. Hauser's work at the project was to do with chimpanzee pathology. He was currently trying to identify the various types of intestinal worms that infected chimps, hence the avidity with which he welcomed our cloacal samples brought in from the field.

We stood together, now, looking at the pathetic remains of the baby chimp laid out on a stainless steel dissecting tray. Hauser's lab had a small generator to power his centrifuges and chill his refrigerators. In a corner a table fan turned its face this way and that, dispensing its breeze, endlessly saying no, no, no. Hauser wore a white coat and trousers, but with no shirt or vest under the coat. Beneath the antiseptic smells of his chemicals and preserving spirits it was just possible to distinguish the thin vinegar reek of his body odour, a noisome seam in the olfactory strata.

He gave a soft grunt and poked at the body with the

end of his ballpoint pen. He lifted a minute leg and let it drop.

'It *is* a chimp,' I confirmed.

'Absolutely. Very young and maybe dead for twenty-four hours. Hard to say. Brains gone, viscera gone. Hardly worth chewing on the rest. Where did you find it?'

'Ah . . . at one of my feeding sites.'

'The very discreet Mrs Clearwater responded.'

I ignored him and laid out my specimen bottles.

'Is there any way,' I began as lightly as I could manage, 'that you could tell if these ones' - I pointed at the bottles - 'had consumed this one?' I indicated the baby's corpse.

Hauser looked steadily at me, thinking. The sweat stood out on his bald head like little sun blisters. 'Yes,' he said. 'Tricky, but possible '

'I'd appreciate it.'

'Then I assume these aren't chimp faeces.' He tapped one of the bottles with his pen. Hauser was no fool – which was annoying.

'God no,' I said. 'At least I assume not.' I tried a laugh and it came out not too badly. But I could sense Hauser's mind at work, testing the implications. 'Just a crazy theory of mine,' I went on, 'about predators.' As soon as I uttered the words I regretted them. I had said too much: Hauser knew better than anyone what chimpanzees ate. He had identified dozens of plant and fruit types from faecal study alone. He would be looking much more closely now. For some absurd reason I suddenly felt guilty about my insignificant duplicity. Why didn't I simply air my suspicions, test my theory on a fellow worker? But I had the answer to that: I knew my colleagues too well to trust.

'No hurry,' I said. 'Whenever you've got a moment.'

'No, I'll get right on to it,' Hauser said, ominously.

I left the lab with some relief. It was hot outside, the mid-afternoon sun burning palely through a thin screen of clouds. No birds sang. All the noise came from the Artificial Feeding Area, and from the volume of pant-hoots, barks and screams it sounded as if there were two dozen chimps scoffing Mallabar's free bananas. And with such a large number present everybody else would be there: Mallabar, Ginga, Toshiro and Roberta Vail, and half a dozen assistants, all observing and notating furiously. Ian Vail would be out in the field, I supposed; like me he was highly dubious about Mallabar's celebrated toy.

I walked back to my tent, doubting whether I had handled the discovery of the dead baby correctly. I should learn to be more craftily evasive, I thought: a bad evasion is tantamount to telling the truth. I was interrupted in my recriminations by the sight of João and Alda waiting for me. No sign at all of Lena, they said. There was no point in sending them out at this stage of the afternoon so I let them go home. I dragged a chair out into the shade of a canvas awning stretched above the tent's opening and tried to write a letter to my mother, but my mind was too busy to concentrate and I abandoned it after three or four lines.

That evening in the canteen I waited until Roberta had left before I approached Ian Vail. His surprise, and then sly delight, might have been touching under any other circumstances, but his evident pleasure that I had initiated a conversation irked me. Our relations were cordial and professional, so far as I was concerned. I was making an innocent enquiry, so why did he have to render it personal, find it implicit with other motives? He set his tray down and turned to give me his full and focused attention.

'Fire away,' he said, his pale-lashed, pale eyes irradiating me with telepathic avowals, I felt sure, but to no effect: Ian Vail did not interest me.

I asked him if there had been any recent births to any of his northern chimps.

'No, there are two pregnant, but nobody due soon. Why?'

'I found a dead baby today. Looking for a mother.'

'How did it die?'

'Accident, I think. I don't know.'

He stroked his chin. The light from the hurricane lamp caught the hair on his forearm, dense and whorly, golden wire. It looked half an inch thick.

'There're a couple of nomadic females pretty far gone,' he said. 'Do you want to check? If Eugene isn't feeding tomorrow we might find them. Shouldn't be hard.'

'Fine,' I said, trying to ignore his boyish grin of pleasure. We arranged to meet at seven in the morning. He would come by in the Land Rover and collect me.

I walked back to my tent, noticing that the lights in Hauser's lab were still on. I realized I hadn't seen him in the canteen that evening and I felt a seep of worry drip through me. Hauser was not known for working late.

Half an hour later, as I was writing up my field notes for the day, I heard Mallabar's voice outside, asking if he might have a word with me. I let him in and offered him a scotch, which he declined. He looked around my tent, and then back at me, as if its contents might provide some encoded clue to my personality. I offered him a seat, but he came straight to the point, standing.

'That body you found today, why didn't you tell me about it?'

'Why should I?'

He smiled patiently, the wise headmaster confronted by the difficult pupil. I always strove for extra confidence where Mallabar was concerned. He worked his charms so thoroughly on everyone else that I made special efforts to show how impervious I was to them.

'Deaths must be logged. You know that.'

'I am logging it.' I pointed to my book. 'I just don't have all the facts yet. Hauser's –'

'That's why I'm here, to pre-empt you.' He paused. 'We have the facts now. It wasn't a chimp.'

'Oh come *on*.'

'Hope, it's a terribly easy mistake to make. I've done it many, many times myself. A partially eaten or decomposed body of a newborn . . . Hard to tell, my dear, hard to tell.'

'But Hauser –'

'Anton just confirmed to me that it was a baby baboon.'

'Ah.'

'I don't blame you, Hope, I want you to know that. You were doing your job. I just wish you had come straight to me with your hypothesis.' Now he took a seat. I wondered what he knew of my hypothesis.

'I must say I thought –'

'I didn't want,' he interrupted again, and gestured at my journal, 'I didn't want you to be barking up blind alleys.'

'Thank you.'

He stood up. 'We're not fools here, Hope. Please don't underestimate us. We certainly don't underestimate you.'

'It looked very like a chimp, I can tell you.'

'Well . . .' he said, drawing it out, relaxed now that I had admitted it. Then he did something extraordinary: he leant towards me and kissed me on the cheek. I felt the prickle of his neat beard.

'Good-night, my dear. Thank God you were wrong.' That smile again. 'Our work here . . .' He paused. 'Our work here is terribly important. Its integrity must be beyond any question. You must understand the potential damage of wild – no, I don't mean wild – of *hasty* theorizing . . . Hmm?' He looked pointedly at me, said good-night once more, and left.

After he had gone I sat down and smoked a cigarette. I had to calm down. Then I finished writing up my field notes: I described the day's events precisely, and made no alterations to the data.

That completed, I left my tent and walked down Main Street to Hauser's lab. The lights were still on, I knocked and was admitted.

'Just in time,' Hauser said. 'You can take these.' He handed me my specimen bottles, rinsed clean.

'What were the results?'

'No trace of meat. Nothing out of the ordinary. Fruit, leaves.'

I nodded, taking this in. 'Eugene's just been round to see me.'

'I know,' Hauser was unperturbed. 'I too thought it was a chimp at first, and I mentioned it to him in passing . . . So we both took a closer look.' He smiled faintly and cocked his head. 'It was a baby baboon. Incontrovertibly.'

'Funny how we both thought it was a chimp, instantly, like that.'

'Terribly easy mistake to make.'

'Of course.' All right, I thought, we'll play it your way. I looked at him searchingly, directly. To his credit he didn't flinch.

'May I have the body, please?' I asked.

'I'm afraid not.'

Why?'

I incinerated it two hours ago.'

THE WAVE ALBATROSS AND THE NIGHT HERON

I sit on Brazzaville Beach in the early morning sunshine watching two gulls fight and flap over a morsel of food – a fish head or a yam heel, I can't make it out. They squawk and strut, their beaks clash with a sound like plastic cups being stacked.

In the Galapagos Islands, the wave albatross mates for life. I have seen films of them smooching and petting each other like an infatuated couple out on a date. And this is no courtship ritual or opportunistic display; these two will cohabit until death intervenes.

One of my gulls gets wise and snatches up the scrap of food and flies away with it. The other lets him go and pecks distractedly at the sand.

In the Galapagos Islands there is another bird called the night heron. The night heron produces three chicks and then waits and watches to see which will emerge the strongest. After a week or so the strongest chick begins to attack the other two, trying to bundle them out of the nest. In the end it succeeds, the weaker chicks fall to the ground and die.

The mother night heron sits beside the nest watching while this struggle goes on and one offspring disposes of the other two. The mother does not intervene.

John Clearwater was a mathematician. It seemed an innocuous statement to make but, as far as Hope was concerned, that was both the root cause of his allure for her and the source of all his enormous problems. She knew he was not particularly good-looking, but then she had never been very drawn to handsome men. There was something facile and shallow about male beauty, she thought. It was too commonplace, for one thing, and thereby devalued. Everywhere she went she saw notionally 'good-looking' men of one type or another: men serving in shops, men eating in restaurants, men erecting scaffolding, men in suits in offices, men in uniforms at airports ... There were many more good-looking men in the world than women, she reckoned. It was much much harder to find a beautiful woman.

Clearwater was of average height but he looked stockier. He was also a little overweight when she met him, and these extra pounds added to the impression of squat solidity he gave off. He had wiry black hair, thinning at the front, that he brushed straight back. He wore unexceptionally orthodox clothes: brown sports jacket and dark grey flannels, Viyella shirts and knitted, patternless ties, but they looked absolutely right on him, she thought. There was a literally careless quality about the way he dressed, and the well-used, well-fitting nature of his clothes ignored fashion and style with a blunt panache that she found far more attractive than the most tasteful and *soigné* modishness.

He had a long, straight nose and bright, pale blue eyes. She had never known anyone who smoked a cigarette so fast. His driven-back hair and his demeanour of restless hurry were both oddly exciting to her and liberating. When she was with him she felt her own potential expand to preposterous lengths. He was indifferent to the ephemera and faddiness of the world, its swank and swish. His tastes, like most people's, were both banal and arcane, but they seemed to have developed under their own impulsion, self-generated, uninfluenced. She found that innocent confidence and self-sufficiency very enviable.

There were disadvantages too. That self-sufficiency made him relatively incurious about her own likes and dislikes. When they did something *she* wanted, she always felt it was an act of politeness on his part, however much he protested the contrary. And his utter absorption in his work, which was of an abstraction so rarefied as to be vertiginous, excluded everyone, as far as she could see, apart from a handful of people in distant universities and research institutes.

She met him, eventually, one June evening at an end-of-term faculty party. She had just collected the typescript of her PhD thesis from the typing agency and the strange joy that the sight of that ream of paper had provoked had encouraged her to drink too much. When she finally found herself face to face with Clearwater she stared at him very intently. He needed a shave – he had a heavy beard – and he looked tired. He was drinking red wine from a half-pint glass tankard filled to the brim.

'So, what's your racket?' he said to her, with no enthusiasm.

'You can do better than that,' she said.

'OK. You've spilt wine on your blouse.'

'It's not wine, it's a brooch.'

He leant forward a few inches to peer at the jet cameo pinned above the swell of her left breast.

'Of course it is,' he said. 'I should have brought my specs.'

'Are you American?'

'No, no. Sorry: *"brawt"*. How's that? I spent four years at CalTech. It can damage your vowels.'

She looked at his clothes. He could have been a prep school master in the 1930s. 'I could tell you'd lived in California. All those pastel colours.'

He looked a little taken aback, suddenly lost, as if a slang word had been used that he wasn't familiar with. She realized that he couldn't believe she was talking about his clothes.

'Oh . . . My *clothes*, I see.'

'Not exactly the cutting edge of *haute couture*.'

'I'm sorry, I'm not interested in clothes.'

Under further questioning he told her that he shopped about once every five years when he tended to buy a dozen of everything – shoes, jackets, trousers. He held up a sleeve to expose a hole in the jacket elbow.

'Actually, this is almost ten years old. Wasn't much call for jackets in California.'

'So what did you wear, when you lived there?'

'Jesus Christ.' He laughed. Then he added more politely, 'Ah . . I don't know. I didn't wear jackets.'

'What about the beach? The sun?'

'I was working. I wasn't on holiday. Anyway, what would I want to go to a beach for?'

'Fun?'

'Listen, I'm thirty-five. Time's running out for me.'

She laughed at this, too long, the drink making her uncontrolled. Then he started to laugh at her laughing at him. It wasn't for a long time that she realized he had been deadly serious.

By the end of the evening he had asked her to go out with him. He did go out, he admitted, and he did drink, in phases, usually when he was changing 'areas of study', as he put it. It was lucky for her, he said without any condescension, that she had caught him on the cusp.

They had sex for the first time about a week later, in the bedroom of her flat in South Kensington. He was living in the Oxford and Cambridge Club, vaguely looking for somewhere to live within walking distance of Imperial College, where his research post was. He came back to her flat the next night and stayed, and the night after that, and stayed. After a dozen nights she offered to put him up until he could find his own place. It seemed sensible. He was still living there in September when, three months and five days after their first meeting, he asked her to marry him.

They had been married for nearly eight weeks when Hope noticed the first change. Summer was over, autumn was well advanced. She came home one cold and frosty evening and opened a bottle of red wine.

'Do you want a glass, Johnny?' she called.

He came through to the kitchen.

'No thanks.' he said. 'I've stopped.'

'Stopped what?'

'The booze.'

'Since when?'

'Since now.'

He opened the fridge. Hope saw what looked like half a dozen pints of milk. He poured himself a glass. He grinned at her. He seemed in an unusually good mood.

'Got to keep my strength up.'

'What's going on?'

'I've found it,' he said. 'I know what I'm going to do next.' He made a little turning motion with his hand. 'Full of amazing . . . The potential. The excitement.'

She felt happy for him. At least, that was what she told herself she felt.

'Great. What is it? Tell me.'

'Turbulence,' he said. 'Turbulence.'

THE ZERO-SUM GAME

Turbulence is John Clearwater's new passion. Hope knows that his old passion, his old love for many years, was Game Theory. He spent four years at CalTech working on Game Theory: the theory of rational conflict. John Clearwater has told her a certain amount about the work he did at CalTech. He started with two-person games – two-person zero-sum games as he put it. A zero-sum game is a game where one person's win is necessarily the other person's loss. 'Like marriage,' Hope said. 'Well, no,' John said. 'Marriage is a non zero-sum game. And emotions come into play. One person's loss may not

*necessarily be another person's gain.' John told her there
was another factor too: he was particularly interested in
games of perfect information, where there were no secrets.
In these games, he said, there was always an optimum
strategy. That was what he was looking for: optimum
strategies. Chess is a game of perfect information, so is
noughts and crosses. Games of perfect information can be
infinitely complex or comparatively straightforward. The
only condition was that there had to be no secrets. Poker
isn't a game of perfect information. Poker is a two-person,
zero-sum game without perfect information. 'Just like
marriage,' Hope said. He still disagreed.*

I was ready, early the next morning, when Ian Vail
came by to pick me up. There was a dirt road that took
you a mile or so into the heart of the northern area. It
saved a lot of time: a fifth to a quarter of my day was
spent in commuting to and fro.

As we drove off Vail told me that he had sent two of
his field assistants ahead at first light with walkie-talkies
to look for the chimps. With a bit of luck, he said, we
might be able to cover most if not all of the northern
chimp population in a day. I was very much aware of
the after-effects of my encounter with Mallabar the
night before. I asked Vail if he had spoken of our trip
to anyone. He looked at me, a little surprised.

'No,' he said. 'Why?'

'Mallabar thinks it wasn't a baby chimp. That body.
He says it was a baboon.'

'And you don't agree.'

'It's not a question of agreeing. I'm right, he's
wrong.'

Vail made a face. 'Look, Hope, maybe you shouldn't tell me any more, you know? Eugene has been extraordinarily . . . I just don't want to have to take sides.'

I smiled to myself: very Ian Vail. 'Oh, don't worry,' I said. 'I'll keep your name out of it. Just a professional disagreement.'

'He must have his reasons. I mean, if you're right.'

'I am and he has. Though I've no idea what they are.'

I sensed Vail's deepening worry: what was he getting into here? To what extent, by aiding me in this way, might he be going counter to his benefactor's wishes?

'It's awkward for me, that's all,' he said feebly. 'With Roberta and all that.'

Roberta Vail. Ian's American wife and Mallabar's amanuensis and uncredited co-author. Roberta worshipped Mallabar - the term was not too strong - and everyone knew it, even though her adoration was couched in terms of proper professional awe. Perhaps, I thought now, it was Roberta's fervent devotion to Eugene that had made Ian Vail try to kiss me that day . . . I realized, also, that Roberta had better not learn of this trip - not because she distrusted her husband (she didn't), but because of its implicit disloyalty to the God Eugene. However, that was one confidence I knew our Ian wouldn't divulge.

We parked the Land Rover and set off up the path into the low hills that climbed towards the grasslands of the plateau. We were now right in the middle of the Grosso Arvore National Park, an area of approximately one hundred square miles. Our particular territory, where the northern group of chimpanzees was situated, was smaller, a strip of forest and scrub approximately ten miles long and two miles wide. It supported a fluctuating population of between thirty and forty chimpanzees — now reduced somewhat by the migration of my southerners.

About half of the northern chimps had been spotted by one of Vail's assistants, so we were informed over our walkie-talkies. We made good progress. It took us only about half an hour to reach them. I noticed how the going here in the north was far easier, there was little of the thick forest or dense undergrowth that I encountered in the south.

We were lucky to find so many of the chimpanzees together at one site. The reason was that three large dalbergia trees grew here and the flowers were in bud. I counted fourteen chimpanzees sitting amongst the branches, grazing avidly on the small sweet bud clusters.

Ian pointed. 'Two of the pregnant females are here. Look.'

Two down. How many to go . . .? We sat down about sixty yards from the trees and watched the chimps through our binoculars. It was about half-past eight in the morning, probably approaching the end of the first feeding session of the day. Already there was a certain amount of calling and excitement. But the chimps were still gorging themselves. Dalbergia buds are a favourite food and the source would only be available for three or four days before they flowered.

I could see through my binoculars that one young female was heavily in oestrus. The pink swelling of the skin of her genital area was remarkably large, a protuberance the size of a big cabbage. The male chimps in her tree were growing increasingly excited and aroused. There was much branch-shaking and displaying, calling and shrieking. But the female kept herself at the very extremity of the dalbergia tree, sitting on thin whippy branches that could not possibly bear the weight of another chimp. Chimpanzees often copulate in trees and occasionally a male would advance out towards her, as far as he dared, and squat down, showing her his erect penis, shaking leaves and hitting branches in his excitement. But the female appeared to ignore him, and munched on contentedly, cramming her mouth with handful upon handful of sweet yellow dalbergia buds.

But eventually, as if she sensed their collective arousal had reached a peak, and the waiting males had suffered long enough, she climbed down out of the tree. And at once half a dozen males and adolescent males followed her to the ground. The air was loud with calling and hooting.

I saw one big male, with a patch of brown fur on his neck, take up the familiar squatting position near her. His legs were spread wide and I could clearly see his erect penis, thin and sharp, about four inches long, almost lilac against the dark fur of his belly, quivering above his bulging scrotum resting on the ground.

I tapped Ian's elbow. 'Is that the alpha male?'

'Yes. N4A.'

'Come on. What's his name?'

'We call him Darius.'

'And the female?'

'Crispina.'

Darius scratched the earth and rapped the ground with his knuckles. He gazed directly, intently, at Crispina, who was half turned away. She raised her lurid rump and backed slowly towards him, looking round from time to time. Darius squatted, almost immobile, swaying very slightly from side to side, the pale tense cone of his penis twitching slightly. He grunted softly as Crispina backed smoothly into his lap.

It was over very quickly. As he thrust, Darius made a harsh grunting noise, and Crispina screamed. After about five or six seconds, and ten thrusts on Darius's part, Crispina leapt away. Darius picked up a bundle of leaves and carefully wiped his penis. But already Crispina had turned away and was presenting her florid rump to another squatting chimp.

I glanced at Vail. He was peering intently through his binoculars. We watched as Crispina copulated with four of the other attendant males. She refused to have anything to do with two of the adolescents, no matter how histrionically they displayed for her. In fact she seemed more interested in Darius, to whom she returned several times, presenting her rump and backing up to him, even, at one stage, hopefully touching his flaccid penis. But he wasn't interested any more, or wasn't aroused. Then, as if on some covert signal, everything seemed to calm down. Crispina lay on the ground and groomed herself; Darius and the other males climbed back up into the dalbergia trees. Vail put down his binoculars and chuckled.

'Fascinating . . . She sure knows what she wants, does Crispina,' he said, with what looked like an ugly smirk on his lips.

'What do you mean?'

'Nothing . . .' He was colouring. 'I mean it's fascinating to see a dominant female emerge in the group again. It's taken a while. Shall we move on?'

We left the dalbergia trees and retraced our steps about half a mile before taking a path that headed north-east. One of Vail's assistants had spotted another, smaller group of chimpanzees feeding on termites' nests. Something about Vail's last remark nagged at me.

'What do you mean about a dominant female emerging *again*?'

'Well, it used to be Rita-Mae, you see. Before she went south. Crispina – what went on there – it was just like Rita-Mae.'

'The copulations.'

'Yes. And favouring certain males. Rejecting others.'

'And you think that's significant. There's some kind –' I searched for the right word – 'some kind of strategy?'

'Ah-ha. Another person who hasn't read my paper.'

'What paper?'

He looked absurdly pleased with himself. 'It's a theory I have. You see, it's not the alpha male that gives the group its cohesion, it's a female. A dominant female. It was Rita-Mae that led the group south, not Clovis.'

This was all new to me. 'How did Mallabar respond?'

'Oh, he doesn't agree. Not at all. He doesn't think the split has anything to do with sex.'

As we tramped along the path towards the termite nests Vail told me more about the article he had written. I didn't listen particularly hard, my thoughts were suddenly back with the dead baby. And Lena. Eventually, to shut him up, I asked if I could see it sometime. He promised to bring it round.

At the termite nests we found Vail's assistant watching a small group of six chimps feeding on the ants. There was a female here who was very pregnant. Vail said that she was one of the two nomads he logged regularly. Neither had been fully integrated into the northern group.

'She's one of the strange attractors,' he said.

'Why did you call her that? Strange attractor.'

'Just an expression. Before Crispina became sexually popular, it was these ladies that stirred things up. They breeze into town, as it were. Is it important?'

'I've heard the phrase before, that's all. In another context.'

We watched the chimps feed for a while and then returned to the Land Rover. My head was full of ideas. I asked Vail to run me through his theory once again. He said that the northern group had been stable, socially speaking, because of the presence within it of a strong, sexually popular female – Rita-Mae. When she left, the younger females could not fill her role and the group began to fragment, socially. Other nomadic females were drawn in – the strange attractors – in an attempt, Vail thought, to find another Rita-Mae. But it wasn't until Crispina started to become popular and favour Darius – who promptly emerged as the alpha male – that the unrest and disruption caused by the schism began to abate.

'But I can see problems ahead,' Vail went on. 'Two of the other females in the group are pregnant and so is one nomad. Crispina is the only one with a functioning sexual cycle. When she becomes pregnant, God knows what'll happen.'

'What does your theory say?'

'I'm afraid that's where it starts to run out of steam.'

Vail dropped me off outside my tent. It was mid-afternoon, hot and silent, apart from the metallic burr of the cicadas. Inside my tent it was stifling. The tin roof was theoretically designed to keep it cooler but I could not calculate why it should. I took off my shirt and wiped myself down. Liceu had folded away my freshly washed clothes in a tin trunk. I opened it and chose a white T-shirt. Then I frowned: the trunk had not been locked. This was not for security; the key hung from a string tied to a handle, but I always asked Liceu to lock the trunk to minimize the risk of any bugs or other clothes-eating insects crawling in.

I pulled on my T-shirt. Perhaps he had simply forgotten. I sat down at my desk and looked at the objects on it: the photograph of my parents, of my sister and her children, the stapler, the red tin mug filled with pens, the scissors, the faceted glass paperweight ... I didn't remember leaving the paperweight in exactly that position. Or the scissors. Or maybe I had. Or maybe Liceu had dusted. I opened the desk drawer. There was my field notebook, rubber bands, paper clips, ruler, my black journal. It all seemed undisturbed. Then a gleam of foil caught my eye, sticking out of a curling-cornered, old paperback edition of *Anna Karenina*. I opened the book. They were still there, my three remaining condoms. But I now knew somebody had been through this drawer. I kept the condoms hidden in the middle of that book, tucked in close to the spine. They weren't there to mark my place.

Hauser or Mallabar . . .? Then I paused. Surely this was getting a little out of hand? I opened my journal: there was my entry, unaltered. *The corpse of a two to three day old chimpanzee infant, partially eaten.* What did I expect?

I placed my hands palm down on the warm wood of the desk. The death of a baby chimp. The sexual popularity of Crispina. Ian Vail's theory. And now somebody was going discreetly through my possessions. Looking for something, or merely confirming suspicions?

'Hope?'

Ian Vail was outside. I pulled back the tent flap and let him in.

'God it's hot in here,' he said. He seemed slightly edgy. 'I'm heading back out again. Brought you this.' He handed me a journal. *Bulletin of the Australian Primatological Association.*

'I didn't know you were a member,' I said.

He grinned apologetically. 'It was the only place that would take it. I think I told you – Eugene wasn't exactly falling over himself to help me get it published.'

I flicked through the journal looking for his article. I found it: 'Sexual and social strategies of wild female chimpanzees'. I read a few sentences.

'A real page-turner,' he said. 'Once I put it down I could hardly pick it up again.' He chuckled weakly at his old joke.

I was looking down at the open pages in my hands, but from the new proximity of his voice I was aware he had moved closer to me. A few seconds dawdled by. I knew what would happen the moment I looked up.

I looked up. He stepped towards me and his hands gripped my shoulders. I turned my face, his lips and nose squashed into my cheek.

'Hope,' he said thickly. 'Hope.'

'Don't, Ian.' I pushed him away. 'What do I have to say to you? Jesus Christ.'

He looked wretched. The blush burning his fair skin, sweat glossy on his forehead. 'I've fallen in love with you,' he said.

'Oh my God ... Don't be so, so *ridiculous*, Ian. For heaven's sake!'

'I can't help it. Today, when ... I thought you –'

'Look. This is not going to go anywhere. I told you the last time.'

'Hope, just give me –'

'What about Roberta?' I turned the knife. 'I like Roberta,' I lied. 'I like you, but that's all. You're not being fair to any of us.'

He had an odd look on his face: as if he had been chewing on some gristle but was too polite to spit it out.

'Please, Ian.'

'I'm sorry. I won't ... It won't happen again.'

He left. I sat down at my desk and thought about him for a while. Then I read his article. It was really quite good.

Roberta Vail was plain and on the plump side. She had wiry, naturally blonde hair that she always wore pulled back from her forehead in a firm, clumpy pony-tail. She wasn't unattractive, but she had a tired slack expression to her mouth. She finished her meal and lit a cigarette. She only smoked when Ian was absent.

'Where's Ian?' I asked, as I sat down opposite her with my tray.

'He's not feeling so good. Not hungry.'

I commiserated and started my meal.

There was a quality about Roberta that always baffled me. Perhaps it was her closed, inert countenance – what was she thinking? Was she happy or sad? Did it matter? Or perhaps it was simply that air of mystery that is associated with certain couples: a nagging curiosity on the part of the observer as to how they could ever have been attracted to each other in the first instance; a fundamental ignorance of what it was that the one found alluring in the other ... This may be a little unfair, I thought. I could see what might be thought interesting or appealing about Ian Vail, but as for what he saw in Roberta, I was stumped. But then, I reflected, we are always on shaky ground when it comes to understanding one man's meat or another man's poison in the sexual arena. I have been wrong more times than I care to think, and my oldest friend, Meredith, confided in me after my marriage broke up, that she had never, ever understood my obsession for John Clearwater. I was amazed – I thought it would be as plain as day to others.

I returned my attention to Roberta who was telling me about something she had observed at the Artificial Feeding Area. I stopped listening altogether when Mallabar and Ginga came in. There was an attitude in Mallabar's bearing this evening that was unusual. He seemed to be bracing his shoulders square; his eyes – I know this sounds absurd – appeared brighter. He went through into the kitchen area and Ginga joined me and Roberta.

'What's going on?' I said.

'Eugene'll tell you. Have you a cigarette?'

I offered her a Tusker; Roberta offered her a Kool. She chose Roberta's. We both lit up and Roberta went in search of pudding. Ginga turned to me and positioned her body so we could talk confidentially. Ginga had a narrow face with thin lips, prematurely lined and aged from too many years under the African sun. She had unusual eyes, the upper lids seemed heavy, as if she were dying to go to sleep but was making a special effort for you. She spoke good English but with a pronounced accent – Swiss–French, I supposed, she came from Lausanne. She was very thin. I imagined that in the right clothes she would look elegant. I had never seen her in anything but a shirt and trousers. She wore no make-up.

She patted my hand and smiled at me. Ginga liked me, I knew that.

'Hope, Hope, Hope,' she said, mock-despairingly. 'Why is Eugene so cross with you? He was in a rage the other night.'

I shrugged, sighed, and told her a little about the transformation of dead baby chimp into dead baby baboon. It made no sense to her, she said.

'So where's the body?' she demanded.

'It doesn't exist,' I said. I inclined my head in Hauser's direction. 'He incinerated it.'

Ginga made a face. 'Well, you know he's been so worried, Eugene,' she said. 'For the project. There is no money, you know? It's terrible.' She reflected a moment, running a hand through her short hair. She took a slow, avid pull on her cigarette, hollowing her cheeks. She exhaled, giving me a half smile, half grimace.

'But I think everything will be fine now.'

'What do you mean?'

'Wait and see.' She pointed.

I turned. Mallabar emerged from the canteen's kitchen with two foil-capped bottles of Asti Spumante. Everyone stopped talking as, with undue ceremony, he assembled glasses, popped the corks and poured out the foaming wine, silencing with histrionic gestures all speculation as to the cause of this rare treat.

So we waited, dutifully, with our charged glasses, while Mallabar stood at the head of the table, head slightly bowed, jaws and cheeks working as if he were actually masticating, tasting the speech he was about to deliver. I sensed people gathering behind me and turned. All the kitchen staff were ranged behind me and most of the field assistants. João caught my glance and mouthed something at me but I couldn't interpret it. Mallabar looked up at the ceiling; his eyes seemed moist. He cleared his throat.

'These last three years,' he began huskily, 'have been the hardest I have ever known in more than two decades at Grosso Arvore.' He paused. 'That we have been able to continue our work is due in large part to you,' he thrust both hands at us, 'my colleagues and dear friends. Under the most trying circumstances – the most trying – and in the face of increasing difficulties, we have struggled on to sustain that vision that was born here so many years ago.'

Now he smiled. He beamed, showing us his strong teeth.

'Those black days, I think we can now say, are behind us. A brighter future beckons at the end of the rainbow.' He nodded vigorously. 'I heard this afternoon that the DuVeen foundation of Orlando, Florida, is to award us a grant of two and three-quarter millions of dollars, US, spread over the next four years!'

Hauser cheered, we all clapped. Toshiro whistled deafeningly.

'We are already recruiting in the States and the UK,' Mallabar continued triumphantly. 'I can tell you that within months the census will be resuming. We are negotiating with Princeton University for two more research fellowships. Many other exciting developments are afoot. Grosso Arvore, my dear good friends, is saved!'

We raised our glasses and, prompted by Hauser, drank to the health of Eugene Mallabar.

After the Asti Spumante we moved on to beer. We sat around the table, exulting in our good fortune, chatting and laughing. Even I, the newcomer, felt cheered, not so much at the news but at the patent elation on the faces of the others, the old-timers. Four more years, a big grant by an important foundation . . . Where one led, others would surely follow, we decided. Hard currency – solid dollars – would soften the restrictions imposed by the government as a result of the civil war. Perhaps Mallabar was right: a brighter future did beckon at the end of the rainbow.

Later, as we were leaving, Mallabar came up to me. He put his hand on my shoulder and left it there. I wondered if he were a little drunk.

'Hope,' he said sonorously, 'I was wondering if you could do me a favour.' He squeezed my shoulder. With his other hand he caressed his beard – I could just hear the rasp of tidy bristles.

'Well . . . What?'

'Could you do this week's provisioning run? I know it's Anton's turn but I need him here. I can't spare him.' He smiled fondly at me, not showing his teeth. 'We have to reassess all our various projects, in the light of the DuVeen grant. We can't waste a moment.'

I thought. He was referring to the fortnightly run into the provincial capital where we stocked up on supplies. It was at least a three-day trip, sometimes longer, and we usually adhered strictly to the rota. I had made it a month ago.

'It would be a special favour to me,' he said carefully, more pressure being applied to my shoulder. 'You would be my goose who laid the golden egg.'

'How could I refuse.'

'Bless you.' A final squeeze. 'Good-night my dear. See you tomorrow.'

I walked slowly back to my tent, wondering if there were other motives behind this 'special favour'. Was it a punishment or was it a way of saying no hard feelings? I strolled past Hauser's lab, and then on my left the vast pale columnar trunk of the hagania tree. A nightjar fluted its haunting five-note call.

Something moved at the entrance to my hut. I stopped.

'Mam, it is I, João.'

I went into the tent and lit the hurricane lamp. João stood outside. I asked him in but he said he had to get back to his village.

'I saw Lena, Mam. I come to tell you.'

'And?'

'She has her baby.'

'Oh.' I had the sensation of a sagging, a falling inside me.

I thanked him, we said good-night and he left for home. I sat down on my bed, suddenly tired. Stupidly, I felt tears smart in my eyes.

NOISE OR SIGNAL?

The man I work with – Gunther – started to go deaf fairly recently. The doctors couldn't explain why but his hearing problems became so bad that he was obliged to be fitted with a hearing aid. He told me that, initially, he found the amplified sound in his head alarmingly hard to cope with. Everything came at him in a rush, he said, trying to explain the effect, sounds were suddenly unfamiliar and new. 'You see, Hope,' he said a little plaintively, 'the problem was that I couldn't tell what was irrelevant and what was important . . . I couldn't tell noise from signal.'

I think: join the club. Learning to listen is like any process of education. You have to sift through a mass of phenomena and discard what is unimportant. You have to distinguish the signal from the noise. When you find the signals a pattern might emerge, and so on.

That was what John Clearwater was attempting to do with his work on turbulence. Here was an area that was all 'noise', completely random and unpredictable. 'Hyperbolic' was a word he used. Was there any pattern in turbulence? Were there any signals being given off? And suppose there were, would pattern form? And what would that tell us about other disorderly systems in the universe? He told me once that he was looking for equations of motion to predict the future of all turbulent systems . . .

The eye sees. It explores the optic array before us. Things shift and change, but the eye searches always for concepts of invariance. That is the way the visual world is pinned down and understood. John was on a different tack: it was variance that fascinated him now – systems in flux, erratic and discontinuous. He was trying to comprehend happenstance, he told me, and write the book of the unruly world we lived in.

On Brazzaville Beach the waves roll and rumble and flatten on the sand in a sizzle of foam. Endlessly, wave after wave. On a beach in Scotland once, John pointed out to sea and said: 'What I want to do is write the geometry of a wave.'

Hope did not notice any further changes in John Clearwater as the weeks progressed. He had stopped drinking but it made no difference to his demeanour. He spent more time away from the flat at the college but his new sphere of interest – turbulence – did not appear to be all-consuming.

In early spring they went to Scotland for a holiday, renting a cold cottage in the Borders near Biggar for a fortnight. They travelled to Ipswich and spent a weekend with John's mother (his father had died a decade previously). She was an old frail grey lady, her back hooped in a pronounced dowager's stoop which made her look up at you sideways, cocking her head to obtain a clearer, oblique view out of one bright eye. She lived with John's brother, Frank, and his wife, Daphne, in a new housing development on the outskirts of the city. Frank was a pharmacist, bald and genial. He and Daphne had two young boys – Gary and Gerry – who were polite and disciplined. To Hope it was a dull and interminable weekend of endless snacks and meals and television, most of which she spent in a state of confused befuddlement, trying to divine John Clearwater's origins in this bland suburban mulch. From time to time she caught herself sneering, and warned herself against being too contemptuous: for most of the world, she realized, this was the Good Life.

She got drunk on the train home to London, drinking whisky and eating chocolates (she was not so slim in those days) and chatted volubly about her life as a schoolgirl in Banbury and Oxford. John found it amusing. He sat opposite her with his bitter lemon, goading her on to more daring revelations.

Her own life at this stage was in something of a

hiatus. Her thesis was complete, immaculate, submitted and she was waiting for the oral examination. For the very first time in her life, it seemed, the future lay open ahead of her, empty and innocuous. She luxuriated in her idleness; it seemed pointless, she thought illogically, to apply for a job with her PhD unexamined. So she read and shopped, visited friends and went to films in the afternoon, repainted their bedroom and looked vaguely for a larger flat. She was happy. Her father had always told her to make sure and recognize that state when it arrived, and acknowledge it. 'It's like money in the bank, old girl,' he would say, 'money in the bank.' She was happy and she recognized that fact, as instructed. Being married had many advantages, she realized, one of which was joint bank accounts. John's salary easily paid for everything.

Hope's thesis was entitled: *Dominance and Territory – relationships & social structure*. She had drifted into ethology almost by accident, after her degree in Botany, judiciously steered in that direction by her supervisor, old Professor Hobbes. But when she felt the urge to study again she realized she had grown tired of laboratories and of animals in cages and so she resumed her botanizing and resurrected some work she had done years before on trees. She thought that it would at least get her out of doors. Professor Hobbes had no objections and he directed her up a few avenues of research that he himself was too busy to explore. She wrote a paper on 'The *Tilia* decline: an anthropogenic interpretation'. Hobbes said it wasn't publishable, but he might find the data useful for a talk he was giving at a symposium in Vienna. Hope had no objections, she was fond of Edgar Hobbes, and all his pupils knew this was part of the *quid pro quo* for his patronage. He had no worries about her doctorate, and neither had she; her work was thorough, exact and surprisingly literate, Hobbes said, for a scientist. Her oral examination was a formality and, eventually, one chilly afternoon, she emerged from her college to walk the streets as Dr Hope Clearwater.

That evening, she and John went out for a celebratory meal. They found a French restaurant in Knightsbridge that was expensive enough to raise the occasion to 'rare treat' status and ordered a bottle of champagne.

'Come on, John,' she said. 'You've got to have one glass. At least.'

'No.' He smiled pleasantly. 'It doesn't agree with me. Not when I'm working.'

'Christ, it's Saturday tomorrow.' She poured him a glass anyway.

He raised it in a toast. 'Congratulations, Doc,' he said, 'lots of love.'

They clinked glasses. She drank hers down in large gulps and watched him set his carefully on the white table-cloth. It fizzed, untouched, brimful, all through the meal.

Apart from his new alcohol-free life, there were no other significant changes in John's life that Hope could easily discern. But, subtly, indubitably, things were different. For a long time she blamed herself for experiencing this feeling, on the grounds that if you persistently go around thinking something is different, this in itself will be sufficient to establish that fact. Covertly, she observed and analysed him, and she had to admit there was very little to go on. Perhaps she was imagining things? They went out together, they talked to each other just as often, they shared enthusiasms and exasperations as before, they made love with the same frequency ... But despite all that, in the end she knew that, in some as yet undefined way, he was not the same man she had met and married.

The victim, the catalyst, the guilty party, had to be – she decided with some reluctance – his work. She almost would have preferred a flesh and blood girlfriend, or some deficiency in her own nature that marriage had revealed, but her rival was mathematics. John was no longer as engaged with her as he had been. She was no longer the main focus of his thoughts. It was this shift that had been nagging at her over the weeks. That portion of his conscious mind that she had occupied, had diminished. He did discuss his work with her, true, but even the broad, simplified terms he employed were not sufficient for her to grasp it fully. She could not understand what he was doing, or what excited him. She made efforts, but the gap between them was not intellectual so much as conceptual – his brain operated on a different level and in a different sphere from hers. As far as his work in mathematics was concerned there was never going to be anything more to share.

But I have my own work too, she thought, and as if to prove it to herself spent three weeks writing an article entitled 'Aggression and Evolution'. She boldly submitted it to *Nature* where, to her surprise, it was accepted. Thus encouraged, she started applying for a few jobs and got her reading up to date. She made a point of discussing her work with John – the latest controversies in ethology, new directions in Life Sciences, as they were now being called – which, to her vague irritation, he found highly interesting. But it made little difference. She saw, in due time, that he was held and involved in what he did in a way that was to her fundamentally strange. It wasn't like 'work' – as she and the rest of the world considered it – at all. She could not understand it, and, she concluded with a dull ache of despair, that meant she would never really understand him either.

THE MARGIN OF ERROR

Should Hope Clearwater have seen the signs? Should she have recognized the early signals . . .?

When a skyscraper is built one of the most obsessively precise jobs is the positioning and fixing of the first, vast, steel girders that form the foundations of the whole airy frame of the building. The margin of error involved in the positioning of these tons of metal is minuscule. It must be no greater than an eighth of an inch. A minute deviation at this stage – a hole drilled a few millimetres askew, an angle miscalculated by a fraction of a degree – can have dramatic consequences later. Eight hundred feet up, that insignificant three-millimetre shift has grown into a fourteen-yard chasm.

John called it the For-want-of-a-nail syndrome. For want of a nail the battle was lost. Something small suddenly becomes hugely enlarged. Something calm suddenly becomes enraged. Something flowing smoothly in one instant becomes turbulent. How or why does this happen? What if, John said, there are small perturbations that we miss or ignore; tiny irritations that we regard as fundamentally inconsequential. These small perturbations may have large consequences. In science, so in life.

Hope has a small perturbation in her life at the moment. A woman from the village behind the beach is careless about tethering her goat. Several times a week it breaks free and makes its way to Hope's garden behind her beach house. Hope watches it now as it grazes on her hibiscus hedge. She has thought about remonstrating, but the woman – called Marga – is a tough, bossy character. Hope can imagine the entire village becoming involved in their dispute, and she needs the village, and in a way they need her. The system is stable. She can spare a few hibiscus flowers.

Hope watched the countryside unreel through the carriage window, dull and grey, green and brown, the hard umber clods of the winter fields dusted with frost. No wonder she felt depressed: a low sky, a drab world, a cold wind ... She wasn't born for English winters she decided; meteorologically she was inclined to the hot south. To distract herself she switched her attention from the view to a mental image of her destination, her friend Meredith's cottage, conjuring up a log fire, a hot meal, red wine and soft armchairs. That was better, that was all right, and she knew an approximation of that was waiting for her. It was just unfortunate that Meredith was so dirty, that she never seemed to clean or dust her home. Hope always worried about the sheets too. There had been a time when she didn't care where or upon what she slept. Even now she would not have described herself as unduly fussy, but these days there was a minimum requirement of whatever bed she found herself sleeping in – clean sheets. She was almost sure that Meredith would not offer her an unchanged bed, but that 'almost' was an insidious concern. Best just to drink a lot, she told herself, and forget.

The man sitting opposite her had a tie rather like one of John's, she noticed. John was away at a convention in New York at Columbia University. It was their first protracted separation since their marriage and she was missing him badly. But not at first. At first she had felt guilty at how much she was enjoying being on her own again, but that sensation had only lasted a day and a night. When he phoned – he phoned regularly – she told him this and he said he was missing her too. She knew he was lying – not lying, perhaps, but merely being nice. He talked with such vigour about the conference and the seminars he was attending, the old friends from CalTech he was encountering, that she guessed that he only started to think about her when he picked up the phone to make his duty call.

Why was she being so unkind to him, she asked herself impatiently? Why was she so ruthlessly analysing their marriage? What did it gain? She took out a cigarette, unthinkingly, and rolled it between her fingers.

'Excuse me,' the man with John's tie said. 'This is a non-smoker.'

'I know,' she said. 'That's why I'm not smoking.'

She was pleased to see that her response had thrown him, rather. Defiantly, she put the unlit cigarette in her mouth and left it there. She rested her chin on her fist and stared out at the cooling towers of Didcot power station as they slowly drifted by. I must be getting addicted, she thought. Bloody John Clearwater . . . She had started smoking in self-defence, and now she found she really quite enjoyed it. She let the cigarette hang sullenly from her lips. There was an old television show, she remembered, where the lead character, a private eye or cop, did the same thing as his personal gimmick, always taking out a cigarette, sticking it in his mouth, but never lighting it. He had a parrot as a pet. Big white one, a cockatoo. It was all rather affected and striven for, she thought, and that unlit cigarette became particularly irritating. She glanced at the man opposite who was reading with rigid concentration, and hoped she was irritating him too.

Meredith Brock was a don, an architectural historian, and one of some eminence, so Hope had come to realize, much to her astonishment. Meredith was an old friend; they had known each other since their schooldays. They were the same age and Hope was slightly affronted that Meredith had made a name for herself so young, albeit in such a recondite area. Her renown had come about as a result of a massive survey of medieval English buildings that she had worked on. The old historian – whose lifelong endeavour the survey had been – had hired her as his assistant to see the books through the presses and had died just as the entire multi-volumed project had been published. It fell to Meredith to publicize and defend the enterprise – it was controversial and nicely opinionated – and because of her age and her looks she had enjoyed a fleeting celebrityhood. She duly became the only architectural historian any lazy editor, producer, or committee chairman could think of and her profile had swiftly risen. It was when Hope had read Meredith's name in two newspapers, heard her voice on the radio, and seen her on television, all in one week, that she realized just how far her friend had come.

Hope looked at her now as she made them both a drink. She *is* pretty, Hope thought grudgingly, prettier than me. But she did nothing to exploit her looks. Her clothes were cheap and out of fashion. She wore too much make-up and very high heels, all the time. Her hair was long but never allowed to hang free, it was always held up and arranged in loops and swags by a combination of combs and clips. Hope thought she was at her most attractive when she had just woken up: hair down, tousled, face clean and mascara-free. They were good enough friends for Hope to be able to tell her this, gently to encourage ideas of a new look, a lowering of heels, a less lurid shade of lipstick. Meredith had listened patiently, shrugged and said what was the point?

'It's no good for people like you and me, Hope,' she had told her, wearily. 'We can't really take it seriously. It's hard enough even making a vague effort. This whole . . .' she picked at her acrylic jersey's appliqué, satin flowers, 'this whole flim-flam.'

Meredith handed her a gin and tonic, one small ice-cube floating, no lemon. Hope picked a wet hair off the outside of the cloudy glass. At least the tonic was fizzing.

'Careful, lovely. It's strong.'

Hope sipped, sat back in the chair and stretched her legs. Meredith threw a log on the fire. A pallid ray of winter sun brightened the cottage windows for an instant, then all was pleasant gloom again.

'So how is Mr Clearwater?' Meredith asked. Hope told her, but did not expand on her own disquiet. It was too early in the day for confidences, they could wait until after dinner. So they talked generally about John, about being married, about not being married, about what job Hope might find. As they chatted, Hope wondered: does she like John? They had met once before the wedding, and possibly a couple of times since. Everything had seemed very cordial, tolerably pleasant. Why not? She looked at Meredith. No, she thought, she probably doesn't.

Meredith went through to the kitchen to organize the lunch. Hope sipped her gin, noticing already the effects the alcohol was having on her. She found her thoughts returning inevitably to her husband. She thought of nothing or no one else these days, it seemed to her. Was that healthy? Should she be worried? What was it about him, she wondered, slightly fuddled, that had drawn her to him, given her such confidence?

The gin, the heat of the fire, the softness of the armchair, were sending her to sleep. She stood up and wandered across the room and looked at Meredith's bookshelves. *Antiquities of Oxfordshire*, *Traditional Domestic Architecture in the Banbury Region*, *Dark Age Britain*, *Landscape in Distress* . . . Suddenly she knew what it was about John; what obsessed her. John had a secret she could never share. John had knowledge that was denied to virtually everyone on earth. She felt her cheeks hot and pressed her glass to them. That was it: John had secrets and she envied him. This was what had fascinated her about him, almost immediately, but she had never really understood it. John and his mathematics, John and his game theory, John and his turbulence . . . she would never, could never know about them. She envied him his secret knowledge, but it was, she saw, an envy that was strangely pure, almost indistinct from a kind of worship. He was at home in a world that was banned to all but a handful of initiates. You gained entrance if you possessed the necessary knowledge, but she knew that it was knowledge that was impossible for her to acquire. That was what made it special. It was magic, in a way. But then a magician might perform some extraordinary trick, that made you gasp with incredulity, but it would be possible for you to reproduce it, if he let you in on his secret, if he showed you how. John could spend a lifetime trying to show me how, she thought, but it would make no difference. If you don't have the right kind of brain then all the effort and study in the world can't help you. So what did that imply? To enter the secret mathematical world John Clearwater inhabited, you had to have a rare and special gift: a particular way of thinking, a particular cast of mind. You either had that gift or you hadn't. It couldn't be learned; it couldn't be bought.

Hope took a book from the shelf and turned the pages, not looking at them, thinking on, feeling the gin surge through her veins. This envy I feel, she thought, it wasn't like admiring someone with a special talent – a painter, say, a musician, a sportsman. Through diligent practice and expert coaching you could experience an approximation of what that talented person achieved: paint a picture, play a sonata, run a mile. But when she looked at what John did, she knew that was impossible. An ordinary numerate person could, by dint of hard work, go so far up the mathematical tree. But then you stopped. To go beyond required some kind of faculty or vision that you had to be born with, she supposed. Only a very few occupied those thin whippy branches at the extremity, moved by the unobstructed breezes, exposed to the full fat glare of the sun.

Hope looked at the book she held in her hands, a

little dazed at the clarity of her insight. She saw a photograph of the aisle of a church, transept columns, glass, vaulting. She smiled: she envied Meredith a little too, but it was a more mundane envy. Meredith had special knowledge. She knew everything about old buildings, the exact names for the precise object. She knew what a voussoir was, the difference between Roman and Tuscan doric, where to find the predella on an altarpiece, what you kept in an aumbry, employed words like misericord, modillion and mouchette with confident precision. But then, Hope thought, so do I. I know the difference between pasture and meadow, can distinguish crack willow from white willow, I know what kind of flower *Lithospermum purpureocaeruleum* is. With time and effort I could learn all Meredith's knowledge and she could learn mine. But John's world, John's knowledge, is beyond me, unreachable.

She walked through to the kitchen, rather chastened by the rigour of her gin-inspired analysis. A roast chicken steamed in the middle of the pine table. Meredith was draining vegetables in a colander. Hope deliberately did not look at the state of the cooker. One of Meredith's several cats leapt up on the table and carefully picked its way through the place mats and cutlery to the chicken, which it sniffed and, Hope thought, licked.

'No you don't,' Meredith said gently, setting a bowl of Brussels sprouts on the table and making no more effort to chase the cat away. 'That's *our* lunch, greedy swine.' She pulled her chair back.

'Sit down, Hope,' she said. 'And bloody cheer up, will you? You look like death.'

DIVERGENCE SYNDROMES

I spend a lot of time walking on the beach, thinking about the past and my life so far. So far, so good? Well, you will be able to make up your own mind, and so, perhaps, will I. My work is easy and I finish it quickly. I have plenty of time to remember.

Fragments of John Clearwater's conversation come back to me. When he was working on turbulence, he told me he had had such good results because he had decided to tackle the subject in a new way. In the past, he said, people tried to understand turbulence by writing endless and ever more complicated differential equations for the flow of fluids. As the equations became more involved and detailed, so their connection to the basic phenomenon grew more tenuous. John said that his approach was all to do with shapes. He decided to look at the shapes of turbulence and, immediately, he began to understand it.

It was at this time that his talk was full of concepts he referred to as Divergence Syndromes. He explained them to me as forms of erratic behaviour. And in a subject like turbulence, naturally, there will almost always be a divergence syndrome somewhere. Something you expect to be positive will turn out to be negative. Something you assume will be constant, becomes finite. Something you take confidently for granted, suddenly vanishes. These are divergence syndromes.

This sort of erratic behaviour terrifies mathematicians, John said, especially those of the old school. But people were learning, now, that the key response to a divergence syndrome was not to be startled, or confounded, but to attempt to explain it through a new method of thought.

Then, often, what seemed at first shocking, or bizarre, can become quite acceptable.

As I stroll the length of this beach I consider all the divergence syndromes in my life and wonder where and when I should have initiated new methods of thought. The process works admirably with benefit of hindsight, but I suspect it wouldn't be quite so easy to apply at a moment of crisis.

It was at Sangui, João's village, that the tarmacadam road began. I turned on to it, heard the empty trailer, towed behind the Land Rover, bump up over the kerb, and settled down for the long drive into town. Normally it took between four and five hours, but that was assuming there were no major accidents on the way, that the bridges were in reasonable repair, that there were no protracted delays at the numerous military road blocks and that you didn't get caught behind one of the supply columns returning from provisioning the federal troops fighting in the northern provinces.

I rather enjoyed this drive – I had done it three times before – and on each occasion relished the buoyant end-of-term sensations it provoked. Turning off the laterite track in Sangui on to the crumbling, pot-holed tarmac of the main road south was like crossing a border, a frontier between two states of mind. Grosso Arvore was behind me, I was on my own for a few days. Almost alone: two kitchen porters, Martim and Vemba, sat in the back of the Land Rover on piles of empty sacks. I had offered them the front seats, as I always did, but they preferred their own company in the rear.

The road was straight, running through dry scrubland

and patchy forest, that spread south from the hills of the escarpment behind me, to the ocean, two hundred miles away. It was early morning and the sun was just beginning to burn off the dawn haze. The routine was familiar. The first day was occupied getting to the town. I would spend the night at the Airport Hotel and the next day would be made up of an enervating round of visits to the bank and department store and the various merchants who provided the project with food and supplies, black market drugs and medicines. Occasionally, there were trips to be made to workshops and garages for machinery to be fixed, or spare parts searched for, and this could add an extra day or two to the trip. But on this occasion I was merely provisioning. A long day's shopping awaited me tomorrow. Then I would spend one further night at the hotel before heading back for home, a much slower undertaking, with the Land Rover and its trailer heavily loaded. Thirty miles an hour was our average speed.

The road ran through an unchanging landscape. Every ten miles or so we would encounter a small village. A cluster of mud huts thatched with palm fronds; a few traders' stalls set out on the verge selling oranges and egg-plant, sweetmeats and kola nuts. The journey was not dangerous – the fighting was distant and only the Federal Army had aircraft – but we were always warned not to attempt it after dark. Ian Vail had broken down once, and was very late returning, but Mallabar had refused to send out a search party for him until the next morning. I was never absolutely clear what we were meant to be frightened of. Brigands and bandits, I supposed: there was a risk of highway robbery after dark. Apparently there were gangs roaming the countryside, mainly composed of deserters from the Federal Army. It was these men that the many road-blocks were designed to deter or catch. Every half-hour or so one would come across these outposts, nothing more than a plank of wood propped against an oil drum jutting out into the road, and beyond it, in the fringe of the bush or beneath the shade of a tree, a lean-to or palm frond shelter containing four or five very bored young soldiers wearing odd scraps of uniform. You had to slow down and halt whenever you saw one of these oil drums. Someone would peer at you and then, usually, motion you onward with a lethargic wave. If they were feeling bloody-minded they would make you step out of your vehicle, examine your papers and make a cursory search.

These were the moments I did not enjoy particularly: standing in the sun beside the Land Rover being scruti-nized by a young man in a torn singlet, camouflage trousers and baseball boots, with an ex-Warsaw Pact AK47 slung over his shoulder. It always seemed especially quiet at that moment. It made me want to shift my feet, or cough, just to break the silence that pressed around me as the soldier examined my *laissez-passer*. In the half-dozen times I had been stopped, never once had another car or lorry driven by. It was as if the road belonged exclusively to me.

On this journey, though, we were being waved through without exception. The mood of the men seemed more jocular, and more than once as I had driven off I had seen beer bottles being raised to lips. I remembered what Alda had told me about the defeat of UNAMO forces. Perhaps this was a pre-armistice re-laxation and the war would be over soon.

We reached the Cabule River by late afternoon. The ramshackle buildings on the far bank marked the outskirts of the town. Our wheels rattled noisily on the metal planking of the ancient iron bridge. The river was four hundred yards wide here. It took a great slow swerve around the town before disgorging its brown water into the dank creeks of its mangrove-clogged delta ten miles away down the coast. The edge of the continent ran straight here – mile after mile of beach and thundering surf. The silty Cabule was navigable only by vessels of the shallowest draught. All the bauxite from the mines – this province's major source of wealth – had to be transported to the capital and its harbour by rail. Bauxite mines, some timber, a few sugar and rubber plantations, sharecropping and the Grosso Arvore national park were all this area of the country had to recommend it.

I drove slowly through the town. On either side of the road were deep ditches. A few brick buildings housed empty shops and drinking dens. In the mud-walled compounds beyond them smoke rose from charcoal fires as the evening meal was prepared. The first neon lights – ultramarine and peppermint – flickered in the snack-bars and on the concrete terraces of the hotel brothels and night-clubs. Music bellowed from loudspeakers perched on roofs or hung from rafters. In the crawling traffic taxi-drivers sat with their fists pressed on their horns. Children knocked on the side of the Land Rover trying to sell me Russian watches, feather dusters, yo-yos, felt-tip pens, pineapples and tomatoes. There were many soldiers on the streets, carrying their weapons as unconcernedly as newspapers. Old men sat on benches beneath the dusty shade trees and watched naked children spin hoops and chase each other in and out of the rubbish tips. At an uneven table two young spivs with shiny shirts played stylish ping-pong, stamping their feet in the dust and uttering hoarse cries of bravado as they ruthlessly smashed and counter-smashed.

The press of traffic nudged its way through the town centre, past the five-storey department store and the mosaic-walled national bank with its swooping modernist roof; past the white cathedral and the brutalist Department of Mines; past the police station and the police barracks, with its flagpole and ornamental cannons, the neat stacked pyramids of cannon balls like the swart droppings of some giant rodent.

Then we turned and headed back north again on the new road to the airport, past the hospital and the exclusive, fenced-in suburbs. We drove past the convent school – St Encarnacion – past the shoe factory and the motor parks. The setting sun basted everything with a gentle peachy light.

The airport was far too large for such an undistinguished provincial capital. Built shortly after independence in 1964, by the West German company that owned and ran the bauxite mines, it was designed to take the largest commercial jets (optimism is free, after all). A sprawling modern hotel was constructed nearby to accommodate all the projected passengers. The bauxite was still being extracted, the mines and the processing plants functioned, after a fashion, but the airport and its white hotel were always heading for decline and desuetude. Five arrivals and departures a day were all it boasted, domestic flights linking other provincial cities. Air Zambia flew in once a week from Lusaka, but the much-heralded UTA link to Brazzaville and Paris became another casualty of the civil war when rumours spread that FIDE – or was it EMLA? – had been sold ground-to-air missiles by the North Koreans.

The war had benefited the airport in other respects, however. Half the federal government's air force was based there now: a near-squadron of Mig 15 'Fagot' fighters, three ex-RAF Canberra bombers, half a dozen Aermacchi trainers converted to ground attack and assorted helicopters. As we drove past the perimeter fence I could see the old Fokker Friendship revving up at the end of the runway about to depart on its evening flight to the capital, and beyond it, in their bays, the tubby, tilted-back silhouettes of the Migs.

At the hotel I said good-night to Martim and Vemba, agreed the time of our rendezvous the next morning, and checked in. The hotel was distinctly shabby these days, all incentive to keep it spruced up having long gone, but, after weeks at Grosso Arvore and my tent, it seemed to me still redolent of a tawdry but alluring glamour. It had a restaurant, a cocktail bar and a half-olympic-sized swimming-pool with a barbecue area. Its rooms were contained in two-storey annexes, connected to the main building by roofed-over walkways which passed through tropical gardens. Scattered here and there were one- and two-bedroomed bungalows for those guests who planned a longer stay. Sometimes, piped Latin-American music was played in the lobby. The staff wore white, high-collared jackets with gold buttons. At the entrance to the restaurant a notice requested, in English: 'Ladies please no shorts. Gentlemen please ties.' Whether it was the ghosts from the heady days of the bauxite factory contractors' ball, or the still-lingering pretensions of the current management, the Airport Hotel (this was its evocative name) had an ambience all of its own. It also had air-conditioning, sometimes, and hot and cold running water, sometimes, both luxuries that were permanently absent at Grosso Arvore.

I walked through the unkempt gardens to my room, unpacked, had a shower and changed into a dress. I felt fresh, cool and hungry.

I strolled along a walkway to the main building. It was now quite dark and the warmth of the night air, after the chill of my room, seemed to lie gently on my clean bare arms and shoulders like a muslin shawl. I could hear some rumba muzak wafting over from the lobby's sound system and from all around me in the grass and bushes came the endless *creek-creek* of the crickets. I stopped and filled my lungs, smelling Africa – smelling dust, woodsmoke, a perfume from a flower, something musty, something decaying.

I turned on to another path and quickened my pace towards one of the cottages. Its windows were shuttered but I could see light shining behind them.

I knocked on the door and waited. I knocked again and it was opened.

Usman Shoukry looked at me, not surprised, but trying not to smile. He was wearing loose linen shorts and a lilac T-shirt. His hair was shorter than the time I had last seen him.

'Look who's here,' I said.

'Hope,' he said, deliberately, as if he were christening me. 'Come on in.'

I did, and he shut the door. When I kissed him I stuck my tongue in his mouth and slipped my hands under his T-shirt and felt his back, running them up to his shoulder-blades and then down, beneath the waist-band of his shorts, my palms resting lightly on his cool, hairless buttocks.

I broke away from the kiss, still holding him to me. His mouth was glossy with saliva. He rubbed it dry with the back of his hand, smiling at me again. I looked at him as if I hadn't seen him for years. The sherry colour of his brown eyes, his slightly askew nose, his thick lips.

'Are you in trouble?' he asked.

'No. Why?'

'I wasn't expecting you for two months.'

'Well, it's your lucky day, then, isn't it? Come on, let's eat before they run out of food.'

THE INVERSE CASCADE

Hope Clearwater buys four parsnips in the market today. She is delighted and very surprised to find them. She asks the trader where they come from. Nigeria, the trader says. Hope doesn't believe her, and questions her scepti-cally: 'Where exactly in Nigeria?' The trader is not pleased to have her word doubted. 'Jos,' she says, and turns away. Hope remembers that Jos is situated high on a plateau in central Nigeria. All sorts of fruit and vege-tables can be grown there because of its cool nights and dry days – even raspberries and strawberries.

The parsnips remind her of a story John told her about an old professor of his. This man had worked for a time on the problem of turbulent diffusion. For his experiments he required a large number of floats that had to be at once highly visible and not affected by wind. For this reason balls – both rubber and ping-pong – would be of no use. After experimenting with turnips and potatoes, the professor discovered that the ideal vegetable was the parsnip. Its rough, conic configuration, and the fact that in the water most of the vegetable was below the surface, made it a stable float and indifferent to all but the severest breezes.

What the professor did was to paint several dozen parsnips white and tip sackfuls of them off a bridge over the River Cam. The white parsnips would float downstream, be caught in eddies, cluster and circle in sideswirls or flow down-river in long bobbing strings, photographed by the professor's assistants standing with cameras on both banks of the river at intervals of twenty yards.

The professor (Hope can't remember his name) had done useful work, John said. The problem was that, despite his imaginative experimental technique, his thinking was too rigid. He believed that turbulence was caused by a cascade of energy from large eddies to small. But John's own work – his breakthrough, as he termed it – had shown that this was only part of the story. In every case of turbulence, in whatever medium, there is also an inverse cascade, a flow of energy from the small eddy back to the large. Hope remembers clearly the day John proved this. He had explained it to her, his voice hoarse with excitement. Disorder, he said, is not simply handed down a chain, some of it is always being handed back again. Once that fact is grasped a great deal that was baffling about turbulent systems becomes far easier to understand.

When John Clearwater came back from America he was on good form. He had met someone at the conference – *a statistician who had helped him enormously,* almost without knowing it. He told Hope about these new avenues that had opened up, new potentials he could now see. Hope laughed with him, with genuine pleasure – with relief perhaps – at this excitement. Once again what he told her - he spent two hours trying to explain it to her – meant little or nothing, but she felt pleased, reassured. That time, after his return from America, calmed her, staunched the thin haemorrhage of anxiety and doubt. All, it seemed, was well again.

He worked as hard as ever, leaving the flat at eight in the morning and not returning, usually, until nine at night, but their hours together seemed to Hope to recapture some of the vivacity and edge of their first months of marriage. Later, when she looked back, she realized that they had merely been going through another phase (she found she could demarcate the phases in her married life as efficiently as a historian – they seemed as precise as the circles of growth in the trunk of a tree). In this particular phase a new enthusiasm dominated – the cinema. They went fairly frequently to the cinema and theatre, whenever the mood took them, or whenever some triumphant *succès d'estime* seemed to demand it. But now John wanted to go out every second or third night. And at first it was fun. His absorption was so intense and single-minded, and the pleasure he took in the cinema so manifestly good for his spirits, that it was a privilege, she reckoned, to share in it. But after six weeks of this, amounting to over two dozen visits – some films were returned to two or three times – she began to find that the strain of accompanying him was growing and she started making excuses.

Part of the problem was that he insisted on sitting very close to the screen, in the front row preferably, and certainly no further back than the third, so that his entire field of vision was dominated by the projected image. At first this was oddly exhilarating, and Hope would emerge from the cinema with her head reverberating like a gong from the big booming pictures, breathless and jangled.

His other idiosyncrasy, however, was harder to take and began to irritate her. He was scrupulous about the type of film they saw. Reviews in as many newspapers as possible were studied and collated, and he built up a small library of film reference books in an attempt to ensure that the film they were going to see would fulfil the demands he made of it. She accused him, jokingly at first, of being the only person she had ever met who sought to entertain himself in a wholly prescriptive way. It was the very opposite of random; he wanted to take no risks. 'How can you enjoy yourself, how can you have fun, without an element of risk?' He paid no attention. It was not a narrow censorship he indulged in – he was very keen on horror films and violent thrillers – it was simply that he believed, with a fundamental zeal, that a true film, a film that was true to the nature of its own form, had to have a happy ending.

'Don't be so ridiculous,' Hope said, when he first put this to her.

'No, honestly ... A film that doesn't have a happy ending is,' he paused, 'is misunderstanding the basis of all cinema.'

'OK. OK. How many counter-examples do you want me to give you? Two dozen? Three dozen?'

'No. Don't you see?' He was enjoying himself. 'Put it

this way. The essence of all art is positive. At root. So in the one great popular art form, *the* popular art form, this motive has to be even more powerful.'

Hope wondered then if he was teasing her. But his expression — candid, intense – belied this. 'Nonsense,' she said. 'Rubbish. What more can I say?'

But he wasn't joking.

And so it went on. And so John only saw those films which did not, as he saw it, demean or betray cinema from its true purpose. Hope came to realize, fairly swiftly, that going to see these films was in a real sense therapeutic for him. They functioned as a kind of drug, and she began to see how his close-up, all-enveloping, dream-fulfilling cinema buoyed him up and kept him floating. Those few weeks of ease she had experienced after his return from the conference began to be eroded once again by the slow drip, drip of worry.

Hope looked up at John's taut, stretched face as he came. She saw his brow crumple and his cheeks concave, and heard a grunting deep in his throat. Then he exhaled and smiled and lowered his head until their noses met. He settled his weight on his elbows as Hope touched his wiry hair. He fitted his head into the angle of her neck and shoulder and exhaled again, his breath warm and moist against her skin. Inside her she felt the small shiftings and slippings as his penis detumesced. She sensed a complementary swelling of love for him in her throat as she dragged her fingers over his head, down across the thick hair that grew on his neck, trailing them lightly across the flaky blur of big freckles on his shoulder-blades, making him shiver.

Catching the thin, sour smell of fresh sweat from his armpits, she slipped her hand into his armpit, feeling the hairs slick and clotted between her fingers. She kissed his neck, pressing her nose into his neck, smelling his own particular scent, his spoor. She remembered thinking once, before she had married, what kind of man she had wanted to live with, and had run through the various types that seemed most commonly on offer – the caring ones, the bastards, the strong ones, the moneyed, the humorists, the saints – and had decided that what she wanted was not a model, or an archetype, but somebody quite different. A man. A person. Different from her.

Hope held and smelt this real person that she had found. Then she slipped her fingers into her mouth and tasted his salt sweat. She reached down his spine to touch the small, flat button of a mole that grew four inches above the cleft in his buttocks and revelled selfishly in the quiddity of this individual that was hers, that she possessed . . . Intimacy made her melancholy and exhilarated. She turned her head and kissed him on the mouth, forcing his teeth apart with a blunt, strong tongue and then sucking his own tongue into her mouth, tasting his saliva.

She pushed him over on to his back and felt his flaccid penis slide wetly from her.

'Ah. Sheets,' he said.

'I love you, John,' she said. 'And don't you forget it.'

'I won't. But I've forgotten the tissues.'

'Then the deal's off.'

It was a Sunday morning. He brought her a mug of tea and then went out to buy newspapers and bread. She shouted at him to put some music on the record player before he left. He couldn't have heard her because the door closed and there was only silence.

She rolled over and sat on the edge of the bed looking down at her lap and thighs, thinking dully that she was putting on weight. She cupped her soft stomach with both hands – she was. She sighed, and then, absent-mindedly, with the backs of her fingers, gently stroked her pubic hair – unusually thick, she thought, a brash, dense triangle – and thought about John, and the cinema, their first wedding anniversary that was approaching, the holiday they were going to take, and how it would be.

She stood up, walked through to the sitting-room and crouched in front of the record player. A thick plank of sun lay across the dining-table illuminating the wreckage of their evening meal, the dregs of wine in the opaque, smeary glasses, the congealed scraps on the uncleared plates.

She put on a record and stood up, humming along. And then, somehow, her mood, a phrase in the music, the sun on the table made the moment magically thicken and hold. For an instant she forgot where she was, her gaze unfocused and she seemed to see John, in her mind's eye, hurrying back to the flat. She saw the sunny street, the shiny cars, the comical way he was trying to read the newspapers as he walked, his arms full of groceries. The shadows the buildings cast were striped obliquely across the street, light and shade. John walked through gloom and glare towards her.

The odd trance passed. She shivered, naked, in the sitting-room. She ran back to the bed and slid between just warm sheets.

USMAN SHOUKRY'S LEMMA

Muhammad ibn Musa al-Khwarizmi was an Arab mathematician from Khiva, now part of Uzbekistan in the USSR. He lived in the first part of the ninth century A.D. *and is remarkable in that he not only gave us the word algebra (from the title of one of his books,* Calculation by Restoration and Reduction *– al-jabr means 'Restoration') but also, more interestingly, in that from his name – al-Khwarizmi – is derived the word algorithm. An algorithm is a mechanical procedure for solving a problem in a finite number of steps, a procedure that requires no ingenuity.*

Algorithms are much-beloved mathematical tools. Computers operate on algorithms. They imply a world of certainty, of rotas and routine, of continuous process. The great celestial machine, programmed and pre-ordained.

However, algorithmic procedures are of little use for phenomena which are irregular and discontinuous. Fairly self-evident, you would have thought, but how often have we tried to solve the problems in our life algorithmically? It doesn't work. I should know.

There is another appellation in the world of mathematics that comes faintly tinged with contempt. A 'lemma'. A lemma is a proposition that is so simple that it cannot even be called a theorem. I appreciate lemmae – or lemmas, maybe – they seem to have more bearing on my world. 'You can't make an omelette without breaking eggs . . .' 'More haste, less speed . . .'

Usman gave me a lemma once.

We were in bed, it was dark and we had made love. The roof fan buzzed above our heads and the room was cool. I could hear only the steady beat of the fan and the noise of the crickets outside. I turned to him and kissed him.

'Ah, Hope,' he said – I couldn't see his smile in the dark, but I could hear it in his voice – 'I think you're falling in love with me.'

'Think what you like,' I said, 'but you're wrong.'

'You're a difficult person, Hope. Very difficult.'

'Well, I am feeling happy,' I said. 'I'll give you that. You make me happy.'

Then he said something in Arabic.

'What's that?'

'It's a saying. What we always say. A warning: "Never be too happy."'

Never be too happy. Usman Shoukry's lemma.

Sometimes I wonder if a lemma is closer, in status, to an axiom. Axioms are statements that are assumed to be true, that require no formal proof: $2 + 2 = 4$. 'A line is a length without breadth.' Life is full of lemmae, I know. There must be some axioms.

Usman said he would be on the beach that afternoon if I wanted to meet up with him after my provisioning trip. As it happened I was finished by half-past three and a hotel taxi took me down to the bathing-beach. I saw Usman's car, parked alongside a few others in the shade of a palm grove, and let the taxi go.

The palm trees here were very tall and old, their tensed, curved, grey trunks looked too slim to hold themselves erect, let alone bear the weight of their shaggy crowns and burden of green coconuts. The ground beneath them was grassless and hard, almost as if it had been rolled and swept. This had been an exclusive beach once and all along the shoreline were the remains of wooden beach houses and *cabañas*. Most had rotted away over the last few years, or had been dismantled for their timber and tar-paper roofs. Locals had settled here and a ribbon of shanties, made from the recycled *cabañas*, lurked in the scrub behind the littoral's treeline. With them had come rubbish dumps and livestock of all kinds. Goats and hens scrounged amongst the palm trees, stray dogs loped along the sand, sniffing curiously at whatever the waves had brought ashore.

One or two of the beach houses were still in good repair. The general manager of the bauxite mines had one, and a few Lebanese and Syrian merchants had clubbed together to keep others functioning. But whatever their efforts, the mood of this stretch of shoreline was inescapably sad, a morose memory of former glories.

I saw Usman standing waist-high in the sea, his torso canted into the green and foamy breakers that rolled powerfully in, smashing and buffeting his body. With particularly large waves he would dive beneath them, hurling himself into their sheer, tight throats just before they crested, and emerge, spitting and delighted, on the other side.

'Usman!' I called and he waved back at me. I sat down on his mat, took off my shoes and lit a cigarette. Behind me, four men played volley-ball outside one of the refurbished beach huts. They were brown – Lebanese, I guessed – wore very small swimming-trunks and played with histrionic abandon, making unnecessary dives for very gettable balls.

Usman came out of the sea, shaking his head like a dog. He had put on more weight since my last visit and there was a soft overhang of flesh at the waistband of his swimming-trunks. He sat down beside me and with delicate, wet fingers helped himself to one of my cigarettes.

'Going to swim?' he said.

'I'm frightened of the undertow, you know that.'

'Ah, Hope. That sounds like an epitaph to me – "Hope Clearwater, she was frightened of the undertow".'

Usman was Egyptian and in his early forties, I guessed. He wouldn't tell me his exact age.

'You're getting fat,' I said.

'You're getting too thin.'

He spoke very good English, but with quite a heavy accent. He had a strong face which would have looked better if he were less heavy. All his features – nose, eyebrows, lips, chin – appeared to have extra emphasis. His brown torso was quite hairless. His nipples were small and neat, like a boy's.

A fly settled on his leg and he watched it for a while, letting it taste the salt water, before he waved it away. There was a milky haze covering the sun and a breeze off the ocean. I felt warm but not too hot. I lay back on his mat and shut my eyes, listening to the rumble and hiss of the breakers. Grosso Arvore, my chimpanzees, and Mallabar, seemed very far away.

'I should have brought my swimsuit,' I said. 'Not to swim. To get brown.'

'No, no. Stay white. I like you white. All the European women here are too brown. Be different.'

'I hate being so white.'

'OK. Get brown, I don't care that much.'

I laughed at him. He made me laugh, Usman, but I couldn't really say why. I sensed him lying down on the mat beside me. We were silent for a while. Then I felt his fingers gently touch my face. Then they were in my hair, brushing it back from my forehead.

'Stay white, Hope,' he whispered dramatically in my ear. 'Stay white for your brown man.'

I laughed at him again. 'No.'

I felt dulled by the warmth and the smoothing motion of his fingers on my head.

'Hey. What's this?' Both sets of fingers were in my hair now, parting the strands to expose my skull. I kept my eyes closed.

'My port-wine mark.'

'What do you call it?'

I explained. I had a port-wine mark, a sizeable spill, a ragged two inches across, above my left ear, a dark prelate's purple. My hair was so thick you had to search hard to spot it. No pictures exist of me as a bald baby. My parents waited until my hair had fully grown in before they put me in front of a camera.

'In Egypt this means very good luck.'

'In England it means good luck too. It's bad luck if it's full on your face.'

He looked resigned. 'I just said it to make you feel good.'

'Thank you.' I paused. 'Actually it does make me feel good. I often wonder what I would've been like if it had been on my cheek.' I squirmed round and rested on an elbow, looking at him. 'You wouldn't be lying here for a start.'

This time he laughed at me. 'Yes. You're probably correct.'

'See. It brings me good luck.'

I lay back again. A clamorous argument was going on amongst the volley-ball players.

94

'Do you want to go to that Lebanese restaurant tonight?' he said. 'I shouldn't be back too late.' He sat up. 'I have to go now.'

'Where?'

'I'm flying.'

'A mission?'

'No. I've got to test the wiring. You know, two days ago, I was on reconnaissance. I pressed the camera button and my fuel tanks dropped off.'

Usman was a pilot in the Federal Air Force. A mercenary pilot, I should say, not to put too fine a point on it. All the Mig 15s at the airport were flown by foreigners, on hire to the government. Apart from Usman there were two British, three Rhodesians, an American, two Pakistanis and a South African. Their number varied. All had signed contracts and theoretically they were instructors. They were issued with uniforms, but did not have to wear them. No discipline was imposed on them. There was a fairly rapid turnover: people who had simply had enough, or casualties. In the year since Usman had been there only one pilot had died while on a mission. Four others had died as a result of mechanical or navigational failures and subsequent crashes. 'Your ground crew,' Usman said phlegmatically, 'is your greatest threat.'

I had met Usman on the first provisioning run I had made from Grosso Arvore. I had arrived at the hotel earlier than expected and, hot and thirsty, had gone into the bar for a beer. The bar room was long and thin and was lined with simulated leather. The chairs and tables were modishly Scandinavian, the chairs organic-looking, a warped kidney-shape with splayed iron legs. The tables were like large paving stones, inlaid with shards of broken, coloured glass. It was very gloomy, and, because of the simulated leather walls, warm. The two ceiling fans were always switched to full blast. The blurred, whizzing propellers produced a stiff breeze that blew your hair about. I had never been in a bar like it and I grew oddly fond of its singular atmosphere.

When I went in that first afternoon the place was empty. Then I saw someone kneeling at the far end apparently searching for something on the floor. He looked up as I came in. He was wearing khaki trousers and a Hawaiian shirt which, for some reason, made me assume he was the barman.

'Good afternoon,' he said. 'I'm trying to catch a frog.'

I waited while he did this. Then he brought it over to show me: a small, livid, lime-green tree frog, its throat pulsing uncontrollably.

'I'll have a beer,' I said. 'As soon as you're ready.'

He pushed the frog out through some louvred glass windows at one end of the bar, before going behind it and pouring me a glass of beer.

'How much?' I said.

'The house will pay.'

Then he engaged me in conversation, in the time-honoured barkeeper to client manner: 'Where are you from?', 'How long are you staying?' Fairly soon I began to suspect he might be a manager – he seemed far too forward and intelligent to be running a cocktail bar at the Airport Hotel. By the time he asked me to have dinner with him that night I realized I'd been had.

'You thought I was the barman,' he said with some glee. 'Admit it. I got you.' He was very pleased with his subterfuge.

'Not for one second,' I said. 'I knew it as soon as you opened the bottle,' I improvised. I pointed to the bent bottle-top lying on the bar. 'No barman in Africa would've left that there. He'd pocket it.'

'Oh.' He looked disappointed. 'You sure about that?'

'Check it out the next time you're in a bar.'

He wagged a finger at me. 'You're lying, I know.'

I kept on denying it and agreed to have dinner that night. I was intrigued by him. He told me his name – Usman Shoukry – and spelled it for me, and told me what he did. After our meal that evening – during which I was introduced to two of his fellow pilots, whose prurient speculation I could sense swirling about me – he walked me back through the gardens to my room.

We stopped at an intersection of two paths.

'That's my chalet,' he said, pointing. 'I was wondering if you'd like to spend the night there with me.'

'No thank you.'

'It's for your own good.'

'Oh yes?' Suddenly I was beginning to like him less. 'I don't think so.'

'No, honestly.' His eyes were candid. 'If those fellows you met tonight ever think we haven't slept together they'll be round you like . . . like flies. Buzzing, buzzing.'

'I'll risk it.' I shook his hand. 'Thanks for dinner.'

He shrugged. 'Well, I warned you.'

But six weeks later, when I returned on my second trip, and he invited me to his 'chalet' again, I accepted.

Usman pulled into the airport and showed his pass to the bored guard. The barrier was raised and we drove through.

'Would you like to see my plane?' he asked.

We stopped by a large hangar, got out and walked towards a row of half a dozen Mig 15s. Here on the concrete apron one really felt the physical force of the heat. I could see the haze rising off the runway, almost as if the rays of the sun were rebounding, corrugating the scrub and palmettos at the perimeter.

Some of the Migs were silver – almost painfully bright in this sun – and some had been painted olive-drab. Here and there a mechanic worked. To one side I saw a row of small trolleys with pairs of teardrop-shaped tanks on them. Usman led me past the first two planes and stopped by a third. He spoke in Arabic to a mechanic, who was fixing something in the under-carriage bay. Usman was wearing a blue shirt over his swimming-shorts. On his feet were rubber flip-flops. I wore shorts and a T-shirt. I felt strange, as if we were Sunday barbecuers inspecting a friend's new sports car in the driveway of our suburban home.

I looked at Usman's Mig. To my eyes it was an ugly plane. It sat low on the ground and was tilted back somewhat, as if on its haunches. The air-intake to the jet was in the nose, a large black hole. On either side of this were twin elliptical recesses, each containing the snub barrel of a machine-gun. We walked round it. The wings were swept back, their leading edges showing a dull gleam of aluminium where the paint had been worn away by the friction of wind and dust. There were dark streaks of oil and grease on the flaps and the soft tyres looked like they needed inflating. I touched the thin metal sides of the plane. It was hot.

'I've been thinking,' I said. 'These planes are made from aluminium and aluminium is made from bauxite.

They dig bauxite out of the ground here. No wait' – he was going to interrupt me – 'what if some of that bauxite is sold to the Russians who turn it into aluminium which is made into Mig 15s? Then they sell the Migs to the air force here who bomb the people who dug the bauxite out of the ground.'

Usman, to his credit, looked uncomfortable for a moment. Then he shrugged. 'It's a crazy world, you know? Anyway, they don't sell any of this bauxite to the Russians.'

'How do you know?'

'I know.' Then he ducked under the wing to see what the mechanic was doing. I touched the plane again, rubbing the palp of my finger over a seam in the metal. This Mig seemed much smaller, close to, than I had imagined, having seen them many times flying in and out of the airport. On the ground and at this proximity their machine-like quality was far more in evidence. I could see all the scratches, dents and stains, the rows of rivet heads, places where the sun had caused the paint to flake and blister. Suddenly it was like any other machine – a bus or a car – a thing of components and working parts, of tubes and wires, levers and hinges. A flying machine.

Usman reappeared.

'What do you think of it?' he said.

'What's her name?' I said facetiously.

'He not she.'

'I thought planes and ships were female.'

'Not this one. This is "Boris". Good Russian name. Big strong bastard.' He gave it a bang with his fist. 'D'you want to sit inside?'

I walked up to the cockpit and peered inside. It looked grubby and very well used, the leather on the seat creased and fraying, the instrumental panel chipped and scarred.

On one side of the cockpit wall hung a curious cloth pouch, like a purse, embroidered with beads.

'What's that?' I said.

Usman reached past me and opened the flap. He took out a small blue-black gun, with ebony panels set in the grip with his initials inlaid in silver.

He showed it to me like an artefact, and then offered it to me to hold.

'It was from my squadron. When I left the air force. It's Italian, the best.'

It felt heavy for such a small gun. The metal was cold.

I gave it back. 'Why do you carry it in your plane?'

'Good luck.' He smiled. 'My special protection. And in case I'm shot down.'

'Don't say that.'

'Here, let me help you climb in.'

'Come on, Usman. I'm hot. I don't know anything about planes. I don't care.'

'Poor Boris,' he said to the plane ruefully. 'She doesn't like you.'

I had to laugh. Jesus Christ, I said, and turned and walked back to the car.

'What are those things?' I said, pointing at the silver teardrops on their little trolleys.

'Gasoline,' he said. 'Drop tanks.'

IKARIOS AND ERIGONE

No Migs fly out of the airport these days. A few months ago the air force moved its main base further south to counter the increasing EMLA *threat. The Airport Hotel is even more deserted than usual, as a result. I eat there once or twice a week, whenever Gunther invites me, and often we are the only diners in the entire restaurant. Which is a shame: the food has improved vastly under the new management. A new manager was appointed some months ago, a Greek, called Ikarios Panathatanos.*

Ikarios is a hefty, balding man who reminds me a little of Hauser. One evening he told me the origin of his christian name. The source is a very minor figure in Greek mythology. The original Ikarios was a farmer who discovered how to make wine from the grapes he grew. For a while he kept the secret to himself, making his wine and drinking it alone, covertly. But he enjoyed the experience so much he decided one day that he should share the pleasure with his neighbours and invited the entire village round to his house to partake of his marvellous discovery.

So the villagers drank their fill. However, as the symptoms of intoxication began to overwhelm them they grew convinced that this was an elaborate plot Ikarios had concocted to poison them. So in a drunken, paranoiac panic they stoned the hapless farmer to death.

But the tragedy did not end there. Ikarios's daughter Erigone, overcome with grief at her father's death, decided to take her own life and hung herself from an olive tree.

That was all Ikarios knew about his illustrious namesake. Ikarios has a pretty little three-year-old daughter whom he has naturally called Erigone. He sees nothing sinister in the connotation at all.

Hope needed a job and Professor Hobbes found her one. He telephoned her one day and suggested she come and see him. Months had gone by since her doctorate had been awarded and she could not satisfactorily explain her lethargy, even to herself. She had published one article and done some reading, but little more. It was as if she wanted someone else to initiate the next stage of her professional career, as if she hadn't the courage to take the next step unguided, of her own volition.

Hobbes was an elderly-looking man, in his early sixties, pot-bellied and moustachioed, who could have auditioned successfully for the role of old codger or benign grandad in a television commercial. The affable looks, however, belied a shrewd and often malicious nature. He was a powerful and influential figure in his field and the various scientific societies he was active in. Each year, from amongst his students, he selected one or two as special favourites and spoiled them blatantly, securing grants, better laboratory facilities and, eventually, jobs, almost as a demonstration of the efficacy of patronage.

In her first year Hope had been chosen as one of the elect. And it was understood too that if Hobbes took an interest in you it extended well beyond the walls of his department and was of no fixed duration, to be terminated unilaterally by him, as and when he felt like it. There were eminent academics around the world who were reminded periodically that the markers were still out and yet to be called in. Hope was well aware, as she first did little, and then nothing, to find a job, that her inertia would not pass unnoticed. When she heard Hobbes's surprisingly soft voice on the telephone, it was with sly relief rather than guilt that she gladly agreed to meet to 'discuss her future'.

'What is going on, Hope?' Hobbes said. 'I mean

just what the hell is going on?' He poured her a glass of wine. It was white and fragrant and perfectly cold. Hobbes had a fridge in his office. He smiled at her as she drank.

'Why didn't you apply for that lectureship in York? I could've rung Frank.'

'I got married.'

'So what?'

'Having got married, I rather wanted to spend some time with my husband.'

'How sentimental.'

'I need a job in London.'

'You should have taken the York job and commuted. Doesn't everyone do that sort of thing now?'

She let him berate her for her naivety for the allotted time, and then said she wouldn't mind something short-term. John was planning to go back to the States, she lied spontaneously, and said that she would not want to commit to anything that would last more than a year. Hobbes grudgingly said he would see what was around.

He called her again within a week. He had two jobs for her, he said, and she had better take one of them. Both were to start as soon as she was ready, both were a one-year contract. Neither was exactly in her area but she was well qualified to do them, and, in any event, he was 'old friends' with both the men in charge. The best one was in Africa, he said, studying wild chimpanzees.

'No, I don't think —'

'Don't interrupt. They're desperate. It's American-funded so you'll be very well paid. And it'll open all sorts of doors for you.'

No, she said, she couldn't go to Africa now. Out of the question.

He told her about the other job. 'One tenth the money,' he said, disgustedly. The advantage as she saw it, though, was that she could do it part-time. It was a survey of an ancient and historic estate in South Dorset, near the coast. An historian, an archaeologist and a geographer had been studying the landscape's history, and they needed an ecologist to complete the picture. 'Dating woodlands and hedgerows, that sort of thing,' Hobbes said. 'Not wildly exciting, but I told them you could handle that. No problem. Don't let me down.'

She duly met the project director, a former student of Hobbes, it turned out, and she was automatically approved. Graham Munro was a gaunt, mild man who was very unlikely, she realized, to challenge Hobbes's estimation of her ability. She would start in a month, they agreed, and she would spend two to three days a week working on location. Munro told her that there was a farm cottage on the estate that she could bunk down in.

Being employed cheered her up, she discovered. She wondered if it had been her joblessness that had made her fractious and worried, rather than John. He was pleased for her too, he said. They made plans for him to come down with her some weeks, if his own work permitted.

In her final month of idleness she suggested they both take a holiday. They decided to go back to Scotland, and rented a small house on an island off the west coast, reached by ferry from Mallaig.

Their house was on the edge of the island's only village. It was a low, single-storeyed, thick-walled cottage with deep-set windows with a view of the harbour and the bay. Inside it was plainly and functionally decorated: white distemper on the walls, brown linoleum on every floor and minimally furnished. There were two armchairs facing the fire and a dining-table with four chairs in the main room. The bedroom had an oak cupboard and a high, iron, double bed. There was a chilly lavatory but no bath; all washing had to be done at the sink in the kitchen, a small room at the back of the cottage that contained a gas stove but no refrigerator. There were working fireplaces in the bedroom and sitting-room, both of which heated the water. The whole place was lit by gas lamps. There was no phone, no television, no radio.

John said it was like living in a D. H. Lawrence novel, but he liked it, and so did Hope. It was austere but it worked. The fires kept the place warm, the hissing gas mantles provided adequate light for reading. The bed was big and hard and there were plenty of grey, prickly blankets. It was curious, but she found that the rigours of keeping the little house functioning imposed a similar discipline on them. They washed up after meals for the first time in their married life, and they never allowed the baskets of peat and logs to empty. They ate solid, simple meals bought from the village store: tinned stew and potatoes, meat pie and baked beans, freshly caught herring and cabbage. After their meal they would sit in their respective armchairs in front of the fire and read for two or three hours, or play chess. Hope had brought a sketch book with her and a quiver of new pencils. She started drawing again.

The older houses of the village were clustered around the simple harbour. The newer and remarkably ugly buildings – the post office, the 'Mini-Market', the primary school and the village hall – were set widely apart on the land behind, placed apparently randomly, facing different directions as if they were ashamed of each other. On a small promontory that jutted out into the bay was an hotel, the Lord of the Isles, that contained the island's only licensed bar. Elsewhere, throughout the island's eight by two miles area, were a handful of crofts – one or two derelict – another semi-village on the north shore and one grand house, surrounded by a small copse of leaning, wind-battered scotch pines, that served its current owner, a Dutch industrialist, as a fifth home. He owned great tracts of the island – hence the derelict crofts – and occasionally helicoptered in with his house guests for a summer weekend. Nobody on the island could understand why he had bought the place.

Very quickly, Hope and John established a routine. They awoke early, after eight hours of sound and dreamless sleep. John lit the fire in the sitting-room while Hope prepared the breakfast. Then they did their chores – replenishing fuel, buying food, preparing a packed lunch. This completed, they set off on their bicycles (hired from the Lord of the Isles) and cycled off – rain or shine – until they found a beach or cove that appealed to them. John was reading nothing but detective novels – he had three dozen paperbacks with him – and as they cycled along he would recount, with astonishing recall and detail, the story of the latest one he had read. Once they had found their beach, and had settled themselves, they prowled around, searching the tidewrack for flotsam and jetsam. Hope sketched, John read or went for walks. They never saw another soul.

They might cycle on after their lunch – their aim was

to have covered the entire shoreline of the island – and they usually returned home about four in the afternoon for tea, and sometimes a siesta. At opening time they would stroll up to the Lord of the Isles for a drink and would linger there until they felt hungry. Then followed their prosaic meal and an evening's reading and drawing. They went to bed when they felt tired, normally before eleven. They made love every night of that holiday, almost as a reflex. The slab, marmoreal cold of their bed had them squirming into each other's arms for warmth and their arousal was immediate and simultaneous. Their sex was as efficient and unpretentious as their surroundings – no foreplay, no experimentation, no undue prolongation of climax – and they were both asleep within minutes of it ending.

On the edge of the village was a hairy, sloping football pitch and behind one of the goalposts was a rusting skip that was the repository of all the village's 'hard' rubbish, as the notice on its side proclaimed. Newspapers, boxes, tins and bottles – anything that the earth could not break down. All the 'soft' rubbish, their landlady, the postmistress, informed them, was to be buried. There was a spade in the wee shed by the back door for this very purpose, she told them, and she would be much obliged if they interred their refuse at least twenty yards from the house. On their third day on the island Hope volunteered to dispose of two plastic bags of hard rubbish if John would take care of the soft.

There was a keen breeze and a fine drizzle that spattered against the hood of her windcheater, but the clouds above were hurrying and broken and Hope could see shreds of indecent blue amongst the grey. She was stiff from cycling and so, after depositing her rubbish, and in an attempt to loosen up, she jogged slowly round the football pitch a couple of times. The island was flat, the roads were well metalled. Only the strength of the wind impeded or assisted cyclist and machine.

Half a dozen cold little boys in sports kit ran out of the schoolhouse and listlessly kicked a too big football at each other, their complaints shrill and protesting. A young schoolmistress, who was clearly indifferent to the rules of soccer, ignored them, hunching out of the wind by the goalposts to light a cigarette. Hope smiled at her as she jogged past and received a cheery good morning in reply. They had seen each other in the Lord of the Isles the night before and no doubt would continue to do so for the rest of the holiday. Hope looked at the little tottering boys with their raw red noses and knees and hurried back to John.

He was not in the cottage so she went to look for him, through the back garden, a stretch of humpy waste ground with brambles and nettles, towards the remains of what she supposed was a wooden privy and a carious dry-stone wall. Beyond that was the heathy spit of land that made up one arm of the bay and beyond that the sun shone on a brilliant cold Atlantic.

John was on the other side of the wall, in his shirt-sleeves, standing in a freshly dug pit, waist-deep, digging. He was unaware of Hope's approach, so preoccupied was he with his task. He looked round when he heard her laughter.

'For God's sake,' she said, 'it's a poly bag of chicken bones and potato peelings, not a bloody coffin.'

He looked, as if for the first time, at his hole and its prodigious depth. His expression was bemused, slightly surprised.

He climbed out, smiling vaguely.

'Got carried away,' he said. Then he dropped his spade. 'Hold on, I've ... I've got to write something down.' He ran into the house. Hope rummaged in the pockets of his jacket, hung on the hinge of the privy door, found his cigarettes and lit one. The sun that had been shining on the sea had moved to the land and it warmed her face as she sat on the stone wall and looked at the hole John had dug. The earth was moist and peaty the colour and consistency of the richest rum-soaked, treacle-infused chocolate cake. The blade of the old spade was clean, its edge silvered from years of abrasion, the handle waxy and worn with use.

She smoked her cigarette and was about to go and look for him when he rejoined her. He was frowning. He picked up the spade and looked at it as if it held some answer to a baffling question. He threw the bag of rubbish in the pit and began to fill it in.

'It's quite extraordinary,' he said as he worked. 'I started digging. And then my mind ...' He paused. 'I started thinking.' He screwed his face up. 'And I worked something out as I was digging,' he said slowly, as if he still couldn't believe what had happened. 'Something that had been puzzling me for ages. That's why I had to go and write it down.'

'What?'

'An equation.' He started to tell her but she stopped him.

He laid the squares of turf over the soil and stamped them down. 'Quite weird,' he said. 'The whole thing.'

That evening, after the meal, instead of reading, John sat at the table and worked, steadily covering the pages of her sketch book with the complex hieroglyphics of mathematical formulae. The next day he had no detective story to recount to her but he was so elated at what he had achieved the night before that he went swimming in the sea, naked, for all of ninety seconds. She folded him in a towel and then in the picnic blanket, laughing at the image he had presented emerging from the waves, white with shock and cold, and his crabbed, crouched stumble up the beach to rejoin her.

'Brass monkeys . . .' his voice blurted hoarsely, his body vibrating like a machine. 'Fucking brass monkeys!' Then he laughed himself, an exuberant bellow, like a blare on a trombone. Hope had never heard him laugh like that before. It was odd to hear the brazen, clear voice of exhilaration.

The following day, as they were about to set off, she came out of the front door and found him tying the spade to the crossbar of his bicycle.

'OK,' she said. 'What's going on?'

'It's an experiment,' he said, smiling. 'I want to see if it'll work again.'

So Hope sat and sketched while John dug a hole. He made it six feet square and, working methodically, pausing for a rest from time to time, he had it five feet deep within two hours. He stopped for lunch.

'How's it going?' Hope said.

'Nothing yet.' He looked vaguely troubled.

'You can't just *arrange* to have a flash of insight, you know,' Hope said, reasonably. 'I'm sure Archimedes didn't start bathing several times a day after the eureka business.'

'You're right,' he said. 'Probably . . . But it was

definitely something to do with the digging itself. The effort. The logic of digging. Shifting volumes ... Seemed to clear something in my mind.' He reached for a sandwich. 'I'll have one more shot at it after lunch.'

He started again. Hope watched him enlarge the hole, cutting turf, stacking it neatly, and then sinking the spade into the dark soil, working the blade, loading it and flinging the earth on to its moist pile. There was something satisfying about the work, even she could see that: simple but effortful, and with instant and visible results. The hole grew deeper. Hope went for a walk.

When she came back he was sitting down making more notes in her sketch book.

'Eureka?' she asked.

'Semi-eureka.' He grinned. 'Something totally unexpected. Three leaps ahead of where I was, if you see what I mean. In fact I can't quite see where it'll join up yet, but . . .' He looked suddenly solemn. 'It's an amazing idea.'

She sat and watched him fill the hole in.

'But this is the boring part,' she said.

'No, no. I'm doing this with gratitude. The hole has worked for me, so I gladly return it to its non-hole state.'

'Jesus Christ.'

'Up yours.' He was happy.

The new idea he had received appeared to satisfy him. He stopped working and started reading detective novels again, and for some days their old routine re-established itself. But on their penultimate day on the island, ignoring her protests, he brought the spade with him again.

'Don't you feel a bit of a fool?' she mocked him.

'Why should I?' he said, with some belligerence. 'What do you know? These ideas I've had this holiday ... I haven't thought like that in years.' He looked at her with some pity. 'I don't give a toss about your sensibilities.'

'Don't worry about me. Dig away.'

He did. He dug without stopping for three hours, this time cutting out a long, thigh-deep trench. She forced him to stop and rest for a while but he soon resumed. There was a 'glimmering' he said. At dusk he gave up, exhausted. 'We'll come back and fill it in tomorrow,' she told him, pulling him away.

They cycled home slowly, freewheeling down the gentle slope into the village. The first yellow lights shone in the windows, the clouds over the mainland were pink and plum, the sea was silver plate.

John seemed unduly disconsolate. She tried to cheer him up.

'Let's eat in the hotel tonight,' she said. 'Get pissed.'

He agreed, readily enough. Then he said: 'I was so close today. I know it. There was something key, something crucial. But I just couldn't get to it.' He made a grabbing movement with both his hands. 'Just out of my reach.'

As Hope leant her bike against the wall, the thought came to her, unbidden, unwelcome, that perhaps her husband was going insane.

CABBAGES ARE NOT SPHERES

Memory from Scotland. John Clearwater in the tiny kitchen preparing a salad of winter vegetables. He has a whole red cabbage in his hand that he is about to chop. Hope sees him staring at it. He holds it up to the light and then turns his head in her direction. He tosses the cabbage to her, which she catches. It is cool beneath her palms and surprisingly heavy. She chucks it back.

'Cabbages are not spheres,' he says.

'If you say so.' She smiles but she doesn't really know how to respond. This is the kind of remark he makes from time to time, cryptic, askew.

'Well, sort of spherical,' she says tentatively.

He cuts the cabbage in half and shows her the crisp violet and white striations, whorled like a giant fingerprint. The point of his knife traces the wobbling parabola of a leaf edge.

'These are not semi-circles.'

Hope sees what he is aiming at. 'A fir tree,' she ventures, 'is not a cone.'

John chops up the cabbage, swiftly and efficiently, like a chef, smiling to himself.

'Rivers do not flow in straight lines,' he says.

'Mountains are not triangles.'

'A tree . . . a tree does not branch exponentially.'

'I give up,' she says. 'I don't like this game.'

Later, after their meal, he returns to the subject and asks her how she would set about measuring, precisely, the circumference of a cabbage. With a tape measure, Hope says.

'Every little bump and weal? Every bit of leaf-buckle?'

'Christ . . . Take lots of measurements, get an average.'

'No precision, though. It's not going to work.'

He leaves the table and starts to jot ideas down in a notebook.

Hope now knows that this set him off down another path. He became preoccupied with the conviction that the abstract precision of geometry and measurement really had nothing to do with the imprecise and changing dimensions of living things, could not cope accurately with the intrinsic raggedness of the natural world. The natural world is full of irregularity and random alteration, but in the antiseptic, dust-free, shadowless, brightly lit, abstract realm of the mathematicians they like their cabbages spherical, please. No bumps, no folds, no dents or dinges. No surprises.

When I turned off the main road on to the laterite track that led to Sangui I had a distinct and unusual sensation of pleasure. Analysing the feeling further, I realized that I was actually looking forward to getting back to work. The two days in the town, and the time spent with Usman, had been restorative. I had needed them and now I was refreshed. Life was all a matter of contrasts, Professor Hobbes used to reiterate. You can't enjoy anything without a contrast to it. I smiled to myself as I thought about him. 'The tide is either coming in or it's going out,' was another of his saws, applied infuriatingly to any complaint or moan. Funnily enough, it always seemed to work. I had gone to his office once to remonstrate about faulty equipment or some other injustice. He had looked squarely at me, patted my arm, and had said: 'Hope, my dear, the tide is either coming in or going out.' I had gone away, pacified, consoled and somehow wiser too, I had felt.

My reflections on the wisdom of Hobbes almost caused me to miss seeing Alda as I drove through Sangui. I caught a glimpse of him waving from the doorway of a hut but by then I was virtually out of the village. I couldn't be bothered to stop, so I tooted the horn and bumped on up the track to Grosso Arvore. I wasn't sure either if it had been a wave of welcome or a request to halt. In any event, I reasoned, if he wanted to talk to me he knew where I would be.

As I parked the Land Rover in the garage I gave three loud blasts on the horn to alert the kitchen staff. Martim and Vemba were already unloading the provisions as I climbed out of the cab. I stretched and yawned, and, as I did so, I saw Mallabar hurry across the road from his bungalow. I looked at my watch – just after four. We had made good time. But I was surprised to see him at home at this time of day, and as he strode towards me I could see he was upset about something. I put on a smile.

'What's up, Eugene?' I asked.

'Hope . . .' He stopped in front of me. 'Ghastly accident. I'm so sorry. I just can't think.'

He was uncharacteristically agitated. As one does at these moments I instinctively prepared myself for the worst possible news. My father or my mother. My sister . . .

'What is it?'

'A fire. There's been a fire. Your tent . . . I can't think how it happened.'

Mallabar related the events to me as we strode up Main Street towards my tent. My huge relief was now being replaced by more mundane concerns. It had happened the night I left, he told me. Toshiro had seen the flames. It seemed that Liceu, the boy who cleaned for me, had carelessly dropped a cigarette stub.

'But Liceu doesn't smoke,' I said.

'Oh yes, I think so.'

We paused beneath the big tree. Through the hibiscus bushes at the curve of the road I could just make out the front of my tent. It looked undamaged.

'Just a small fire?' I said, hopefully.

'Not that small.'

We moved on. 'Where is Liceu?'

'I sacked him. Immediately.'

My tent was in fact half destroyed, the back half. The front looked fine but the back consisted only of a charred supporting pole and a few shreds of burnt canvas. The tin roof was buckled and blistered. To one side stood a sorry pile of my damaged possessions. The bed – ruined; my clothes trunk – carbonized.

'My clothes.' I felt a sudden lassitude descend on me.

'I'm so dreadfully sorry, Hope.'

I ran my fingers down both sides of my face.

'We got a few bits and pieces out,' Mallabar said. 'And I think you had some clothes being washed.'

We walked inside. My desk was badly scorched but still standing. After some tugging I managed to open the drawer. Black soaked lumps. Cinders. My letters, some books. All my field notes and journal.

I walked around my ruined home. I had lived here for almost a year.

Mallabar's concern was palpable; he was practically wringing his hands. 'We'll get it fixed up. Back to normal. Soon as possible.'

'All my field notes have gone. And the journal.'

He winced with sympathy. 'Damn. God. I knew it – I

saw the desk. Didn't dare to look.' He gave a sad laugh. 'I was praying you'd taken them with you.'

'Worse luck.'

I moved into the census building. It was a long, thin, prefab hut – army surplus, I guessed – that at one time had housed eight census workers in the good old days. I set up my makeshift quarters at one end. A new bed was provided and a folding canvas chair. That, and my few clothes returned from the laundry, made up my reduced stock of personal possessions. In some respects my new home was better than my old one – I had wooden boards under my feet for a start – but it did not raise my morale. I felt incredibly temporary, all of a sudden, like someone passing through who had to be put up for a night.

My colleagues were upset for me and full of commiserations that evening in the canteen. Mallabar promised again that my tent would be repaired as soon as possible and Ginga donated a desk and a bright green rug to give me something to work on and to cheer up the hut a little. They were kind, but in the end the misfortune was mine and only a mishap to them. Even the destruction of my field notes was of minor significance. My job at Grosso Arvore was no more than a watching brief; the main body of work at the project would be unaffected by the loss of my data.

I asked Toshiro, who had raised the alarm, what exactly the sequence of events had been. He told me he had been working alone in the lab, had gone to the back door for a breath of fresh air and had seen the smoke. He ran over but by then the back of my tent was well ablaze. He shouted for help and had snatched

a few bits and pieces (a wash-stand and enamel basin –
where were they?) from the front before the heat drove
him off. Others arrived, and buckets of water ferried from
Hauser's shower stall had eventually doused the flames.

'Lucky we had Anton's shower there,' he said. 'Otherwise everything would have gone.'

'Where was Hauser?'

Toshiro frowned. 'I don't know. No, actually, I think
he had gone to the feeding area.'

I swear to you it was only then that I first thought
that the fire might have been deliberately started. You
may think me unduly naïve, but Mallabar's anxiety and
the patent sincerity of his sympathy had me convinced.

'Was Eugene anywhere near?'

'Well, yes. After me he was the first one there. In fact
he thought of using water from the shower.'

Hauser absent from his lab and Mallabar close at
hand. A fire started by an allegedly careless smoker
who was now sacked and not present, or able, to defend
himself. No serious damage caused, and minor in-
convenience to the victim. But a year's data gone up in
smoke. I thought further: in theory I should not even
have been away – I had accepted advancement up the
provisioning rota as a 'favour' to Mallabar.

I was clearing my tray when Hauser came in. He
marched straight over to me and put his hands on my
shoulders. For one horrible moment I thought he was
going to hug me, but an inadvertent and automatic
stiffening on my part must have informed against the
wisdom of this course of action, and he contented
himself with a sorrowful, intense look into my eyes.

'Ach, Hope,' he said. 'It's a bastard thing. Really a
bastard.'

He was good, as good as Mallabar, but it didn't matter: I was already plotting my revenge on them both.

He went on to enquire about my bits and pieces. Had I lost this? Could he replace it with that? I happily accepted the loan of his transistor radio.

The Vails had asked me round to the bungalow for a drink. I had been quick to accept; I was not particularly looking forward to my first night in the census hut.

We sat – Ian, Roberta and me – and drank some bourbon. Roberta had made great efforts with their two-roomed cottage. It was comfortable and homey, with cane chairs and bright overlapping rugs on the floor. The walls were painted light blue and were hung with pictures – local naïve oils – and photographs of previous research projects they had been involved in. Ian in Borneo with orang-utans. Roberta graduating, clutching her rolled diploma in two tight fists. Ian and Roberta at the Institute for Primate Studies in Oklahoma, where they had met and married.

That evening, Roberta was strangely relaxed and fussed over me in a rather maternal manner. She brought out a pack of her menthol cigarettes and smoked one, delicately. I could sense Ian's resentment crackle round the room at this little act of domestic defiance. I puffed away at my pungent Tuskers and soon the air was hung with rocking blue strata of smoke. Roberta steadily became tight on bourbon and started bitching warily about Ginga Mallabar, testing me out to discover whether I was friend or foe. My pointed neutrality encouraged her, and we were then regaled with a year or two's worth of hoarded resentments and grudges. Ginga was manipulative. Ginga commandeered the huge proportion of Mallabar's royalties. Ginga's needless and inept meddling with agents and publishers had delayed publication of the book by over a year, and so on. I sat and listened, nodding and saying things like 'My God' and 'That's a bit excessive' from time to time. Eventually, she stopped and rose slowly to her feet, announcing she had to visit the little girl's room.

She paused at the door on her way out. 'We should do this more often, Hope,' she said.

I concurred.

'I think it's bad the way we all slink back to our homes in the evening. It's so . . . So British. No offence.'

'None taken,' I said. 'In fact, I agree.'

'Well, that's one thing you can't blame Ginga for,' Ian Vail said, with acid pedantry.

'And why not?'

'Because she's Swiss.'

'Same difference.'

'For God's sake!'

I could sense the row – that would inevitably take place after I had gone – was now boiling up dangerously, and so chipped in with some banal observation about how the very geometry of the camp site precluded easy social toing and froing – instancing its linear development along Main Street and the almost suburban concern for domestic privacy evidenced in the placing of the various bungalows and huts, etc. etc. The bourbon made me articulate and authoritative.

'You know, Hope, I never thought of that,' Roberta said, frowning, and going off into the night to the latrine.

Ian opened the front door for a moment to let some

smoke out. The bungalow was screened and two moths took the opportunity to flutter in.

'To my knowledge,' Ian said, in a thin voice, 'she hasn't smoked for three years. What's got into her?'

I decided it wasn't worth correcting him. Roberta's little secret was safe with me.

'Leave her alone, Ian,' I said. 'She was enjoying herself, that's all. God, but she's not too fond of Ginga, though, is she?'

He wasn't listening. 'She *was* relaxed, wasn't she . . .?' he said, as if surprised. He looked at me and gave me an apologetic smile.

'I only say that,' he explained, 'because she's always been a little frightened of you.'

'Of *me*?'

'Oh, yes.' He gave an edgy laugh. 'Aren't we all.'

I decided not to follow up this remark any further. I reflected on something Meredith had once told me; one of life's great verities, she had said: the *last* thing we ever learn about ourselves is our effect.

I slept well in the census hut, lulled by the bourbon, no doubt, and oblivious to the many rustlings, scurryings and crepitations that emanated from the further reaches of the long room. The place was full of lizards, and something – I hoped it was a squirrel – was living in the ceiling space. Before I fell asleep I heard the tick and scratch of sharp claws on the plaster board as it scampered to and fro, to and fro above my head.

I was woken by João's knock at six in the morning. We went to the canteen for some tea and to collect my packed lunch. João said he hadn't seen Liceu for a few days – he was very upset at the sacking, and had gone away. I suggested that whenever he came back we should meet up.

As we crossed the Danube I broke the bad news to João about the loss of my field notes and journal.

'A whole year,' I said, ruefully. Now that I was heading out to work, the loss was suddenly painful. 'We'll just have to start again.'

'Well, I don't think is necessary,' João said, trying not to smile. 'I have my own notes. Plenty. Every night I make Alda copy. For his training. You know he is not so good for writing.'

'From the time I came? Everything?'

'Just the daily journal.' He shrugged. 'Of course, some days I am not with you.'

'But I was either with you, or Alda ... And Alda has his notes?'

'Oh yes. I check him every night.'

I let the smile grow on my face. 'I'll come and get them,' I said. 'Tonight.'

'Of course.' He was very pleased with himself. 'So nothing is waste.'

'What would I do without you, João?'

He laughed at me, averting his face and making a tight wheezing sound. I clapped him on the shoulder.

'Well done, João,' I said. 'We're going to be famous.'

We came to a junction in the path. Back to work.

'All right,' I said. 'Where do we start?'

'Ow.' João smacked a palm against his forehead. 'I forgot. Lena and her baby, I saw her. She have a boy.'

'Let's go and find her.'

We found Lena at midday with a few other members of the southern group. They were resting in the shade of an ironwood tree. Lena was nursing her new baby and around her lounged Mr Jeb, Conrad and Rita-Lu. There was no sign of Clovis, Rita-Mae, Lester and Muffin.

João and I approached a little closer than usual, settling down only thirty feet or so from Lena. Her baby was almost hairless, and blue-black in colour. Conrad was grooming Mr Jeb, but I noticed from his regular glances towards Lena that he was clearly fascinated by the baby. Rita-Lu lay idly in the grass. She looked half asleep. I noticed a fresher pinkness on her rump and possibly some signs of swelling.

'We need a name,' João said softly, 'for the baby.'

I thought for a while. 'Bobo,' I said, finally. I had no idea why. João wrote it down on his record sheet: 'Bobo, male, son of Lena.'

Conrad stopped grooming Mr Jeb and slowly made his way over to Lena. She was leaning back against the trunk of the ironwood tree. Bobo clung feebly to the hair on her belly – through my binoculars I could see his tiny fists clutching tufts of fur – and sucked hungrily on her right nipple. Conrad moved closer, and Lena gave a small bark of warning.

Conrad sat down a few feet away and gazed at them both. Then, with Lena watching him intently, he reached forward very slowly across the gap between them and touched Bobo's back. I had always assumed that Clovis had impregnated Lena, but now I had a funny feeling that Conrad might be Bobo's father. Then Lena got up and moved away from him. I saw that the placenta was still hanging from her and the black loop of the umbilical cord was still connected to Bobo.

I shifted my position slightly and the noise I made caused Conrad to turn and look at me. With his white sclerotics, Conrad's gaze was always the most disturbing I had ever received from a chimpanzee. The whites around the brown iris made his eyes as meaningful as any human's. I looked at his black muzzle, the wide thin slit of his mouth and his heavy brows . . . he always seemed to be frowning, Conrad, a rather solemn and dignified character, not given to displays of frivolity. He came towards me a few paces and made some pant-hoots. Then he sat down and stared at me for a full minute, unswervingly. I looked into his eyes for a second or two, and then turned away.

Then, in the distance, I heard more hooting and barking. The other chimps hooted in response. Soon a crashing of branches heralded Clovis's arrival, followed by Rita-Mae, Lester and Muffin. Like Conrad, Clovis was very curious about Bobo, but Lena would not let him come close, barking and grimacing and even, at one stage, climbing into the ironwood tree. Clovis gave up and moved away. However, when Rita-Mae approached, Lena was much less anxious, even going so far as to lay Bobo down in the grass. Rita-Mae peered closely at him, seemingly fascinated, and stroked him gently once or twice. Then Lena gathered him up and moved away again to the periphery of the group.

After resting in this way for a couple of hours, the chimpanzees roused themselves and moved off northward, João and I following behind. They halted at a fig tree above the banks of the Danube, where the river cut a deep ravine through the foothills of the escarpment. We watched them feed for a while. I watched

Rita-Lu repeatedly touching her genital area and sniffing at her finger. She was coming into season.

That evening I walked down the track into Sangui to collect all João and Alda's field notes. João had said that he hoped Liceu might be there.

João's house was one of the largest in the village, and one of the few to be made of concrete. He was sitting on the narrow verandah with a small baby on his knee. He told me this was his third granddaughter. I took the baby while he went to collect the papers. She was naked, fat, and almost asleep, drugged by her feed. She had small, gold earrings in her long, soft lobes and around her hips was a string of tiny multi-coloured beads. Her belly button was a small hard dome, the size of a thimble. I stroked her hair and thought of Lena and Bobo.

João came back with his wife, Doneta, who relieved me of her grandchild. João had a great bundle of papers, mainly copies of the daily analysis sheets. He turned up the light on the verandah lantern and I quickly sifted through them.

'Is this everything?' I asked him.

'Even today's follow,' he said.

This was ideal. 'Is Liceu coming?' I asked. I was keen to get back home with this material.

'He is already here. Liceu!' he called into the darkness of the compound. After a moment's pause, Liceu stepped uneasily into the circle of light cast by the lantern. Liceu was a teenager, about sixteen or seventeen, a constantly grinning, rather gormless boy who had wanted desperately to be a field assistant but who had neither the aptitude nor the patience. He came forward reluctantly, his face heavy with hurt and resentment, and started immediately and with belligerent conviction to protest his innocence. I let him go on for a while and began to piece together his version of events.

He had been tidying my tent, he said, and he had taken my dirty clothes to the camp laundry to be washed. He had been sitting chatting in the cooks' compound when he had heard a commotion and run out to find the tent well ablaze. No, he said, he had not seen any sign of Mr Hauser or Mr Mallabar.

He had no idea how the fire started.

Doneta brought us all a mug of sweet tea. I lit a cigarette and offered one to João. He accepted. Liceu was still fulminating at the injustice of his dismissal in an unpleasant droning way when I casually offered him the pack. He said at once, 'No thank you, Mam,' and carried on talking. Two seconds later he stopped, realized what I had done to him, and looked at me accusingly.

'Ah Mam, you know I don' never smoke.' He sucked air disapprovingly through his teeth. He spread his hands. 'Tell her that, João.'

João confirmed this. I reassured Liceu, and apologized for testing him in that way. If I had not known it before, I did now: the fire in my tent was not the result of one of Liceu's cigarette butts.

Later, I walked back alone up the track to Grosso Arvore, hefting a thick bundle of daily field records under my arm. The oval pool of light from my torch shone four feet ahead on the ground as I searched for snakes and scorpions, its beam freckled with dancing night insects. I wasn't entirely sure what I was going to do with all this data, to tell the truth, but it seemed to me clear that if Mallabar and Hauser wanted my records destroyed, then it would be prudent for me to try and reproduce some copy of my own research, however patchy. Something Roberta had said also nagged at me: if Ginga had delayed publication of the book for a year, did that imply that its publication was now imminent? And could that explain the panic and unseemly cover-up of the dead baby chimp? Also, all this talk about money was intriguing. Mallabar had been made wealthy by his work at Grosso Arvore; I wondered how much he would receive around the world for the successor to *The Peaceful Primate* and *Primate's Progress*?

I sat up late that night in the census hut analysing and summarizing the information in João and Alda's field records. To be secure, I really required copies of all these, but the nearest photocopiers were a six-hour drive away ... Perhaps I could volunteer to do next week's provisioning run again? I smiled to myself. Usman would be very surprised.

Around midnight I came to the final day's notes. There was João's sighting of Lena and her new baby ... I turned the page: here, Alda had seen six unidentified male chimpanzees in southern territory. I frowned – they must have been northerners. I checked the map references. According to Alda's estimations they were well south of the Danube.

I stood up and paced around the census hut. This was most unusual. Since the community split no northern chimps had ever travelled that far south ... I yawned, went back to my desk and tidied up my papers. I wondered if Ian Vail had noticed this migration; if it was temporary, or if the little band of northerners were still in the south?

I undressed, went to bed and forgot about it. That

night I dreamed of Hauser, emerging naked from his shower stall and scampering across the grass to my tent with a box of matches in his hand. He struck match after match and held them to the canvas in vain. Then suddenly Mallabar appeared, unzipped his fly, and pissed on the side. His urine ignited like blazing gasoline and soon the tent was burning fiercely. Then with horrible squeals Lena fled from it, Bobo clutched to her belly, her placenta bouncing and dragging on the ground behind her . . .

I remembered this dream vividly the next morning and wondered vaguely what my unconscious was trying to convey: Hauser could barely strike a light, while Mallabar pissed like a flame-thrower. It made no sense to me.

When João arrived he said he felt ill – a fever, he said. I sent him home. I picked up my provisions from the canteen and headed south to look for Lena and Bobo. I found them towards mid-morning, with all the other members of the southern group present, at the half-dead fig tree. I noticed that Lena's placenta had dropped free in the night and that only six inches of dry, shrivelled umbilical cord hung from Bobo's hairless belly. Rita-Lu's sexual swelling had also grown and both Mr Jeb and Clovis were intensely interested in it, sniffing and inspecting her genital area whenever possible. Mr Jeb even squatted down and presented his spiky erection to her, but she screamed at him and he scampered off, promptly. The males generally seemed less curious about Bobo today, but Rita-Mae and Rita-Lu constantly approached Lena and her son. Lena was cautious, but she allowed them to hunch over the baby, peering at him and touching him gently from time to time with their fingers.

I took up my position and observed them for almost three hours. My head was full of suppositions and hypotheses about the fire, and the possible role in it played by Mallabar or Hauser. I had temporarily hidden the field notes beneath the mattress of my bed, but the census hut was not well blessed with hiding-places and I realized, on reflection, that beneath the mattress was the first place anyone would search. I wondered whether I would be wiser leaving them with João until I had had copies made, but couldn't decide. All the time, I asked myself, fruitlessly, what on earth was going on.

Then I heard a warning bark that snapped me out of my circling speculations. I looked up. Lena, holding Bobo to her, was now sitting in a low branch of the fig tree. Rita-Lu was approaching her, on the ground, one hand held out. Behind Lena, I saw Rita-Mae climbing higher in the tree. Lena bared her teeth at Rita-Lu. I wondered what I had missed, the mood was now so clearly tense and hostile. Rita-Lu persisted, arm held out, inching closer, as if she wanted to pet Bobo. Lena screamed furiously at her, the noise shrill and ragged, and stood up on the branch, as if she were about to jump to the ground and run off. But before she could move further, Rita-Mae swung down through the branches of the tree above her and threw herself on to Lena's back. All three fell six feet to the ground.

At this commotion, the other chimps began to scream and display but none intervened in the fight. As Lena hit the ground, still clutching Bobo, Rita-Lu immediately grabbed her free arm and sank her teeth into her hand, working her jaws violently, chewing on the flesh of her palm. Lena screamed in agony, and with rapid jerking movements tried to pull her hand free.

Rita-Lu hung on and I saw Lena's blood falling from the sides of her mouth as her head was jerked to and fro. Meanwhile, Rita-Mae had leapt on Lena's back again and was trying to rip Bobo from his mother's grasp. Then she backed off and lunged and snapped at Lena's rear, her teeth gashing her bare rump badly.

At this new attack, Lena dropped Bobo, her head arched back in a shriek of pain. She whirled round and leapt on Rita-Mae, snapping and punching with her fists. Rita-Lu immediately seized the baby and climbed with it up into the tree. Lena tore herself away from Rita-Mae and raced after her child. She bit Rita-Lu on the shoulder and tore Bobo away from her. Now Lena had Bobo, but Rita-Mae was in the tree beneath her and was snapping and biting at her feet while Rita-Lu, above her, repeatedly hit her about the head and shoulders with her hands. Lena held one arm above her head to protect herself. Rita-Mae, with a sudden lunging movement, grabbed Bobo and shimmied down the tree to the ground with the baby, while Rita-Lu kept up the attack.

Bobo was making a shrill keening sound, his thin arms batting the air uselessly. Rita-Mae bounded away from the tree, holding him out at arm's length with one hand. Then she squatted on a rock and drew him into her breast as if she was going to cuddle him.

It was at that moment that I knew what she was about to do. I screamed at her: 'Rita-Mae! Rita-Mae!' But I was just another sound in the cacophony of sounds, and she didn't hear me, or was not bothered by my desperate shouts. Bobo wriggled and squirmed in her grasp, then Rita-Mae hunched forward and bit strongly into his forehead. I heard a distinct cracking sound as the frail skull was crushed by her teeth.

Bobo died instantly. At this, Rita-Lu immediately broke off the fight with Lena, retreating higher into the fig tree. Lena lowered herself slowly to the ground, exhausted and bleeding from the bad wounds on her hand and rump. The noise subsided.

I looked round. Rita-Mae was eating Bobo. She tore into his belly and pulled out his entrails with her teeth. She flung his guts away on to the rocks. Rita-Lu, meanwhile, climbed out of the tree, circled round Lena – who started to scream, loudly and monotonously – and rejoined her mother. They both fed on Bobo's body while Lena screamed vainly at them. Then, abruptly, she stopped. She seemed to lose all interest; all her outrage disappeared. She gathered up some leaves and dabbed at the wound on her rump with them.

Rita-Mae and Rita-Lu continued to eat the baby. Lester came up to his mother but she pushed him away vigorously. The other chimps also seemed to grow indifferent to what was going on. Only Lena kept staring at Rita-Mae and Rita-Lu. Then she left the tree and made her way over the rocks towards them. She stopped about six feet away, and watched them silently as they ate her dead baby. Then she began to whimper and extended her hand. At first Rita-Mae ignored this gesture. Lena circled around the two of them. She found a fragment of Bobo's entrails on a rock, picked it up, sniffed it and let it fall. She whimpered again. Rita-Mae dropped Bobo's body and went towards her. Lena whimpered submissively. Rita-Mae embraced her, holding her in her arms for a full minute. Then she released her and returned to the baby's corpse. Lena sat and watched Rita-Mae and Rita-Lu for the rest of the afternoon as they fed idly on the body. At dusk, when they moved off to their nesting site, Rita-Mae draped the shreds of Bobo's body over her shoulders like a scarf.

Mallabar's face remained still and emotionless as I told him what I had seen. We were in the census hut, alone, the evening meal was over. I sat on the bed, he sat by the desk. I finished talking. He looked down, I could see his jaw muscles working busily beneath his neat beard.

'Was the field observer with you?' he asked, formally.

'No. He was ill so I sent him home.'

'So there was no other witness.'

'For God's sake, I'm not on trial. I saw –'

'I'm sorry, Hope,' he interrupted me. 'Deeply sorry that you should feel this way.'

'Feel what way? What're you talking about?'

'I'm prepared, just this once, to accept that the shock of the fire and the loss of a year's research may explain this . . . this fantastical story.'

He looked at me, his face full of concern. I said nothing.

'On a personal level,' he went on, 'I can only record my deep hurt that you should feel such resentment and bitterness towards us here, your friends and colleagues. And whatever you may think, we are your friends.' He stood up. 'You've changed, Hope.'

'Good.'

'No it's not. And I'm sorry for you.'

This made me mad, but he started speaking again before I could interrupt.

'I'll overlook this now,' he said, 'but I must warn you that, if you persist in these fabrications, if you repeat them to anyone outside this room, I will have to terminate your employment here, immediately.' He paused. 'As for myself, I won't speak of this to anyone. At all.'

'I see.'

'Do you understand?'

'I understand everything.'

'Then you're a shrewd person, Hope. So please don't let this foolishness continue.' He stopped at the door. 'We won't talk about this again,' he said, and left.

I worked hard that night. By the time I went to bed I had most of my article drafted out. I was pleased with my title too: 'Infanticide and cannibalism amongst the wild chimpanzees of the Grosso Arvore project'. The peaceful primate's days were over.

FERMAT'S LAST THEOREM

A Peano Curve. The Weierstrass Function. The Cauchy Condition. L'Hôpital's Rule. A Möbius Strip. Goldbach's Conjecture. Pascal's Triangle. A Poincaré Map. The Fourier Series. Heisenberg's Uncertainty Principle. A Cantor Dust. A Bolzano Paradox. A Julia Set. Reimann's Hypothesis. And my favourite: Fermat's Last Theorem.

What are these things . . .? Why am I so curious about them . . .? What is it about these names, these oddly poetic appellations, that is so beguiling and fascinating? I want to know about them, understand them, find out what they do, what they imply.

And this, I suppose, is every mathematician's secret dream. To have a function, a number, an axiom, a hypo-

thesis named after you ... It must be like being an explorer on a virgin continent, naming mountains, rivers, lakes and islands. Or a doctor: to have a disease, a condition, a syndrome called after you. There you are on civilization's intellectual map. For ever.

Fermat's Last Theorem.

Now, bear with me. I love the ring of this one, it sounds so good. Let's see what we can make of it (I found it hard too: formulae have a narcoleptic effect on my brain, but I think I've got it right). Take this simple formula: $x^2 + y^2 = z^2$. Make the letters numbers. Say: $3^2 + 4^2 = 5^2$. All further numbers proportional to these will fit the formula. For example: $9^2 + 12^2 = 15^2$. Or, taking the proportionality downward: $12^2 + 5^2 = 13^2$. Intriguing, no? Another example of the curious magic, the severe grace, of numbers.

Along comes Pierre Fermat in the seventeenth century, a civil servant whose hobby was mathematics. He wondered if this same proportionality would apply if you raised the power above two. What if you cubed the numbers? Would $x^3 + y^3 = z^3$? The answer was no. It never worked, no matter how high he raised the power. So he produced his notorious Last Theorem. THERE ARE NO POSITIVE WHOLE NUMBERS, WHATEVER, WHERE 'N' EXCEEDS TWO, SUCH THAT $X^n + Y^n = Z^n$.

For four hundred years no one has been able to prove or disprove Fermat's Last Theorem, and they have checked every power of 'n' from 3 to 125,000. Intriguingly, Fermat himself said at the end of his life that he had a proof, though it was never found when his papers were searched after his death. What I like about Fermat's Last Theorem is that it remains one of those conjectures about the world which are almost indubitably true, that no one

134

*would ever deny, but which, in the final analysis, we can't
actually, physically prove.*

Hope trudged across the dewy field towards the hedgerow. It was eight in the morning and a grey haar off the
sea lay over the downlands that stretched along the
coast in this part of Dorset. She checked her map to
make sure she was in the right place and veered over to
a corner of the field. Reaching the hedge, she hooked
the end of her tape measure over a protruding hawthorn
twig and unreeled the tape for thirty metres. The hedge
was thick, perhaps six feet across at its base, and was
growing on a small bank. At first glance it looked like
an ancient hedgerow to her, and in that case, she reflected, it should conform to her dating theory. She
walked slowly along its length. Predominantly hawthorn, but there was a fair amount of elder and blackthorn mixed in there too. On closer inspection she
found some field maple, dogwood and, just within the
thirty-metre sample area, a small patch of holly. She
noted this all down on the map and in her record book.
Six species in thirty metres: according to the theory this
hedge had been here for approximately six hundred
years. She took a small sample of the soil for the
geologist and then made another quick search for
brambles, but there were none in this section. She sat
down on a stile and wrote it all up.

The survey of the Knap estate was well advanced.
Much of the archaeological work was already completed: the ancient barrows, the deer enclosure, the
Celtic field systems, had all been thoroughly examined,
mapped and described. The ecologist who had done the

initial work on the hedgerows and woodland had resigned for some reason – hence the job vacancy – but Hope had found so many inaccuracies and inconsistencies in his estimations that she had told Munro she would have to start again from scratch. It meant that she had much more work to do than she had been contracted for, but it kept her busy, and for that she was grateful.

Her own approach to the problem of dating was based on a simple formula she had devised, namely, one shrub species in a hedge equalled a hundred years. She made many trial counts on hedgerows whose age was known (the earliest detailed map of the estate was dated 1565) and her method had proved to be surprisingly accurate, with an insignificant margin of error. So she had set about dating all the unmapped hedgerows with some confidence, and already she had discovered that there were many more medieval hedgerows than had hitherto been imagined. Feudal and Saxon field systems were revealed where previously eighteenth-century enclosure fields had been believed to exist. The landscape history of the estate was far more complex and thorough than had been envisaged. As a result of her efforts, 147 new hedgerows had been classified as level one. In conservational parlance: they were of ancient and abiding historical interest and to be preserved at all costs.

To her vague surprise, Hope found she was thoroughly caught up in her work, in a way she would not have imagined possible. Sure, it was routine and methodical, but there was a profound satisfaction in that routine and method when it allowed her to draw clear and irrefutable conclusions.

Another bonus was that she was out of doors all the

daylight hours, walking the downlands and the fields in all weathers. In the weeks she had been there, she had lost weight – almost a stone – and she felt markedly fitter. Now she had almost finished classifying the estate's hedgerows and Munro was encouraging her to move swiftly on to the many woods and coppices.

She was keen to do so. She had forgotten this facet of her personality: the dogged application of, and exultation in, her expertise. This was what she had trained herself to do; this was why she was educated. Problems were presented to her and she found a way to solve them. It was a feature of her character which, when it was not required or employed, she somehow forgot. It did not feature in her private conception of herself. The fanciful, wishful version of Hope Clearwater tended to downplay the professional scientist in her.

Now she was working again she enjoyed and savoured the unrelenting rigour of her approach to her task, the unswerving persistence of her routine and the evident success of her experimentation. In her work she was achieving something irrefutably concrete. However recondite, however parochial, she was adding a few grains of sand to that vast hill that was the sum of human knowledge. She was discovering aspects of the English landscape that were unknown or hidden; and what pleased her most was that she could prove she was right. As her steady documentation of the estate increased and as the maps were redrawn and dates corrected she developed a quiet but strong pride in her abilities. Her latent self-confidence – never far below the surface – re-emerged into the clear light of day again.

Munro was pleased, and said so. But he had other

priorities, largely directed by the need to complete the project on schedule. Hope was stubbornly resisting his attempts to hurry her along as she had developed another dating theory that was even more precise and she was impatient to try it. Munro was not so enthusiastic, as it might mean more delay. Her theory was that the number of bramble sub-species in a hedge would follow the same pattern as shrub-types, and she had proved the efficacy of the method to Munro very neatly one day, in an attempt to make him vote her more funds (with a few assistants she could cover the entire estate in two months, she reckoned).

Munro was impressed but as yet undecided. He would see if there was any chance of hiring an assistant or two, he said, but he reminded her that the estate had fifty-three named woods and coppices and all but twelve of them were dateless.

She left the field and set off down a farm track towards Coombe Herring, a small village on the estate. There was a long ditch and bank there that ran up to the edge of the village that the project's archaeologist had classified as part of the enclosure of an early seventeenth-century deer park. There was a problem in dating the hedge on the bank as it was almost entirely hawthorn. Out of curiosity Hope had done a bramble test on it and it had turned up a count of ten sub-species. She felt sure, as a result of this, that the ditch and bank belonged to a construction that was significantly older than the deer park – an old parish or manor boundary perhaps, or even a barrow mound. When she put this supposition to the archaeologist – a lean-jawed, pale-faced man called Winfrith – he had almost lost his temper with her. He reminded her that he had spent months plotting and reconstructing the configuration of the deer park, and he informed her that he had no intention of redrawing his maps because of a 'bunch of brambles'. She planned to take several more examples from thirty-metre sections and confound him with the evidence.

She walked through the small village and up a sunken drove road that rounded a hill and eventually led on to East Knap, the village where she was living. It was a cool day, even for September, with a fresh east wind and the sky low and dense with packed clouds. She climbed up the bank off the road, went over a stile and cut through a small wood of coppiced hazel to the disputed bank and ditch.

She measured out her first thirty-metre section and with a pair of secateurs began to collect samples of the profusion of brambles that grew amongst the hawthorn. She worked steadily and carefully, placing the samples in plastic bags and labelling them. The wind stirred her hair, and her nostrils were full of the scent of earth and leaf mould disturbed by her feet and the dusty green smell of the hedge.

She picked a bramble and ate it, her mouth full of its winey, sour taste. She could hear birds singing and the restless thrash of the hedgerow elms above her being hustled and bothered by the wind. Through the gaps in the hawthorn she could make out the gentle rise of the coastal downs and sense, rather than see, the chill of the Channel beyond. Behind her back the landscape of Dorset unfolded. Its gentle hills, its fields and woods, the shallow valleys with their farmsteads and villages. Her mind was calm and full of her task and all her senses were stimulated as she crouched at the foot of a hawthorn hedge in a landscape she had come to know as intimately as any in her life. No wonder she loved her work, she thought, no wonder – she added guiltily – she hardly ever thought of John.

The project office was in the stable block of Knap House, a long attic room above a row of loose-boxes. Every Friday there was a meeting to report on the individual progress of each project worker. Munro chaired it, invariably diplomatic and mild. Hope arrived a little late to find Munro and Winfrith waiting for her. She gave Munro, a soil geologist, the soil samples she had taken that day and sat down at the round table. Winfrith had motored in for the meeting from Exeter where he spent most of his time these days working with the project's historian, a woman called Mrs Bruton-Cross, whom Hope had met infrequently. These were her three colleagues, but she dealt mainly with Munro, who supervised and collated all their respective efforts. To all intents and purposes she worked on her own from Monday to Friday. Munro would telephone her in the evenings if he had anything of note to impart.

The meeting lasted its usual half-hour and Winfrith left at once for Exeter. Munro made her another cup of coffee.

'Here Saturday, Hope?' he asked her. 'Marjorie and I were wondering if you'd like to –'

'Sorry. Going up to London, I'm afraid,' she said quickly, trying to keep the relief out of her voice. She had had one dinner with Graham and Marjorie Munro in their little cottage in West Lulworth and that had been sufficient. It had proved to be an eternity of strained conversation and wineless food. The one small sherry she had been offered – and had consumed – before dinner had turned out to be the solitary alcoholic component of the evening's entertainment. As she ate her way through Marjorie's special casserole (recipe happily provided if requested), Hope had been seized by such a craving for booze that she made an excuse (flu coming on) and had left before coffee, making straight for the nearest pub before it shut.

'Shame,' Munro said, genuinely. 'Marjorie was looking forward to meeting John.'

'Oh, he'll be down again,' Hope said vaguely. 'I'll give you plenty of warning.'

'Say hello to the Big Smoke for me,' Munro said.

'What?'

'Say hello to the –'

'Sure. Certainly.'

She drove back to East Knap and packed her bag and had a bath before leaving for the station at Exeter.

She sat in the train drinking beer and looking out at the dusky landscape. She missed Knap more each time she left it, she realized. Had she stayed she would have worked on all weekend. She didn't need a break; these trips to London were proving to be something of a chore. And she found she was growing to dislike the city with its noise and dirt. She poured more beer into her plastic cup. But something was wrong, she said to herself: surely she should be happier at the thought of being with John again?

On Saturday morning John sat in his pyjamas staring out of the kitchen window at the towers of the Natural

History Museum that rose above the chimneys and gables of this part of Kensington. He was making little clicking noises with his tongue and tapping his chin rhythmically with a forefinger.

Hope watched him over the top of her newspaper. He had kept this up for almost ten minutes now – just staring out of the window and making clicking noises.

'D'you fancy a film this afternoon?' she asked, refusing to be irritated.

'Can't, I'm afraid. I'm going into college. I've some computer time booked.'

Hope forced herself to speak reasonably. 'How long will you be?'

'Should be back . . .' He turned and looked at her, then cocked his head, figuring. 'Early evening. All being well.'

'OK.' She stood up. She put on her raincoat and picked up her bag. 'I'm going out.'

'Fine. See you later.' He looked back at the towers of the Natural History Museum.

Sunday was better. They went for lunch with some friends from the college, Bogdan and Jenny Lewkovitch. He was a plump, fair-haired Pole; Jenny was English, petite and self-effacing. They lived in Putney and had two young children. Over lunch, John was lively and amusingly malicious about their colleagues.

Bogdan was a physicist. John had said on the way to lunch that, despite this fact, he respected his mind. 'Which,' he added, 'is pretty unusual for me, because normally I don't have much time for physicists.'

'Why?' Hope said, wondering vaguely where he ranked ecologists who dated hedgerows in Dorset.

'Why? Because they refuse to admit – most of them – that what they do is basically all about mathematics. They think they're doing something grand with their expensive machines, something in the world. But it's all mathematics, really.'

They were driving down Fulham Palace Road towards Putney Bridge. Hope looked out of the window at the trees in Bishop's Park. The sun was shining and the horse chestnuts were just beginning to turn yellow. She thought of the work that lay ahead of her in the woods and coppices of Knap and longed to be back there. For the first time she felt a little sorry for John and his clean, airless world of perfect abstractions.

'Don't you think that's a little childish?' she said.

'What?'

'My discipline's better than yours. Na-na-nana-na.'

John smiled. 'Ask Bogdan. If he's honest he'll tell you I'm right.'

That evening they made love.

'You're a difficult bugger,' she said, kissing his long nose.

'I know,' he said. 'Just as well you're not, or we'd be in deep shit.'

'Yeah.'

He slipped his hand across her belly, fitted his palm briefly to her hip bone, then ran it up over her ribs to cup a breast.

'Bones, bones, sharp angles,' he said. He flipped back the sheet. 'Hey. Your tits are getting smaller.'

'I'm not fat any more.'

'All that tramping around the turnip fields of Darzet,' he said, in a stage West Country burr.

'You should be pleased.'

He lay back smiling to himself.

'How's the work going?' he asked.

'My God, I don't believe it. You really want to know?'

'Sure.'

'Let me tell you about this fascinating technique I've developed for dating hedgerows.'

'Oh yes?'

'It's all to do with counting the number of sub-species of brambles. You see –'

'Good-night.'

As she unlocked the door to her cottage in East Knap on Monday morning, Hope felt an agreeable shifting in her gut, an excited tightening of her sphincter. She realized she was glad to be back. She felt somewhat guilty about this because, all things considered, the weekend had been quite a success, after the difficult Saturday. But it was hard to contradict or suppress the palpable sensations she was feeling.

She busied herself about, first unpacking and then making herself an early lunch of a corned beef sandwich. As she ate, she remembered that John didn't like corned beef. He couldn't stand the smell of it, he said. He didn't like her to eat it either – he claimed he could smell it on her breath hours later . . .

She sat at the kitchen table and thought about him and their marriage and her new ambivalence, the slight but steady distancing from him that she felt more and more as the weeks passed. Perhaps the fault lay with her, she wondered. Perhaps she shouldn't have married him? Or anyone, come to that. She had always assumed she would be married. She had always been quite confident that one day she would encounter someone with exactly the sort of strange allure she demanded. She knew herself, or so she thought, and she knew that she required someone different, someone odd and very intriguing, even to the point of being difficult . . . Just like John, in fact.

Perhaps she had rushed things, been too sure of herself? She thought back to that first meeting, that moment when she had said, yes, that's the one. She had *known*, as if by pure instinct, that he would be right, was worthy of her . . . She looked at her half-eaten sandwich. My God, she thought, maybe I'm a victim of my own arrogance? That to marry John was the ultimate act of selfishness in a fairly selfish life?

She stood up and went to put on her boots and coat, telling herself to stop interrogating herself so incessantly. It had been a good weekend. Don't sink it under a huge cargo of analysis.

She looked at her watch. Little Green Wood awaited her.

All week Hope worked in the woods and coppices of Knap estate. She found this job even more amenable than the hedgerow dating. The weather was fair but cool and the leaves on the trees were just on the turn. She loved the woods at this time of year, the pale, lemon-juice rays of the sunshine spread through the thinning canopy of leaves dappling the ground, and the air was always cold enough to make her breath condense. In the beech woods and the hazel coppices, with the sky screened and the horizon invisible, she felt even more cut off from the world and its hurry. Only occasionally was there the sound of a car or a tractor in a nearby lane, or the pop-popping of someone out with a gun. Otherwise she was alone with the shifting shadows and sunbeams of the ancient woodlands, hearing nothing but the endless hushing of the coastal breezes in the branches above her head.

John liked the cottage, he said, but he had only stayed there once before, shortly after Hope's arrival at Knap, and before she had been truly settled in. Now she was, emphatically and comfortably, and over the weeks she had come to think of it as very much *her* home. But when John came to stay again he moved around it, naturally enough, with total ease and unconcern, just as he did in their London flat. For some reason, this familiarity, this lack of any by-your-leave, vexed her. She was watchful of him as he moved about the rooms, as if he were a clumsy guest. She found the way he took cushions from the armchairs to make himself more comfortable on the sofa, the way he raided the fridge and larder for his huge 'snacks', finishing off her biscuits, drinking almost all of her orange juice, leaving half-empty, skinning mugs of coffee on the mantelpiece, stupidly irksome. She was not a fanatically tidy person herself, but the smallness of the rooms in the cottage forced her to be neat. Now, with another large adult in the place, who didn't possess her sense of propriety, it began to feel cluttered and messy.

'Do you think you could hang your jacket up?' she asked him, after they had returned from a walk and he had slung it over a chair-back.

'Don't be so obsessive. Why?'

'Makes the place look untidy.'

'No it doesn't.'

'It does. I hang mine up.'

'It's just a jacket on a chair. I haven't been sick on the carpet.'

'It's just something I happen not to like.'

'You hang it up then. Christ, you'd think we were about to be inspected.'

They bickered and niggled at each other through the week-end. Then John announced he felt like staying on for a couple of days. Hope said that would be fine; they could go on to her parents' house together on Wednesday.

'What on earth for?' John said.

'I've been telling you for weeks. Ralph's seventieth birthday.'

'Oh. Is there a party?'

'Yes,' she said with exaggerated patience. 'A big party.'

'Count me out, then. God, you know I can't stand that sort of do.'

'Fine,' Hope said, vaguely surprised that she wasn't more annoyed. 'Suit yourself.'

Sometimes John came out with her into the woods as she worked. He was no trouble; he said he was quite happy watching her move around, measuring and collecting. Occasionally, he would wander off on his own and explore the estate. There was one place he found that he was particularly fond of, not far from the remains of the old Jacobean manor house.

Here, a small valley had been turned into an ornamental lake, now rather reedy and silted up. The original panorama had been spoilt by a Forestry Commission conifer plantation on one side of the valley, but the approach to the lake, which was made by a long clear ride, or chase, still had a strange enchantment.

Now, you walked through a beech wood along the overgrown path of the ride. On your left-hand side was the small stream that fed the lake. It had been dammed and built up so that the water fell in a series of ornamental ponds and falls. Just before the lake was reached, and while it was still screened from view by the beech trees, the path kinked right so that you had to go round a dense stand of green-black yews.

And then, suddenly, the vista was revealed. The silver sheet of water, full of sky, and, beyond, grassy meadows set with old oaks and limes. At the far end of the lake was a carefully planted avenue of elms that was intended to carry the eye to a distant monument, a column of pink granite, on the summit of a hill a mile or so off, but that had never been built.

Hope knew about the lake, of course, but had never approached it from the direction John had found. He took her to see it.

'Now isn't that clever?' he said pointing to the stand of yews, as he walked her round it. 'Just when you think you're there, you have to stop, turn, go round, and then: *bingo*! Expectation, frustration, and then double the effect because you've momentarily forgotten what you came to see.'

*

Hope's parents still lived in the house where Hope had spent the greater part of her childhood. It was in Oxfordshire, not far from Banbury, a straight long house in a small village not too disfigured by drab council houses or bijou retirement homes. Hope caught a bus there from Banbury, for nostalgia's sake, and allowed the old images of her past to unreel in her mind as they drove south towards Oxford, ducking off to the side here and there, as they visited the villages east and west of the trunk road.

She left the bus at the green and walked past the church, the graveyard and the row of yellow alms-houses, turning left up a shaded lane, beech nuts crunching beneath her feet, towards her family home.

The capacious front lawn was occupied by a large blue and white striped marquee. A lorry had been backed down the drive and men were unloading gold-painted bentwood chairs and round chipboard table-tops. From inside the tent she could hear her mother's and her sister's voices clamorously instructing the workmen where to place their loads.

She slipped by the lorry and let herself into the house. She placed her case down at the foot of the stairs and walked through the sitting-room and dining-room into the kitchen. There were flowers everywhere and the air was filled with the smells of blossom and beeswax polish. Through the kitchen window she could see her father at the end of the leaf-strewn, rear garden burning something in the incinerator at the edge of the orchard. She went to join him.

Hope's father was tall and lean. His hair, which had been dense and glossy all his life, had started to thin rapidly in the last two years, a fact which he pretended to make light of but which in reality upset him considerably. He had always been unduly proud of his hair, and in the many photographs of him as a young man, which were placed about the house, it was the feature of him one noticed first. He had known a brief but lucrative period of fame as a West End matinée idol before the Second War, but even in those days he would never have been described as conventionally handsome. None the less, people thought of him as handsome, he had a reputation for his looks, because he had exactly the kind of hair – swept back in a smooth shiny parabola from a clear forehead, with a not too pronounced widow's peak – that handsome men were expected to have. No one really noticed his rather small eyes, or the somewhat too thin lips, or whether he had a moustache or not (that came and went like the seasons) because everyone's gaze settled at once on that proud, almost indecently lush head of hair.

Even grey it had looked good, but now it was falling out and all that glory was gone. In defiance he had grown a beard – an affectation he had hitherto loudly despised – only good for hiding a weak chin, he thought – but it was a patchy, curly thing, as if his body had expended all its energy making superb, pedigree hair for nearly seventy years and wanted a rest from the job.

Hope walked up quietly behind him. He was wearing an ancient jacket, the tweed so worn it hung like a shawl from his square shoulders, jeans – improbably – and a pair of horrid tawny suede shoes.

'Hello, Ralphie,' she said. Some of his friends still pronounced it 'Rafe' but, since retiring from the stage in the fifties, plain Ralph Dunbar it had been to most people, including his family.

He turned with no surprise (she was the only person who called him that) and came towards her, solemn-faced, arms wide.

'Hopeless, darling Hopeless,' he said.

She kissed his bearded cheek and he squeezed her to him strongly.

'Happy birthday,' she said. 'I haven't got a present, I'm afraid.'

'To hell with that. How do I look?'

'Great. But I can't stand that beard.'

'Give it a chance, girl, give it a chance.'

They wandered back to the house, arm in arm. Her father smelt of woodsmoke and a faint musky perfume. He was always experimenting with different colognes and aftershaves.

'So glad you've come, Hopeless. Now I've got you all here.' He sniffed. 'Christ, waterworks. Here we go.'

Hope had never known anyone, man or woman, who would cry so easily. It was as much a part of his repertoire of emotional responses to the world as a frown or a chuckle.

He wiped his eyes and hugged her passionately again. 'It's a funny old world, but a great old life,' he said. It was one of his familiar expressions. 'Wonderful. Grand old life.' They had reached the kitchen door. He turned towards her.

'Where's John, by the way?'

Hope always looked intently at her sister, Faith, whenever she had the opportunity, searching for lineaments of her own looks in her sibling's. Was there something familiar, possibly, in the slightly belligerent jut of her lower lip? A correspondence in the bold arc of the eyebrows? Would anybody think, seeing them side by side, that they were related . . .? As far as Hope was concerned there was no resemblance at all, apart from their laugh, which was identical. As soon as it had been pointed out to her, Hope had endeavoured never to laugh in that way again. It was their deep laugh, the uncontrolled explosion of merriment. There were times when Hope could not restrain it, and she laughed like her sister. Two factors prevented people from commenting on it, however: Hope and Faith saw very little of each other and they had entirely different senses of humour.

She didn't dislike Faith, it was just that the gulf that had begun to grow between them in their late teens was now so wide as to be insurmountable. Ten years ago, shortly before her sister married her husband, Bobby Gow, she announced to the family that she did not want to be known as Faith any longer: henceforward her new name was to be Faye.

'Such a shame John couldn't come,' Faith/Faye said to her now. 'The whole point was to get the entire family together.'

They were sitting in the kitchen, drinking tea. Ralph was back in the garden. Her mother was supervising the flower arrangements in the marquee. For an instant Hope thought about making an excuse for John – pressure of work, a conference – but decided to tell Faye the truth.

'Actually, he hates these sort of occasions. Runs a mile from them.'

'Charming.' Faye gave a baffled smile. This was clearly aberrant behaviour of the highest degree.

'I mean to say,' Faye said. 'It is his father-in-law's seventieth birthday. Daddy's very upset, you know. He's not showing it but I think he's jolly hurt.'

'Ralph couldn't care less. Anyway, I don't think he likes John particularly.'

'Nonsense! Hope!' In Faye's world, members of the same family loved each other unreservedly, for all time.

'I don't think any of you like him.'

'That is not fair,' Faye said, a little flustered, playing for time, unused to all this candour. 'John is ... Of course we like him. We just haven't seen much of him, that's all.'

Hope let her go on protesting. Faye had a pretty face – even-featured – with a small perfect nose that Hope coveted. Hope had her father's nose, long and very slightly hooked. But Faye treated her prettiness almost as an embarrassment. She cut her straight, dark hair short, severely and unadventurously, parted neatly on one side. She wore minimal make-up. Her clothes were the uniform of her class and status – the box-pleated skirt, a blouse or silk shirt, little waisted jackets, plain, low-heeled shoes. Hope had once suggested she let her hair grow and Faye had retorted that, to her, long hair always looked dirty. Hope accepted the implied insult without reproach.

Faye had three children – Timmy, Carol and Diana – and was married to a solicitor, Bobby Gow, with a practice in Banbury. Every time Hope contemplated the life Faye led she was always appalled by its waste, its lack of even faint excitement, its rigid cultivation of the norm. They had been good friends in their teens – Faye was three years older – but approaching adulthood had soon separated them in almost every regard.

Hope suspected that her sister's life – superficially serene, blessed and prosperous – was in reality a long catalogue of large and small dissatisfactions. And she could see her restlessness with this lot, and the endless compromises she had to make to live with it, hardening her year by year. For Faye, the passing of time only signalled the mounting, overwhelming unlikelihood of her life ever being different; the steady retreat of alternatives to her current existence – however whimsical, however minor – ever being explored.

Hope felt sorry for Faye, sinking in the quicksand of prudence, moderation and propriety, but she knew that was the one emotion, the one act of sympathy, she could never express. Faye would rather *die* than have Hope feel sorry for her. That was not the way the world was meant to be organized: the whole purpose of putting up with this dullness, this inevitability, this pretence, was to allow Faye to feel sorry for Hope. Not the other way round, most definitely. So Hope said nothing, and Faye felt safer for a little longer.

Hope tinkled her teaspoon in her cup as she stirred in more sugar. A silence had fallen.

'Where's Timmy?' Hope said. She liked Timmy, Faye's eight-year-old son. He was a solemn, sweet boy with odd, obsessive interests.

'Well, he's not here.'

'Where is he?'

'Away at school. Since last year. Hope, really, I don't think you listen to a word I say.'

The family assembled at seven before the guests arrived. They toasted Ralph with champagne. Ralph raised his tumbler of whisky in response and delivered a tearful, polished, and extravagant hymn of praise to his 'own special darlings'. Hope noticed how avidly he swilled down his drink and presented the glass for more. At this rate he wouldn't see dessert. Hope watched her mother stiffen slightly, but only for a moment. Her mother, Eleanor, was dressed smartly in pink and cream, even her blonde hair had a faint strawberry rinse through it. She was an attractive woman who, in her fifties, had recognized that the addition of a little weight would be more advantageous to her appearance than the effort of constant dieting. So she had let herself grow a little plumper. Her skin was fresh and she carried the extra pounds with aplomb. Hope could see that even now she was desirable. She had large breasts and the general impression she gave was of a cosseted, elegant softness. She spent a lot on her clothes and jewellery. She was bright and shrewd. Hope saw her discreetly remove Ralph's glass as he fussed over Faye's little girls.

'Super you could come,' she heard Bobby Gow's voice at her side. She turned. 'Shame about John.'

'Well . . . Us lot. All the locals. I'd run a mile if I was him.'

Bobby Gow gave an edgy smile and looked uncertain. Was she joking or was she serious? If he disagreed, would she think him stuffy? If he agreed with her, would it seem disloyal . . .? Hope could sense him going through the options.

'All work and no play,' he said finally, inanely, and gave a little laugh.

'So. How's life, Bob?' Hope said.

He frowned and smiled weakly. 'Fine, fine . . . well, you

know, can't complain. Soliciting away.' Hope was sure he had said this to her on every occasion they had met.

'How's Timmy getting on?' She was beginning to feel exhausted already.

Gow waggled his hands, signalling indecisiveness. 'I'm afraid he's taking a bit of a while settling in. But it's a good school.' He swallowed and looked at his champagne. 'Fundamentally. Anyway,' he went on, 'do him good to get away from Mother.'

'Really? Why?'

He didn't answer. 'We miss him terribly, though, old Timbo. Specially the girls.'

'I bet they do.'

'Anyway. There we go.' He pulled a smile. He looks like a man in agony, Hope thought, dying to escape me.

'How about a refill,' he said abruptly, snatching her glass away. He went in search of more champagne and Hope turned to her nieces, Carol and Diana, pretty in their party dresses. She wished she liked them better.

Hope was wearing an old black velvet dress with long sleeves and a V-neck. She had pinned her hair up loosely round her head and at her throat she wore an old pearl choker that belonged to her mother. She idled unnecessarily in the kitchen, reluctant to rejoin the throng in the drawing-room again. Most of the guests had arrived by now, about eighty all told, and the volume of noise was growing by the minute as they drank champagne and guzzled canapés.

Little Diana came into the kitchen with an empty tray and Hope gave her a new one filled with miniature vol-au-vents.

'What're these, Auntie Hope?' Diana said.

'Vol-au-vents. And please don't call me auntie, Diana, OK?'

'What should I call you then?'

'Hope. That's my name.'

'But Mummy says –'

'Tell Mummy I don't mind. Off you go.'

Hope followed her out. The room was tight with people. The men, young and old, in black tie; the women – so many blondes – painted and lacquered. The noise was insufferable.

'Hey, Hope! Hope Dunbar!' someone drawled loudly at her elbow.

She looked round. It was a young man, fair-haired with a flushed, bright face that she vaguely recognized. She couldn't remember his name. He kissed her cheeks.

'How are you? Haven't seen you for . . . God, how long? You committed matrimony recently, didn't you?'

'Yes, I did. I mean I am married.'

'Been away? You're very tanned. D'you ski?'

'No. I spent all summer working out of doors.'

'Really?' He was genuinely astonished. 'What are you? Some sort of riding instructor or something?'

'I'm an ecologist.'

'Oh . . .' A worried look came into his eyes. 'Sounds great. Anyway –' He began to look around the room. 'Where's hubby? Love to meet him.'

Hope stood beside her mother as the guests filed into the marquee. Round tables had been set out in a semi-circle facing a wooden dance floor. On a dais beyond that, the band's instruments stood – piano, drums, a double bass leant against a high stool, and a saxophone held in an iron frame – awaiting their musicians. The tables were covered in pink cloths, the marquee was lined in ruched bands of pink and white material, and white flower arrangements stood on truncated doric columns here and there. It looked pretty and tasteful. Everyone knew where to sit. Eleanor Dunbar smiled sweetly at her guests as they moved by.

'It looks lovely,' Hope said.

Her mother looked at her. 'So do you,' she said. 'In an untidy sort of way.' She gestured at Hope's hair. 'Should've let me put it up for you.'

'I'll be back in the woods tomorrow. It's hardly worth it. Should we sit down?'

Her mother held her back a second. 'Keep an eye on Ralph, will you, darling?'

'What do you mean?'

'Well, I have to table-hop and while I'm away he'll drink too much.'

'It is his seventieth birthday.'

She didn't smile. 'Of course it is. But I don't want him falling down drunk before the main course. Just . . . watch him for me.'

They moved towards their table.

'He seems all right,' Hope said.

'You haven't been here for a while. He's not funny any more.' Her mother's face was expressionless. Hope felt a sudden tightness, a coiling, inside her.

'I am sorry, Mummy,' she said. 'I'm so sorry.'

Her mother stopped, looked at her and smiled formally.

'Don't pity me, Hope. I won't have that.'

Hope felt a real depression settle on her when she saw

she was sitting between Bobby Gow and a man called Gerald Paul, an old friend of the family. He was a retired theatrical agent whom her mother had worked for before she married Ralph. Hope rather suspected that they might have been lovers in the past. Perhaps they still were, for all she knew.

Bobby Gow actually turned away from her when she sat down so she was obliged to talk to Paul. He had a thin, wide mouth full of what looked like brown impacted teeth, set at all angles. Oddly enough, his breath did not smell disgusting, only slightly sweet, as if he had rinsed his mouth with vanilla essence.

'Wonderful to see Ralph looking so well,' Paul said, looking across the table. 'And your mother. Gorgeous creature.'

Hope looked at her parents: her mother, licked by the salacity of Paul's gaze; her father, listening, his hand constantly stroking his beard . . . To his left, Faye gave Carol a sip from her glass of champagne. Paul was reminiscing about 'wonderful Eleanor'. Hope closed her eyes and felt a sudden desire to be in Little Barn Wood. She decided she would leave the room while the speeches were made.

She took a deep breath and spooned out a ball of avocado from the pear in front of her. A waiter came and leant over her mother, then circled the table to her.

'Mrs Clearwater, telephone for you.'

She excused herself and went through to the sitting-room. It must be John, she thought, as she picked up the receiver. It was Graham Munro.

'What is it, Graham?' she said, interrupting his apologies.

He explained. That afternoon three of the Knap

estate farm workers had been passing through the beechwood near the old manor house when they heard an unusual noise. On investigating, they discovered a man digging a 'trench system' – Munro's words – on the lake bank. Apparently some forty yards of trench over three feet deep had been dug. The workers challenged the man and remonstrated with him. Then they frogmarched him to the estate offices.

'It seems he became violent and tried to run away at that stage,' Munro said, his voice sonorous with unspoken apologies. 'I'm afraid the men had to restrain him, forcibly.'

'Is he all right?'

'Just cuts and bruises. I'm told.'

'Haven't you seen him?'

The estate office, having established John's identity, phoned Munro in West Lulworth. He, in turn, telephoned John and told him to go to the cottage and wait for him there.

'Unfortunately,' Munro said, 'I couldn't go straight away, and by the time I got to your place there was no sign of him.'

'What do you mean?'

'He'd gone. The lights were on and the front door was unlocked.' He paused. 'That's why I thought I should phone you. There was a note as well.'

'What does it say?'

'I can't read it. It's just a scrawl. It does say "London" on it, though. I think.'

'He's probably gone home. Thanks, Graham.'

When she hung up she thought instantly: stupid, stupid bastard. And then, selfishly, that here was the perfect excuse to flee the party. Her mother came out to find her and Hope explained the problem, saying only that John had fallen ill and that she thought she should go straight home. For a moment Eleanor looked like she was going to protest, but she thought better of it.

'Well . . . Just say goodbye to your father before you go. I'll get him for you.' She leant forward to give Hope a kiss.

Hope felt her mother's soft breasts squash against her and her nose was filled with the scent of rosewater perfume. She held her for a while.

'Come down and see me will you, darling? When it's quiet. Just spend a little time with me.'

'Of course. Very soon.'

'I never see you these days.' She looked at her fixedly. 'I miss you.' Then she smiled. 'I'll get Ralph.'

Hope went upstairs and packed her case quickly. She didn't bother to change. She pulled on her coat and took the combs out of her hair.

Ralph was waiting for her downstairs. She told him quickly what the problem was.

'I suppose you'd better go,' he said glumly and grudgingly and kissed her. 'What's wrong with John? Has he gone mad or something?'

Hope managed a laugh. 'No, of course not. Why do you say that? He's just working too hard.'

'Big mistake.'

She squeezed his arm. 'Have a lovely party.'

'Fat chance.' He walked her to the door. 'Trouble is,' he said, 'I'm so fucking bored. That's why I drink. I know your mother isn't happy, but I just can't help it, you see.'

Hope thought he would begin to cry at this, but his eyes were clear and his voice firm. 'I hate this,' he said.

'Come on, Ralphie. Enjoy yourself. All your family's here. We all love you and so do all your old friends.'

He looked at her. 'All my old friends ... What a crowd of shits.'

She caught the stopper from Banbury to Oxford. She would be in plenty of time to catch one of the last trains up to London. She sat in the overlit, overheated compartment looking out at the black countryside and seeing only her own reflection in the window staring back. She thought about John and forced herself to recognize that eccentricities were becoming problems, and that quirks of behaviour were developing into warning signs ... But there was a reluctance in her to take this recognition any further. And when she started to ask herself what she should do next, she seemed to run into a thick smog of inertia and apathy. Nothing was clear; no direction out seemed obvious.

That mood gave way to something colder: a kind of anger began to grow in her. She had not bargained for this. She had not expected this turn of events. Her brilliant, unusual man was not meant to fall ill in this way, to become unstable and troublesome.

She confronted her selfishness in the same way as she faced her image in the black cold glass of the railway carriage and told herself to reconsider. To her vague alarm she realized she was not prepared to do so.

At Oxford station she had a wait of twenty minutes. She sat in the grimy cafeteria amongst the usual collection of lovelorn teenagers, very poor people and mumbling drunks and felt her anger still lodged hard within her, like a brick beneath her ribcage.

No, she said to herself, this is *unfair*. What right did he have to behave like this? To be so perverse and heedless? She thought of him now, waiting for her in the flat, and tried to imagine what mood he would currently be occupying: breezy and indifferent, perhaps? Or zany and amused? Or mute and helpless, or sulky and withdrawn...? She knew them all by now, she realized, far too well. And she could hear in her head the respective monologue being played out. I didn't mean ... I never thought ... I wasn't sure ... I don't give a damn ...

She felt weary and careworn, in the way one often does *before* the big job of work is tackled; that sense of premature or projected exhaustion that is the breeding-ground of all procrastination.

The London train pulled in and pulled out again. Hope sat on in the squalid buffet, thinking, and then took a taxi to Meredith's cottage. There were still lights on upstairs in the bedroom. Meredith came to the door, tousled and bland in her dressing-gown.

'What the hell are you doing here?'

'Copping out.'

THE HAPPINESS OF THE CHIMPANZEE

João told me a story one day while we were out in the field. We were watching Rita-Mae with Lester and Muffin. Muffin was playing with Lester, Rita-Mae joining in from time to time, tumbling the baby over, or checking Muffin when the fun became too rough. It was quite obvious to me that, as they romped and scampered, the young chimpanzees were enjoying themselves; they were having a good time. They were, not to beat about the bush, happy.

On our walk back to camp João told me this curious fable that he had heard from his father.

Two hunters, Ntino and Iko, were out strolling one day through the forest. They came across some chimpanzees who were playing in the branches of a mulemba tree.

'Look at the chimpanzees,' Ntino said, 'look how they swing so easily through the branches. This is the happiness of the chimpanzee.'

'How can you know?' Iko said. 'You are not a chimpanzee. How can you know if it is happy or not?'

'You are not me,' Ntino said. 'How do you know that I do not know the happiness of the chimpanzee.'

I never found the remains of Lena's baby. We searched all the nest sites we came across, hoping to discover some shred of skin or tiny bone that I could present as exhibit A, but we failed completely to discover whatever Rita-Mae had done with the raggy scrap of a body she had carried off over her shoulder, that afternoon under the fig tree.

For several days after the killing we saw nothing of Lena either. And then one day she turned up again. She kept her distance from Rita-Mae, but otherwise there seemed no real change in her attitude to the others, or theirs to her.

Indeed, the same apparent normality also existed between me and my colleagues. I told no one, apart from João and Alda, of the killing, and I was pretty sure Mallabar had been as discreet as he had promised. There was still a good deal of residual sympathy around for me as fire-victim – which did not diminish – and which, I supposed, was the best evidence that he had kept his word. Mallabar himself was perfectly cordial. I did not apologize or retract my story, but he acted as if I had done so: a momentary aberration for which he had forgiven me.

I kept smiling and each night worked on my paper.

One morning I left the camp early and set off for a rendezvous with Alda. As I passed the Artificial Feeding Area, I heard my name called. Mallabar was standing in the middle of the cleared area of ground. He waved me over.

It was just after six and the sun had not yet risen above the treeline. The light was the colour of white wine and the air was cool. As I walked over, I checked to see if there was anyone in the hides but they were empty. This was the first time we had been alone together since I had told him the news of Bobo's death. I offered Mallabar a cigarette, which he declined. I lit up myself. I noticed there were three big yellow chandeliers of bananas propped against the concrete feeding cages.

'You're off early,' he said.

'I've got to check on something,' I replied, trying to be as cryptic as possible.

'I was wondering if you'd like to join us here today.'

I glanced at the bananas. 'Big feast?'

'Yes. My American publisher's arriving and I want to show him our chimps.'

'I've got too much to do today. Sorry.'

'Shame.' He shrugged. 'You'd like him. Might be useful to meet. Good man to know.'

'Another time. But thanks anyway.'

'You don't approve of all this,' he said abruptly.

'What?'

'The AFA.' He gestured at the cages and the bananas. 'Hope, the stickler.'

I looked at him. 'It's a machine. An artificial and bountiful food source switched on and off at your whim. I don't think . . .' I paused. 'It's got absolutely nothing to do with life as wild chimpanzees live it, that's for sure. You attract two dozen chimps here and let them gorge. It's unnatural. You've dumped a banana machine down in the jungle. You're playing God, Eugene. It's not right.' I smiled at him. 'But then I'm sure you know all the arguments against.'

'Most of them formulated by me.' He sat down on the concrete cage and leant back, crossing his legs. He was very relaxed, very sure of himself. I dropped my cigarette on the ground and stepped on it.

'Hope, I like you,' he said.

'Thank you.'

'Despite our . . . methodological differences you're exactly the kind of person we need in this team.'

I waited. He flattered me some more. Now that the war was virtually over, he said, and the new grants were coming through, Grosso Arvore would soon be back to its original size – in fact it would probably expand. He was thinking of opening another station, another camp, ten miles to the north. I happened to be precisely the type of person he imagined running it.

The first rays of sun had cleared the tree-tops and I felt their warmth begin to spread across my face. I wondered vaguely, and not for the first time, if Mallabar had a sexual interest in me. I certainly had none in him, but I knew that for some men such indifference was a powerful aphrodisiac.

'Is that a job offer?' I asked.

He lost his composure for a second.

'Well . . . Let's say, let's say it's a, a distinct possibility.' He stood up and rubbed his hands together as if he were washing them.

'I just wanted to let you know how I felt,' he went on, his assuredness rushing back. 'And how things lay ahead. There are no flies on the early bird. There's a future for you here with us, Hope, something considerable.' He let his hand rest momentarily on my upper arm, and looked me candidly in the eyes. I felt the hot glare of his sincerity. 'I want you to understand that,' he said.

'It's understood.'

Alda met me at our prearranged spot and led me east to the area where he had seen the six unidentified male apes. There were no cut trails out here, just ancient bush paths, but the further east we went, and as the ground began to rise slightly, so the vegetation thinned.

He showed me the path where he had spotted the chimpanzees. He had followed them for ten minutes before he had lost sight of them in the undergrowth. I checked our approximate position on the map. If these had been northern chimps, then they had crossed the Danube and advanced almost a mile into southern territory. When Alda had lost them, he said, he thought they had been heading back north again. He showed me where this had happened. The Danube was eight hundred yards away through a thick screen of trees. It was a reasonable assumption.

Looking at the map again, I thought it was another reasonable assumption to conclude that these chimpanzees had made an exploratory incursion, an arc swinging through the southern area covering a mile or two . . . An analogy kept nudging itself into my head.

'You say they were all males?' I asked Alda.

'Yes, Mam. I think. And they move very slow – looking here, looking there – and they make no noise. No noise at all.'

To me this sounded exactly like a patrol.

That evening I typed the final draft of my article. It was twenty pages long, short on scholarly apparatus, but very readable. I knew that whomever I submitted it to would publish it, such was the inflammatory and controversial nature of its contents. In the end I decided to send it to a magazine called *The Great Apes*. It was a monthly, with a sound academic reputation and a fairly wide popular appeal. Also, I knew one of the editors there.

I sealed the article in an envelope, addressed it, and then sealed it in another envelope which I addressed to Professor Hobbes, with a covering note asking him to forward it to the magazine. I was taking no chances.

Two days later, when Toshiro was on the point of setting off on the provisioning run, I handed him my package. He accepted it without a second glance and added it to the pile of the project's mail on the seat beside him.

The article complete, I spent more time analysing and transcribing João and Alda's field notes. I noticed another discrepancy. Quantifying the travelling distances of the individual chimps over the last three or four weeks, I realized that they were diminishing. Plotting them on the map, it was at once obvious that the ranging area of the southern chimps had shrunk quite dramatically, by about 35 per cent.

Something strange was going on, but I wasn't at all sure what. It was in the light of these observations that I called a halt to our normal procedures of observations and follows and instituted the watch on the Danube. Each day, João, Alda and I would take up our positions, about a mile apart, on the southern slopes of the small valley cut by the Danube as it flowed down from the escarpment, east to west. We each found prominent viewpoints overlooking the river and between us were able to cover a significant amount of ground.

We watched without any result for three days. Then, on the morning of the fourth day, at about half-past nine, João called me up on the walkie-talkie. I was in the middle, João was a mile to the east.

'They comin', Mam,' he said. 'I think seven, maybe eight. They comin' your way.'

He said they had just passed a big mafumeira tree, which I could see from my position. I told João to keep following and went to meet them.

There were seven chimps, moving cautiously along the ground on all fours, loosely spaced out in a column. Their complete silence and concentration were eerie and disturbing. They were led by Darius, whom I recognized at once. There was one female, anoestrus, in the rear. They were coming straight towards me.

The ground cover was patchy, so I moved off the path to give them a wide berth. I circled round to rejoin João who was following about a hundred yards behind. He looked unhappy and grim. Neither of us had ever seen anything like this before.

We followed the chimpanzees for about an hour as they moved steadily, ever deeper, into southern territory. Then they halted at the side of a narrow valley with a stream running through it and climbed into a veranista tree. They sat there for forty minutes, still and silent, watching and listening. There was no sound or sign at all of my southern chimps.

Eventually the intruders climbed down from their tree and headed back north at a quicker pace. When they got to the Danube valley they burst out into a loud chorus of hoots and barks, running frenziedly across the stream, drumming on the trunks of trees, breaking off branches and shaking them in the air. Then they were off, deep into the northern territory, still screaming and whooping at each other.

'I don't like,' João said. He was still upset and troubled, frowning intently. 'I don't like at all, at all.'

'It's so strange,' I said. 'What are they trying to do?'

'I fear too much, Mam.' He looked at me. 'I fear too much.'

I asked Ian Vail if I could come out with him once more and spend a few days with the northern chimpanzees. He readily agreed, but when he asked me why, I said only that some strange individuals had been spotted in the south and I thought they might be his chimps.

I spent two days in the north with him and saw most of the males that belonged to the group. The composition of the northern group was in fact very male-dominated. There were three mature females but two of them had just given birth and would not resume their sexual cycles for two to three years. The only 'available' female was Crispina. The other members of the group were four prime males, half a dozen adolescents (male and female) and a couple of old males. In the early days before the group split the sexual balance had been more normal, but the departure of Clovis, with three mature females – Rita-Mae, Rita-Lu and Lena – had, so Ian's theory went, destabilized the community. One other young female had also disappeared eighteen months previously, exaggerating the imbalance further. She may have been killed by a predator, or possibly lured away by the other chimp community to the north of Grosso Arvore. Since my last visit Crispina's sexual cycle had finished. There was every chance that she might be pregnant.

Ian thought the patrolling in the south was highly significant.

'I'm sure they were looking for Rita-Mae,' he said, casually. 'She was very popular.'

'It didn't look like it.'

'Is she in oestrus?'

'No. But her daughter's about to start.'

'Ah-ha. What about the pregnant one?'

'She . . . the baby died.'

'Well, she'll start her cycle again.' He thought. 'What do you call the alpha male?'

'Clovis.'

'He'll have his hands full.' He gave a leering grin. It

was at moments like this that he was easy to dislike. I changed the subject.

'Have you got photos of your chimps?'

'Mug shots? Yeah, masses.'

We were sitting on a rock in the afternoon sun. At the foot of some trees ahead of us, some chimps were searching for termite nests. I waved away a couple of circling flies and wondered briefly whether to tell Vail about Bobo's killing. I decided not to, in the end, because of Roberta and her connection to Mallabar.

Vail was looking at the foraging chimps through his binoculars. He was wearing khaki shirt and shorts and suede ankle boots. His legs were brown and dusty and covered in small scratches. Blond hair grew thickly on his knees and lower legs. Perhaps I should tell him, I thought again? I needed an ally, after all. But he had warned me off once before.

'Do you know anything about Eugene's new book?' I asked.

'Well, yes. Roberta's correcting the proofs at the moment. It's huge.'

'God. What's it called?'

'*Primate: the society of a great ape,*' he said in a sonorous American accent.

'They've got proofs . . .? When's it out?'

'Four months, five months.' He turned and smiled sarcastically at me. 'So we might as well pack up and leave. It's very much the "Last Word", if you know what I mean.' He unslung his binoculars from around his neck. 'Better find another area to write about.' He stood up. 'What were you doing before you got into this lark, anyway?'

'Hedgerow dating.'

'Oh yes?'

'Always has been a bit of a conversation stopper.'

We were walking back to the Land Rover. I decided to go a little further.

'Ian, do you think ... I mean, how aggressive are these chimps? Violently aggressive, I mean.'

He stopped and looked at me quizzically. I could see he was trying to guess what was behind the question.

'I don't know,' he said. 'Not really aggressive. No more than you or me.'

'That's what I'm worried about.'

'What do you mean?'

'I'm not sure, but I'll tell you if something comes up.'

We watched three more northerner patrols. They crossed the Danube at more or less the same point, and each time penetrated ever deeper into the south. With the aid of Ian Vail's photographs I was soon able to identify and name the individuals. The groups were always led by Darius and there were always a few adolescents with them (whom I found harder to single out), and usually three other mature males: Gaspar, Pulul and Americo. From time to time an old male called Sebastian would accompany them. These five were the nucleus of the northerner patrols.

It was when they crossed the Danube that their normal noisy chimpanzee demeanour changed. They became tense and careful and almost completely silent. Their sweeps into the south grew longer and more extensive. Often they would stop, climb trees and watch and wait. It was obvious to me they were looking for my chimpanzees.

Our watch on the Danube, and the shadowing of the northern patrols, meant that I had lost contact with the southern group. One day I sent off João and Alda to try and locate them. We knew now where the northerners tended to cross the river; I could watch it effectively on my own.

This time, they came over at about four in the afternoon. I heard them before I saw them – the sound of vigorous drumming on tree trunks. Then I saw Darius, fur bristling, displaying aggressively, shaking branches and shrieking. Then the other chimps joined him, calling, shouting, hurling rocks into the Danube. Then they crossed the river and fell silent. Darius led, and strung out behind him were Pulul, Gaspar, Sebastian and Americo – and one adolescent that I couldn't recognize. I followed them as best I could. They saw me of course, but they were completely habituated to human observers. All the same, I remained a prudent forty or fifty yards behind them.

They moved south, cautiously, for an hour. Then they stopped on the edge of a small rock cliff to watch and wait. At this point João came through faintly on the walkie-talkie – I had the volume low, and he was at the limit of his range – and told me that he had seen Clovis, Rita-Mae, Lester and Rita-Lu. There was no sign of Muffin, Mr Jeb, Conrad, or Lena.

I took out my camera and took some photographs of the group on the cliff edge. Their concentration was intense. Nearby, there were fruits on chavelho bushes but none of them seemed interested in eating. They watched. They smelled the air. They listened.

Then I noticed that Darius's attention was now focused on a small grove of date palms about five hundred yards away. I called up João.

'Where are you?'

'Far in the south, Mam. Near the bamboo.'

'Rita-Mae and Rita-Lu?'

'They are here. I can see them.'

I relaxed slightly. If Ian Vail was right, and the object of these patrols was sexual, then these northerners were miles adrift.

Suddenly, Darius gave a soft grunt and bounded off his rock, down the cliff face, and disappeared into the undergrowth beyond. The others followed immediately, moving fast. It took me a little time to find a place where I could slither safely down the cliff, and by the time I had reached the bottom the chimps were lost to view. Ahead I could hear them crashing through the undergrowth. I found a path that appeared to head towards the palm grove and ran off up it.

I must have been about a hundred yards away from the palms when I heard the warning hoots of a southern chimp. And then I heard a second chimp respond. I stumbled over a root and fell, grazing my knee badly. I stood up and limped-ran in the direction of the noise. All at once, there was a mad bellowing of screams and barks and a persistent shrill screeching, all the panicky hysteria of a fight. Then, as I reached the first trees of the palm grove, I saw a chimp fleeing, swinging away through the branches of a huge alfonsia tree. In the glimpse I had, it looked like Conrad.

I moved forward cautiously. Through the trunks of the palm trees, I could see excited chimpanzees milling about. Then I saw Mr Jeb, surrounded by the northern chimps. He was crouching low, his teeth bared and screaming. The northern males standing around him displayed, rearing up, hair bristling with bravura aggression. Darius held a dried palm frond in one hand with which he lashed the ground, making guttural pant-roars at Mr Jeb. Mr Jeb's response was feeble and pathetic. As he writhed and shook, his withered arm flopped uselessly around. His bald head and stringy goatee made his threatening gestures look sham and nugatory. But he roared as bravely as he could, peeling back his lips to expose his worn old teeth, and hurling pebbles with his good arm at the encroaching gang of northerners.

Then they charged him. Darius, twice Mr Jeb's size, felled him easily and sat on his chest, holding down his arms. Gaspar clutched his feet and Pulul and Americo jumped on his head repeatedly. Then Gaspar leant forward and sank his teeth into Mr Jeb's scrotum, producing a horrifying scream of pain from the old chimp. But the battering he was receiving from the others stunned him, and his body slumped. One by one the others let go.

Then Darius grabbed both his legs and dragged him violently to and fro along the ground, running backwards and forwards. In the course of this, Mr Jeb's head hit the trunk of a date palm and gobbets of blood spurted from his nose. Darius stopped at once and licked and slurped at the blood that dripped from his nostrils.

Darius moved away, after a while, and the other chimps gathered round to gaze at Mr Jeb's inert body. He lay face down, quite motionless. Then he stirred. He raised his head and gave a small whimper. He sat up and with his good arm tried to push himself upright, but he fell over at once, his entire body shivering.

Pulul approached, sat on Mr Jeb's back and started

twisting his leg round and round. I saw, rather than heard, the break. All natural tension suddenly went from the limb. Pulul then gnawed at the toes, biting one of them off, and nearly severing two others. Mr Jeb made no sound while all this went on.

Pulul backed off, eventually, screeching. Then they sat and watched Mr Jeb as he lay there for a full five minutes, before Darius stalked up and prodded him several times with a finger. There was still no movement from the old chimp. Darius seized one leg, the broken one, and dragged him a couple of yards, turning him over, face up. Then he began to hit him in the face with his fists, again and again, for two or three minutes.

Darius stopped, moved away, and suddenly, at great speed, the northern chimps were off, bounding and scampering away through the scrub.

I looked at my watch. The attack on Mr Jeb had lasted nearly twenty minutes. I felt exhausted, aching with tension. I stood up awkwardly – I hadn't moved at all during the attack – and walked over to Mr Jeb.

He was still alive. I could see the fingers of one hand moving slightly. A V-shaped gash on his bald head had flipped back a triangle of scalp that shone a bright pinky-orange against the dusty grey-black of his skin. The blood had congealed on the wound on his scrotum and already there were blow-flies crawling on it. But it was his torn feet that particularly distressed me: I could see the bone gleaming white at the stump of his severed toe.

I felt a kind of breathless shock boom through me, making me gasp and gulp at the air as if I was drowning. I turned away and took deep breaths, exhaling slowly. 'Oooh, Mr Jeb,' I heard myself saying. 'Poor Mr Jeb.'

Then I walked back to him, knelt and touched his shoulder gently.

He opened his eyes. One of them was just a slit, almost closed by dark plummy contusions. He looked at me.

I was too close, and stepped back a few yards. Mr Jeb began to shiver, and tried again to raise himself up but he was too weak. Then he began to haul himself away along the ground, using his good arm and one good leg, making for a dense thicket of undergrowth. He left an irregular furrow in the dust, speckled with his blood.

He crawled deep into the thicket. I tried to follow for a way, but it was too dense and thorny for me. I backed out with a bad scratch on my arm. I sat down, with my back against a tree, and rested there for a minute or two. It was late in the afternoon and dusk was not far off, I realized; I should think about returning to camp. I opened my bag and took out some antiseptic ointment which I spread over my scratch and grazed knee. As I replaced it, I saw my camera.

I had taken no photographs of the fight. And now Mr Jeb was dead or dying in an impenetrable clump of thorn ... What was happening in Grosso Arvore, I asked myself? Already the revelations of my article were out of date. Those northern chimps had come to kill and, most disturbingly, to inflict pain. As far as I was aware this was without precedent.

I heard a soft pant-hoot – *hoo hoo hoo* – and looked round. Conrad crouched, staring at me, twenty feet away. I felt stupid relief, and an absurd sense of welcome.

'Conrad . . .' I said out loud.

At this he was off, bounding through the under-growth.

Then I saw him a few seconds later, climbing a pale-trunked lemon-flower tree that hung over the thicket that hid Mr Jeb's body. He edged out on the furthest branches and sat there peering down into the tangled bushes where Mr Jeb, no doubt, was dying slowly, in enormous pain.

I was late getting back to camp. I went straight to the canteen to allay any suspicion. I told no one what had happened, explaining away my scratches as the result of a fall during a follow. I ate my stringy chicken and sweet potato with unaccustomed pleasure and asked one of the cooks to bring me a bottle of beer. It was barely cool but I felt a powerful need for some alcohol. So I ate my meal and drank my warm beer. I had just lit a Tusker when Ginga came over.

'Hope, are you all right?'

'Fine. Why?'

'You look . . . not very well.'

'Just tired.' I smiled at her. 'Long hard day. And I think one of my chimps is dead.' I still don't know why I said this to her. I think I had to eke out something of what had built up inside me. I told her I had come across the scene of a fight and had found a blood trail leading into a thorn thicket.

'How do you know it was a chimp?' she said.

'There was another in a tree above the thicket. Sort of keeping guard.'

Ginga shrugged. 'Maybe a leopard?' She squeezed my hand. 'My God, if you knew how many dozen chimps I've lost since we came here. Dozens.'

'I know. It's just that there aren't many in the south. One gone and you notice it.'

'Have you told Eugene?'

'No. I was going to try and recover the body. To be sure. Anyway...' I stubbed my cigarette out and changed the subject, ingenuously. 'I hear the book's due out soon.'

She glanced sharply at me for an instant, then relaxed. 'Yes. We're correcting proofs...' She paused, then said reflectively, 'It's going to be very big I think. Ten languages already. But good for us all. After this war, you know, we'll be back on the map.'

'I'd love to see it.' I said this as off-handedly as I could.

'So would everybody. But you know Eugene. Nothing is seen 'til he's ready.'

She rose to her feet and we said our good-nights in a perfectly friendly manner. I didn't know why I should have thought this, but I knew that the growing friendship between me and Ginga would go no further. I was sure that from then on she would never fully trust me again.

PULUL

Cruelty. (Kru.elti). n. (1) The quality of being cruel; disposition to inflict suffering; delight in, or indifference to, another's pain; mercilessness, hard-heartedness.

When Hope thinks of Mr Jeb's slow death, she remembers most vividly the way Pulul sat on the old chimp's back, twisted his leg until it broke, and then tried to bite his toes off. It was a cruel act; it looked cruel. But did he know what he was doing? 'Delight in, or indifference to, another's pain.' If it was cruel, then it was deliberately done. If it was deliberately done, then blind instinct has to be ruled out, some level of cognitive awareness must be involved.

Hope knows (how do you know?) that this was the evil in the chimpanzee. Pulul wanted to inflict pain, as much as possible.

'I don't want to talk about it!' John shouted at her. 'Don't you understand?' His hands were clamped to the back of a kitchen chair. He began to bang it on the floor in rhythm as he repeated himself. 'I don't want to talk about it! I don't want to talk about it!'

'All right! *Shut up!*' Hope yelled at him. 'Just shut up!'

They faced each other across the kitchen table. She had spent the night with Meredith in Oxford and had come back to London on an early train. John had been out. So she phoned the college and was told that he was in his room working and didn't want to be disturbed. He came back in the evening at about half-past seven. He greeted her as if nothing had happened. 'How was the party?', 'How were your folks?' She allowed him to keep this up for a minute or two and then demanded an explanation of what had gone on at the lake. At which point he began the crescendo of evasion that culminated with them both screaming at each other.

'All right,' she said quietly. 'We won't talk about it.' She went over and put her arm round him. 'I was just worried about you, that's all.' She kissed his face and felt the tension in his body begin to ease and his breathing slow. He pulled back the chair he was still holding and sat down on it.

'Christ,' he said wearily, 'I've got to take it easier. Got to relax.' He rubbed his eyes, hard, with the heels of his hands. Then he let his head fall back, exposing his throat, and exhaled. He began to rotate his head to and fro in semicircular movements, to ease the knotted muscles on his shoulders. Hope stepped round behind him and began to massage his neck with her fingertips.

'So anyway,' he said. 'How was the party?'

'Horrible.'

She told him how awful it had been, inventing freely, not bothering to recount her premature departure and the night at Meredith's.

'Ralph was miserable. My mother was tense as hell about his drinking. Faye and Bobby ... God, I feel sorry for that girl.' She stopped her massage and went to pour herself a drink.

'You were well out of it,' she said over her shoulder.

'Bobby Gow,' he said, thoughtfully. 'What a cunt.'

'Bobby?' She was surprised at the muted vehemence.

'Yes. He's a stupid, screwed-up, English cunt and he's married another. What do you expect?'

She had not turned round. She kept her gaze fixed on her wineglass. She had never heard him talk like this before.

'Well,' she began, careful not to provoke him. 'I think she wanted a life, a kind of life that was completely different from Ralph and Eleanor's. I think that's it.'

'Ralph and Eleanor. Don't get me started on them. Pair of repulsive, hideous –'

'Why don't we nip out? Get a bite to eat?'

They walked along the Brompton Road to an Italian

restaurant they often went to. They were greeted with noisy welcome by the superhumanly jolly waiters. Hope often felt a spontaneous sympathy for these men. Whatever their cares and woes, their domestic tragedies or personal failures, they were compelled to contribute to and create this cheery ambience of facetious bonhomie, all *'Ciao bella, ah la bellissima signorina!'* and *'Amore, amore!'* But tonight this carefree farce was exactly what she required and she was glad to see that the preposterous informality worked immediately on John. We need to be distracted for a while, she thought, have some other people around us, steer the conversation in different directions . . .

The restaurant was crowded but a table was found for them near the back. Half-way through their main course John suddenly seemed to recall what he had said about her sister and brother-in-law.

He apologized. 'Christ. I didn't mean that, really.' he said, earnestly. 'It was unfair. Very unkind.' He screwed his face up. 'But I think it's good that I recognized that – don't you? That I could, you know, look back and see that I was wrong?'

'Look, it doesn't matter. We all fly off the handle.'

'But I can criticize myself. That's good, isn't it?'

'Yes . . . Yes. We should . . . we should all do that a bit more.'

And then he began to talk about what had happened at the lake. He had enjoyed himself there so much, he said, and he had decided to spend more time with her. He didn't need to do so much work on computers. It was good, he said, just to reflect, to let the brain work unprompted.

'You see,' he went on, 'I haven't been coming down

because I've been worried. Worried that I'm losing something.' Then he told her about the way mathematicians were divided: that out of ten mathematicians nine would think in figures and one would think in images. It was the ones who thought in images that produced the most startling work.

'Take me,' he said. 'I was always a figure man until I started working in turbulence. Suddenly it changed. I started seeing answers, solutions, in *shapes*. It was unbelievable.'

He began to tell her about hydrology, about fluid dynamics, how no one could understand how turbulence arose from the differential equations for the flow of fluid. The erratic behaviour and discontinuities threw the calculations out of the window. Everyone was attempting to tackle turbulence by analytical methods, by writing ever more complex equations, he said, trying to explain the hyperbolic activity of turbulent fluids and gases.

'I was plugging away, too,' he went on, 'and getting somewhere. My thinking . . .' he made a sweeping gesture with one hand, 'my thinking was on the right lines, I could see that. But then suddenly there was a change. I don't know how it happened, but I started looking at the *shapes*, the shapes turbulence made, and then things began to fall into place with all sorts of fascinating ramifications.' He paused. He had an odd look in his face, as if he were smiling and frowning at the same time.

'The funny thing was, and this is what is worrying me, it only seems to have lasted six months or so.' He started to score the white table-cloth with the tines of his dessert fork. 'I seemed to lose the knack. I would look at shapes and think figures.'

Then he told her that in Scotland the digging he had done – for some inexplicable reason – had rejuvenated the imaging power.

'Just the exertion, maybe. The physical effort.' He shrugged. 'Or maybe just the fact that I was cutting a shape in the ground. A square, a rectangle. It all seemed to come back.'

He paused. She looked at his pale, worried face, his eyes on his plate of unfinished food. Frowning. Thinking. She saw the force of that thought distorting and buckling his features. He exhaled shakily, a catch in his breath.

'But it's going again, getting weak,' he said. 'I just have to face up to it. I had the gift for a few months. On loan.' He shook his head, his nostrils pinched. 'And the work I was doing, God, you wouldn't believe . . . Incredible.' He looked up at her at this point and she saw his eyes were brimful of tears.

'You see, at Knap, I thought maybe if I tried digging again, something might come back.' His voice had gone quiet. 'You don't know how terrible it is, to have something, that kind of power, and then have it taken away from you.' He made a strange sound – half grunt, half retch – in the back of his throat. 'I try to force myself, force my brain to go on, but it's not . . .' His entire body seemed to give a shudder and his face went bright red. He closed his eyes and pressed his chin into his chest. For a moment, Hope thought he was going to vomit.

But he wept. He put his hands on the table, hunched forward and let the sobs blurt from him. He made a strange, panting, wailing noise, his mouth hanging open, tears, snot and saliva dripping from his face.

'Jesus, please, John!' Hope was round the table and crouching by him, her arm round his bucking shoulders. She was terrified by the sound he was making, as if it were a prototype form of weeping, unfamiliar and unrecognizable. 'Johnny, darling, stop please! *Please!*'

The whole restaurant had fallen immediately silent, disturbed and unsettled. Beneath her hands, Hope could feel the muscles of his shoulders locked and quivering. He was letting his sadness run from him, she thought. She could almost sense it coiling about her – a thin and ethereal flux – like a gas, a turbulent gas, flowing from his mouth, nose and eyes.

Somehow, with the help of a couple of waiters, they got him up and draped his coat over his shoulders. The staff was concerned for him, but they wanted him out. As she led John through the restaurant, she was aware of the rapt and troubled faces of the other diners staring at them both. What was this abject misery, they seemed to be demanding? This was a man: why was he so afflicted? What shocking tragedy had reduced him so? To her shame, Hope felt a hot embarrassment envelop her like a shawl.

The cool air outside was a help. John took a few unsupported paces down the street and then turned towards a dark shop window. He rested his forehead against the cold glass. Hope whispered to him – endearments, reassurances – and put her arms around him.

'Ach, God, Hope,' he said. 'I'm a fucking mess. You've got to help me.'

'Of course I will, of course. You'll be fine.'

'You know, I think that was good for me. In a funny sort of way I feel better.'

'Come on, let's get you home.'

Back at the flat she helped him undress. He seemed calm, but he moved slowly, like a man with terminal exhaustion. As he climbed into bed she saw that his face was slumped and set in unfamiliar angles and planes that made him look ten years older. His eyes were swollen and shadowed.

'I've got to sleep,' he said.

'You'll sleep, don't worry.'

'No. My head's boiling. I'll just lie here thinking. I've got some pills in my briefcase.'

She went through to the sitting-room, opened his briefcase and took out some folders and notebooks. He carried pills for every eventuality, she knew, it was a habit he had acquired in the States. She found some Librium, antacid, anti-histamines and some sleeping-pills.

She gave him two. The plastic capsules were yellow and white.

'You and your damn pills,' she said with a resigned grin.

'See? Sometimes they come in handy.'

He swallowed the pills and pulled up the blankets to his ears. She crouched by the bed and stroked his wiry hair. She kissed him, reassured him, and made brief plans about his coming down to Knap to rest. Soon he began to drift away.

'We'll be OK,' he said loosely. 'We'll work it out.'

She switched off the light, closed the door and went back to the sitting-room. She locked the Librium and sleeping-pills in a drawer of the bureau and made herself a strong scotch and soda. She sat down at the table and began to repack his briefcase. She was weary herself, aching-limbed, but with an odd background sensation of restlessness.

Her eyes fell on the untidy clutter of John's papers and

print-outs. Strange jottings and diagrams, scribbled calculations. Amongst the detritus she counted two napkin, a cardboard lid from a cigarette pack and the torn-off cover of a Penguin book. She looked at the crabbed, tiny figures: to think that someone can read this stuff, she thought, picking up loose papers, actually make sense of these numbers and squiggles ... She shook her head, ruefully. This was the magic she was in awe of, she had to admit, the runic language of the mathematician. It was uncanny, other-worldly. She picked up a scrap of paper, torn from a memo pad. There were some words written on it – *Euler's gamma functn. def.* – and below that:

$$t^{-\gamma} = [\Gamma(\gamma)]^{-1} \int_0^\infty \gamma^{-(\gamma-1)} \exp(-t/\gamma)d\tau$$

What kind of bizarre and extraordinary mind dealt in this type of discourse, used these symbols to communicate crucial ideas ...? Idly, she turned the sheet over. There was another scribbled note here, not in John's handwriting:

Darling J,
Come at four. He goes off to Birmingham for *three* (!) days, from tomorrow.
Can you stay a night? Please try. Please, please.
XXXXX

THE ONE BIG AXIOM

On Brazzaville Beach the time passes slowly, easily. On the days when I am not working I eat my meals, swim, read, walk, sketch, write. The day does not hurry by. The view is familiar, the seasonal changes, negligible. Brazzaville Beach during the rains is little altered. The palms are there, the casuarina pines . . . the waves roll in. This is my time, personal and private. Whatever is going on out there in the world, with its hurry and its business, is something else. Its progress is marked by time, too, by clocks and calendars – civil time – but on the beach the days move by to the tick of a different clock.

'Civil time', as the chronologists call it, has always been based on the rotation of the earth. But our sense of 'private' time is innate. Neurologists think that this sense of time, which is always of the present moment, is conditioned by our nervous systems. As we grow older, our nervous systems decelerate and our sense of personal time dawdles correspondingly. But civil time, of course, tramps on remorselessly, its divisions constant and inexorable. This is why our lives seem to pass more quickly as we age.

So I try to ignore civil time on Brazzaville Beach and instead measure my days by the clock-like systems in my own body, whatever they are. I am pleased with this idea: if I can ignore civil time, as I age, and as my nervous system slows, the sense of the passing of my life will become ever more attenuated. I wonder, fancifully, if I have a notion here that I could call the Clearwater Paradox – after Zeno's – with me, as Achilles, always slowing down, never quite able to catch the tortoise of my death, no matter how close I come.

No. There is one thing we can be sure of – the one big axiom: when my nervous system shuts down entirely, and it will, my personal time will end.

I dived in and swam a couple of strokes underwater, enjoying the moment of coldness and the silence. I kept my eyes closed because of the chlorine, opening them after I had surfaced, then turning on my back and swimming a slow backstroke to the shallow end. As I swam I saw Hauser climbing up to the top of the three-tier diving-board. He was wearing very small cerise swimming-trunks, almost invisible beneath the solid tureen that was his belly. He stood at the end of the board, rose on tiptoes and pretended to dive. I heard the faint jeers of the others and some ironic slow handclapping. Hauser bowed elaborately and climbed down.

My hand touched the end of the pool and I stood up. I smoothed my hair back with my hands and wrung the long hank dry behind my neck. As I did so, Toshiro, who was sitting on the edge, his feet dangling in the water, looked candidly at my breasts. I looked back at his, equally candidly. I had always imagined Toshiro to be fit and muscled, but his torso was soft and pudgy, like an adolescent boy with puppy fat, his breasts pert cones with brown nipples.

'Why don't you jump in?' I said.

'I can't swim.'

I waded over to the steps. 'Do you want me to teach you? After lunch?'

He looked surprised. 'Well . . . Yes please. Can you?'

'We can make a start. It's ridiculous a man of your age not being able to swim.'

I climbed out. Hauser, who had been the dummy hand, had rejoined the bridge game. Mallabar, Ginga and Roberta were staring at the spread fans of their cards. Some way off, Ian Vail sat in the shade of an umbrella reading a paperback. I returned to my lounger and dried myself down.

We were on our 'works outing', as Mallabar had

whimsically christened this trip. We had travelled fifty miles from the camp to the Nova Santos Intercontinental Hotel. The Nova Santos was only half completed when the civil war had begun, and further work had been abandoned since then. It was designed to be a luxury hotel, with five hundred bedrooms, olympic swimming-pool, tennis courts and an eighteen-hole golf course, the first and most important symbol of the country's rejuvenated tourist industry. Now it stood, a new ruin, waiting for the end of the war and for new funds to be available, a sad reminder of what might have been.

The hotel was positioned on a small hill and looked out, over a view of monotonous orchard bush, northward to the dusty distant slopes of the Grosso Arvore escarpment. The curving drive up to the entrance portico had been built, as had the portico itself, the lobby and reception area, and, mysteriously, the swimming-pool. Everything else remained in the state it had reached when the money had run out. From my lounger, I could see the grey concrete bricks and the rickety bamboo scaffolding of a half-finished residential block. Already vines and creepers had climbed high up the three-storey sides, and plants and weeds grew as high as the ground-floor window ledges. The area cleared for the tennis courts had been planted with cassava and yams by the families of the skeleton staff who remained behind, and the golf course consisted of a few sun-bleached, termite-gnawed, black and white stakes hammered into the ground here and there. But the power lines that had been run out to the hotel from the national grid had never been dismantled, and the Ministry of Tourism paid the staff and kept the pool functioning, waiting for better days. The thick teak slab of the reception desk was burnished and gleaming with polish, and the cool terrazzo floors of the lobby were regularly mopped down and free of dust. One could even order a drink, as long as it was beer.

Mallabar had announced we were to visit the Nova Santos a few days previously. This was something he had treated the team to periodically whenever he felt we could benefit from a day off and a complete change of scene. We had set off on the two-hour drive in good spirits, transported to the hotel in two Land Rovers – the project members crammed into one, the cooks and the barbecue gear in the other.

I could smell charcoal smoke now, as I lay in the sun. It made me hungry. I sat up and sipped at my beer, looking round at my colleagues. It was odd to see them all in their swimming-suits – on vacation, as it were – these familiar people were, in their almost nakedness, made strange to me again. Apart from Hauser, of course. However repugnant his cerise thong might be it was a relief not to have to look at what it concealed. Mallabar wore absurdly boyish sawn-off jeans. He was lean and tanned (where and when did he sunbathe?) with a curious two-inch wide stripe of hair running vertically from throat to navel. By contrast, Roberta was almost unnaturally pale. Her skin was milk white, with a subcutaneous blueness about it. She wore an old-fashioned, two-piece swimsuit – wide shorts and a top with a flap hanging down from it like a fixed curtain, that exposed only two inches of creamy, plump midriff. Her breasts were large and mobile. She appeared quite unselfconscious of the amount of cleavage she had on show. It was Ian who seemed embarrassed for her. He had been moody and taciturn all day, and had not even bothered to change into his swimsuit. He sat in the shade, wearing shorts and a T-shirt, some distance away, reading intently. He hated sunbathing, he had said, and the heavily chlorinated water irritated some skin complaint he suffered from.

Ginga wore a minute, pea-green bikini. She was very thin, almost emaciatedly so, the twin triangles of her top appeared creased and empty. I noticed the luxuriant hair in her armpits, dense brown divots, and the tiny scrap of material over her groin could not hope to conceal the spreading scribble of pubis that underflowed on to her inner thigh. I knew that Ginga did not care: on the journey to the hotel, she had reminisced enthusiastically of the nude beaches on the Isle de Lerins off Cannes where she and Mallabar had spent some summer holidays in their early married life. The bikini was no more than a gesture to propriety.

And me? What was Dr Hope Clearwater wearing? I had chosen carefully. I was the earnest head girl, the keen captain of the school swimming team, in an opaque black one-piece that – I trusted – gave absolutely nothing away.

The weather was fine, just a faint haze obscuring the perfect blue of the sky. We lounged around; the bridge game came to an end; we ate lunch. We had grilled chicken and some big, freshwater prawns, fried plantain and baked sweet potatoes, a huge tomato and onion salad and some rare lettuce. Plenty of fruit and plenty of beer.

After lunch there was more sunbathing. As promised, I tried to teach Toshiro to swim but he refused to put his head underwater, so I gave up after ten minutes.

I returned to my book but was distracted by the sight of Mallabar oiling himself. I had never seen anyone oil himself so fastidiously. He oiled every visible inch of his body: he oiled the crevices of his toes and the backs of his hands. Then he asked Ginga to oil his back but she said no – she was reading and didn't want her hands to get greasy.

'Ask Roberta. Ask Hope,' she said.

Mallabar turned to look at me, eyebrows raised, questioningly. He read my answer in my expression and called out to Roberta instead.

'Roberta? Could you do me a favour?'

No one's back was ever oiled with such lingering diligence. Mallabar lay face down on his towel, eyes closed, while pale, plump Roberta crouched over him as she massaged the lotion in, to and fro, to and fro.

I walked over to Ian Vail, still under his umbrella, still reading. Half a dozen empty beer bottles stood on a low table beside him. I sat down on the end of his lounger. He drew his feet up to give me more room.

'Hi,' he said.

'How're things?'

'Fine. What about you?'

'Fine. In fact I've quite enjoyed myself.'

'So've I - getting mildly pissed on weak beer.' He held up his paperback. 'Have you read this?'

'No. After you.'

'It's not bad.'

'Talking about books,' I paused. 'How's Roberta getting on with Eugene's?'

'Nearly finished, I think.'

'Have you read it?'

He coloured slightly. 'No. I'm not allowed to. Eugene prefers it that way. And you know Roberta . . .'

'Sure. No, I suppose I can understand that.' I wondered if he had seen her oiling the master, her white hands smoothing Mallabar's brown back.

I looked away and watched Hauser pad doggedly across the concrete towards the diving-board. You've done that trick already, I said to myself, we're not going to find it quite so amusing second time around.

'What do you think,' Ian Vail said, lazily querying, 'what do you think our chimps will be doing today, now that we're not there to observe them?'

I nearly told him, almost a reflex answer to an idle question: killing each other. But I checked myself. Hauser had reached the topmost diving-board and he stalked to its end, chest inflated, every inch the champion, and spread his arms wide.

'Oh no, not again,' I said wearily. Then, to Vail, 'See you later.'

I strolled back to my seat, my eyes on Hauser and his pantomime.

Hauser leapt out into space, almost swooped, in a perfect butterfly dive, horizontal for an instant, then – in kind of mid-air check – his arms came together, his head dipped, and, with a precise and practised effort, he hitched his tubby legs into a vertical plane and sliced cleanly into the water with hardly any splash. Bubbles seethed.

'My God,' I said, in tones of cheated astonishment, and joined in the applause. Hauser surfaced, and waved.

I reached my lounger and took off my sun-glasses. I saw that the cooks had almost finished dismantling the barbecue. The coals had been doused in the halved oil drum that acted as the grill, and it was being carried off to be emptied somewhere. A boy was packing the plastic plates and knives and forks away in an orange box.

I walked to the poolside and climbed down the chrome ladder into the turquoise water. I pushed off and glided under. There, I opened my eyes wide and I felt the chlorine begin to sting almost at once. I swam a little more, surfaced and climbed out. My eyes felt raw and peeled. I towelled myself down and rubbed my eye sockets vigorously. I put on my sun-glasses and collected my bits and pieces.

'Eugene?' I spoke to Mallabar as he lay basking. He turned and held up a forearm to shadow his eyes. 'I'm going back with the cooks,' I said. 'Chlorine's got to me.'

He stood up. I raised my sun-glasses and showed him the damage.

'Ouch,' he said. 'I did warn you.'

'I wasn't thinking.'

'Wash your eyes with milk,' Ginga said. 'They'll be better in a couple of hours.'

I took her advice. When we returned to camp, I fed my smarting eyes on a weak solution of powdered milk and it seemed to work. Within ten minutes my world was still deliquescent but I could see without it stinging.

I stood in the middle of Main Street, alone, thinking. It was by now about five in the afternoon and I reckoned I had a two-hour start on the others. It was curious to be the only person in the camp, with the shadows lengthening and none of the usual sounds from the canteen or the kitchen area. I was standing opposite Hauser's lab; to my left was the huge tree and beyond it, round a curve in the road, were my own – still unreconstructed – quarters. Diagonally to my right, through a gap between a nim tree and a grove of frangipanis, I could see the purple bougainvillaea on the end of the Vail bungalow. I took one more swift glance around, crossed the road and walked confidently towards it.

The front door was unlocked. We never locked our houses. I pushed the door open and stepped into the sitting-room. It was neat and tidy, even the papers on the desk were arranged in piles, notebooks stacked, edges flush. For some reason I was sure that Roberta wouldn't keep Mallabar's proofs there. I went through to the bedroom. It was simply furnished and smelt fresh and perfumed. There was a bright Mexican-looking coverlet on the bed and a vase of zinnias on a table beside it. Clothes were hung in an unattractive zip-up plastic wardrobe printed with a fish and shell motif. Along the wall beneath the window was a row of boxes and trunks. I checked them all: full of papers, back numbers of journals, old log books. One trunk was locked. I looked under the bed. I unzipped the ward-robe. No sign of any proofs.

I returned to the sitting-room and went through the desk drawers – nothing. I began to feel foolish: if the proofs were in the house she would be bound to keep them locked up. But for all I knew she might collect and return them daily from Mallabar himself. I wondered if I had time – if I had the courage – to search Mallabar's bungalow . . .

I walked over to the bookcase. Piled beside it was a

great stack of papers, folders and two bulging concertina files. I opened a folder: it was full of data from the Artificial Feeding Area. I put it down. There was obviously nothing here. I looked out of the window and sighed.

I saw Roberta Vail walking up the path to her front door.

I carried it off well, I must say. When Roberta opened the front door I was standing by the bookcase with a book open in my hand, like a browser in a shop.

'Hi, Roberta,' I said with huge nonchalance. 'I thought I heard you.'

She was very surprised. As her expression moved rapidly through shock, outrage, and suspicion to feigned good manners, I turned away and carefully replaced the book on the shelf.

'Must borrow that off you sometime,' I said, smiling. 'Where's Ian?'

Ian was right behind her and came in just at that moment.

'Hope?' he said, stupidly, and looked nervously at his wife.

'Hope was ... Hope was waiting for us,' Roberta explained to him.

'Oh,' he said knowingly, as if this were an everyday occurrence.

'I popped round to borrow that article,' I said to him.

'What article?'

'The one you were telling me about the other day,' I said, very directly.

'Ah yes,' he said, slowly, obviously lost. 'The article . . .'

'What article?' Roberta said.

'The one about sexual strategies,' I said, getting impatient at Vail's obtuseness. As I uttered the words I regretted them. Roberta looked at me sharply.

'In chimp society,' I continued.

'Oh *that* nonsense,' Roberta said, with heavy sarcasm.

'I'll dig it out,' Ian said, finally catching on. 'If I can still find it.'

'That'd be great,' I said, walking to the door with a smile. 'See you later.' I left.

There was no meal in the canteen that night as the cooks and kitchen boys had been given the evening off. I spent the time alone in the census hut reviewing my plans for the next day. I reread the article I had sent off to England, and wondered how Mallabar would react when it came out. I realized that, with Mr Jeb's death, its conclusions had already been superseded.

Later, I stepped outside for a breath of fresh air and stood alone in the dark for a few moments listening to the crickets and the bats. I was about to go back inside when I saw the light of a torch nodding down the road. I crept over to the hibiscus hedge and in the dim backwash from the beam saw that it was Roberta Vail. She went to Mallabar's bungalow, knocked on the door and was admitted.

The next morning, I was up early and off before any of the others had emerged. I took João to the site of Mr Jeb's killing. I told him only that I had found Mr Jeb badly injured, and that he had crawled away into the thorn bushes to die. We stood peering into the undergrowth. There was a distinct reek of putrefaction in the air.

'Look,' João said and pointed. 'Conrad.'

Conrad sat in the lemon-flower tree, looking down at us, and the spot where Mr Jeb was decomposing.

'I think leopard,' João said grimly, spitting on the ground. The smell was bad. 'We get leopard here.'

'No,' I said. 'I think it was chimps.'

He looked at me as if I were mad.

'I think,' I went on carefully, 'that I saw chimps – the northerners – nearby. I heard the noise of a fight.'

'I don't think is possible, Mam,' he said respectfully, but with complete conviction.

I took out my notebook. 'Well we'll just log it as "unknown predator". How's that?'

João remembered something. 'Oh yes, Mam, Dr Mallabar wants my papers. All the notes I gave you.'

'All of them?'

'Yes, Mam.'

'Did he say why?'

'He say for the archive.'

Mallabar had talked vaguely about this project in the past: a store-house of all the work done at Grosso Arvore since its inception. All his own papers would be gathered there as well as those of the other researchers. It would be the greatest repository of primate lore anywhere in the world, he claimed. At the same time, its potential as a money-earner was not overlooked: it could be sold to some university or institution, a benefactor's name could be added ... anything was possible.

'Did you tell Dr Mallabar I had your papers?' I asked João.

'Yes, Mam.'

I saw from the rota on the bulletin board in the canteen that Ian Vail was meant to be doing the next provisioning run. I drove up to the northern area straightaway and one of Vail's assistants told me where I could find him.

It was mid-afternoon and the humidity had built up considerably. The air felt heavy and moist. The seasonal rains were not far off now. Over the last week, from the mountains beyond the escarpment, we had heard the distant rumbles of thunder as the clouds darkened and the weather fronts massed. I walked up a baked, well-worn path through waist-high grass, dry and bleached blonde, waving at the flies that buzzed around my head. There was no wind or breeze at this hour of the day, and every leaf and blade of grass in the scrub on either side of me seemed to hang limp and exhausted.

I saw Dias, Vail's chief assistant, sitting in the shade of a fitinha palm. He put his finger to his lips and pointed at a grove of trees. I peered into the dappled gloom and saw Ian, about forty yards off, sitting in front of a tripod-mounted camera with a long telephoto lens. I picked my way carefully towards him, trying not to step on twigs or dead leaves. It was very quiet under the trees and, for all the shade, it felt hotter and more oppressive.

Ian Vail looked round when he heard me coming. His face did not exactly light up in his usual shy smile of pleasure. I felt a little guilty; I hadn't spoken to him since that afternoon Roberta had caught me in their bungalow. Still, I thought, I could cope with his bruised feelings.

I crouched down beside him. Thirty feet away two chimps were feeding at a termites' nest. I recognized Pulul; the other was a young chimp, barely adolescent. Pulul was delicately inserting a long stem of grass into the termites' nest, wiggling it around, withdrawing it, and then eating the swarming termites that were clinging to its length.

After a few more goes, he stopped and let the adolescent chimp try to copy him. But this chimp was using as its tool a blade of grass which, as it was thrust into the nest, kept buckling, and could not reach the ant-rich depths of Pulul's thin stem. The adolescent's fishing attempts only rewarded him with a rare termite or two.

Soon, he threw his blade of grass away and then searched the ground for a more suitable implement. Pulul watched him silently. Ian started photographing. The adolescent found a twig about eighteen inches long with a few dead leaves attached. It stripped the leaves off and inserted the twig deep into the termites' nest. When it was extracted its tip was busy with ants.

Ian turned and looked at me. 'Every time I see that, it amazes me,' he said, somewhat formally, jerking his thumb in the direction of the chimps. He appeared edgy and a little embarrassed. I told him what I had come for and he agreed to exchange places on the rota with me.

'But why do you want to go in again?' he asked. 'Hell of a drive.'

'I have some things to do that can't wait.'

'Oh.' It didn't satisfy him, I could see. He began to dismantle and pack his camera.

'Listen, Hope,' he began. 'About the other day . . . It was very awkward for me, all that stuff about the article.'

'It was all I could think of.'

'But what were you doing there in the first place?'

I paused. Perhaps now was the time for candour. 'I was looking for the proofs of Mallabar's book.'

'Jesus Christ . . .' He shook his head in astonishment. 'But why? What difference –'

'I just wanted to see what he had written. What his line was.'

'I still don't –'

'I think he's gone badly astray.'

Ian Vail looked at me patronizingly. 'Oh come *on*.'

'There are fundamental . . . misconceptions, I'm sure.'

He picked up his camera and tripod and stood up. 'Don't be ridiculous.'

'Oh yeah? What would you say if I told you chimpanzees were capable of infanticide and cannibalism?'

His face went bland for a second as he took this information in.

'I think,' he said cautiously, 'I think I'd have to say you were mad.'

'Fine. Now, what would you say if I told you one group of chimpanzees was capable of attacking and brutally killing another chimpanzee?'

He decided not to provoke me this time. 'I'd say: prove it.'

'I've seen it happen.'

I told him about Rita-Mae and Bobo. I told him the way in which his northern chimps had attacked and killed Mr Jeb. The detail I employed in my accounts unsettled him. These were clearly not the spontaneous ravings of a deranged mind.

'My God,' he said, worriedly, when I finished. 'I can hardly . . . Have you told Mallabar?'

'I tried. He doesn't want to know.'

'I can sort of understand that . . .' Ian pursed his lips, thinking hard. 'Yeah, I can see why. Jesus.'

'Look, I don't know what's happening here – in Grosso Arvore – but something very strange is going on with these chimps.'

'You're not kidding.'

'I mean, I'm seeing things that, theoretically – if the whole Mallabar line is correct – could never happen.'

We were walking back down the path. Ian was very thoughtful. I decided to embroil him further.

'I think your article is some kind of clue,' I said. 'At least it's the only hypothesis that has any kind of plausibility. I think it's all to do with the split, with Rita-Mae leaving with Clovis. I think,' I had to smile, almost in panic, at the boldness of my idea, 'I think your northern chimps want her back, and, in order to get her, they're prepared to kill all the southern males.'

'Jesus, Hope.' He looked anguished. 'This is crazy. We're primatologists, for God's sake. What you're talking about sounds like . . . like the Trojan Wars.'

'I don't know anything,' I admitted. 'But I'm seeing things. I'm witnessing things that are completely extraordinary. Your northern males are patrolling in southern territory. They attacked two chimps, quite deliberately, completely unprovoked.' I paused. 'They got one and they killed him, trying to cause him as much pain as possible. It was horrible.' I thought again. 'Actually, I almost said inhuman. In fact it was all horribly *human*, what they did. They wanted him dead and they wanted to hurt.'

We walked along the path, not really thinking where we were going, Dias following a few discreet paces behind, just out of earshot.

'You realize,' Ian said, 'exactly what this does to Mallabar. Everything he's worked for.'

'Look, I've not just invented all this simply to embarrass him, for God's sake.'

'I know . . . But it's so *odd*. So out of the blue.'

'It happens sometimes, you know.'

'But it doesn't fit the data.'

'Isn't that what they said to Galileo? How do we know what's "odd"? What's "out of the blue"? We don't.'

He rubbed his face with his hands. He seemed suddenly exasperated. 'You've got to tell him.'

'Oh, *sure* . . . Look what happened when I found the dead baby. Face it, Ian, if I tell him he's been wrong for the last twenty years what do you think he'll do?'

'I suppose you're right . . . Too much is riding on it.'

'Exactly. He'd discredit me. Cover it up. Call me a fraud, or something.'

'He'd have to delay the book.'

'At least. Please.'

'What're you going to do?'

'I'll have to prove it to him. Somehow.'

We had reached the place where the Land Rovers were parked. I hadn't quite finished.

'Don't tell anybody about this, Ian,' I said. 'Nobody . . . and that means Roberta.'

'Of course not. Don't worry.'

But I did worry. 'Don't get me wrong, Ian. You

mustn't even *hint*.' I looked at him squarely. 'I would know at once, you see, if you did. And if you did . . .'

I left the threat unspoken. It was a calculated risk, this threat, even left implicit, but necessary, I was convinced. I could see at once from his face that he knew what it was. But I also registered in his abrupt shock and surprise that I had, for an instant, held a mirror up to him, and afforded him a glimpse of how the world saw Ian Vail, and it had hurt him.

I knew what would come next.

'Bitch,' he said. 'Don't worry, bitch.'

'I'm sorry,' I said. He had every right to be upset. 'I just have to be sure.'.

I climbed into the Land Rover and started the engine and drove away from him. As I bumped down the track to Grosso Arvore, I wondered if I had made a mistake. On balance, I thought, probably not.

The next day, at sunset, I stood at the perimeter fence of the airport and waited for Usman to fly in. The air force officer at the main gate said he was due back from a mission shortly. I thought about returning to the hotel to wait for him there, but decided to stay. It was cooling down nicely and the sky was shading from an ice blue into a washed-out lemon. Unusually, there was no orange or pink in the light. It looked like a sunset better suited to Antarctica or some frozen tundra.

I had stopped my car not far from the military entrance to the airport. As at any site where there was a flow of traffic and the coming and going of people, a small community had established itself. Opposite the gate on the other side of the road were a few stalls selling food, and beyond the ditch some shacks had been erected. In a year or two it would have grown, piecemeal, into a village. In front of one of the shacks an old mammy was cooking something on a brazier, and the smell of the charcoal smoke, seasoned with a peppery spice, was carried to me by the breeze that blew off the ocean. I climbed out of the Land Rover, assured the stallholders I was not here to buy anything, and sat on the bonnet and smoked a cigarette.

When I saw the three black specks flying in from the east I jumped off the bonnet, stepped over the ditch and stood by the perimeter fence, my fingers hooked into the diamond-shaped mesh, waiting for my aviator to land.

There were three Migs, two silver, one olive drab. They flew over the airport and then banked round to make their approach. With an uneven, jerky movement their wheels came down and at surprising speed and almost carelessness they landed, one after the other. They taxied to their allotted spaces on the apron. I waved, and then felt a little foolish. These men were not returning from a vacation.

I drove the Land Rover up to the gate and waited for Usman. After about twenty minutes I saw his car – a beige Peugeot – emerge from behind some quonset huts and drive out of the entrance. I tooted the horn and when he stopped, I left the Land Rover and walked up the verge to his car. You might at least get out to welcome me, I thought, but he made no move.

'Hello,' he said, looking at me. 'My God. My lucky day.'

I did not bend to kiss him. 'Just passing by,' I said.

He still had pressure marks on his cheeks from what I

assumed was his oxygen mask – symmetrical, ogival scars. He looked tired and his eyes were restless.

'Are you all right?' I asked.

'Yes, I'm fine. But we lost one man today. Dawie. You know, the South African.'

I remembered him vaguely: small and alert, with fine thinning blond hair. 'What happened?'

He rotated a hand carelessly. 'We were flying back, four of us. We flew into some cloud and only three came out . . . Navaid failure, I suppose.'

'Like Glenn Miller.'

'Who?'

'Doesn't matter. I'm sorry . . . Anyway, I'm here for two nights.'

'Have you been to my room?'

'No. Why?'

'Good.' Some animation returned to his features. 'I've got something special to show you.'

I followed him back to the hotel. Then he made me wait outside his door for five minutes. I paced up and down watching the bluey darkness creep over the hotel gardens and hummed along to the tune of 'The Girl from Ipanema' which I could hear faintly from the lobby. Then I heard Usman call my name.

'Can I come in?'

'Yes, yes.'

I opened the door. Usman stood in the middle of the room. All the chairs had been pushed to the walls to make space. At first glance I thought three large, white moths were flying around him. I closed the door behind me quickly. But looking closer I saw that they weren't moths at all. They didn't bob and flutter; their circuits were too fixed. They moved slowly in wide and narrow circles, like flies patrolling a room, and there was a distinct buzzing noise emanating from them. I stared at them: they had wings and a tailplane, and what looked like an undercarriage. They looked like miniature flying machines, culled from a Victorian inventor's notebook.

'What the hell are they?' I asked.

'The smallest powered aeroplanes in the world.'

He reached out and carefully picked one from the air with a delicate plucking motion, and held it out to me. It was like a tiny precise glider, fragile, rather beautiful, made from doped tissue paper and slivers of matchwood. The wingspan was about two inches. Beneath the wing, in a meticulous harness of glue-stiffened threads, was a horse-fly, its wings a hazy blur of movement.

'Watch,' Usman said and held the minute aircraft at arm's length. He let go and it dropped four or five inches before resuming its normal flight pattern, meandering, weaving round the room.

'I need you as a witness,' he said with a grin. 'I'm going to send it off to that book. You know, that book of world records. Stand here.' He positioned me in the centre of the room. 'I need a photograph.'

He went into the bedroom to fetch his camera. I stood still and watched the tiny aircraft circle me, hearing the angry constant hum of their insect power-plants.

Their fly instinct, I guessed, controlled their movements; they seemed to avoid each other easily, and they altered course whenever they flew too close to a wall. They never attempted to land or settle on anything. The contraption on their backs, I supposed, precluded that sort of manoeuvre, and somehow, I supposed again, they must have been aware of that. So they would

209

cruise on endlessly until fatigue – fly fatigue – set in and they would spiral to the carpet.

I stood there while Usman took several flash photographs. I held my hand as close to the planes as possible to convey the scale.

'Can you set them free?' I asked.

'No. They're glued in place.' He smiled. 'They're pilots for the rest of their life.'

'They're rather beautiful. To look at,' I said.

He took one more photograph.

'What now?'

'They die in combat,' he said. He picked up a can of fly spray. PifPaf it was called, a yellow can with crude red lettering. He pointed it at one of his aeroplanes and enveloped it in a cloud of spray.

'Like poor Dawie,' he said.

For a while the plane flew on as normal, but then it began to judder and sideslip and in a second or two it fell fluttering to the floor like a leaf. He aimed at the other two.

'No, no, Usman,' I said quickly, 'don't do that.' I opened the door. 'Give them a last flight to remember.'

I picked one out of the air and Usman captured the other. We stood at the threshold of the bungalow and launched the little aircraft into the night. At first, away from the inhibiting cube of the room, they seemed perplexed and flew to and fro in tight trajectories of three and four feet. But then one of them very suddenly climbed up and away and we soon lost sight of it as it flew beyond the glow from the bulb above the front door. The other continued to zigzag for a while longer and then it too, perhaps caught by a gust of wind, seemed to bank off and up, and soared away into the huge expanse of the night.

We went back inside and Usman showed me his drawings and preliminary models. In a cupboard he had a jam-jar buzzing with horse-flies which he had collected with a butterfly net on the beach. He put them into a killing jar for a second or two, to drug them into immobility, before gluing them into the harness. It was the precise angle at which they had to be fixed in this that had taken him so long to calculate. It had been a matter of trial and error, he told me, and it had taken many days to find the exact position where the forward motion of the horse-fly's wings, properly directed, did not work against, or cancel out, the natural aerodynamics of the carefully cut and moulded paper wings.

He showed me a fly-less flying machine. Unbelievably light it lay in my palm like a husk, the ghost of a dragonfly. The wings were beautifully worked, curved in section to provide lift, and the tips were folded up. The tailplane was disproportionately large, an unusual V-shape. It was this feature that made the plane fly straight, he said. It took a lot of effort for the fly to turn the machine. That was why the movements seemed so studied, their turns so deliberate and slow.

So the horse-fly was sedated, fitted into harness with its wings free to move, and then glued in place, tilted back slightly. Usman showed me his drawings, immaculate as an architect's plans. I signed and dated the statement that I had witnessed these machines in powered, sustained flight. I was surprised and impressed; the drawings were not to scale, larger than life. They had a curious, surreal beauty.

'You've obviously had a lot of time on your hands,' I said. 'I thought there was a war on?'

'I thought it was finished. Then we flew three missions in three days after nearly a month off.'

'What's happening?'

'I don't know. UNAMO has broken out of its enclave.' He shrugged. 'All I know is that it's UNAMO now. Not FIDE or EMLA.' He smiled. 'But we can't find them anywhere. Come on, let's go and have dinner.'

I lay in Usman's bed, waiting for him, naked. I felt calm and in control. The chimpanzees, the northerners' patrolling, Mallabar and his book, were not forgotten, but safe in their context, and therefore easier to cope with.

'Have you washed?' Usman called.

'Yes,' I said.

He was scrupulous about this: he liked us both to wash our genitals before we made love. He said it was polite.

I slipped out of bed and went to the bathroom door. Usman stood in the bath sluicing soap off his groin with water from a jug. He stepped out and dried himself. His penis and scrotum were oddly dark, almost charcoal grey against the caramel of his belly and thighs.

'What're you looking at?' he said.

'Your fat stomach.'

He sucked it in and slapped it. 'Muscle,' he said, trying not to smile. 'Solid muscle.'

As he towelled himself dry, I could see he was growing aroused. I think he liked me to be forthright and uninhibited. Once, when he had been showering, I had come into the bathroom and had a shit. I hadn't given it any thought but Usman told me after he had been shocked and exhilarated.

'See you later, Fatso,' I said. I went back to bed and waited for him.

*

The next morning I was up early. I typed a long post-script to my article (on a typewriter borrowed from reception) about the killing of Mr Jeb. Usman took this and all of João's field reports to an office at the airport and had them photocopied. I made a bundle of these copies and left them with Usman for safe keeping. Not all the material from Grosso Arvore would be stored in the Mallabar archive.

Then I met up with Martim and Tunde, the kitchen staff who had travelled down with me. We did our chores and shopping and I ran the various small errands that the others required. I went to the central post office, just down the hill from the cathedral, and posted my afterthoughts to my friend at the magazine. I waited for forty minutes in a hot glass cabin as the operator tried to connect me with London. Eventually the light flashed above the telephone informing me that the connection had been made. I shouted hello into the receiver for a while but all I heard was the fizz and crackle of the ether.

Back at the hotel I found the copied field notes and a message from Usman to meet him at a refurbished beach house for a late lunch.

Offshore, I could see – miles away – a big storm system lurking, a great toppling continent of cloud with mountains and plateaux, cliffs and chasms. We sat on a wide wooden deck, eight feet above the sand, looking out at the view. The sun was shining, but the presence of the offshore clouds made the day and the beach and the creaming breakers seem threatened and imperma-nent.

Usman had borrowed this beach house from a Syrian merchant he knew. It was freshly painted but only half repaired. The jutting deck was strong, with new timber and supports, but when you opened the door to go into the house you discovered that the roof had collapsed. But it was fine on the deck. It caught whatever breeze there was and we were high enough from the ground to escape the sand-flies.

Usman had prepared an odd lunch of garlic sausage and a sweet potato and onion salad. There was some bread and processed American cheese and a pineapple. We drank beer from a cool box.

We sat on aluminium chairs – an aluminium table with the lunch on it was between us – and rested our feet on the balustrade, watching the waves tumble in. Usman told me that the Syrian had offered to sell him the beach house.

'What's the point?' I said. 'You won't be here much longer.'

'But it's very cheap. And anyway I've got nothing to spend my money on.'

'Don't you send it home?' I had never really questioned Usman about his domestic arrangements.

'I send some to my brother and sisters, of course.'

'What about your wife and children?'

He looked at me, then laughed. 'Ah, Hope. I'm not married.'

'I don't mind.'

He took a long pull on his beer, still smiling, amused at me.

'I was too dedicated to get married,' he said.

'Dedicated to what?'

'To outer space.'

He told me he had trained for many years to be an astronaut. When the Russians opened their space programme to certain third world countries – notably India, Viet-Nam and Egypt – Usman had been one of the six Egyptian Air Force pilots selected for initial training. He had spent four years at Baikonur itself, he said, waiting for the day. Then the six had been reduced to two, Usman and one other. There was always a back-up, he said: two Indians, two Vietnamese, two Egyptians. No one knew who would be chosen.

'I knew it would be me,' he said matter-of-factly. 'You see, it was my dream to go in space. I talked to the others who had been, who had looked down on the world. I saw the photographs . . .' He smiled, sadly. 'I think that was my mistake. The photographs were so beautiful, you see.' He screwed up his face, wincing at the memory of their beauty. 'I stopped being the perfect technician. I even began to write poems about the earth, seen from outer space. I think that was my mistake.'

'So they chose the other one.'

'I was there right up to the blast-off. In case something went wrong with him. But it didn't.'

'That's sad.' I felt full of love for him, then.

He made a resigned face. 'And now the Americans go to the moon.'

'So you can speak Russian?' I asked, trying to change the mood.

'Oh, I've forgotten most of it . . . But it was a long time, you know, to be there, to be so obsessed with one thing, and then not getting it . . .' He pinched the bridge of his nose. 'When I came back to Egypt, nothing was the same, I couldn't settle. I had to leave the air force.' He turned and smiled. 'I saw an advertisement, looking for

"Instructors". So here I am fighting someone else's war.'

'Don't you have a home?'

'I have a small flat in Alexandria. My cousin's living there just now.' He stood and hitched up his swimming-trunks. 'It's not really a home. That's why I'd like to buy this place.'

'Well you should buy it. If it'd make you happy.'

He came round the table and kissed me.

'Hope. Clever Hope. It's not so simple. I don't think one old beach hut can make me happy.'

In the night, very early in the morning, before dawn, someone came to the door to wake him. I heard them talking softly for a while, then Usman got dressed. There was a mission to be flown at dawn, he said. They had to go now to be briefed. A UNAMO column, he said, heading for the marshes and river systems in the north. I was still half asleep when he kissed my cheek and said goodbye.

'When you come back, Hope, next time. I'm going to buy that beach hut. We'll stay there.'

I left the hotel for the run back to Grosso Arvore a few hours later. Just as I was turning on to the road that led past the airport, I heard the rip of jet engines and saw six Migs take off, two by two, afterburners orange, and climb up and away into the misty blue air of the morning.

THE COSMIC DAWN

Hope feels sorry for Usman and his lost dreams of space flight. She too has seen those photographs of the home planet shot from high above our misty atmosphere. She can understand his longing to be up there in the infinite blackness, spinning through the vacuum of space at five miles a second, looking down at the blue and white ball.

To watch the raspberry colours of a cosmic dawn. See the furry haze of the fragile biosphere. Check out the moonrise and the moonset, climbing rapidly like a bubble in a glass of water, falling like a ping-pong ball off the edge of a table. Observe the vast spirals of plankton blooms in the oceans, hundreds of miles across. Count the sixteen sunrises and sunsets you see every twenty-four hours as you orbit the beautiful planet ... Maybe he might have gone further out and had his eyes lit by earthshine, or – who knows? – seen the earthrise itself, blue and lazy, over the sallow moon surface, like those American astronauts he so envied.

Usman's dreams were out of this world. They could be hard to live with.

Hope made a plan. She would watch John in secret, covertly, over a weekend to see what happened. So she telephoned, said she was coming home and then, late on Friday evening, rang him again to cancel. An important meeting, interviewing Winfrith's replacement, her presence required. John said he was sorry; he had been looking forward to her coming.

So she took a train up to London, hired a car and drove to one of those anonymous large hotels off the Cromwell Road and booked herself a single room.

On Saturday morning she drove to their street and parked. She saw John emerge from their flat, alone, and walk to college. She watched the college, almost uninterrupted – she had to eat and relieve herself – until seven in the evening, when he went home. He did not leave the flat again that night, and had no visitors.

She was up early enough on Sunday morning to see him returning from the newsagent's with the Sunday papers. She felt strange to be spying on him in this way, to be looking at a person you know intimately as others see him. Facets of John's appearance that had grown familiar now seemed singular again: his neutral, unfashionable clothes, the tight fit of his jacket, his wiry driven-back hair. When he walked he rolled slightly from side to side, almost a swagger. He smoked constantly.

The afternoon was bright, cold and crisp, but warm in the sun. At about three, he left the flat with a ragged bundle of newspapers and a notebook. He walked to Hyde Park. He sat on a bench and read for a while and then jotted something down in his notebook. Then he wandered down to the Serpentine and strolled around, stopping to gaze at the last intrepid boaters of the year and the model yacht enthusiasts.

He looked pale and thin-faced and, despite her resolve and her anger, she felt a pity for him grow in her, almost enough to make her run over and say, hello, it's me, I came up unexpectedly ... But not quite enough. She hung back and watched him until he went home, stopping on the way to buy food. She sat in her car outside the flat until ten and then returned to her hotel. She telephoned him.

'Hi, it's me,' she said. 'How are you?'

'Fine, fine.'

'Have you tried to call? I've been out.'

'Ah, no. I was just about to.'

'Telepathy.'

'Yeah. Must be.'

'Are you all right? You sound a bit . . . down.'

'No, actually,' he said. 'I'm fine.'

'What've you been up to?'

'Read the papers. Went for a walk in the park.'

'Nice day?'

'Yeah. Coldish.'

'Funny to think of you in London, doing these things, without me.'

'Just a walk in the park.'

'Miss me?'

'What? Yes, of course.'

'Why don't you come down this week? Wednesday, Thursday.'

'I might, actually.'

They talked on in this way for a while and then said good-night. She thought he had sounded depressed, even though he denied it. She decided to wait one more day and telephoned Munro to tell him, making some excuse about a dental appointment.

The next morning she was outside the flat by eight, sitting in her car, munching a sticky bun and drinking coffee out of a plastic cup. By ten o'clock there had been no sign of John and she began to wonder if she might have missed him. Perhaps he had gone to work especially early? Perhaps he'd slept in? After some thought, she decided to ring the doorbell, just to see if he answered. There was an answer-phone device at the main door. Their flat was on the fourth floor. John would not see her even if he leant out of the window.

She left the car and crossed the road. As she approached the front door she heard her name called. She stopped abruptly, her shoulders hunching automatically with guilt. She turned. It was Jenny Lewkovitch. Hope told herself not to be stupid: this was her front door; after all, what could be more natural.

'Hi,' Jenny said, smiling. 'I forgot you lived round here. For some reason I thought you lived in Notting Hill.'

'No,' Hope said; she rummaged in her bag for her keys. 'Number 43.'

'I'm looking for a cheese shop,' Jenny said. 'Meant to be an amazing cheese shop near here, isn't there?'

Hope pointed. 'Bute Street. Three along.'

'Great.'

There was a pause. Hope could not think of anything to say. She felt her face grow hot.

'Well . . .' Jenny said. 'See you later. Are you going to that college do? Saturday?'

Hope opened the front door.

'No. I'll be in Dorset.'

'Oh well. Say hi to John. See you.'

She left. Hope closed the door and stood in the dim hall, feeling absurdly foolish. She had been unbelievably tense and awkward, she realized, God knows what Jenny had thought. She sorted through the mail, picking out their letters. I have to go up now, she told herself, this is ridiculous. If he's here, I'll say I've had to come back for a meeting.

She ran up the stairs.

As she reached the landing below their floor she heard the door to their flat open and John said, 'Miss Punctuality.' Hope's pace slowed. She turned the corner and looked up the last flight of stairs. John stood in the doorway, smiling broadly. When he saw her it faded, but only for a second.

'Hi,' he said. 'Thought I heard you.'

Hope felt cold. She felt a tightness travel up her spine to constrict her scalp.

'Miss Punctuality,' she said. 'Who's that?'

But she didn't need to ask. Now she knew who XXXXX was.

'I needed somebody,' he said, flatly. 'You weren't here.'

'Jesus Christ. All my fault.'

'She's not happy. Bogdan's . . . He wants to leave her. And I was miserable. Christ, you know how miserable I've been.' He seemed to poke and prod at his face, as if it was going numb. 'What can I say? All these clichés. Me, her, a moment. A kiss. So fucking banal.'

The thought of Jenny Lewkovitch kissing John made her want to vomit.

'I don't even like her particularly,' he said. 'Don't particularly fancy her.'

'That's meant to make me feel better?'

'It's not a . . . grand passion. It was just something that happened. We fell into it.'

'Our bed.'

'Don't do the bitter sarcasm number, please.'

He looked down at his hands on the table.

'Everything's going wrong,' he said in a quiet voice. 'Everything. I'm sorry.' He took a deep breath. 'It's contemptible. Inexcusable. I'm weak. I'm a liar.' He shrugged and looked at her. 'Now you're here, I'm baffled at myself. I can't understand what made me do it. Now you're here.'

Hope thought of that moment in the park yesterday and of her upwelling of sympathy for him. She pushed her chair back and went round the table to him. He tensed as she approached. Even then she wasn't sure what she might do. From somewhere came the urge to hit him.

'Life's too short,' she said, and bent to kiss his cheek.

They talked about it. Hope confessed she had been watching him for two days. He was unsettled by that news. He said he would never have expected her to be quite so devious. Hope said she would never have expected him to have an affair with Jenny Lewkovitch.

They went for a walk and had a meal in a restaurant. They tried talking about other things, then they acknowledged to each other that they were trying to talk about other things and so talked about the affair a bit more.

The day progressed with a strange lethargy.

Of all the emotions that Hope experienced, the most bizarre was a sense of disappointment. Disappointment that he could have betrayed her with someone so ordinary, so mundane as Jenny Lewkovitch. She recalled their encounter at the front door. Her awkwardness; Jenny's breezy, brazen calumnies. The cheese shop . . . The chit-chat . . . she saw again Jenny's small face, her funny, pointed chin, her fringe, her bulky artisan's clothes. She tried to imagine, from a man's point of view, what there might be about Jenny Lewkovitch that could be described as sexually attractive. She failed. Perhaps it was simply a matter of mutual need and mutual opportunity . . .? But how dull, she thought, and how disappointing. And in any case where does that leave me?

*

By the evening of that slow day John's mood began to change. During the afternoon he had made an effort, had looked closely at his behaviour and taken responsibility for the consequences of what he had done. As it grew dark, Hope sensed him beginning to withdraw into himself.

At half-past six he switched on the television and settled down to watch a quiz show, notebook in hand.

'Why are you watching that crap?' she asked.

'I'm interested in them.'

'Game theory? Again?'

'Ah . . . Yeah. Sort of.'

She let him watch. She went into the bedroom and changed the sheets. Shouldn't *he* be doing this? she thought, allowing herself to feel a little bitter. Shouldn't *he* be slightly more aware of *my* feelings? Surely this job was one for the adulterer, not the adulteree . . .? Then she told herself to calm down. The whole plan, she reminded herself with some irony, was not to pretend it hadn't happened but to get its importance – its *lack* of importance – in perspective . . .

She stuffed the sheets into a plastic bag. She wouldn't have them cleaned, she thought, she would just throw them away. An expensive symbolic gesture, perhaps, but no less satisfying for all that. And she –

'Hope?' John called from the sitting-room.

She went through. He was still watching the quiz game intently, with the volume turned so low as to be almost inaudible. He glanced at her, then back at the screen. She waited patiently.

'I'm all ears,' she said.

'I think . . .' He paused, eyes still on the game. 'I think we should stop all this.'

'What? Television?'

'This farce.'

'I'm not with you.'

He stood up and switched the television off.

'Us. The marriage,' he said. 'I can't take any more of it.'

John moved out. She didn't throw him out, exactly, but at times she consoled herself with the thought that she had. In fact she left him in their flat and went back to Dorset, assuming he would be gone when she next returned.

Before she left she telephoned Bogdan Lewkovitch and said she wanted to talk to him. He suggested they meet in a café near South Kensington tube station. He was waiting there when she arrived. It was a dark, old-fashioned-looking place, with cracked oilcloths on the table and run by a staff of stout old ladies. They drank milky coffee from scratched perspex cups.

Bogdan was a large man with fair, untidy hair and, oddly for someone of his age, he still suffered from acne, he always had a few pink spots on his neck and jaw beneath his ears. He had a brisk and direct manner and often caused inadvertent offence in the college. Hope liked him. While they talked he ate three pastries, triangular sticky cakes studded with nuts as big as gravel.

'It's about John, isn't it?' Bogdan said, almost at once, munching.

'Yes.'

'What can I tell you? Each day he's different.' He picked some crumbs off the table with his forefinger 'That's part of the charm, of course.'

He told her that John's work on turbulence had started well but he had moved on too quickly. Conclusions he had drawn from a study of fluid dynamics he had then tried to apply more generally to all types of discontinuities. But here the sums did not quite add up. Those promising avenues were revealed as dead ends. Lucid and attractive formulae generated prolix answers of babbling complexity.

'And so he got very depressed, for a while. Which is natural. We could all see it. But then,' he winced histrionically, 'we all go through that. That kind of frustration.'

Bogdan said that the first really bad sign was when John started working piecemeal, almost at random, on other topics – irrational numbers, tiling, topology – 'Even the dread world of physics attracted him for a week or two,' Bogdan said, with a sarcastic smile.

'And now he's back on game theory,' Hope said. She told him about the quiz show.

Bogdan said that, initially, John's work had been astonishing. He had read a paper that everyone regarded as completely novel and exciting. The trouble was, Bogdan said, there were no laws of trespass in the world of science. Many people were working simultaneously, all over the world, in John's area. All types of turbulent, discontinuous phenomena were being analysed: weather systems, economic markets, radio interference. John was not alone, he said. He ordered more coffee.

'But the cruel irony is,' Bogdan said, 'that those first months of work John did on turbulence seemed to have opened doors for the others, but not for John. He's like . . . you know, a guy who invents an engine that runs on steam but finds out that James Watt reached the patent office first.' He shrugged. 'Happens all the time. Even when you're dealing in nothing but abstract ideas – concepts' He snapped his fingers. 'Someone on the other side of the world comes up with identical proofs.'

'So. John's got so far but can't go further.'

'Yeah, and it's killing him, I guess. It would kill me. You see, he thinks someone else is going to snatch the prize.'

'What can he do?'

'Nothing. He just has to accept it. We all tell him, but you know, I think that's what's causing his problems.'

Hope frowned. She wasn't sure if this explained why he had slept with Jenny.

'I bumped into Jenny the other day,' she said. 'How is she?'

Bogdan was eating. He swallowed and swilled down some coffee and then told her, with some eagerness, that they were thinking of getting divorced.

'I'm seeing someone else,' he said. 'In Birmingham. I'm very happy with her.'

'Oh. Great.'

'But, you know, I'm worried about the children, etcetera, and all that.'

Hope said she understood.

'And Jenny,' Bogdan said. 'I think maybe she has a lover here in London. But I don't know who.'

For an instant, malice prompted her, urged her to try for a small revenge, but she resisted. Instead she told him vaguely about her troubles with John and how they were going to separate for a while. There was no one else, she said, it was a question of warring temperaments. They both felt that some time apart might be the answer. Hope wrote down her telephone number in

Dorset and gave it to Bogdan. She asked him to keep an eye on John.

'Let me know if things get worse,' she said.

'Oh sure. I see him every day. I'll call you.'

They left the café. It seemed very bright outside after the brown gloom. Hope flinched as a bus thundered by. Bogdan kissed her farewell and reassured her once more.

'Everyone's getting divorced,' he said wryly. He paused. 'They're funny people, mathematicians,' he said. 'You should have married a physicist. We're not quite so crazy.'

THE CALCULUS

The calculus is the most subtle subject in the whole field of mathematics. It is concerned, I read, with the rates of change of functions with respect to alterations in the independent variable. It is the foundation of all mathematical analysis.

I'm lost. But I'm still attracted by this idea of its subtlety and importance. I like the fact that we apply the definite article to it. The calculus.

A simpler definition tells me that the calculus is the study of continuous change, that it deals with growth and decay, and I begin to understand why it is such a crucial tool. Growth, change and decay . . . That applies to all of us.

But its key defect, it seems to me, is that it cannot cope with abrupt change, that other common feature of our lives and the world. Not everything moves by degree, not everything ascends and descends like lines on a graph.

The calculus requires continuity. The mathematical term
for abrupt change is 'discontinuity'. And here the calculus
is no use at all. We need something to help us deal with
that.

The rains threatened, but still they never came. João
and I kept up our watch on the Danube but saw no
further incursions. Meanwhile, Alda logged the movements of the other members of the southern group as
best he could alone.

After several days sitting in my hide overlooking the
river ravine, hot and sticky and pestered with flies, I
decided further vigilance was fruitless. As a result of the
attack on Mr Jeb, I assumed, Clovis had led the southern group further south almost to the edge of the
escarpment. Their core area was now a good two miles
from the Danube, any patrolling northerners would
have to cover a vast area of the forest in order to find
them.

I was away from the camp most days from dawn to
sunset. I often arrived at the canteen late, as the others
were finishing their meal, and in this way managed to
keep my social contacts to a minimum. After abandon-
ing our surveillance at the river I spent a morning going
over the data of Alda's follows, trying to plot the extent
to which the core area of the southern group had
moved and how confined it now was. It was clear at
once that they were wandering about far less, spending
much more time together as a group and rarely ventur-
ing off on their own or in twos. Except for Lena.

Alda had done two follows on Lena. She had left the
group one day and had gone off foraging on her own.

At the end of the day she had constructed a sleeping-nest about half a mile from the others. She had returned to the group the next morning and then, two days later, had wandered off again. Alda had last seen her at four o'clock one afternoon high in a dalbergia tree. Since then she had not been seen. When I superimposed Lena's movements on a map of the others' it was obvious she was ranging as widely as she had ever done, oblivious, it seemed, to any risk.

The three of us spent the next two days with the southern group. There was still no sign of Lena. The other chimps seemed quite relaxed; there was no evidence of excessive caution or fear. The only significant change since I had last seen them was that Rita-Lu was now fully in oestrus. We saw Clovis and Conrad copulate with her, Clovis many times, but Conrad only once. Even then Rita-Lu jumped away from him after three or four thrusts and Conrad ejaculated into mid-air. Rita-Lu still presented to Conrad but he seemed subdued and quiet. It was as if, with Mr Jeb gone, Conrad had lost his natural desire. Even Muffin showed some interest in Rita-Lu but she would chase him away.

Clovis ministered to her most often. Rita-Lu's swollen, shiny rump infallibly aroused him and he would break off his feeding or grooming whenever she presented to him and squat down, thighs spread, his testicles – big as tennis balls – resting on the ground, like hairy tubers at the root of some thin, lilac-stemmed flower drilling upwards towards the sun.

One morning when I met João and Alda they told me that a man from a village south of Sangui had informed

229

them that he had heard the sound of chimpanzees fighting in the bush. I took out a map and they showed me where the village was. I plotted the most direct route there.

We walked south through the forest for over three hours. We were now near the edge of the lush vegetation that marked the southernmost precincts of the national park. The escarpment here took a ninety-degree turn east. Due south was a wide, flat, rift valley of featureless orchard bush and small villages, scattered miles apart. The province we were in was very underpopulated and those people who lived on the fringe of the park had no necessity, as yet, to move up the green slopes of the escarpment in search of better pasture or more arable land. A few fields of maize and cassava had encroached here and there, a certain amount of timber was felled for firewood but the human population posed little threat to the habitat of the chimpanzees.

We emerged from the treeline, tired and a little foot-sore, and surveyed the view spread below us. To our left the forested hills of the escarpment swung east for twenty miles and then rolled southwards once more. The grey clouds of the ever-impending rains hung above the distant hilltops, but above us the sky was blue, badged with round, white, stationary clouds. The pie-bald, dusty bush stretched out for miles before us. At our feet lay the small nameless village with its irregular fields cut from the bush haphazardly, the green maize plantations almost indecently fresh-looking in the midst of so much dusty aridity. In the far distance a band of darker vegetation crossed the plain, the riverine trees of a tributary of the massive Cabule.

We ate our lunch. Alda pointed to the river in the

distance, and where it emerged from a valley cut in the hazy hills, and said, 'There, is FIDE. And beyond. And there,' he gestured north behind our backs, 'there is UNAMO.'

'Look,' João said. 'Aeroplane.'

He pointed. I saw, coming from the west, high up, making contrails like spilled salt, two jet fighters. Migs, I supposed. I had never seen them in our skies. Usman told me they rarely flew missions in the north. They passed above us and disappeared into the haze. Seconds later we heard the rumble of their engines.

We went down to the village. Round mud huts, thatched with straw, the matting walls of compounds. João spoke to one of the old men lounging beneath a shade tree and a small boy was deputed to lead us to the approximate scene of the chimpanzee fight.

We crossed a patch of even waste ground. At one end a football goal stood, a few shreds of net still hanging from it.

'For the missionaries,' João said. 'They were here before the war.'

Men and women working in the fields looked at me curiously as we walked by. Then the ground started to rise and the bush closed in on us once more. The small boy pointed to a clump of cotton trees on the edge of the ridge above us. The noise came from there, he said, and left.

It took us another half-hour of further climbing to reach the cotton trees. We spread out and began to search through the grass and bushes beneath them. I found many discarded seeds of the fruit. They were nutty flat discs about an inch across, like small mango seeds, surrounded by a pale yellow, fibrous flesh in a fuzzy, suede-like casing. From the amount of seeds on the ground I would have thought that the entire southern group had been feeding here. There were many torn leaves and broken twigs on the ground as well but nothing that indicated anything more than the usual careless and untidy feeding of a group of hungry chimpanzees.

Then João called out. I ran over to him.

Just beneath the lowest branches of a large bush was a severed arm. The right arm of a young chimpanzee that seemed to have been crudely torn off at the shoulder. I looked at it: it could only be Muffin's. Alda was peering under the bush. He reached in with a stick, hooked it on to something and tugged. At once there was a great noise of buzzing and the bush came alive with thousands of blow-flies, hard and shiny. It was as if handfuls of gravel were being flung at the leaves. The bush shivered and vibrated as the flies fought to escape. I backed away while Alda pulled his shirt over his head and plunged in to haul out the body.

It was Muffin. Something had been eating him recently, something small and carnivorous, a bush rat perhaps, and his stomach had been opened to expose his viscera, slimy and swollen. His face was battered and cut, just as Mr Jeb's had been, and his left foot and leg below the knee was missing. The bloody, congealed socket of his right arm was filled with swarming ants. There was no stink but, as Alda heaved him out, some of his guts fell from the hole in his stomach with a moist slither.

I gagged and felt saliva swirl into my mouth. I felt faint and shocked. Muffin: neurotic Muffin who hated to leave his mother. I turned away and spat and took a deep breath. I opened my bag and removed my camera.

*

It was a long walk back home. I had wanted to bring Muffin's body but it was too badly torn to carry for such a long distance. As we trudged homewards I had plenty of time to think. I wondered what to do. Mr Jeb and Muffin were dead. Lena was missing but I was now convinced that she too had been attacked and probably killed. Let's assume, I reasoned, that three of my southern chimps have been killed by the northerners. I had no doubt that Muffin was the latest victim. I had a vivid memory of Pulul sitting on Mr Jeb's back twisting his leg round and round until the ligaments and tendons gave and it broke. The thinner limbs of a small adolescent would be no problem for a mature adult. A full-grown male was incredibly strong: I had seen them snap branches as thick as an arm with almost casual ease. They could have torn Muffin apart as easily as you or I would wrench a drumstick from a roast chicken.

Three chimps were gone; only five were left: Clovis, Conrad, Rita-Mae, Rita-Lu and baby Lester. There were seven mature males in the northern group and several enthusiastic adolescents. What chance did my depleted band have against them? And there was another problem, no less perplexing: what should I tell Mallabar? For the first time I began to regret so precipitantly sending off my article to the magazine. Events had moved faster than I could ever have imagined. Suddenly, revenging myself on Mallabar no longer seemed my highest priority.

'I don't quite see what you're saying,' Mallabar said, slowly.

We were in his bungalow, it was about nine in the

evening and we were sitting in his study. This room was a small shrine of self-importance. The walls were covered with framed citations, photographs, honorary degrees and diplomas, but the room's furnishings were simple to the point of austerity: two metal filing cabinets, a square wooden table as a desk and a couple of canvas director's chairs. Mallabar pre-empted all criticism of the egotistical decor by classifying it as his fund-raising room. Important sponsors could see what results their patronage had achieved, and the spartan facilities reassured them that nothing had been squandered.

I sat in a canvas chair looking at several framed magazine covers featuring the man behind the desk opposite me. He had a faint smile on his face, but it was only a polite formality. His mood was not benign.

I began again.

'I want to take a female, from the south, and reinstate her in the northern group.'

'Hope, Hope,' he said, leaning forward urgently. 'You don't understand. This is not a zoo. We can't move animals from cage to cage, as it were. To do what you want would be ... out of the question. This is a *wild* environment. What you're proposing is an act of engineering.'

I resisted the temptation to point out the engineering required to build the Artificial Feeding Area.

'I still think we should do it.'

'But you haven't told me why.'

'To ... to avert trouble.' I held up my hand to stop him interrupting. 'Northern males are making regular patrols into the south and –'

'I don't like that word "patrols",' he said.

'That is what they are,' I said emphatically. 'I've seen

them, and . . .' I paused for a second, 'there has been aggression.'

He stiffened. 'What do you mean?'

'Three of my chimpanzees have been killed. And two, for sure, have died as a result of violent attacks.'

'That is a forest out there, my dear. Full of wild beasts.'

I ignored his sarcasm. 'I have a horrible feeling,' I was treading very carefully here, 'that they have been attacked and killed by the northern chimps.'

'Stop now!' he shouted. He stood up, very angry. 'Don't say another word. For your own sake.' He was shivering slightly, even though he had a tight pursed smile on his face. He put both hands on his desk and lowered his head for four or five seconds. When he looked at me again there were, I could swear, tears in his eyes. It was very impressive.

I sat there and listened to him, knowing that I had gone as far as I could, and that to go further would have been the end of my career at Grosso Arvore. So I listened as Eugene Mallabar ran through his autobiography for me, sketched out his ambitions and dreams, and summarized the enormous efforts and sacrifices he had made over the last two and a half decades. All this, it transpired, was a mere preamble to what he had to address to me. He and Ginga, he reminded me, had not been blessed with children. As a consequence they were inclined to look on all those who worked at Grosso Arvore as members of their large, extended family. People came for a year or two, they lived and worked here, and eventually returned to America or France or Sweden or wherever. But they never forgot what they had shared, and they never forgot Grosso Arvore (I was tiring rapidly now). Everybody was admired and cherished, everyone was special, they were all working together in common purpose.

'Take yourself, Hope. You are, and I make no secret of it, a very special member of our family. The exceptional circumstances of your arrival, at a time when our fortunes were particularly low, were very, very important to us. You answered our call at our time of need. You came to us . . .'

He paused for effect. I had a ghastly premonition of what he was going to say next and he did not disappoint me.

'Ginga and I think of you with great fondness. It . . . it would not be going too far to say that I myself like to think of you as my daughter . . . There's something about you, Hope, that stimulates my, our, parental love. So,' he paused again, turning his head to one side as if to hide a tear from me, 'so I hope you will take what I am about to say in the spirit of a father talking to a much-loved, but young and inexperienced daughter.'

He looked at me for approval. I kept my face rigidly neutral.

'I have been studying chimpanzees for twenty-five years,' he said. 'Now you arrive here and you see certain things, certain occurrences which are unfamiliar to you, and you make an interpretation. Too fast. Too eager. You count your chickens before you leap.' He came round his desk and leant back against it. He linked hands and pointed his joined fists at me.

'These . . . these allegations you've made are pure speculation. You are jumping to conclusions based on the patchiest data. Bad. Bad science, Hope. Whatever you may think is happening is *wrong*. You are wrong, Hope. I'm sorry. I know, you see. I know more about chimpanzees than any living person, more than any person in the history of mankind. Think about it.' He smiled, incredulously.

'And yet you are challenging me.' He spread his hands. 'That's why I get angry. You're too bold. The advancement of understanding goes A B C D E F G. You go A B and then you jump to M N O. It can't be done, it can't be done.'

He came towards me and put both hands on my shoulders. He pushed his dark face close to mine.

'Don't torment yourself with these wild speculations, my dear. Observe and note. Observe and note. Leave the interpretation to me.'

He leant forward and pressed his dry lips to my forehead. I felt the sharp prickle of his neat beard on my nose and cheeks. I said nothing.

He led me to the door, smiling fondly at me. I realized he had enjoyed himself enormously.

'Thank you, Eugene,' I said flatly. 'I understand now.'

'Bless you.' He squeezed my arm. 'We shall do great work here, Hope. You and I.'

I walked out into the moist warm darkness of the African night with a new sense of purpose.

Two days later, I was returning to camp from a long follow of the surviving members of the southern group. Clovis and Rita-Lu had moved away from the others leaving them feeding on date palms. I left João and Alda and followed Clovis and Rita-Lu. They travelled north for about half an hour. Then they stopped. Rita-Lu presented and Clovis copulated with her. Then they rested in the shade, Clovis idly grooming Rita-Lu.

With the transfer of the core area further south much more of our working day was given over to travelling than before. I carried on observing until about four in the afternoon before I decided it was time to head back to camp. I called up João on the walkie-talkie, gave my location and told him I was going home and that he and Alda should do the same.

Ten minutes after leaving the two chimpanzees, I came to an area of the forest that I called the 'glade'. It was a place where the character of the forest changed dramatically. Here there were huge stands of bamboo, with diameters at their base of twenty to thirty feet. Their mass was such that they blotted out so much of the sun so that the vegetation beneath their spreading crowns was untypically sparse. The only trees that seemed to flourish in this perpetual twilight were thin spindly thorns – locally called rat thorns because the bark on their trunks was curiously incised, rather like a rat's tail. In this shade the rat-thorn trees grew relatively straight, up to a height of twenty feet. The trunks, branchless for two-thirds of the way, were studded with soft, warty, brown thorns. At the top, their crown of branches and leaves was substantial and undernourished-looking. Because of the absence of ground cover, this was the only area of the reserve that looked as if it might have been planted out. The rat-thorn trees did not crowd together, and with their clean, branchless trunks they resembled poles hammered into the ground. The glade looked, I thought, like a surreal orchard, planted to produce some as yet unheard-of fruit.

I reached the glade and walked quickly through the rat-thorn trees. I knew where I was now, not as far from home as I had thought. The main pathway which we had cut deep into the southern area was only three minutes' walk away.

I stopped abruptly. I had seen something moving in the gloomy recesses of the glade. I left the path and moved behind a stand of bamboo to wait.

The northerners were moving at a faster pace than usual, almost a lope, in rough indian file, with Darius leading. They had never come this far south before.

They passed about sixty feet from me, unaware of my presence. They were as silent as ever, but this increased speed made them seem more sinister, somehow. This new pace signalled lack of caution, the old tentativeness had gone.

I radioed João and said I was going to follow and set off, trailing them at a distance of forty to fifty yards. While we were in the glade I could keep up with them, but as we left it I began to fall behind. Then I realized why they were moving with such confident deliberation. They knew where they were going. They were heading directly to where I had left Clovis and Rita-Lu. They must have seen them from some vantage point.

Then I heard shrieking and squealing from up ahead, all the ugly noises of aggression and fear. I swung to my left. There was a narrow ravine nearby, cut by a small stream, along whose eroded edge the going would be easier. As I ran I fumbled in my bag for my camera. I had to have photographic evidence of a chimp attack if I was ever to refute Mallabar. The noise ahead was growing steadily more intense and now I could hear the violent thrashing and breaking of branches.

But trying to run and extract my camera from its case meant that I could not properly judge where I was going. One foot went too near the edge of the gully, the ground gave way and I fell, tumbling and slithering twenty feet of near-vertical incline to its bottom, coming to rest in a rubbery clump of pepper cress that grew in the stream bed.

At first I was a bit stunned and disorientated. I stood up and sat down heavily, straight away. I crawled up the stream a way to find my camera, which was dirty but undamaged.

Getting my bearings, I realized that the noise of the fight had moved on, further upstream. I walked up the ravine for a hundred yards trying to follow it. Then it seemed to burst out anew on the bank edge high above me. I could glimpse in the trees and bushes the flailing, rushing bodies of several chimps, but could not recognize them. Then suddenly it was quiet again. Then some hooting, then some furious screams. Then silence.

The banks of the ravine here were very steep and with little vegetation growing out of the stony exposed earth there were few handholds. I walked downstream looking for an easier route out. I found a place where some creepers and lianas grew down the bank face from the forest above. I grabbed the thickest, tugged strongly on it to see if it gave, and began to climb up, hauling myself hand over hand.

I was half-way up when I heard a noise – a slither of earth and pebbles – I looked up to see a rock the size of a medicine ball bounce down towards me. I had no time to avoid it or protect myself. My seeing it and its fall by me were virtually simultaneous. I felt its warm breeze brush me, it may even have touched my hair, and then heard it bury itself with a thunk in the damp sand of the river bed. Big clods of earth, dust and shale followed it. This did not miss me. I hung on to my liana and hunched my head into my shoulders.

When that had passed I lowered myself to the stream bed carefully, and shook the dirt from my hair and clothes. I washed my face in the trickle of water and walked downstream to a place where I could climb up unaided.

I walked slowly back through the glade and joined the main path that led to the camp. Only then did I remember the fight and wondered what had happened to Clovis and Rita-Lu. I stopped and deliberated for a while whether to go back and search for them, but I realized that this late in the day any solitary efforts I could make would be a waste of time.

I set off again, turned a corner and met Roberta Vail.

It shocked me to see her there. I felt the breath driven from my body.

'My God,' I said. 'Jesus, Roberta . . .'

'There you are,' she said, matter-of-factly. 'Eugene wants to see you.'

We walked back together. She seemed to me to be almost unreasonably calm, though I realized that might simply be in contrast to my own jangled and unsettled state. She said she didn't know what Mallabar wanted to see me about. He was away somewhere and had radioed back to camp asking her to find me and bring me to him. The Land Rover was waiting. All she knew was that he had something to show me.

'How did you know where I was?' I asked.

She tapped the walkie-talkie strapped to her belt. 'I called up João. He told me you were heading back, so I came down the path to meet you.' She glanced at me. 'Why are you so dirty?'

'I had a fall. I slid down the side of this ravine.'

'Got to be more careful, Hope.'

'I know.' I had an idea. 'Did you hear any chimps?'

She paused. 'Ah . . . no. I didn't. Did you?'

'Yes. A hell of a din. I was trying to follow. That's when I fell.'

'No, I didn't hear anything.'

I can't say why – perhaps it was because she seemed so incurious – but I thought she was lying. And a suspicion entered my mind then, like a thin splinter worked in to the palp of a finger, small but indisputably there, that – perhaps, possibly, conceivably – that rock the size of a medicine ball that had missed my head by an inch or less had been dislodged by something else, and not by the exertions of my over-eager climb.

Back at camp we got into a Land Rover and were driven, first to Sangui, and then south, heading, I soon realized, for goalpost village. By the time we arrived it was almost dark and the headlights were switched on. In the village we were directed on, and soon we saw Mallabar's Land Rover and a group of about two dozen villagers gathered round the goalposts.

I opened the door and climbed out. I felt stiff and weary. There was a cool breeze blowing and carried on it was a distinct smell of wet earth. It would rain tonight.

Mallabar left the crowd and strode toward us. I could tell from his posture and the conviction of his walk that he was both excited and pleased with himself.

'Hope. Sorry to drag you down here. But it's important, you'll see.'

He led me back towards the crowd. Hauser was there; he smiled and greeted me. I felt suddenly apprehensive, as if these people were now my enemies. The crowd parted and I saw why I had been called here.

Strung up by its hind legs to the crossbar of the goalposts was a large, dead leopard. In the glare of the headlights the white fur on its groin and belly looked almost indecently clean.

'There, Hope.' Mallabar presented it to me triumphantly as if it were some exotic *hors d'oeuvre*.

'There's your predator. That's what's been killing your chimps.'

FAME

Hope is more honest with herself since she came to live on Brazzaville Beach. She can admit to herself now, that, almost from the day she saw Bobo being killed, and certainly from the death of Mr Jeb, there were other motives forcing her to act in the way she did. Alongside her alarm and her shock had been another sensation: excitement. She felt lucky, almost blessed. It was Hope Clearwater who was witnessing these extraordinary events. What was taking place at Grosso Arvore was unparalleled, revelatory – no matter what explanation might be offered up later. And Hope was aware, from very early days, that there was every chance that it would be her name for ever associated with this new knowledge and understanding.

Hence the urge to have something in print; hence the

reticent and scrappy way she proceeded with Mallabar. If
she told him too much, if she shocked him into sacking
her, then the killings and the fate of the southern chimps
would either be misconstrued or go undocumented. Or,
worse still, someone else would break the news to the
wider world. Though she was reluctant to admit it for a
long time, Hope was in thrall to a vision of the future in
which her name glowed with lasting renown. She had to
be very careful that she did not throw this opportunity
away.

Five Acre Wood. Hazel, sallow, beech, hawthorn,
maple, sycamore, blackthorn, birch, oak, ash and elm.

The elms were dying.

When Hope pried away the friable, seamed bark she
saw the shallow, vermiculate grooves running along the
wood beneath. They looked too small scars to injure
great trees like these. But the evidence was irrefutable.
Even now, with winter almost arrived, and only a few
yellow leaves clinging on, Hope could tell which were
the dead, diseased branches: twigless, furry with lichen,
and without the true whip and give of live boughs in the
wind.

She walked through Five Acre Wood. It was a cold
day with low heavy clouds, mouse grey, dense. The stiff
breeze spat drops of sleety rain. All around her the
wood seemed to sway and heave in the wind. She was
well wrapped up but her cheeks and nose were numb
from the cold. Beneath her feet the path was wet and
muddy and the clayey loam stuck to her boots in a
thick, ochre rind. As she made her way through the wet
underwood, the blackthorn and the hawthorn scratched

at her oilskin. A strand of hair that had escaped from her woolly hat flapped annoyingly in front of her eyes.

The wind was blowing in cold off the grey tossed Channel, sweeping up the cliffs and across the downlands and winter fields to tug and worry at the trees of Five Acre Wood. The light was cold and neutral, with a urinous hint of yellow that probably meant snow that evening.

Hope thought with pleasant anticipation of her small cottage. The Raeburn heater in the kitchen stuffed with wood and coal; logs burning in the grate of the sitting-room fire; upstairs in her chilly bedroom an electric heater buzzed, her bed hot from the wire grid of her electric blanket. Everything went full blast in the cottage these winter evenings; she was careless about her fuel bill. The windows would weep with condensation, the hot water pipes would ping and shudder as the Raeburn bulged with heat ... And what would she have for dinner? she thought. She was putting on weight again, making big spicy stews for herself – lamb and chicken, oxtail and pork – slathering potatoes with butter and salt. But these days she did not care.

All this fantasizing about her cottage and her evening meal made her suddenly want to be back indoors and out of the cold. She was heading for Green Barn Coppice, one of the five remaining areas of woodland that she had still to date and classify. She had intended to make a start today, but she felt tired and buffeted by all this raw weather.

She picked her way carefully down a bank, slithery with fallen beech leaves, on to the drove road that led to the quarry pits and Green Barn Coppice. She stopped. If she turned right instead of left she could cut through

Blacknoll Farm to East Knap and be there in fifteen minutes. She stood for a moment in the muddy lane, her brain dull with the effort of thought, trying to goad herself into making a decision. What the hell, she thought, the coppice will be there tomorrow, and I've got a lot of potatoes to peel. She turned right, into the wind, and walked down the lane towards the farm.

Since she and John had separated, Hope had been back to London only once. John had cleared out all his belongings but had left the flat dirty and untidy. So she had spent an afternoon houseworking, hoovering and dusting and wiping down surfaces, as if attempting to expunge John's smell from the place, and remove all lingering traces – stray hairs, fingerprints, toothpaste smears – of his presence.

She bought some flowers, a new bedside lamp and a whistling kettle. She threw many things out: some ugly glasses with a sailing-ship motif, a thin rug, a blackened frying pan, a bathroom blind with two waterstains the shape of New Zealand. All these changes were more than cosmetic. She saw them as punctuation marks: a full stop here, a new paragraph there. Her life had changed now, and these alterations signalled that fact. She was not returning to a former state, she felt, this was the next step. Many of the bits and pieces she discarded had no association with him or with their life together; she simply wanted the atmosphere in her flat to be subtly different – the old place made new, for whatever was coming next.

Having spent all Saturday effecting all this, she went to visit him on Sunday in a calm and confident frame of mind. He was living in a street that ran behind the Albert Hall, a high redbrick cliff of a Victorian terrace. He had rented a tiny, one-roomed, furnished flat under the eaves. It was cluttered with cardboard boxes full of his possessions which he had made no attempt to unpack. There was a long table which he had pushed up to the dormer window. The view took in the top of the Albert Memorial and a section of Hyde Park. The table was covered with papers and files. When she came in he kissed her firmly on the mouth. She had expected some shyness or awkwardness, but his mood, like hers, was brisk and confident. He went into the kitchenette to make her a cup of coffee.

'Nice view,' she said, looking out of the window. A fat, grey pigeon sat on the guttering two feet away preening, and making its soft cry. She rapped on the glass and it flew away.

'What?' he said, returning with two steaming mugs.

'Pigeon. Can't stand them.'

They sat down.

'Look busy,' she said, indicating the papers.

'I'm getting a lot done,' he said. 'Amazing. Funny what a change of scene can do sometimes.'

She sipped the hot coffee, recognizing the mug she was drinking from as hers. They chatted on, not at all sadly or wistfully, but almost in a mood of quiet self-congratulation. They had done the right thing, John said. Hope agreed. He knew they would get back together again, but he just had to go a little further on his own. Once this body of work was over, then they could reassess everything and start anew.

'I miss you,' he said with a smile. 'All the time. And I can't imagine not being with you.'

'Good. Exactly. That's what I hoped you'd say. I can't imagine it either.'

'But I think it's best this way, for the time being.'

'Yes. Get things on an even keel again.'

'We had fun, didn't we. *Have* fun,' he said, sounding a little surprised. 'Together, I mean. Don't we?'

They rationalized further, adultly. Hope made the point that the Dorset job had perhaps come at the wrong time, had meant they spent too much time apart, had forgotten something of what it was like to be together. When she was finished it would be the perfect opportunity to make new plans.

'Perhaps we could go back to the States,' he said. 'You wouldn't mind?'

'No. Well, as long as it was somewhere nice. I have to get a job as well.'

'That can be arranged. You'd be amazed.'

They explored this option for a while and each enthused the other. It was a definite possibility, they concluded.

When Hope left she was cheered up, more optimistic. When his work was going well he was a different person.

At the door he said, 'I think I'm close, this time. There's something taking shape. A new set.'

A set? Hope thought. What was a set? But she humoured him. With her spread fingers she framed an invisible title, a plaque in the air.

'The Clearwater Set,' she proclaimed. She saw she had said exactly the right thing.

He smiled, momentarily exhilarated, then lowered his gaze, immediately modest.

'If only,' he said quietly. 'My God, if only.'

When he looked up she saw the ache of his ambition in his eyes for a second or two.

248

'Don't push yourself, Johnny,' she said. 'It doesn't matter to me, you know. I'll be happy if there's a Clearwater Curve or a type of triangle or half a theorem, whatever.' But she saw she had inspired him.

He shook a pair of crossed fingers at her. 'Don't worry,' he said, with a kind of breathless glee. 'We're practically there. The big one. The Clearwater Set.'

She returned to Knap relieved and relaxed. To her surprise she found she could think unmoved and objectively about the affair with Jenny Lewkovitch. She was not bothered any more by his infidelity. He was too unusual a person, she felt, his motives in life, in the way he dealt with others, were strange and one-off. Even his adultery, she told herself, came into a different category from other people's betrayals. But then she wondered if she were fooling herself, being less than honest, self-deluding. She thought about it, seriously, and decided that, in all objectivity, she was not being unfair.

Her new mood lasted for a few more days. All the data on the hedgerows came back from the typist and the marked-up Ordnance Survey maps were sent off to the cartographers. It was an impressive and thorough piece of work, Munro told her, shyly. She happily accepted his compliments: he was right. She had examined and classified 475 hedgerows. Of these 121 had been graded as level one: ancient hedgerows of crucial ecological importance which were to be protected and conserved. Now her work on the woodland was almost completed, Munro asked her to stay on to classify the ecology of the estate's watermeadows and some areas of downs and heathland. The work would take her through the following summer. She asked for some time to think about it.

But she found that the act of considering her future brought in its train a mild depression which refused to be shaken off and, indeed, steadily deepened. She told herself it was simply the effect of concluding one job and having to start the process of finding another, but as the days went by and nothing improved she realized her disquiet was more profound than that.

She telephoned Bogdan Lewkovitch and asked how John was. Bogdan reported that he was in very good form, as far as he could tell, working hard and fairly jolly and sociable. Then a day later John called and asked if he could come down to Knap for a weekend. Hope said no, immediately, making up some excuse. She felt guilty at first, but then she was irritated by his asking. He knew perfectly well that the cottage had one bedroom and one bed, so where did he expect to sleep? With her? If so, what was the point of officially separating if you saw each other at weekends to make love?

This call and her annoyed reaction to it prompted a further clear-eyed reassessment of her marriage. Was he incorrigible or merely wayward? Would he ever change? Was she doing the right thing? As she could provide no satisfactory answers to her own questions, her anger gave way to a more pervasive melancholy. So she thought about her marriage, and John, and herself, as she tramped the lanes and droveways of the estate, moving from one sodden wood to another, solitary and brooding, distracted only by her measurements and classifications and her dreams of enormous meals.

*

She walked through Blacknoll farmyard. It was empty apart from a damp bedraggled collie who picked its way through the brown puddles, barely glancing at her. The tearing noise of a drill biting into metal came from a big asbestos barn. It was funny, she thought suddenly and for no particular reason, but she wasn't missing sex. Weeks had gone by since the last time she and John had made love but she wasn't missing it at all.

She was still pondering this phenomenon as she unlocked her cottage door and changed out of her damp clothes. She put the kettle on the Raeburn's hob to boil and wondered vaguely if this was a sign that, genetically, she was Old Maid material. Perhaps she was exhibiting the symptoms prematurely . . .? This is what Meredith claimed had set in with her, recently. Except in her case she wasn't the least worried about it. In fact she was almost exultant: complete contentment with one's own company, Meredith said, was a rare and real achievement. Every need – emotional, intellectual and physical – could be catered for, single-handedly and fulfillingly, by the correctly inclined person. Blissful self-sufficiency was how she described it.

Hope recalled the last time she had stayed with Meredith, after the disaster of Ralph's seventieth birthday party. The next morning she had watched Meredith's routine carefully. First came the leisurely descent from the bedroom about nine, still wearing nightdress and dressing-gown; then the radio was switched to Radio 3 and turned down low. The juice of three oranges, freshly squeezed and chilled with ice-cubes, was gulped down standing at the sink. Then came the move to the kitchen table with a pot of coffee, two slices of brown toast and lime marmalade and a packet of cigarettes. There was no conversation. A newspaper, the *Telegraph*, was glanced through briskly and then folded back to the crossword. Then Meredith sat, drank coffee, smoked and did the crossword until it defeated her or she defeated it, a period that tended to last approximately half an hour.

Hope had looked at her hunched over her paper, cigarette held at her right ear – a cursive rope of smoke climbing to the ceiling – a slight smile or a frown on her face depending on what progress she was making with the crossword. It was as if she were stimulating her brain cells for the day ahead, like an athlete warming up before a race. It was a ritual – and sacrosanct – Meredith said, the best time of the day.

Hope wondered if she could ever be like that, or if, conceivably, she already was? Could she achieve that state of contented self-absorption day after day, month after month? But even if she could, did she want to? She remembered Meredith warning her once about an unsettling mental affliction she called the Curse of Brains. Was this its other face, the compensatory benefaction: the ability to enjoy being alone?

Hope chopped carrots and onions and prepared the other ingredients of her powerful stew. When it was on the hob and cooking, she opened a bottle of claret and put some music on. She sat down in front of the fire with a glass of wine, a novel, and as she read she smoked a cigarette. So far, so good, she thought. This was all right. No complaints.

The phone rang.

It was Bogdan Lewkovitch.

'What's wrong?' she said.

'It's John, I'm afraid. He's ill.'

THE CLEARWATER SET

This is difficult. This is not straightforward. The Clear-water Set. I said it to John as if I knew what I was talking about. I had fanned the glowing embers of his ambition with my casual remark but I had no idea what the Clearwater Set was or what it was capable of.

And how he wanted it! How he longed for his name to merit a separate entry in dictionaries of mathematics. 'John Clearwater, English mathematician, inventor of the Clear-water Set.' But what was it? Or rather, what would it have been? The answer is: a simple formula. A formula that would fix an endless series of points on a complex plane. From the reiterated numbers that the formula would generate – like grid references and co-ordinates on a map – you would be able to plot an image on a piece of paper or a computer screen. If you plotted the image that John's numbers gave you, an extraordinary shape would emerge. It was magic.

He tried to explain it to me once, using an old analogy.

What are the dimensions of a ball of string, he asked me? The answer is: it depends on your point of view. From a mile away a ball of string will appear dimensionless. A point. A full stop. Moving closer you can see that the ball is three-dimensional, solid, shadowed. Closer still and the ball has resolved itself into a two-dimensional mess of filaments. Place a filament under a microscope and it transforms itself into a three-dimensional column. Mag-nify that – hugely, monstrously – and the atomic structure of the filament is revealed: the three-dimensional thread has become a collection of dimensionless points again. The short answer is: the position and scale of the observer determine the number of dimensions of a ball of string.

The Clearwater Set, John told me, would be able to

reproduce this subjectivity endlessly. He was trying to write a simple algorithm that would reproduce the magical, infinite variety of the natural world. Extreme complexity would emerge from the simplest formula.

Or put it the other way round: behind all this teeming variety would lurk one simple instruction. For some reason I understood it better expressed in that manner. I could see what excited him. He always said that the most profound joy for any scientist was when the abstract workings of the mind found a correspondence in nature, in the world we live in. This was as true for a mathematician, he said, as for any chemist or physicist. That moment, he said, was the most acute of all the intellectual pleasures available to man.

A set, a ball of string, magnificent variety and complexity governed by a simple rule. I could not understand the detail of what John was doing but I could see the direction in which he was headed. To weld the world of mathematics to the world we live in; to blend pure abstraction with the randomly concrete. If he could write the Clearwater Set he could die happy. But, as I realized this much, I saw that the final stages were eluding him. He had gone so far and then stopped. He urged himself on but remained fixed and immobile. It was as if he had single-handedly invented the internal combustion engine but his mind finally balked at the design of a carburettor. The assembled mass of components sat there on his laboratory bench, inert, waiting only for the final touch to roar into animated life.

Clovis had a cut on his ear, but otherwise both he and Rita-Lu seemed unscathed by the attack I had heard, but not actually witnessed. It had scared them, though. The remnants of the southern group huddled together constantly now, never wandering off any distance alone. As they foraged for food they were noticeably more watchful and jumpy. They would survey a prospective feeding area for up to an hour before advancing forward to eat, never lingering for long. Even now, resting, Clovis flat on his back, Conrad grooming Rita-Lu, Lester gambolling around Rita-Mae, annoying her, Conrad would pause for a while, every now and then, and look around, listening for unusual noises.

I heard a faint crackle of static on my walkie-talkie. I had the volume turned low, so as not to alarm the chimps. I backed off, out of earshot. It was Alda.

'They are comin', Mam.'

'How many?'

'Eight. Nine.'

'OK. Get João. Come down here as fast as you can.'

I felt a burning, like indigestion, in my oesophagus, and a cold agitation seized me. I recognized the symptoms: I used to experience them with John at his worst moments. It was the physical correlative of a crucial indecision, a growing panic of inertia in the face of several demanding options. What should I do here? Should I frighten away my chimps, run at them waving my arms...? But if I did that, all those months of habituation – of trust – would be gone at once, at a stroke, and I would never get close to them again. One part of me encouraged this course of action, but I knew all it would do would be to postpone events, or possibly make them worse. At least here, with the four adults grouped together, they provided more of an opposition to the northerners. The chimps sprawled in the shade of three piper trees – small trees with drooping branches that cast good shade – oblivious to the approaching danger. I waited anxiously with them: perhaps they would not be spotted this time.

I waited for forty minutes. Then Conrad heard something. He rose up on his hind legs and spread his arms, his fur bristling. The other chimps immediately prepared to move, but they milled around waiting for Clovis to lead them, but he seemed uncertain and confused, uttering soft pant-hoots.

Then Darius charged out of some bushes above them, upright, teeth bared, arms windmilling. He bounded powerfully into and through the group, knocking Conrad violently out of the way. The other northern chimps followed close behind, screeching and screaming. I saw Pulul, Gaspar, Americo and Sebastian.

The two groups faced off, displaying, roaring and grimacing at each other. Darius charged at Clovis, followed by Sebastian and Pulul. There was a confused scrum of flailing arms and legs in a cloud of dust as the four chimps fought. Then they had Clovis pinned down. Pulul bit his leg and tore a long ribbon of skin off his thigh.

Meanwhile, the others advanced, led by Americo. He grabbed Rita-Mae and threw her to the ground, sending Lester flying from her back. Americo stamped viciously on her head. Rita-Lu, at the same time, crouched shivering, presenting her pink, swollen rump to the other males. Suddenly their aggression waned, became half-hearted. Then Clovis, by some mighty effort, broke free from Darius and Sebastian and leapt into a piper tree. He snapped off a branch and shook it at the northern males, his hair erect, screaming shrilly.

All fighting stopped and a sudden calm descended. Lester ran to Rita-Mae, Conrad crept under the piper tree. Only Rita-Lu was left surrounded. The males gathered round her, inspecting her rump, touching and smelling. Then all at once the northern group was off, with Rita-Lu running with them, up a small gully and into the trees. I could hear their whoops and screechings and the hollow reverberations as they drummed on the tree trunks they passed.

Two days later João saw Rita-Lu return to the group. She was unhurt and was welcomed back unequivocally. João led me to where he had left them feeding. The same watchfulness was there but otherwise nothing seemed to have changed. Only Clovis was obviously in some discomfort; the shred of skin that Pulul had torn from his left thigh dangled like a garter from his knee. The pink flesh that was exposed looked raw and smarting. Clovis constantly interrupted his feeding to dab the wound with bunches of leaves and grass.

Then I saw something else that made me even more alarmed: Rita-Mae seemed to be developing a sexual swelling, the skin on her rump was markedly pinker and looked stretched and shiny. Theoretically, she was still anoestrus, still lactating. Lester was too recently born for her cycle to have resumed. But it was not unheard of for lactating females to experience infertile sexual swellings for some years, before the cycle properly restarted. Infertile or not, it made no difference to a male chimpanzee. I felt a sudden deep pity for my southerners. Now there would be two females in oestrus. I looked at Clovis, Conrad and Lester and wondered how long these males, mature and immature, had left to live. Much though I disliked the idea, I thought I should go back and see Mallabar again.

Since the leopard had been killed, Mallabar had been exceptionally cordial towards me, with the relief of a man who had doubted for a while but had had his faith convincingly restored. My other colleagues, however, and by contrast, had grown more guarded. They were not entirely sure what had been going on, but it was clear to them in some way that I had been rocking the boat, generally making trouble. I would have to be watched more closely.

So I went to Mallabar's bungalow again, that evening after our meal. Roberta was leaving as I arrived. I noticed she had touched her eyelids with blue, and there was a sweet talcy smell of perfume about her.

'Ah, Hope,' she said, a little inanely, as if I were exactly the person she expected to encounter on the Mallabar threshold. I smiled back and said her name, Roberta, in a falling cadence. She held the door open for me. I went in.

Ginga was there too. She went to the kitchen to make me a cup of coffee. Mallabar flourished me into a seat.

'I want you to do me a favour,' I said, not wasting any time.

'Of course.'

'Spend the next few days in the southern area with me.'

'Hope,' he said, a little wearily. 'Really, I thought we –'

'No. There are some things you should see for yourself.' I felt surprisingly tense. I sat on the edge of the chair, rigid.

'All right, all right.' He spoke calmly and looked at me with some curiosity. 'Do me good to get back in the field.'

Ginga reappeared with the coffee and stopped in the doorway.

'Everything all right?' she said. 'Hope?'

'Hope's asked me to spend a few days with her in the south,' Mallabar said, talking about me as if I were slightly simple.

Ginga nodded. 'Good,' she said. 'Excellent You haven't been out in the field for a while. Do you good.'

I spent the next three days with Mallabar as we watched the five survivors of the southern group going about their daily business. He asked me what had happened to Clovis's leg. I said I had no idea. We observed, we followed, we logged the data on the survey sheets and in our journals. Mallabar reminisced about the early days at Grosso Arvore. He told me about the efforts he and Ginga had made to habituate the chimps to their presence. It had taken him ten months to get within twenty yards of a chimpanzee without it running off. He talked of how, for the first three years of their married life, their home had been an army surplus tent. How months could go by without seeing another soul. At first I wondered if these memories, unprompted by me, were a series of oblique rebukes; if he was gently reminding me that half his life had been spent at Grosso Arvore, in these hills and forests, and that my allegations were jeopardizing everything he had set out to achieve. But after a while I realized it was genuine nostalgia. Indeed, he was quite good company and it was fascinatingly instructive to observe the chimpanzees with him. I saw that he had an understanding of these apes that was profound and, there was no other word for it, full of love.

He looked at Clovis and remembered him as an infant. He knew his siblings and how his mother had died. He had seen Rita-Lu the day she was born. He had photographed Conrad's white sclerotics, as he had peered through a screen of grasses one day, and had produced thereby one of the most haunting covers ever seen on *National Geographic*. And for the first time, too, I really sensed the personal bafflement and hurt in him, caused by the schism in the community he had studied for so long. For unknown reasons, some of those chimpanzees that had happily swarmed round his banana-dispensing machine had suddenly lost interest in it and had migrated south. He hadn't seen Rita-Mae – or SF2 as he referred to her – he said, for over two years. Baby Lester, he confessed, he had only known through photographs. To me he seemed like the benevolent chief of a tribe grown too large and complex for him to understand. Its motivating forces, its factions and feuds, allegiances and enmities, were too difficult to quantify and relate to. He confessed as much to me one after-noon.

'It was all very mystifying,' he said, 'terribly upsetting, really.' He laughed. 'I just couldn't understand why they were doing this to me. And to be suddenly confronted by your ignorance when you felt you knew everything – well, nearly everything. It shakes you up, I tell you.'

'King Lear,' I said.

He looked at me. 'Good God, let's hope not. What an analogy.'

'No, it was just ... that same sense of mystification. Getting something so wrong. I know what you mean.'

'Do you?' He smiled, he was thinking of something else. 'That's a comfort.'

On our second morning out João led us to a cluster of sleeping-nests far south of the Danube. The northerners had spent the night here, he said. I realized the colonization was entering a new phase; now the chimps were not even bothering to return home as night fell.

'It's not surprising,' Mallabar said. 'They know there are too few chimps to use this area to the full. It was the same when we had the polio epidemic. The core area shrunk, more chimps came down from the north.'

We were walking through the forest to the blasted fig tree. I was hoping we might find some northern chimps there. It was too close to the Danube, now, for my southerners. It was a sticky, still afternoon. The occasional breeze brought with it the wet earth smell of impending rain.

'It'll rain tonight,' Mallabar said, inhaling deeply. 'I love that smell.' He glanced at me and smiled. 'I'm glad you asked me out, Hope,' he said. 'I'm going to do this every two months or so – spend a few days in the field – I'm losing touch.' He went on almost garrulously to berate himself for the amount of administration and paperwork he was obliged to do. A manager was what he needed, he said, which would allow him to spend more time out in the bush with the chimpanzees.

The blasted fig tree was empty, but chimps had been there recently, as the ground was covered with half-eaten fruits. I paced about feeling edgy. Northerners feeding in this tree, which I had come to associate so much with my chimps ... It was almost like having your house burgled. This was my territory, mine and my southerners'; now it was home to strangers and no longer felt the same.

On the third day the northerners attacked again. It had rained in the night, as Mallabar had predicted, and the forest was wet and visibly steaming in the sunlight, the paths mushy beneath our feet. We wore lightweight oilskins and wellington boots. Occasionally we could hear the distant noise of thunder but Mallabar still wasn't sure, he said, if this was the true start of the rainy season.

João had located our southerners in a grove of lupus trees. The fall of rain had brought out their pale yellow, sticky flowers overnight, and all the chimps were sitting in the branches grazing on them. Rita-Mae lay on a low branch, on her back, one leg dangling, with Lester squatting on her stomach. She seemed to have eaten her fill; from time to time she would reach out, pluck a lupus flower and give it to Lester to eat.

The forest was still dripping from the drenching it had received. Everywhere was the sound of water falling on leaf as the movements of the chimps shook droplets free. And in the background there was still the noise of thunder, as the night's cloud systems moved south towards the coast, heavy furniture being shifted in the room above. We sat and watched the chimps in the sultry, moist heat. The atmosphere was soporific. Mallabar yawned again and again. It was infectious, we both yawned simultaneously.

He turned and smiled at me, and seemed about to say something, when he was interrupted by a crash of vegetation. Pulul or Americo – it was too sudden for me to tell – hurled himself out of the nearby bushes and leapt up and grabbed Rita-Mae's hanging leg. With a scream she and Lester fell the ten feet to the ground. To the left, Sebastian and Darius were up another tree after Conrad, who brachiated recklessly from his position into an adjacent tree, missed his grip and half-fell, half-tumbled through the branches to the ground.

Meanwhile, Gaspar had grabbed baby Lester by one leg and was whirling him round and round in mid-air. Observing this, Darius jumped down and seized the baby from Gaspar, who readily surrendered him.

Darius held Lester by both legs and thrashed him violently against the knobbled length of an exposed root. I saw Lester's skull literally explode under the force of the blow and bits of brain and bone were scattered widely. Then Darius thwacked the limp body against a trunk two or three times before flinging it carelessly away.

Conrad and Clovis made their escape, shrieking and calling. Rita-Lu adopted her half-crouched, presenting position and watched as Pulul and Americo and a couple of unidentified adolescents pummelled and stamped on the supine body of Rita-Mae, who had been badly stunned by her fall in the first charge. Then, as if on some invisible signal, they stopped and gathered round Rita-Lu. Darius drummed on a tree and they were off again, like the time before, running and whooping, Rita-Lu in their midst.

Rita-Mae was not dead. When they had gone, she stood up, shivering, and immediately fell over. She made a feeble hooting noise as if calling for Lester. She rolled over, managed to regain her feet once more, cast around a couple of times as if making a cursory search for Lester and then loped off with some awkwardness into the undergrowth after Clovis and Conrad.

The fight had lasted only a few minutes. I felt myself begin to unfreeze. I looked round at Mallabar. His face was sallow, bloodless; his beard looked suddenly black and coarse. He was biting his bottom lip, staring in front of him as if he were in terrible shock. I touched his shoulder; I could feel it shuddering beneath my fingers.

'Jesus,' he said. 'Jesus Christ.' He kept on repeating this.

I thought it best to leave him alone for a moment or two and went to look for Lester's body. I found it hanging in a thorn bush. The head was a loose bag of pulped tissue and bone, the small limbs bizarrely misshapen and broken in many places. Carefully, I lifted him out and placed him on the ground. I turned, Mallabar was walking towards me.

He stared, clearly horrified, at Lester's body.

'Did you see,' he said, in a small voice, 'that alpha male, what he did? Did you see?'

I felt enormously sorry for the man. 'I know,' I said. 'It's very shocking. Nothing prepares you for the violence. Even me.'

'What do you mean?'

'This is the third fight I've seen.'

'Third?'

'Yes.' I spread my hands apologetically. 'Eugene, this is what I've been trying to tell you. This is what's been happening here.'

'*Been* happening?' he said distractedly, as if lost in other thoughts.

'I've been trying to tell you. But you –'

He raised his fist to shoulder level, arm bent, and took a step towards me.

'What have you been doing here?' he said in an urgent trembling voice. 'What have you been doing to them?'

'What're you talking about?'

'It's you. It's something you've done to them.'

'Come on, Eugene, don't be stupid!'

He lowered his fist and hung his head for an instant.

'I blame myself,' he said. He looked up. 'I should have had you supervised.' Then he screamed at me, madly: 'WHAT HAVE YOU DONE? WHAT HAVE YOU DONE?'

I took a step back. I had felt his spit on my face.

'I haven't done a thing, you fool, you bloody idiot!' I shouted at him, angry myself. 'I've just been watching them.' I pointed at Lester's broken body. 'It's what *they're* doing. They're killing each other!'

He had raised his fist again. His eyes were wide.

'Shut your fucking mouth!' he shouted. 'Shut your fucking mouth!'

'No! The northern apes are wiping out my southerners. One by one. Now you've seen it with your own eyes, you stupid bloody fool, and you –'

He tried to hit me. He hurled a punch, full force, at my open face. If he had connected he would have broken my nose. Squashed it flat. Crushed bones and shattered teeth. But somehow I managed to jerk my head away and down and the punch hit me on the shoulder. I heard, distinctly, the knuckle bones in his fist crunch and break as the force of the blow spun me round and right off my feet. I fell heavily to the ground. My shoulder burned, hot with pain. I felt it had sprung from its socket. I grunted through clenched teeth, flinching, looking round expecting another attack.

Mallabar was some distance off, scrabbling in the undergrowth looking for something. He was flicking his right hand curiously, fingers spread, as if they were wet and he were trying to shake water from them. He stood up, he had a stick in his left hand. He ran over towards me.

'Eugene!' I screamed at him. 'Stop, for Christ's sake!'

I ducked.

He hit me across the back. The stick broke under the blow, but, because it was left-handed, it had not as much impact as it might have. He grabbed at me, and I pushed wildly at his face, scratching. At the same time, somehow, I caught hold of two of the broken fingers on his right hand and pulled them back with as much savage effort as I could muster.

He bellowed with pain and let me go. I ran.

I sprinted off down the path through the dripping forest towards the camp. I thought at first I could hear his running footsteps behind me, but I never looked round. I ran for fifteen minutes and then halted, doubled over, my body aching with effort. I sank to my haunches, hand on a tree trunk for support. I tried to calm down. I felt a hot drumbeat throb in my right shoulder. I slipped my jacket off and unbuttoned my shirt. My shoulder was pink flushed and already slightly swollen. I could see four darker circles in a row, the imprint of his knuckles. Very gently, I eased my shoulder joint. Very sore, but mobile.

I dressed and headed off again. I crossed the Danube and walked into camp past the feeding area. I could hear the noise of chimps coming from it. I turned left to cut past Mallabar's bungalow, making for the census hut. On my left were the garages and workshops. I saw a Land Rover parked there with its bonnet up and Ian Vail leaning inside fiddling with the engine. He stood up, wiped his hands on a rag and closed the bonnet with a vengeful but satisfied bang. I remembered: it had been Vail's turn to do the provisioning run this week. By rights he should have left hours ago.

'Hi,' he said, as I walked over to him. 'Bloody fuel pump.'

'When're you off?' I asked.

'Are you OK, Hope? You look –'

'When're you off?' My voice was trembling.

'Now.'

'Ten minutes. Five minutes. I'm coming with you.'

I went back to the census hut and threw a few essentials – passport, wallet, cigarettes, sun-glasses – into a canvas hold-all. I hadn't thought at all what to do, but seeing Ian Vail about to leave, I knew suddenly I wanted to be with Usman for a while and talk about beach huts and tiny aeroplanes. I would let some days pass and either return and face Mallabar, or else send for my things and leave.

I climbed into the Land Rover beside Ian. The two boys were already in the back. He looked puzzled and concerned.

'Listen, Hope, are you sure –'

'I'll tell you everything. Just give me a little while.'

He started the engine and we moved off.

'Stop,' I said. I thought. 'Five more minutes.'

I jumped out and ran to Mallabar's bungalow. I

entered and called for Ginga. There was no reply. I sat at Mallabar's desk and wrote him a brief note:

> Eugene,
> You should know that I have written an article on the cases of infanticide, cannibalism and deliberate killing that I have witnessed at Grosso Arvore. I have submitted it to a journal for publication. I am going into town with Ian Vail. I will be in touch in a few days.
>
> Hope

I sealed this in an envelope, marked it confidential, propped it on his desk and went to rejoin Ian Vail in the Land Rover.

'Good Christ,' Ian said, with a tone of shocked awe in his voice. 'Good God Almighty.'

He looked stunned, sandbagged. I had just finished telling him everything that had happened. We had been driving for over two hours. I had sat silent for the first hour and a half, collecting myself.

Ian exhaled. 'Ooh God,' he said, worriedly. 'Ooooh God.'

He was beginning to irritate me. I supposed this was a good sign.

'Come on Ian, I haven't killed him. Get things in perspective.'

'No. But it's all too . . . There's too much to take in. I keep thinking of other things. Jesus. I mean, quite apart from Eugene hitting you like that.' He glanced at me. 'The chimps. Pretty earth-shattering.'

'You're not excusing him.'

'No, no. He's obviously gone mad, or something. I mean, I think you're absolutely right to get away for a while. He's got to get a grip on himself. Still,' he shook his head. 'What those chimps did . . .'

'Look, no one was more amazed than me.'

'Darius, Pulul, Americo, the others?' I had forgotten that Ian would think of them as *his* chimps.

'Yes,' I said. 'All of them.'

'Bloody hell. You know what this means?'

'Yes.'

'Set the cat among the pigeons. No two ways about it.'

I looked out at the road and felt fatigue flow heavily through me, weighing me down, making me drowsy. My shoulder still ached and throbbed, and there was a hot weal across my back where Mallabar had caught me with the stick. I arched my spine and massaged my shoulder.

The road in front was straight and gently undulating, cut through a landscape of open scrubby savannah with the occasional acacia here and there. The sun hammered down on the black tarmac, causing the road ahead to vanish in a wobbling liquid horizon. Over to the east, some miles away, a tall thin column of smoke slanted upwards – a bush fire perhaps. I peered ahead. Out of the shimmering horizon appeared a few deliquescent black dots – four. Like two colons set side by side. They shivered and joined silkily, making an eleven. As we approached they turned into two soldiers standing by an oil drum with a plank inclined across the road from it. Our first road-block.

I pointed it out to Ian, who was still clearly thinking about his chimpanzees, and we began to reduce speed.

When we were about a hundred yards off I saw one of the men begin to flag us down. Ian changed gear noisily and slowed further. At the side of the road I saw other figures standing.

'Ian,' I said. 'Stop and turn back.'

'Hope, don't be stupid.'

'No, you've got time, stop ... All right, speed up. Drive through.'

'Are you crazy? Just a bloody road-block.'

We slowed to a crawl and stopped a few yards short of the oil drum and plank. Two very young, tall soldiers with Kalashnikov rifles walked towards us. I felt a draining in me, as if my blood were being sucked to my ankles. One of the soldiers – no more than boys, really – was wearing shorts and heavy boots that made his legs look ridiculously thin. The other wore camouflage trousers. Both had identical grey track-suit tops with hoods on the back.

'Morning,' Ian said, with a relaxed smile. 'Sorry. Afternoon.'

'Please to get out.'

I climbed out slowly. After the thrum and noise of the engine, the landscape now seemed eerily quiet. I could hear the tick and ping of the cooling metal and the soft alarmed mutters of Billy and Fernando, the two kitchen staff who had been travelling in the rear. I glanced at them: they stood there, their possessions hugged to them, they knew something was not quite right as well. But Ian was still smiling and at ease. I looked across the road. Under a thorn tree was a lean-to: four poles with a palm frond roof. The other men stood there, peering at something on the ground.

One of the boy-soldiers with us turned and beckoned

to the group beneath the tree. On the back of his track-suit top I saw printed in red letters the words '*Atomique Boum*'. I took a few steps to the side and glanced at the other soldier. His had the same message too.

The other men wandered over to inspect us. I saw that they were all young, teenagers, in an odd mixture of military and civilian clothes. They were, apart from one, unusually tall, all over six feet. They were led over by the short man, whom I saw, as they approached, was older as well. Apart from him all the others sported the same track-suit top.

The short man was wearing pale blue jeans with the cuffs turned up and a camouflage jerkin that was too large for him. He had a beard, a patchy goatee, and much-repaired, old-fashioned spectacles, the sort with dark frames at the top that shade into transparency around the lower half of the lens. One of the arms of his spectacles was neatly bound to the hinge on the frame with fuse wire. The other arm appeared home-made, carved from wood.

He walked around the Land Rover, inspecting it, and stopped in front of me. I was a good two inches taller than him. He had a pleasant face, made more studious by his spectacles, a broad nose and full, shapely lips. His skin was dark, very black with a hint of purple beneath the surface, it seemed. He had a mottled pink and brown patch on his neck and cheek below his left ear. A scar perhaps, or a burn.

He took hold of my elbow and steered me gently round the Land Rover to stand beside Ian. Ian was still smiling, but I could sense his unease beginning to uncoil within him. This was not a normal road-block, he now realized. This *politesse*, this scrutiny ... These tall, silent boys with their track-suit tops.

'One moment, please,' the bearded man said, and went over to Billy and Fernando. They stooped quickly and touched the ground with one hand. A brief conversation ensued, which I couldn't hear, then I saw the bearded man clap his hands and make a shooing gesture. He did it again, and slowly Billy and Fernando backed off, their faces alternating expressions of apprehension and incredulous relief. Then they turned and ran. I heard the noise of their bare feet slapping on the hot tarmac for a while. We all watched them go, running back up the road to Grosso Arvore.

The small man turned to us and extended his hand, which we duly shook, first Ian, then me. It was dry and very calloused, hard like an old lemon.

'My name is Dr Amilcar,' he said. 'Where are you going?'

I told him.

'I'm so sorry,' he said, looking at us both, 'but I have to take your Land Rover.' His English was good, his accent educated.

'You can't leave us here,' Ian said, boldly, stupidly.

'No, no, of course not. You will be coming with me.'

'Who are you?' I said, blurting out my question.

Dr Amilcar removed his spectacles and rubbed his eyes, as if considering the wisdom of a response.

'We are . . .' He paused. 'We are UNAMO.'

DEATH OF A PROPHET

A friend of Usman – one of the other pilots (Hope has forgotten his name) – told her a story about the civil war in Nigeria, the Biafran war of 1967-70.

By 1970, the war had reached a state of near stasis, a conflict of mere attrition. The rebel heartland had shrunk, but further progress was agonizingly slow. The war had developed into a siege. It was stalemate. But then, suddenly – this man said – it was all over in days, with a speed that no one could ever have predicted.

After the war the explanation for this collapse of the rebel forces emerged. The Biafran army, outgunned and outnumbered, fought with tenacity and desperation, even for men who know their cause is lost. This zeal and effort was the result of superstition. The majority of the officers were under the sway of spiritualist priests. These priests, or 'prophets', were so integrated in the structure of the army that many of them were officially attached to military units. By 1970 their influence was so powerful that officers refused to order attacks or lead their men in battle unless the prophets deemed it opportune. Officers regularly left their units at the front line to attend prayer meetings organized by the most influential prophets in the rear.

General Ojukwu, leader of the Biafran regime, realized he was on the verge of losing complete control of his army and tried to curtail the spiritualists' influence. His first move was to arrest one of the most charismatic and popular prophets, a Mr Ezenweta, and accuse him of 'vicarious murder'. At a military tribunal he was found guilty and swiftly executed.

The morale of the Biafran army collapsed totally and immediately. Soldiers simply refused to fight and either ran away or stood aside as the bemused Nigerian army advanced unopposed, occupying town after town without firing a shot, rifles slung, singing loudly with relief. The execution of a fetish priest for vicarious murder lost the

war for the Biafrans. The death of Mr Ezenweta fore-
shadowed the death of his country.

In mechanics, systems that lose energy to friction are
known as dissipative. In most systems that loss is gradual,
measurable and predictable. But there are other dissipative
systems that are ragged and untidy. The friction grips,
and then suddenly eases, only to grip again. If you con-
sider life as a dissipative system, you will understand what
is meant. The most dissipative system anyone will ever
encounter is war. It is violently uneven and completely
unpredictable.

The morning after Bogdan Lewkovitch had telephoned
her, Hope received a letter from John. At once she saw
that his handwriting was different, slanting acutely forward, hard to read.

Darling Hope,

Forgive this flood of letters but it helps it really does to
pen things down. Rather than endlessly garble on and on
garbling thoughts into half thought out words. It really
does help.

I'm well here, and for the first time the docs are doing
something for me. It's not much fun, but it's working and
that surely is the main thing. Getting better from an illness,
after all, is not meant to be 'fun'. The fun can come along
when you're 'better', not during the 'getting'. And we did
have fun, didn't we, darling girl. Remember Scotland? Remember that funny little chap who used to pelt us with
stones as we cycled past and you shouted that if he did that
again you'd cut his balls off? That fixed him.

But in the end 'fun' is not enough. There is play and
there is work. And I see now – or at least the docs are

helping me to see – that the problem with me over the last few months is that I've been screened from my work. There's been a sort of screen, like a gauze screen, between me and what I'm trying to achieve in my field. It stopped me from seeing clearly. I'm sorry to say, my darling, that you were that screen. You were the shadow between me and the light. That's why I went with Jenny L., you see, I didn't know it but I was trying to push you out of the way. Trying to break the screen. I didn't know it was there at the time, of course. The docs are helping me see these things now. Helping me see why I acted in the way I did.

Anyway, that is why we had to part, so that my way ahead was no longer obscured. I could see where I was meant to go, but not clearly, and that was what was frustrating me and making me ill. Clarity of vision is vital in my field. You can't do mathematics in a mist. (What kind of landscape am I in with my misty fields? You know what I mean!)

What I hope will happen here is that clarity will return – and it is returning, I am beginning to do good work again. When it comes back, the docs say that it will be different and that you won't screen or obscure the way ahead anymore. Then we can be together. And after this treatment, the docs say they have this great drug which will keep my eyes bright and beady.

Come and see me. I'm fine. I'm getting better. I'm at Hamilton Clare's neuropsychiatric hospital in Wimbledon. Ring up my doc, Doc Phene, and he'll tell you when to come.

Con amore,
John.

The gates to Hamilton Clare reminded Hope at first of the approach to a municipal crematorium. But beyond the low, cream-coloured walls, with their neat borders of geraniums, were rolling lawns and grouped poplars which looked more like the campus of a teacher-training college, she thought, or a model secondary school.

The buildings of the hospital had been constructed in the fifties from a pale grey brick and were uniformly and unattractively boxy, every window the same size. They could have been a barracks or civil service offices. Closer to, she saw that they were already looking shoddy, and the wet weather had marred their sides with darker swags and streaks of moisture, like camouflage on a battleship.

Inside there were brighter colours and framed prints of sketchy London views on the walls, but the uniform right angles everywhere, and the low ceilings, kept the mood of the place fixed at institutional rectilinearity. Hope's own spirits had been low on the journey up; Hamilton Clare sunk them still further. As she sat on a hard chair outside Dr Phene's office, waiting, she began to wish - selfishly - that she hadn't come.

When Bogdan Lewkovitch had phoned he told her that John had not come into college for three days. He didn't answer his phone and, when a member of the department had gone round to knock on his door, John had screamed obscenities at her.

A doctor was summoned and the door broken down. John was found in a 'very disturbed state', dehydrated and starving. He had been taking amphetamines and had not slept or eaten for over seventy-two hours. The flat was in a very unkempt, not to say squalid, condition, Bogdan added diplomatically. John was taken to Charing Cross Hospital where he was put on a saline drip and slept for twenty-four hours.

He recovered quickly and seemed completely normal. He apologized unreservedly to his colleagues for the distress he had caused. He then told everyone he was taking two weeks' sick leave. Confidentially, he had confided to Bogdan that he was checking himself into a clinic to seek psychiatric help for his condition.

Dr Richard Phene was a younger man than Hope had been expecting. For some reason she had been imagining slightly too long grey hair, a thin face, a bow tie and a blue suit with too wide pinstripes. How this image of John's doctor had established itself in her mind she could not say.

Phene's hair was greying, but was neatly parted and short. She guessed him to be in his early forties, but his skin was as fresh as a boy's, and scarcely lined. He spoke in an unbelievably quiet, formal voice, almost without moving his lips, that had her leaning forward in her chair in an effort to catch his words, breathing shallowly so that the faint noise of her inhalations wouldn't drown him out.

'Your husband,' he whispered, 'is clearly manic depressive. But the great advantage, from our point of view, is that he recognizes this. That's half the battle. He asked Dr Fitzpatrick –'

'Who is Dr Fitzpatrick?'

'His psychiatrist.' Phene looked at Hope's blank face. 'You didn't know?' He took in her ignorance of this fact with a little cough and a brief examination of his spotless blotting pad. He began again.

'John has been a patient of Dr Fitzpatrick for some weeks. He – John – asked Dr Fitzpatrick to have him admitted here for treatment. John had decided on his own course of treatment – which is enormously encouraging. Enormously.'

'And what course of treatment would that be?'

'A course of electro-convulsive therapy.'

'You're joking.'

'I beg your pardon?' Phene was offended. He did not joke, Hope saw.

She heard a rushing noise in her head, like a train. She started again. 'I thought . . . I thought nobody had that nowadays.'

Phene sat back and considered her observation seriously, as if he were leading a seminar on modern psychotherapy. 'It's less common, true. But it does have its adherents. I would have to say that it's not part of the repertoire in contemporary clinical practice, but,' he gave her a tight pursed smile. 'in special circumstances we feel it may be beneficial. Especially if the patient requests it.'

'Even if the patient is manic depressive?'

He smiled sorrowfully. 'Mrs Clearwater. "Manic depressive", I know, sounds grave. But mania takes many forms, mild and strong. Some of the most lucid and charming people I've met have been manic depressive . . .' He chuckled at some memory of a lucid and charming person.

'But what if I object to the treatment?'

'With great respect, I don't really think you can. As it were.'

Dr Phene paused at the door to John's room.

'I should say,' he began, in an even quieter voice, 'that John, ah, underwent some therapy this morning. He may seem a little disorientated, vague . . .' He made a parting gesture with his clenched fingertips. 'Some memory loss? But it wears off, in due course.'

'How reassuring.'

She saw him decide to tolerate her sarcasm. He showed her the door with a clean, flat palm. 'Do go in, no need to knock. If . . .' He paused. 'If you'd like to talk after, do come along.'

He left her.

Hope stared at the door for a few seconds, then knocked and heard John's surprised 'Come in'. She closed her eyes, opened them, put on a smile and turned the door-knob.

He was sitting at a desk in a room that looked like the sort one would find in the plusher range of motel. Pale grey jute walls, orange curtains with a 'modern' design, smooth pine furniture. He jumped to his feet when he saw her, and to her huge relief he looked unchanged. He kissed her cheek, they hugged, and he pulled up a chair for her. They talked for a while, circuitously, about the progress he was making, and how – they were both sure about this – his admitting himself to Hamilton Clare had been the right thing to do. Absolutely.

As they talked, Hope studied him more closely. She noticed that he looked a little pale, and that on his temples was a slight greasy shine. He seemed to be blinking at a somewhat faster rate than was normal.

'What's it like?' she said suddenly, interrupting him. 'Is it sore?'

John smiled with relief. 'No. No, not at all.' He grinned, all at once he seemed more relaxed. 'No whiff of burning flesh, either . . . It's like – there's a noise in your head, a kind of whooshing, shrilling sound, and you feel as if you're being given a really good shake. You know, *major* vibration. I just have a couple of electrodes here.' He touched his temples. 'They rub on a graphite salve. You can have them all over the place, I think, if you want. But I just have them on my temples.'

'Johnny, I just feel that –

'No, really. It's helping. I know it sounds sort of inquisitorial. A torture, agony, all that. But it just gets everything . . .' He scooped the air with his hands. 'Fizzed up. I feel so much better than I did.' He yawned. 'Makes me a bit fuzzy though, for an hour or two.'

'Well, you look good,' she said, striving for a chirpy bonhomie. 'Have you had your hair cut? You look a bit thinner, somehow.'

They talked on. After the ECT, John said, they wanted to give him Lithium, to keep him stable. He was looking forward to being on Lithium, he said, it was the fluctuating of moods that got him down. He wanted to talk only of himself, she realized, his illness, his prognosis.

'I thought I might come down to Knap for a while,' he said. 'Get my sea legs.'

She thought: no. No you won't. I don't want you there. Then she felt ashamed.

'Of course you must,' she said, a weakness overcoming her. She was thinking: I thought we were meant to be separated. I don't want to –

'The docs think that it'd be useful –'

'Please don't call them the "docs", Johnny.'

'Oh. OK.' He looked hurt. 'Sorry. Dr Phene thinks I'll need some peace and quiet.'

'Of course.' She made an effort. 'Great. Well there's masses of peace and quiet at Knap. No shortage of that. Stroll by the lake, that sort of thing.'

'Lake?'

'The lake by the old manor . . . where you dug the trenches.'

He pulled down the corners of his mouth as he thought.

'A lake?' he said. 'Are you sure? I don't remember a lake.'

ECT

I enjoy the beach in bad weather too. The waves hammer in, hurling themselves at the sand, the pines and the palm trees sway and thrash. Falling coconuts hit the beaten ground beneath them with a noise like a wooden mallet on a paving stone. Soft and hard at the same time. I take my longest walks in such windy, rainy weather, three miles south to where the mangrove creeks begin, where the silt from the Cabule gives the green water a curious mauve tinge. Then I turn and walk home. Out at sea enormous electrical storms flicker and pulse, too far away for me to hear the thunder.

The theory behind electro-convulsive therapy is that psychopathic behaviour is caused by aberrant brain patterns. By submitting the brain to electric shocks of 70 to 150 volts muscular contractions are provoked in the cortex which unsettle the psychopathic patterns and allow healthier ones to take their place. During the treatment the patient might spontaneously urinate, defecate or even ejaculate. Possible side-effects include panic, fear, memory loss, personality change and poor concentration.

There is no satisfactory explanation of just how this ECT *is meant to work. In medical parlance the treatment remains 'empirical'.*

Ian and I sat in the back of the Land Rover along with seven of the boy-soldiers. We faced each other. wedged against the cab. furthest away from the open back with its juddering ochre square of receding landscape. Through the rear window of the cab I could see Amilcar at the wheel. I felt cramped and uncomfortable and very hot. We were driving on a dirt road and were thrown about as we bounced over ruts and pot-holes. I had no idea where we were going: we had driven back up the road in the direction of Grosso Arvore for a few miles. and had then turned off on to this track. which seemed to be leading us roughly north-east. Amilcar had a map spread out on his knee. but I could not make out any details through the dusty window.

The boys in the rear with us did not speak a great deal to each other. Their expressions were solemn and serious, and their remarks to each other terse and to the point. Not all of them were armed; there were only five Kalashnikovs between the nine of them. One of the boys had a bandaged arm and they all looked tired. They reminded me of a photograph I had seen once. of a group of passengers rescued from a sunken liner or ditched aircraft, sodden. sitting huddled in blankets, exhausted, faces set and eyes lowered. showing nothing of the exhilaration of rescue. all chastened instead by whatever ordeal they had been through in the water. These boys conveyed the same sense of having undergone such a profound experience. Perhaps that was why they were behaving with such propriety towards us. I could hardly believe we were hostages; we were treated more like guests.

I glanced over at Ian. opposite me. He appeared upset and preoccupied. and he was chewing nervously on his lips. There were white flecks of dry saliva at the corner of his mouth. I caught his eye, and gave him a slight smile. He nodded briefly and then looked away.

I shifted my position, bumping against the boy on my right. He was the one in shorts and big boots who had flagged us down. His thin brown thigh was pressed against mine. He had long delicate fingers, curled around the chipped and scratched gun-metal of his Kalashnikov's barrel. He gave a faint smile of apology and told the boy next to him to move down. The row shuffled and rearranged itself. I gained an inch or two of extra space.

I considered myself; analysed how I felt. My shoulder was still sore, but I was not frightened. I was tense, certainly not at ease, but these lanky boys with their rationed guns and the diminutive Dr Amilcar did not frighten me.

I looked across at Ian again. He was leaning forward, elbows resting on his knees, head hanging, the very picture of a man in decline. Dr Amilcar had never once mentioned the word 'hostage' or 'prisoner' or 'kidnap'. Somehow that refusal to classify us made me less worried. I had a strange confidence that we would remain unharmed.

I thought of Mallabar, briefly. Of what had taken place in the forest; of what he had tried to do to me. In a way he was responsible for my current plight. If I hadn't fled the camp. If Ian's Land Rover hadn't been delayed departing . . . The 'if' clauses wound backwards through my life towards the day of my birth, tracing my personal route through the forking paths of happenstance and whim, my selections, willed and unwilled, from the spread deck of infinite alternatives and choices that the world and its time offered. I could hardly blame Mallabar.

We drove on for another two hours on a succession of small bush tracks. The land was dry and bleached and the road surface friable and powdery. Often the view through the rear was nothing but an opaque screen of khaki dust. I considered that, from the air, we would be visible for miles, trailing this plume - this nebulous spoor – behind us. I thought suddenly of Usman. Usman in his Mig in the pale blue upper reaches of the sky, looking down on this corner of Africa and seeing our wedge of red dust inching across the landscape . . .

I smiled to myself as we bumped and bucked along – Amilcar was driving as fast as he could – and I felt my sweat run down my sides beneath my shirt. I hit the warm yielding shoulder of the boy on my right, and then the hard frame of the cab on my left, as we swayed and shook in unison. Ian Vail looked up and caught my eye. His features were drawn, like a man who has had no sleep, and his lips were so dry they were beginning to crack.

'Are you all right, Ian?' I asked.

He nodded. I could see his tongue working behind his cheeks, trying to coax some lubricating saliva from his parched glands.

'We'll be OK,' I said. 'I'm sure.'

Ian nodded again and looked down.

When we stopped we had driven continuously for over four hours. The boys clambered stiffly out of the cab and went into a huddle around Amilcar. We were allowed out of the Land Rover. I rubbed my numb buttocks and stretched and stamped. I felt curiously serene, distanced from what was happening to me, as if I was taking each minute, each second and observing it dispassionately for whatever information it might yield.

Ian, I could clearly see, was occupying a different pole of experience. For him each tiny division of time passing was pressing down on him as a further weight, a burdensome reminder of his plight, a growing freight of potential danger and hurt. He looked stooped and word-less, suddenly a smaller, frailer man, all his efforts devoted to maintaining the functioning of key compo-nents of his body – heart, lungs, bloodflow, musculature. All that was important to him now was that he should not collapse.

Amilcar led us over to the shade of a small mango tree and invited us to sit down. He was courteous and firm. We sat cross-legged on the earth with two boys to guard us and watched him and the others climb aboard the Land Rover and set off once more.

A few flies hummed around us. I looked up into the dark centre of the tree above my head but saw there was no fruit. I would have liked a mango, to have sunk my teeth into its juicy yellow flesh. But it was not the season. After the rains, if they ever came. My stomach rumbled and I felt my hunger shift inside me like something alive.

I looked around at the countryside trying to divert my attention from my appetite. We had left the savan-nah and were now in a flat terrain of bush and thin forest. The track we had been driving along was old and partially overgrown. I could see no hills in the distance, only a milky haze. The green slopes of the Grosso Arvore escarpment were far away. It felt warmer and stickier here too. If we kept heading north or northeast, I reasoned, trying to recall the geography of the country, we would soon reach the myriad watercourses and tributaries of the Musave River, beyond whose far bank was the frontier. Around it were thick forests and acres of marsh and mangrove. A detailed map I had once seen had shown a tormented writhing of silted creeks and dead-end lagoons, oxbow lakes and seasonal mudflats . . .

I tried to remember other information. There had been some oil exploration in the delta, I thought, before the civil war. And some policy of retraining the local fishermen to grow rice, to which end marshes had been drained, rivers diverted, irrigation systems installed. Whatever had been achieved would have been undone by the war, in any event. And further up the Musave, I seemed to recall, was a huge copper mine, run by a Belgian company.

The Musave River Territories were the main source of UNAMO manpower and the thick jungles and mangrove-clotted waterways of the river were the original UNAMO heartland. I looked over at our two guards. They were dark-skinned, long-necked boys with small round heads. The people from the River Territories were ethnically of different stock from the rest of the country, and Christians too, I seemed to remember.

I felt frustrated and angry with myself. UNAMO. UNAMO . . . Who were they? What were their objectives? Hadn't Alda told me they had been defeated by an alliance of the Federal Army and FIDE? There had been a big battle, Alda had said – it seemed like years ago now – so who was Dr Amilcar and where was he taking us? Was this a fleeing remnant of the destroyed UNAMO army, or some kind of flying column, an insurgent force?

Ian tapped me on the arm.

'I need to pee,' he said.

'Well . . .' I felt a squirm of irritation inside me. What did he expect *me* to do about that? 'Why don't you ask the boys?'

He looked at me as if I were mad. 'The *boys*? Jesus . . .' He stood up and indicated his need to them. They only let him move a few paces away. He turned his anguished face towards me.

'Go on,' I encouraged. 'For heaven's sake, Ian.'

He urinated, head bowed, the patter of his water crackling on the carpet of dead mango leaves. He shivered and buttoned his fly. He came back and sat down in silence, his face distorted with embarrassment.

'We've got to get used to this,' I said, consolingly. 'We have to be more . . . relaxed with each other.'

'I know,' he said. He reached out and squeezed my hand. 'Thanks, Hope. I'm sorry. This . . . It's just taken the wind out of my sails, rather. I'm so –' He stopped. 'I'll pull myself together.'

'I really don't think they want to hurt us,' I said. 'They're just kids.'

'The kids are the worst,' he said, fiercely. 'They don't care. Don't give a damn what they do.' He was shivering, his voice was a rasping whisper.

'Not this lot, surely,' I said.

'Look what they've got written on their fucking jackets! *Atomique Boum*. What the fuck does that signify? Some kind of commando? Some kind of death squad?' He was beginning to panic.

'For Christ's sake.' I stood up. The two boys were lounging at the fringe of the shade cast by the mango tree. They were talking quietly to each other, their weapons on the ground, their backs half turned away from us. I walked over to them.

'Where has he gone, Dr Amilcar?' I said. They spoke briefly to each other in a language I did not recognize. I suspected only one of them spoke English. One had understood me. Beneath each eye were three small vertical nicks – tribal scars.

'For gasoline,' he said. 'Please to sit down.'

I pointed at the other one's track-suit top.

'What does this mean?' I asked. *'Atomique Boum.'*

'Volley.' He smiled.

'Sorry?'

'It is our game. We play volley-ball. We are the team Atomique Boum.'

'Ah.'

I felt an odd subsidence in my gut, a hollow feeling that made me want to laugh and cry at the same time.

'It's a good game,' I said. Lost in Africa, prisoners of an armed volley-ball team.

'Very good,' he agreed.

Then the other one said something, more sternly. The boy with scarred eyes smiled apologetically, and motioned for me to return to my place. I rejoined Ian. Anxious Ian.

'Relax,' I said. 'We've been captured by a volley-ball team.'

Dr Amilcar came back after an absence of about an hour and a half. We all climbed into the rear of the Land Rover to discover our space was to be shared with five jerrycans of petrol. It was a much tighter squeeze. We set off once more, still heading north.

We stopped before sunset and made camp. The boys lit a small fire and cooked up a kind of grainy porridge, yellowy grey in colour with a bland, farinaceous taste. I ate mine with some enthusiasm. Ian began to eat, but then had to go behind the Land Rover to shit. I felt confidently costive, my bowels locked solid. I went to urinate, though, just to show Ian I was sharing his discomfort. I walked out a little way into the bush, accompanied by a boy. He stood a discreet few yards away in the gathering gloom, as I lowered my trousers and pants and squatted down behind a bush, feeling dry grass stems scratch my buttocks. When I came back, Ian asked me needlessly and solicitously if I were all right.

Throughout the day, Amilcar had pointedly kept himself to himself, rarely talking to us. Now, after we had eaten, he wandered over to join us, with two blankets under his arm, which he handed to us. Then he took off his spectacles and cleaned them with a scrap of chamois leather. His eyes were small and slightly hooded, and without his glasses he looked more innocent, the goatee suddenly something of an affectation and not, along with his spectacles, a symbol of his intellect.

He sat down cross-legged, facing us.

'There's a problem tonight,' he said, reasonably. 'My boys have to sleep – they're exhausted. So, I can't guard you. But,' he paused, 'I don't particularly want to tie you up.'

'I promise we won't try to escape,' I said at once. 'You don't need to worry.'

'Hope!' Ian rebuked me, outrage driving his voice high.

'Come on, Ian,' I said, exasperated at him. I gestured at the bush. It was black like a wall, alive with insect noise. 'You going to run off into that?'

Amilcar watched us bicker. 'You could run,' he said. 'I wouldn't come to look for you. I think you would die.'

'We won't run,' I said.

'Why have you kidnapped us?' Ian demanded sharply. 'We've got nothing to do with anyone. The government, UNAMO, nobody.'

I felt it was time that I showed some signs of agreeing with Ian, so I said, frostily, 'Yes. Exactly.'

Amilcar pouted his full lips, thinking.

'Actually,' he said slowly, 'I don't know. Maybe I should have left you at the road?' He stroked his beard. 'Maybe I thought if we met Federal troops it would be useful . . .' He shrugged. 'When we get to the front line, I'll probably let you go.'

I looked at Ian as if to say: see?

Amilcar stayed on talking to us. He was in loquacious mood and told us quite candidly what had happened and what his plans were.

He had been cut off from the main column of UNAMO forces in the south after the heavy fighting at Luso. It had been a running fight, he said, rather than a battle. Nobody could claim a victory. He and the Atomique Boum team had spent the last weeks laboriously making their way back to base. We were indeed heading for the Musave River Territories, much faster now thanks to the Land Rover. It was still a difficult journey. The UNAMO enclave in the River Territories was currently being attacked by two columns of troops: the Federal Army and some FIDE units.

'What about EMLA?' I said.

'They are in the south, far in the south. FIDE thinks, you see, if they finish us in the north, then they can return to the south with the Federals and finish EMLA.'

'Will they?'

'No. But maybe they will attack EMLA later in the year. I don't care. I only care about UNAMO. The others are worthless. Everyone is paying for them – America, Russia, South Africa. Only UNAMO is independent. Truly.'

'But after Luso?'

'So they caught us a bit there. And so we retreat, to rearm and re-equip.' He smiled broadly, showing his teeth. '*Reculer pour mieux sauter*. You understand?'

I congratulated him on his French. Then he spoke a few sentences to me in French and I realized he was in fact virtually fluent. I admitted defeat and felt foolish. Amilcar told us he had studied at the Faculté de Médecine at the University of Montpellier for three years before completing his studies in Lisbon, after he won a state scholarship there.

'But I came home when the war started,' he went on. 'Before I could finish my internship.' The disappointment appeared momentarily on his face. He had organized and worked in field hospitals for the UNAMO columns for two years, before steady attrition had necessitated his own move into the guerrilla army.

'I was at Musumberi,' he said, 'for six months. There were many refugees and we had a school there. When I wasn't working in the hospital I was the coach for these boys.' He gestured at them, most of them now curled in blankets around the embers of the fire. 'My volley-ball team. They are good players.' He stopped. 'But now they are tired. And they are depressed. Two of their fellows were shot three days ago. We were surprised in a village, and when we were running away . . .' He didn't finish. 'It's a team, you see? And these boys were the first ones we have lost.'

He paused, reflecting, making little clicking noises with his tongue. He looked up and scrutinized us both.

'It was a mistake. To bring you. I'm very sorry. But now you have to stay on, for a few days only.'

'Well . . .' I was about to say something consoling but I glanced at Ian. His face was set tight, full of frustration and anger.

'You are both working at Grosso Arvore?' Amilcar asked. 'With the monkeys?'

'Chimpanzees. Yes,' I said.

'With Eugene Mallabar?'

'Yes.'

'A great man. He has been a great man for this country.'

Amilcar wagged a finger at us. 'So, are you both doctors?'

'Yes.'

'Of science,' Ian said, with abrupt pedantry.

'So we are three doctors,' Amilcar chuckled. He clearly found the situation very amusing. 'Here in this bit of forest we are three doctors.' He stood up. 'I won't tie you. If you want to go, you can go.'

MINONETTE

*In Massachusetts, in 1895, a man called William G.
Morgan invented a game called Minonette. The only
equipment required was a rope stretched across the gym-
nasium or shed or barn and the inflated bladder of a
basketball. The two teams on either side of the rope
batted the ball to and fro. Points were scored or lost
whenever the batted bladder hit the ground. No catching,
throwing or hitting of the ball was permitted. Anyone –
old or young, fit or unfit – could play Minonette almost
anywhere, indoors or out. No special equipment, skills or
dexterity were required. It was very cheap.*

*Minonette seems to me to be, quite possibly, the most
democratic game ever invented. As further evidence of
this conclusion it possesses one of the most thoughtful and
unselfish rules in any sport.*

*I learnt about it this way. During a game a high ball
was hit over the net. One of the receiving team from the
back of the court yelled 'Mine!' and pelted forward to
intercept it. Suddenly, one of his team-mates flung himself
at him and wrestled him to the ground. Meanwhile, another team-mate, better positioned, intercepted the ball
himself, batted it back over the net where it fell simply to
the ground, the other team having been wholly distracted
by the fight on the other side of the court.*

*A point was duly awarded and a hot debate ensued. It
was decided when Amilcar consulted his tattered coaching
manual and rule book for guidance. The question was
quickly resolved. In Minonette no penalty is awarded if
one player actively holds or restrains a team-mate from
committing a fault such as running into the net or crossing
into the opponents' court. Which is exactly what would*

have happened, it was argued, if the first player's hectic, foolhardy rush for the high ball had not been checked. Play on, Amilcar said.

In 1896, a year after the game had been invented, the name Minonette was dropped in favour of the more prosaic 'volley-ball'. But the courteous, helpful rule remains.

'No. What I did was this. You know that in volley-ball you have to rotate the players, so that in a game everyone plays in every position?'

'Yes,' I said.

'So, normally in a team you have a mix of sizes: some small agile players for the back line returns, and some tall ones for the blocking and smashing. But in my team I only chose the tallest boys.'

'And that made a difference?'

'We won everything. Atomique Boum was unbeatable. You see, when you are a boy it doesn't matter if you are tall or if you are short. OK, if you are a man, it is important. A small man can retrieve a low ball more easily than a tall man. But with boys such a difference isn't really there.' He was enthused. 'Even if I found a very good player who was small, I wouldn't let him in the team. With Atomique Boum, whatever the stage of the game, the other team could not change their tactics. After every point we would rotate the players and each time the front line players were tall. Every time the blocking wall was there. Every time there was one tall fellow to spike it.' He illustrated. 'Chack-chack-chack. *Atomique Boum!*'

It was about an hour after sunrise. We had been

travelling for three days now and a pattern to our day had established itself. We were wakened before dawn, a fire was lit and breakfast cooked – invariably a porridge of various textures, ingredients and flavours. With the first glimmerings of light we were on the road and we would drive without stopping for three to four hours. Then, in the heat of the day, we lay up, the Land Rover parked under a dense tree or else camouflaged with brushwood and branches. During these rest periods some of the boys would go off foraging for food. Amilcar seemed quite happy to let them go to nearby villages. 'They all like UNAMO here,' he would say. Our diet was occasionally improved, as a result, by the addition of chicken or goat, sweet potato or plantain. We ate only twice a day, at dawn and sunset, and the portions were always fairly meagre.

During our protracted midday halts the time would crawl by. The further north we progressed, the closer we approached the great river delta, so it grew more humid. We would lie or sit in the shade for hours, sweaty and uncomfortable, waving vainly at the flies which swarmed round our salty bodies, occasionally stirring to drink some water or relieve ourselves. Beyond the circle of shade we lay in, the sun smashed down on the baking earth, and in the sky great boiling ranges of cumulus massed inexorably only to disperse – like a miracle – at the end of the afternoon.

In the hours before and after noon while we rested, there were many planes in the sky, jet fighters and transports. It was the aircraft that made us hide in the day. We were too far from the base, Amilcar said, and the pilots refused to fly in darkness; consequently they concentrated their activities around the middle of the day. I told him that the pilots were experienced. Of course, Amilcar said, but they can't trust their instruments. If they can't see, they won't fly. So we drove at the day's beginning and at its end.

Amilcar let Ian and me sit in front, now. Most of the time he drove himself, occasionally squeezing a fourth in on the bench seat when one boy or other had local knowledge of the way. The countryside was unchangingly scrubby, with clumps of trees and the odd small rocky hill, and threading through it the faint dusty tracks and rutted lanes we followed. There were no signposts on these makeshift roadways and in our three days of driving we had never seen or heard a hint of another vehicle. Occasionally we would reach a fork or a junction and Amilcar would stop, descend, talk to the boys, make a choice and drive on. At this stage of the journey he used no map or compass. I asked him how he knew the way, and he replied simply that it was UNAMO country we were driving through, as if it were sufficient explanation.

In the days of our travelling Ian's mood had not improved. He remained taciturn and cast down and often seemed close to tears. I tried initially to rally his spirits, but talk of the camp, of what the others would be doing, of official search parties and so on, only seemed to depress him further. He was losing weight rapidly, also. We all were, but Ian seemed unable to keep any food in his system for more than an hour or so. I suspected that he was still in some form of delayed shock; I hoped he would come out of it in due course before his health gave way completely.

One factor he could be sure of was that Amilcar and his Atomique Boum team posed no physical threat.

Amilcar was garrulous and charming; the boys were gentle and lugubrious. Privately, Amilcar told me that they still had not recovered from the death of their team-mates.

My own mood was more complex and bizarre. Sometimes, I felt jaunty and spry, as if I were privileged to be taking part in this extraordinary adventure, especially so now that I knew Amilcar planned to release us. At other times a resigned, stoical lassitude infused me. Then I felt that this interminable journey through this dry and scrubby landscape was some kind of curious dream, a heady reverie of capture, a fantastic, benign kidnapping in which I felt part victim, part accomplice.

On our third evening, Amilcar called a halt a little earlier than usual. The Land Rover was parked beneath a thin acacia and covered in brushwood. A small fire was lit and a pot of maize porridge, with some fish heads in it, was set to stew.

Then the boys hammered two stakes into the ground and tied some rope between them. The perimeter of the court was scratched out with the point of a machete. They divided into two teams of four. Before they occupied their respective courts and the game began, they lined up. Amilcar led them in their team chant.

'*Atomique?*'

'BOUM!' they shouted.

'Atomique?'

'BOUM!'

'Atomique?'

'BOUM! BOUM! BOUM!'

Then a ball was produced from someone's pack, and they played while the light lasted. I watched them dive and set, smash and dig, saw their repertoire of shots, their jump sets and lob balls, their floaters, dumps and dummy spikes. For the first time the boys' reserve left them, and they shouted and cajoled, argued and exulted in the soft evening light, their thin lanky bodies casting thinner and lankier shadows.

At one stage, Amilcar joined in and flung himself about heedlessly, hurling himself after ungettable balls, leaping as high as he could in the air to make a spike, constantly calling out advice and criticism, exposing flaws in their tactics.

Ian and I sat on the ground and watched, bemused at first, but eventually joining in, applauding loudly whenever some particular act of agility or stylish bravado merited it. It was only later when it grew too dark to really see, and the game broke up, that I realized we had been sitting six feet away from the small stack of set-aside Kalashnikovs. The boys trooped off the court, laughing and breathless, their faces glossy with sweat, and picked up their guns as idly as if they had been towels or kitbags.

'I'm glad we played,' Amilcar said. 'Tomorrow is going to be difficult.'

From where we parked the Land Rover, just off the dirt track, I could make out – through the intervening screen of trees and bushes – the pale grey stripe of a tarmac road. I sat in the front of the cab with Ian. The boys all stood outside, edgy and cautious, their guns held ready. Amilcar had advanced eighty yards through the bush to the road. We were all waiting for him to return. We waited an hour, then a bit longer. Eventually he came back, stepping briskly through the undergrowth.

'They're coming,' he said.

He ordered everyone into the Land Rover and we sat and waited again. Soon I heard the noise of the engines and the slap and clatter of tracked vehicles on the tarmac. Then, through the trees I saw a half-track, moving quite slowly. It was leading a convoy of about a dozen lorries. The first four were open-topped and I could see they were filled with soldiers. At the rear came two civilian lorries and I could hear, distinctly, across the patch of bush, the clinking shudder of thousands of bottles.

'What is it?' I said, baffled.

'Beer,' Amilcar said, dolefully. He was suddenly depressed. 'There will be an offensive soon.'

The convoy passed and soon too did its noise. We sat on for a while, then Amilcar sent a boy up to the road to check that all was clear. I asked Amilcar to explain the connection between beer and a new offensive.

The Federal Army, he said, was a conscript army, made up of reluctant young men who had no real desire to fight, and who were governed by a powerful urge towards self-protection.

'Nobody wants to get hurt or killed,' he added. 'Which is normal.' These young men only stayed in the army to earn some money and eat well. In combat zones there was a further incentive: free beer and cigarettes. The Federal Army would not advance one foot without copious supplies of beer. The chiming glass on board that convoy signalled one thing alone: they were planning an assault on the UNAMO front.

Amilcar gripped the steering wheel with both hands. 'They will be advancing,' he said darkly. His mood had changed. 'Two maybe three days.' He started the engine.

'But what about FIDE?' I said aimlessly, like someone trying to make conversation at a cocktail party.

'Oh, FIDE ... FIDE isn't here,' he said. 'It's just that they have stopped fighting the Federals so that they can move more troops up to the River Territories.'

I thought it was a curious war when two lorries full of beer presented more threat than any number of heavily armed men.

One of the boys stood in the middle of the road and waved us on to it. With a lurch and a bump we left the track and moved on to the metalled surface. I felt old sensations: it was like that moment when you left Sangui and hit the main highway south.

We drove up the road in the same direction as the convoy. It was a good road, with wide, mown verges and deep drainage ditches on either side. It ran straight and true through the thickening forest. We were driving at some speed and for a moment or two I thought we might catch up with the beer lorries.

'Careful,' I said to Amilcar. 'Unless you're thirsty.'

'You realize,' he said evenly, 'that if I could destroy that beer UNAMO would be safe for weeks.'

All the same, he slowed down.

After another two minutes, he braked suddenly. Ahead, about four hundred yards away, we could see a vehicle, apparently stuck in the ditch. As we drew closer we saw it was a wrecked lorry, partially burned, with the remains of whatever cargo it had been carrying strewn along the verge: sacks of groundnuts, baskets, kettles, pots and pans.

We halted by the wreck. From my seat I could see a corpse in the driver's seat. I had a glimpse of teeth, top and bottom rows, empty eye sockets and a curious rippled, foil-like texture to the skin. I looked down at once and saw the other body on the ground, bloated and impossibly tight, and somehow incomplete.

I clamped my lips together with my fingers.

Amilcar's expression was enraged.

'It's disgusting,' he said quietly and emphatically. 'It's disgusting how they do this.'

He left the Land Rover, went round to the back and was passed a jerrycan of petrol. He took a deep breath, like a man about to dive underwater, and, averting his face, sloshed petrol generously over the corpse in the cab of the lorry and then the corpse on the verge.

He retreated a few paces, turned and exhaled with a whoosh of expelled air. Then he darted forward and set the two bodies ablaze.

They burned immediately, the long flames pale and almost transparent in the sunshine.

Amilcar climbed back into the Land Rover.

'There's no need for that,' he said, his face calm again. 'Nobody should be left like that. Nobody.'

We turned off the road soon after that on to another dirt track and bumped on, still heading north. I could see that the land around us was lusher and wetter. We were now in thickish forest and we drove over or forded many small streams, reduced to trickles in this dry season. When the rains came I saw that these tracks would be impassable.

Around mid-afternoon we reached our destination. The track entered a large clearing and before us was a low, single-storey building with a corrugated asbestos roof. It was made of mud, but the walls had been painted with white distemper. At the main door was a crude portico with a cross above it and on the entablature was inscribed: S. JUDE.

Behind the building was a small compound with a patchy matting fence and a few mud store-rooms or servants' quarters. There was also what had at one time been a sizeable vegetable garden, now largely overgrown with weeds, except for a few young paw-paw trees and some spindly stands of maize and cassava.

Ian pointed to the name on the building.

'Patron saint of –'

'I know,' I said. 'Don t remind me.'

'It was a mission school,' Amilcar said, misunderstanding our exchange. 'We can stay here, we'll be quite safe.'

The first thing they did was to move the Land Rover undercover. They demolished the gable end of a mud hut and the Land Rover was backed carefully into the shell. Ian and I were taken into the mission school and shown our room.

It smelt mouldy and abandoned. At one end was a row of built-in cupboards and a blackboard. The cupboards were veined with the small raised earth tunnels of termites. The wood was dry and rotten. The cupboard doors broke as easily as toast.

Ian's mood seemed to improve immediately, now that we had stopped travelling and were finally housed. He went through the cupboards busily – and pointlessly, I thought – looking 'for anything that might be useful'. Two days previously he had been badly bitten on the cheek by some insect, and he had scratched the bite into a scab. His beard had grown also, a golden fuzz on his jaws and cheeks. The sore and his beard and his considerable weight loss made him look quite different, less soft and nice. I saw the emergence of an alternative Ian Vail, nastier and leaner, tougher and more capable, not entirely to be trusted.

On the other hand, by contrast, my own strange insouciance of the last few days began to evaporate. It was replaced by a dull, unshiftable depression. For me, because we were no longer on the move, and were living in a building, the brute fact of our kidnap was brought home emphatically. Our curious journey, the games of volley-ball, our polite and tolerant travelling companions, were now all behind us. We were now being held in a house in the middle of a shrinking rebel enclave surrounded – I imagined – by an advancing, beer-fuelled army. Coming to a halt had brought me to my senses: no wistful fantasy could be constructed around our present circumstances.

I still had no fear of Amilcar or the Atomique Boum team, but for the first time since our capture I became very conscious of just how filthy I was. Sleeping out in the open, eating vile food cooked on fires, being continually on the move, had distracted me. A bit of dirt was unexceptionable. But now, in this abandoned school, I felt rank and stinking. My skin had a layer of dust on it. My clothes were grubby and sweat-infused. My hair hung in thick greasy ropes. My teeth and gums felt furred and clogged as if lichen was growing in my mouth. I went straight to Amilcar and demanded some sort of washing facilities.

There was a well behind the school in the compound and two buckets of water and a hunk of pink soap were provided. I washed my hair and immediately felt better. One of the boys gave me a chewing-stick and I cleaned my teeth with it. Ian stripped to his underpants and tried to wash himself down. Now I was marginally cleaner, I found my clothes unsupportably dirty. I was wearing a khaki shirt, a pair of jeans and some lace-up, suede ankle boots. I had nothing else with me apart from the shoulder bag I had packed the day we left Grosso Arvore. Ian was worse off. When Amilcar had ordered the two kitchen boys out of the Land Rover, Billy had unreflectingly picked up Ian's overnight bag which had been stowed in the back. He had had it in his hand, we had remembered later, as he had run off up the road to safety.

Our buckets were refilled and I washed my shirt and jeans. When Ian took them out to lay them in the sun to dry, I quickly washed my pants and brassière, wringing the water from them as best I could, and putting them back on just before he returned.

We sat in our room waiting for our clothes to dry. I felt self-conscious in my underwear and sat stiffly by the wall with my legs drawn up. The bruise from Mallabar's punch discoloured my shoulder like a tattoo, a lead-grey and sludge-brown flower with four purple dots. It was very tender to the touch.

As I sat there I was aware of Ian's flickering gaze from across the room. His eyes kept returning to me, making me more ill at ease. I felt annoyed with him for this little susurrus of prurience. He was fine: his pale blue boxer shorts were as revealing or as unrevealing as swimming-trunks. Irritated by my own modesty I deliberately stood up and walked to the window to look out over the sun-baked, grassless patch of earth in front of the building.

'Should be dry soon,' I said nonchalantly.

'Give them half an hour.'

But as I stood there I found myself wondering

whether the dampness of my pants would make them cling more tightly to my buttocks, and, if I turned around, would the thick triangle of my pubic hair be pressing, bluey, through the moist gusset . . .

I turned and walked quickly back to my blanket and sat down, my legs crossed, my interlocked hands resting modestly in my lap.

There was nothing either of us could think to say. It was hot in the room. Our mutual embarrassment seemed to make it hotter. I felt the sweat begin to seep from my pores. My hair began to cling wetly to my shoulders.

Ian stood up, trying to think of something to do. He went to rummage needlessly again in the cupboards. He found half a ruler.

'Not much use,' he said, holding it up.

'Not unless you want to measure something short,' I said, without thinking.

For a second or two we tried to ignore the double entendre.

'Well, we won't go into that,' Ian said, and laughed. So did I, sort of. At least it eased the tension. We began to talk again: about our plight, about the options open to us, about whether we should try to escape. Outside our clothes dried quickly in the sun.

That night we were given a meaty stew and a big mound of doughy pudding to eat. When I asked what the meat was I was told 'bush pig'. It was stringy and lean with a strong gamey taste. Whatever it was it acted as a powerful aperient on my crammed immobile gut. I went outside and shat copiously behind one of the sheds.

I felt purged and unsteady, and for a moment or two stood quietly in the dusk, the air full of the smell of woodsmoke from the fire our supper had been cooked on. Something about the light and the smell and my moment of weakness brought back strong memories of Knap and John Clearwater, and, for the first time since our capture, I felt my emotions begin to overwhelm me and I sensed the salt of tears tart at the corners of my eyes.

When I went back inside Amilcar was in our room talking to Ian.

'I have to go tonight,' he said. 'To headquarters.'

'What about us?' Ian said. 'When are you going to let us go?'

'I have to talk to General Delgado about you. What to do. What's safest,' he shrugged. 'Maybe we can fly you to Kinshasa or Togo. It depends.'

'Fly?' I said.

'We have one airstrip, beyond the marshes. The planes come in at night.'

'But I thought –'

Amilcar interrupted him politely. 'I'll be back in two days. Everything will be settled then, and you can go home.' He shook hands formally with us. 'I'm leaving six of the team here. Please don't worry. You're quite safe.'

I slept badly that night. I had finished my cigarettes days before, and from time to time a tobacco craving would overwhelm me. I lay wrapped in my blanket, my head on my shoulder bag, dreaming of a pack of Tuskers. I could hear mosquitoes whining and lizards and rodents scurrying about somewhere, and also the deep and rhythmic surge of Ian's breathing. Like a tide I thought, like the wash of wavelets on a pebble beach . . .

I threw off the blanket and quietly left the room. I went outside to the back verandah that overlooked the compound and the kitchen garden. A lantern hung from a rafter and three of the boys were sleeping beneath it in a row. A fourth leant against a pillar, his gun slung over one shoulder.

'Evenin', Mam,' he said.

'Isn't that light dangerous?'

'There are no planes for night.'

I saw I was talking to the young boy with scars under his eyes. He called himself Comrade October-five, he had told me, out of respect for the day General Aniceto Delgado had declared the Musave River Territories independent in 1963, and had unilaterally seceded from the republic.

'What's your real name, October-five?'

'That's my name.'

'What was your name before?'

He paused. 'Jeremeo.'

'Have you got a cigarette?'

'We don't smoke. Only Ilideo.'

'Where's he?'

'I'll go and look for him.'

October-five came back with half a cigarette. He found a match and I lit up. I drew in the sour, strong smoke avidly, feeling my head spin, and exhaled. Whatever brand this was it put Tuskers to shame.

The night was warm. I sat down on the steps and stared out into the blackness. From somewhere in the compound a cock gave an untimely half crow.

'What time is it?' I asked.

'I think about three.'

Despite the nicotine I began to feel tired. A few more minutes and I would sleep. I asked October-five what was tomorrow's programme. He said they would have to wait to receive orders from Dr Amilcar. The one event that was scheduled was a meeting with the comrades from the village committees in this district. We talked vaguely about UNAMO and General Delgado. October-five had taken part in the fighting at Luso.

'We would have won,' he said confidently, then reflected. 'I think. Except for the planes and the gasoline bombs. We shoot at them but we have no ...' He searched for the word.

'Missiles?'

'Yes. But General Delgado is buying us some good missiles.'

'Atomique Boum,' I said. He smiled.

I went back to our room. Ian slept undisturbed.

The next morning we watched from a distance as the comrades from the village committees met. Ilideo presided. He was a lighter-skinned, thick-set boy who was trying to grow a small moustache without much success. They talked for a while, the Land Rover was inspected, and then we were led out. The comrades of the village committees were both men and women, all middle-aged, I noticed, and all thin and raggedly dressed. They looked at us with resentful curiosity. Some questions were put to Ilideo.

'They want to know if you are Cubanos, South African, or Tugas,' Ilideo said.

'We're English,' Ian said proudly.

'Tell them we're doctors,' I said.

This news brought smiles and a few good wishes. Then Ilideo declared the meeting closed, and the comrades of the village committees drifted off in various directions up the forest paths that led away from the mission school clearing.

In the afternoon, the Migs came. It was a hot, still day and we were sitting out on the verandah at the back of the school waiting for the sun to go down and the evening breezes to pick up. We never heard them coming, they seemed to arrive simultaneously with their noise. They came in low, three of them, at about a hundred feet. The rip and battering sound of their jets was shocking, palpable. We saw them for a split second, then they were gone, out of sight, somewhere over the forest, the dispersed rumbling echo of their engines all about us. Ilideo ordered us inside.

The planes came over again, higher and more slowly. I saw them clearly this time, silver Migs with tear-drop pods under their wings. They banked and circled once over us and then flew away.

Ilideo said they deliberately came in low like that. It made people – children mainly – run instinctively out of their houses. There were so many deserted villages in this region, he said, and the planes did not want to waste their bombs or cannons on empty houses.

We did not venture outside for the rest of the day. If the planes had come in from the opposite direction they would have seen us, lined up on the verandah waiting for dusk.

I thought of Usman, and wondered if he had been

flying. What if I had run out, waving? I felt chilled and unhappy: for the first time the grimmer reality of Usman's 'job' was apparent to me.

Ian came into the room. Daily, he was more chipper and buoyant. He said that he had been talking to Ilideo and the others and it was clear to him that they were fighting some kind of fantasy war. They spoke, he said, as if the UNAMO heartland was impregnable, uninvadable.

'They've got no idea what's going on,' he said, in almost outraged tones. 'They talk about "the front" but there is no front. There's several hundred men marching up a road towards a town wondering if anyone'll try to stop them. Tragic.'

He lowered his voice. 'I think we've got to get out of here ourselves, Hope.'

'No, I don't think so.'

'Listen, everything Amilcar's talked about – you know, handing us over when we're through the lines, flying us to Togo – it's fantasy. We could just walk out of here tonight. The Federal Army's on the doorstep ... We just have to walk down that road, heading south. We're bound to find them.'

'I'm not walking down any road.'

'What's going to happen then, for God's sake?'

'We'll wait till Amilcar gets back.'

He looked around the room, hands on his hips, an exasperated smile on his face.

'You don't really, seriously, think he's coming back, do you?' Ian looked at me, parodying incredulity, his eyebrows raised, his mouth open. The sore on his face had scabbed over and his pale beard was softening.

'Of course he'll be back. This is his team.'

'You're as bad as them. Jesus Christ.' He shook his head and chuckled. He looked at me intently. 'Incorrigible Hope. I'd forgotten what you were like.'

I leant back against the wall, closed my eyes and fanned my face with the lid from a cardboard box.

It was very hot that day in the mission school, the sun seemed to press down fiercely on the asbestos roof, cooking up the air inside. I thought of cutting my jeans off at the thigh to make some shorts, but I knew I would regret it: their protection was better than an hour or two's comfort.

I walked slowly through the musty rooms of the mission school, waiting for dark. I tried to find a pace that required a minimum of exertion, but that at the same time might generate the sensation of a breeze, imparted by my motion through the air. The air in those rooms seemed to congeal around me, almost as something semi-solid, as if I were wading through a tank filled with a transparent jelly that yielded easily but was everywhere in clammy contact with my skin.

The boys sat and watched me as I glided to and fro through the empty rooms. They lounged at the angle of the walls and the floor, inert, backs hooped, knees bent, only their eyes moving, following me, their dark faces lacquered with sweat.

The coolness that came with the night was a sweet relief. Then a stiffish breeze developed out of the south. I stood in the centre of the mission school clearing, feeling it tug gently at my clothes and stir my hair. I wondered if it might rain. Rain in Africa is always preceded by a sudden breeze. But tonight I could not smell the ferrous reek of an approaching storm, and up above my head the stars shone confidently, unobscured by clouds.

I strolled back to the school and cadged a few puffs of his cigarette from Ilideo. As we smoked, I asked him, innocently, when Amilcar was due back. He said the next day, definitely. It was time to move on, to pull back to the heartland, he said.

He gave me the cigarette stub to finish and I wandered back to our room. It was lit by a candle and Ian was there, lying on his blanket, palms clamped behind his head, legs crossed. I thought he looked at me a little oddly as I entered. I told him about Ilideo's total confidence that Amilcar would return the next day.

'Not a shadow of doubt,' I said.

Ian rolled on to one elbow. 'OK. But if – if – he doesn't show up, then we have to make a move. We can't hang around with these boys.'

I sighed. 'So, we run off. They won't come looking for us. We could wander around for weeks. Do you know where to go?'

'But the Federal Army –'

'Is where? You don't know where we are. We step out of this clearing and we're lost.'

That seemed to deflate him somewhat. He lay back again, frowning. I carefully stubbed out the cigarette butt; there was just enough left for a draw or two later, if I should need it. I unrolled my blanket. I had stuffed my canvas bag with grass to make a crude pillow. It helped me sleep a little better, but tonight I did not feel tired at all. I lay down out of a sense of boredom and obligation, not fatigue. My hair was beginning to itch again at the roots: I should have washed it today – if Amilcar came back tomorrow and we set off on our travels again, God knows when I'd have another chance. I sat up and scratched my head with both hands. Ian looked at me.

'You're being very up and at 'em,' I said. 'Why don't we just wait? Amilcar'll let us go in the end.'

It was as if I had given him a signal. He was on his feet at once, pacing about. He ran his hands through his hair, tugged at an ear-lobe, hitched up his trousers several times.

'Listen, Hope,' he said seriously. 'There's something I've got to talk to you about.' He waved his hands. 'It's been on my mind for a while.'

'Spit it out,' I said, but I had no real desire to talk.

'When we were captured . . . My, my behaviour those first few days. I feel very bad about it. I was useless.'

'Forget it. It's not important.'

But he wouldn't forget it. He wanted to talk about it. He wanted to explain himself and apologize. He could not account for what had happened to him. A total collapse of his spirits, he said, something he had never experienced before. During those first days he had either felt completely numb, he said, or terrified. When his brain was working, all he could think about was death. Being killed or dying slowly. He was convinced we were both going to be shot. He kept imagining what it would be like, the sensation of a bullet entering his body . . .

He came and sat down beside me, leaning back against the wall, face raised to the ceiling. Now he started to compliment me, to praise my coolness and composure. I interrupted him to tell him I had felt just as strange; how it was as if I were participating in some kind of bizarre dream, and because of that had never faced up to what was really going on.

'I was fantasizing,' I said, trying to make him feel better. 'At least you were aware of the risks. I felt I was on some magical mystery tour.'

But no, he wouldn't accept that. If it hadn't been for me, my example, my strength, God knows what would have happened to him. He carried on talking, analysing the various stages of his decline and trying to pinpoint the moment when he had begun to recover.

My concentration began to waver, as I realized he was not particularly interested in a dialogue. This was something he had to talk out of himself. I began to feel drowsy, my brain acknowledging only the occasional word in his apologia – 'desperate' . . . 'unthinkable' . . . 'debt' . . . 'emotional turmoil' . . . I moved my head slightly, and heard the drying grasses stuffed in my canvas bag crackle and shift. I let my right hand slip from my chest on to the blanket and, absent-mindedly, with my left I raised the front of my shirt an inch or two and blew down into its warm interior, feeling for a moment the fleeting chill of my exhalation on my clammy breasts and stomach.

Then Ian's hand was on my cheek and neck, and I felt the prickle of his beard on my forehead and the dry pucker of his lips as he began to peck at my face.

'Hope,' he said, softly, 'God, Hope . . .'

And then he was lying on top of me, squirming and moaning, his wet mouth chewing at my throat, all the while muttering his stupid endearments: 'Hope, I love you . . . You saved me . . . I couldn't have got through without you . . .'

I felt drugged and slow, both arms pinioned by his weight. I felt his lips and tongue move across my jaw to squash on my tight, closed mouth. I heaved and bucked, twisting my torso violently sideways, freeing a hand and hitting out wildly at his head.

I threw him off and he rolled clear. He pushed himself up on his haunches, slowly, as if he were in great pain.

'Don't cry,' he said, urgently. 'Please don't cry.'

'Don't worry,' I said, harshly, composing my features. Something in my expression must have made me look as if I were about to burst into tears.

'Fucking stupid,' I said. 'Stupid fool.'

I had a distressing vivid picture in my head of the two of us on the blanket, him between my spread legs, sweaty and grubby on the dirty grey blanket, the boys in the next room listening to our grunts and moans.

'I'm sorry,' he said.

'Stupid bastard.'

He crawled silently over to his blanket and lay down. I saw his hand reach to pinch out the candle flame. I lay there in the darkness, stiff with anger, railing at this man's incorrigible vanity, his woeful ignorance. What did I have to do to make things any plainer?

I dreamt there was a knocking on the door, a dry and insistent rapping, and woke almost as my unconscious mind recognized it for what it really was.

Ian was already scrambling across the room to the window. I heard the bullets ripping into the asbestos roof making a wild clattering noise. I hauled on my shoes and crawled over.

At the window with Ian I could see nothing, just the

clearing, the bare circle of earth, still, empty under its soft grey wash of starlight, the surrounding forest opaque and dark But my ears were loud with the toc-toc-toc of the gunfire and the ceramic clatter of shards of asbestos flying, as if someone was dropping bathroom tiles on to a concrete floor. Aiming too high, I thought, automatically. Something Amilcar had said pushed its way into my mind: all African soldiers aim too high.

'Jesus Christ. Jesus!' I heard Ian say. 'They're here.' He grabbed my hand. 'Let's go!'

We scurried to the door. Now there was a new sound. The boys were firing back. In the main room two boys – I couldn't see who they were in the darkness – were firing blind, out of the windows, leaning back, heads averted, Kalashnikovs propped jerking on the sill, as they emptied their magazines, willy-nilly, into the night. Through the windows I saw for the first time the yellow lances of tracer, light spears hurled everywhere.

Crouching, we raced out of the back door. October-five was there, flattened against a wall. To the right, the direction he was staring in, I saw the mud building that held the Land Rover disintegrating, it seemed, in kicking clouds of dust, and I could hear the metallic thunk and clang as bullets punched through the tin sides of the vehicle.

October-five waved us to the left. His eyes were wide. He shouted something, but I couldn't hear what he said. We crawled up the verandah and slid off the end into a tangle of weeds that marked the old border of the kitchen garden. As one's mind will, I started instantly to think of lesser dangers, snakes and scorpions.

Then the firing stopped for a second or two and, from all around the clearing's perimeter, it seemed, I heard raucous, argumentative shouting. Then a boy fired from the school building and the shooting started again. Small chips of asbestos roofing began to fall down on top of us.

Ahead, we could see an empty third of the mission school clearing. The road in was at the other end and the road out was close by it too, angling off acutely. In plan, the two roads were like a bent arm, the clearing, the school and its outbuildings like a swollen growth at its elbow. Many forest paths led out of the clearing. A wide and well-worn one was no more than twenty yards away from us. I could see it now as I lay flinching and edgy in the weeds, its opening a darker patch of star shadow against the neutral grey-black of the perimeter trees.

'There,' I said to Ian, pointing.

I heard a noise behind me and twisted round. I saw three of the boys hurtle out of the back of the house and scamper through the maize and cassava plants of the kitchen garden to disappear into the black bush beyond.

'That way?' I said.

'No,' Ian said. 'Come on.'

We stood up and, bent over, ran for the path opening. I was unaware of anyone shooting at us. All fire seemed to be concentrated on the mission school. We ran into the undergrowth, me leading, and on down the path, a pale stripe weaving in front of me. I kept running at full speed. I ran for as long as possible – two minutes, ten minutes? – before a cruel stitch in my side made me stop. I bent over, writhing. Something inside me seemed to be trying to prise my ribs apart. I sank to my knees. I could still hear the firing from the mission school.

'Come on,' Ian said, stepping past me and setting off again at a jog.

I hunched after him, limping, canted over to favour my stitch-wracked side. Through my blurry eyes and in the gloom of the forest, I sometimes lost sight of him up ahead, and began to panic, then I would see his legs moving against the paler stripe of the path and I would push myself on again.

Sometimes the forest thinned and the night sky and a horizon would reveal itself to us. Sometimes we ran through groves of tall trees with long columns of silver trunks. The path was clear and wide. We would come to a village before too long, I was sure.

Then I ran into Ian, solid in the middle of the way, his elbow hitting me square on the left breast, a hot coin of pain.

'Shut up!' he said, as I gasped. 'Listen.'

I could only hear my own noises. The suck of my lungs, the throb in my head, the ebb and flow of blood. I tried to stop breathing, to breathe slowly, shallowly, to pick up and sieve the other sounds of the night.

Voices.

Men's voices arguing, not raised, but the sound of an urgent serious dispute.

'Amilcar?' I said stupidly. 'Who is it?'

'Back,' Ian said. 'Get back!'

Ahead, the path curved. I saw a torch-beam through the intervening bushes. I heard many feet, the chink and swish of weapons on webbing.

We turned back and started to run again. We had gone ten paces when there was a shout and the torch-beam whipped up to illuminate our fleeing backs and flying heels. I heard confused bellows of surprise behind

and shouted orders. The path swerved. The firing
started. We were in darkness again. Somewhere to our
left the sound of leaves and branches being shredded,
ripped apart.

'Faster!' Ian screamed at me, close at my back.

On my right were trees. Trunks, slim, straight, evenly
spaced. Planted out. I turned into them, instinctively,
Ian following. It was like being in an explosion. Beneath
our feet was a deep layer of leaves, parchment dry, large
as plates, crisp as water biscuits. I thought I heard Ian
utter a sob of frustration, but I kept on running down
the long aisle of tree trunks. I saw the torch-beam
playing over to my left, then it homed in on me.

Ian had jinked one aisle over, and was abreast of me,
drawing further ahead. I thought I heard the sound of
gunfire above the reverberating crunch and shatter of
our footsteps. Then I did hear the shouts and whoops
of my pursuers as I ran for my life, my crazy jerking
shadow silhouetted on the brittle leaves ahead.

I glanced over at Ian and saw him grab a tree trunk
and wheel himself off diagonally. I did the same, thinking: how sensible. The firing was clear and loud now. I
could hear the vicious axe-thunk of bullets hitting tree
boles.

Our change of direction meant that the torch-beam
had lost us. I could see it flicking around aimlessly. Too
many trees in the way now. I stopped for a second,
holding on to a trunk. Pounding, crunching feet behind,
crazy shouts, crazy firing. I started running again. I
could just make out Ian, labouring somewhat, about ten
yards ahead of me. Somehow my stitch had gone and I
seemed to have more strength. I started to gain on him.

Then I went over on my ankle and fell. As I tumbled

and rolled I screamed his name. *'IAN, STOP!'* I looked up for him, my ankle felt wobbly and loose, as if the joint had gone and there was only water there. *'HELP ME, IAN!'* I think he stopped. I think he was coming back for me. But then the torch-beam found him, and I saw only his blind, dazzled eyes for a second. As I screamed the guns started firing. I saw chips of tree trunk big as half-bricks flying, then Ian ducked out of the beam and was gone. I heard his crunching footsteps disappear in the approaching crescendo of our pursuers' running boots.

I hunched down in the leaves, sliding beneath the layers of dead leaves, like huge potato crisps, feeling for the cool soil beneath. They would not find me if I kept still, I knew. They would have to stand on me to find me.

My nose touched the earth, my nostrils filled with its musty, mouldy smell. I sunk my fingers into it as if I were on a cliff face, clinging on. I kept my head down and stayed absolutely still.

In seconds I heard them all around me, running and tramping, calling out to each other as they chased after Ian. I heard them firing and shouting, the noise gradually dying away. It was quiet, and soon my ears were filled with the sounds in the leaves themselves, the tiny rustlings and crepitations. I felt ants and grubs on my face, and something small and four-footed scampered by me. I started to count and had reached over two thousand before I heard them returning. But they were some way off and came nowhere near me. They were still shouting and calling to each other angrily. Did that mean they had caught Ian or that they had missed him? And if they had caught him, I wondered what they would do with him . . .

Long minutes after they had gone, and there was no more noise, I sat up. Only now I felt the pulse and ache of my ankle. Still sitting, I pushed myself backwards until I hit a tree trunk. I leant back against it and rubbed the crown of my head against its rough bark. I settled down in the forest, in the blackness, and waited for dawn.

THE NEURAL CLOCK

Lying alone, in the dark, in her house on the beach, Hope often remembers that night. When the memories become too vivid she leaves her bed and goes through to her tiny kitchen for a drink. She switches all the lights on in the house and tunes her radio to the BBC World Service, or to some local 'batwque' music station.

That night, in the grove of trees, seemed to her sense of subjective time – her private time – to crawl by with intolerable slowness. The refusal of the earth to turn faster, to bring the light round to this corner of Africa, to initiate civil time once more, seemed to her almost a personal insult.

And in the dense blackness of that interminable night, she was highly conscious of the clock-like systems in her own body. The beat of her heart, the inflation and deflation of her lungs. But she knows now that our sense of private time is not formed by the pulsing heart or the breathing lungs but by the neural impulses of our brain.

A neuron transmits a pulse at about fifty times a second, and the impulse travels down the branching tree of the nervous system at a speed of approximately fifty metres a second. This neural timekeeper is never at rest for one instant; throughout our entire life the neural race never quickens or slows. Its regularity and constancy fulfil all the requirements for the definition of a clock.

If this is indeed how our sense of personal time originates – by the ticking of the neural clock at fifty times a second – then one intriguing consequence of the theory is that other primates – whose neural impulses function identically to ours – should have a similar sensation of personal time also.

Hope sits in her bright, loud house and looks out into the darkness towards the sound of the waves. It seems strange, but not inconceivable, that Clovis should have had a sense of his life passing by – a finite sequence of present moments – just as she does.

As the blackness of night slowly cleared I saw that we had been running through a large plantation of teak trees. They were about thirty feet high and their big, flat, wrinkled leaves, the size of tennis racquets, hung motionless in the cool, still air of early morning. There was no undergrowth beneath the trees. The carpet of dead leaves was six inches thick – nothing grew here. I stood up and leant back heavily against the tree, causing the dry leaves above me to rattle. I was facing the way I had been running. All around me I could see the damage done to the level leaf floor by the running boots of the soldiers. None had come very close to me.

I tested my ankle cautiously. It was slightly swollen, but could just about take my weight. A sprain, then. I dusted myself down, shook the twigs and leaf fragments and other living creatures from my hair and clothes, and limped off to see what lay beyond the teak plantation.

It took me five minutes to reach the edge. All the way I followed the tracks through the fallen leaves left by the soldiers. Beyond the plantation edge was thick bush. Had Ian escaped, or had they caught him at the boundary? If he had reached the bush they would never have found him.

The sun was rising on my right-hand side. I turned to face it and walked along the edge of the plantation. After about three or four hundred yards I came to a fire-break in the trees. From the fire-break, running out into the bush was an overgrown track. I set off up it, noticing that nothing had driven down here since last year's rains. Creepers grew across the twin wheel ruts and the central stripe of turf was thick with weeds and knee-high grass. Every now and then I stopped and listened, but I heard nothing, only the calls of birds, loud and fresh – orioles, hornbills, doves.

A forest path crossed the track, well-trodden and dusty, like the one we had been running on the night before. I decided to follow it, still heading east into the rising sun.

The tree cover began to thin after half a mile or so. I passed one or two brackish pools stuffed with reeds. I was thirsty by now, but was not about to risk drinking out of these slime-fringed swamps. I limped on, scratching at my bites, trying to ignore the questions that yammered in my head, trying not to recall the expression on Ian Vail's face in my last glimpse of him, before he ran away and left me.

The landscape was changing around me. It was markedly greener and lusher. There were patches of tall, sedgy grasses, thick clumps of rushes and bamboo. One had the sense of a brimming watertable inches below the surface. On either side of the path were groves of palms and palmettas and curious, jagged-looking trees with tortured pale bark and tough viridian leaves that looked as if they had been cut from polished linoleum. We were in the Musave River Territories.

At about midday, very tired, my throat raw and cracked, I heard a curious clucking in the undergrowth. I crouched down and lifted a trailing branch. It was a scrawny startled hen with three chicks. A hen. I let the branch fall. There must be a village nearby. I continued down the path.

I saw the sagging thatched roofs some two hundred yards off, but it was suspiciously quiet, even though a few wisps of smoke appeared to be rising from cooking fires. I advanced cautiously. The path merged into the beaten grassless earth of the compound. The place hardly merited the description of village, really; it was just a cluster of huts around an old shade tree. There were no animals, I saw, so I assumed it was deserted, but there was a smell of smoke about, and underlying that a sour nutty reek that was unfamiliar to me.

I passed the first hut and peered round the corner into the open space around the shade tree.

Three dead bodies blazed there, tall, pale yellow flames wobbling along their length. The corpses were swollen but already charred sufficiently to make sex or age or manner of death impossible to determine. The smell coming off them seemed to pour down my throat – porky, nutty, sour and mineral all at once – like a foul medicine. I dry-heaved convulsively, three or four times, in an involuntary spasm. I spat copious saliva. Somewhere in my dehydrated body a little fluid remained, clearly. My cracked throat eased, my tongue was slick and moist.

324

'Amilcar!' I shouted. 'It's me, Hope!'

A man came out of a hut. At first I did not recognize him and I felt my body lurch with alarm. But then three of the Atomique Boum team appeared behind him and I gave a little whimper of relief. I limped towards them. I felt like crying; I felt I ought to cry, in a way, but I was too tired.

'Hope . . .?' Amilcar said. I could see he was utterly and completely surprised to see me. He smiled, moved his head and the sun flashed off the new silver frames of his spectacles. Everything he wore was new. He looked incredibly smart in a new camouflage uniform, all green, brown and black lozenges, creaking with starch. He wore a funny little kepi-style hat, with a protective sun-flap at the rear, also camouflaged, matching his tunic and trousers.

'My God,' I said. 'What an outfit. Amazing.'

'I've been promoted,' he said, pointing at the pips on his epaulettes. 'I'm a colonel now. And this,' he pointed at the three boys, 'is my battalion.'

We laughed.

We left the village with its still smoking corpses towards the end of the afternoon. We had caught the scrawny hen, cooked her and eaten her along with an old tough yam and some unripe plantain. The three boys were October-five, Bengue and Simon. They were silent and subdued, their faces solemn and watchful. These were the three we had seen making their escape across the kitchen garden. Nobody knew what had happened to Ilideo and the others. 'I'm sure they got away,' Amilcar said with breezy confidence. 'They'll be moving back, like us. We'll meet up, don't worry.'

I told him of my own experiences, of the attack and then the chase. Amilcar used my story to bolster the boys' morale. Look, he told them, twenty men, armed men, were chasing Hope and she got away. The implication being that if I could do it anyone could. The boys said nothing; they looked searchingly at Amilcar as he spoke, as if keen to trap him in any equivocation, but his sincerity and his confidence were manifest. Later, I caught the boys glancing at me covertly, as if my presence guaranteed the safety of the other members of the team.

I walked beside Amilcar as he led us out of the village. The boys trailed behind us, gunless, hands in pockets, sometimes talking softly among themselves.

'How did those people in the village die?' I asked.

He said he didn't know. Perhaps a patrol. As far as he knew – as far as General Delgado's intelligence was aware – units of the Federal Army were massing at two roads that led into the UNAMO heartland, but they were miles away.

'So, it must have been a patrol,' he conceded, with a frown. 'But I still don't understand how they attacked the school. And at night. It's not like them. Did you see any whites, among the soldiers?'

I said I hadn't.

'There are more mercenaries now, in the army. Maybe it's them. From Rhodesia and the Congo.'

He went on speculating. Once all the UNAMO forces had withdrawn behind the huge marshes that fringed the River Territories there would be a stalemate. The Federals could not advance. UNAMO could regroup and rebuild. In any event, he said, looking at the sky, when the rains came all fighting would necessarily stop.

And then in the south EMLA would launch their offensive: in the south you could fight during the rains. So the Federals would have to withdraw and the UNAMO columns could move out into the field again.

I looked at him, smart in his new uniform, as he talked with tranquil confidence about this chain of events as if they were inevitable and preordained. I glanced back at his 'troops', the remains of his personal UNAMO column, three frightened and confused teenage members of a volley-ball team, and wondered if all zealots saw the world in this simple way, devoid of any connection to the evidence on hand. Or perhaps he had gone mad.

Before dusk we came to another deserted village, one without any corpses to burn. We searched the huts for food but found nothing.

Just beyond the village was a road, tarmac, in bad repair. We climbed up on to it and looked up and down its deserted length. The light was soft and dusty and the first bats were out, ducking and jinking over our heads. Amilcar told me the lie of the land.

To turn left, north, would take us to the causeway which crossed the great marsh. There we would rejoin the regrouping UNAMO forces. To turn right, south, would lead us to one of the two Federal Army units that were preparing to advance up this road sometime in the next two or three days.

'And I assume that last bit of information is for my benefit,' I said.

He shrugged and turned away. 'If you want to go you can go,' he said, suddenly surly. 'I don't care.'

I put my hands on my hips and looked around me. We could be almost anywhere in Africa, I recognized.

The scene was at once typical and banal. A pot-holed road running straight through low scrubby forest, a scatter of decrepit huts, a strange dry smell in the air of dust and vegetation, a big red sun about to dip below the treeline, the plaintive chirrup of crickets.

'I'll stay with you a little longer,' I said, not wanting to walk alone down that road to meet the Federal Army. I punched my fist tiredly in the air. *'Atomique Boum!'*

The boys smiled.

We reached the causeway a mile further up the road, in the last of the fading light. It was about three-quarters of a mile long and ran straight across a wide expanse of marsh. The causeway looked solid and well constructed. The road surface was intact and the gradient of the banks was precise and maintained for its entire length. Here and there beneath it were large concrete culverts to permit the flow of water in times of flood.

We walked across it briskly. A big white heron took off and shrugged itself effortfully into the evening sky. It was liberating to be in open space again, to have a large sky above and a sense of horizons receding. I began to realize, also, why Amilcar was so confident. It would not be difficult to defend this road.

Amilcar was preoccupied. 'These boys,' he said discreetly, disappointedly, 'they are not true soldiers.'

As we approached the end of the causeway our pace faltered. It was almost dark now. Amilcar told us to wait and walked forward into the gloom. Then we heard him shouting – a password, I assumed. After five minutes he came back, mystified. There was no one there, he said.

We proceeded onward.

At the end of the causeway was a small village – the usual huddle of mud huts on either side of the road. One hut had been demolished and its remaining thatch appeared burned. There was no evidence of other damage.

On either side of the road were abandoned trenches, and in one sandbagged emplacement an anti-tank gun. It had a very long, slim barrel and it smelt new, of milled, turned metal and fresh rubber from its tyres. Its breech mechanism glistened with oil. To one side was a tidy stack of flat wooden boxes. As we explored we found more boxes and crates of abandoned equipment and ammunition. In a hut we discovered a hundred Warsaw pact Kalashnikovs, tied up in bundles of ten like awkward faggots of wood.

'Where is everybody?' Amilcar wondered aloud. 'What happened here?' He sounded baffled and hurt, as if this abandoned village and its profligate waste of weaponry were designed as personal slights.

We foraged further and came across bags of rice and tins of pickled mackerel from Poland. The boys cooked up an oily stew of fish, rice, cassava and some leaf that Amilcar stripped from a bush.

Then Amilcar rearmed the Atomique Boum team, giving them each a new Kalashnikov and draping them with shiny bandoliers of redundant machine-gun bullets. 'It looks good,' he said. 'It makes them feel strong.' He sent October-five out to the gun pit to keep watch on the causeway and the other two volunteered to accompany him. He was pleased at this development.

'You see,' he said, after they had gone. 'Now we are home they will fight.'

We sat together in a hut, a lantern burning in the middle of the floor. We sat on piles of rubberized, olive-drab ponchos we had found. Amilcar was in talkative mood, and reminisced for a while about his past ambitions. He would never have worked in the capital, he said, not like the other doctors with their private clinics and Mercedes Benzes, all lobbying for jobs in the World Health Organization so they could live in Geneva. He would have stayed in his province, he said, and helped his people.

'God will return me there,' he said simply. 'When the war is over.'

'God?' I said. 'You're not telling me you believe in God?'

'Of course.' He laughed at my astonishment. 'I'm a Catholic.' He reached into his camouflaged tunic and pulled out a crucifix on a beaded chain. 'He is my guide and protector. He is my staff and my comforter.'

'I never thought for a minute.'

'Are you a Christian?' he asked.

'Of course not.'

'Ah, Hope,' he shook his head sadly. He seemed genuinely disappointed in me. 'It's because you are a scientist.'

'It's got nothing to do with being a scientist.'

We started talking about my life, what I did, what I had done before. I told him about my doctorate, my work at Knap, Mallabar and the Grosso Arvore project. I talked animatedly, in a succinct and authoritative way. It seemed to me as if I were recollecting a vanished world, that I was summarizing some historical research project I had completed a long time ago. Professor Hobbes, the college, the Knap field study, Grosso Arvore and the chimpanzees seemed to have absolutely nothing to do with me any more.

From time to time Amilcar would interrupt me to make a point.

'But Hope,' he said at one stage, 'let me ask you this. All right, you know a lot. You know many obscure things.'

'Yes. I suppose so.'

'So let me ask you this: the more you know, the more you learn – does it make you feel better?'

'I don't understand.'

'All these things you know – does it make you happy? A better person?'

'It's got nothing to do with happiness.'

He shook his head, sadly. 'The pursuit of knowledge is the road to hell.'

I laughed at him. 'My God. How can you *say* that? You're a doctor, for God's sake. What rubbish!'

We argued on, good-naturedly. I sensed he was taking up positions for forensic effect, to prolong the debate, so I indulged him. Occasionally he would say things that made me pause, however. At one stage he asked me many questions about the chimpanzees, why we were studying them so intently. He seemed genuinely amazed – and this time I don't think he was pretending – that I had spent month after month in the bush watching chimpanzees and recording their every act and movement.

'But why?' he said. 'What's it for?'

I tried to tell him but he didn't seem convinced.

'The trouble with you in the West is . . .' He thought about it. 'You don't really value human life, human beings.'

'That's not true.'

'You value a monkey more than a human. And look at you: I hear you talk about a tree, about some kind of hedge.' He pointed at me. 'You value a tree more than a human being.'

'That's ridiculous. I –'

'No, Hope, you have to learn,' he kept jabbing his finger at me, 'you have to learn that a human life, any human life is worth more than a car, or a plant, or a tree . . . or a monkey.'

THE WEIGHT OF THE SENSE WORLD

I went out walking on the beach today. It was fresh and breezy and my hair kept being blown annoyingly across my face. For some reason, my thoughts were full of Amilcar and his mad moral certainties. I was distracted from them, fairly ruthlessly, when I trod on a fat blob of tar the size of a plum. It squashed between three toes of my left foot, clotted and viscous like treacle.

The next hour was spent in a frustrating search for some petrol or spirit to clean it off. There was none in the house so I had to hobble through the palm grove to the village. I bought a beer bottle full of pink kerosene from one of the old trading women and, eventually, with some effort and enough cotton wool to stuff a cushion, I managed to remove all traces of oil from my foot.

Now I sit on my deck, feeling stupid and exhausted, looking dully out at the ocean, a strong smell of kerosene emanating from my left foot, my toes raw red and stinging from the crude and astringent fuel.

The weight of the sense world overpowers me some days, today clearly being one of them. I seem unable to escape the phenomenal, the randomly human. It's at times like these that the appeal of mathematics, and its cool abstractions, is at its most potent and beguiling. Suddenly I can understand the satisfaction of that escape, savour something of the acute pleasure it gave to someone like John. All the itch and clutter of the world, its bother and fuss, its nagging pettiness, can wear you down so easily. And this is why I like the beach – blobs of tar notwithstanding. Living on the extremity of a continent, facing the two great simple spaces of the sea and sky, cultivates the sense that somehow you are less encumbered than those who live away from the shoreline. You feel less put upon by the fritter and mess of the quotidian. It is fifty yards from where I sit now to the foam and spume of the last breaker. There is not very much between here and there, you think, to distract you.

I remember something Amilcar said to me that night as we talked. I asked him what would happen if UNAMO were defeated. He refused to admit it was possible.

'But what if?' I said. 'Hypothetically.'

'Well . . . I would be dead, for one thing.'

'Are you frightened?'

He pushed out his bottom lip as he thought about it. 'No,' he said.

'Why not?'

'Because what cannot be avoided, must be welcomed.'

I was never sure, in our discussions that night, if he was simply trying to provoke me. We talked on and the subject changed. He started to tell me about a girl, a French girl, he had met in Montpellier, whom he had asked to marry. She had said yes, and then three weeks later had said no. He never saw her again. He asked me if I were married. I said no. He smiled and screwed up his eyes.

'So. What about Ian?' he said.

'What about him?'

'I think he would like to marry you. Why don't you marry him?'

'You must be joking.'

He found this very funny. Still laughing, he went outside to check on the boys in the gun pit. Alone in the hut I thought about what Amilcar had said, and realized that we had blithely assumed Ian was still alive. If he were, I doubted that marriage to me would be on his mind.

When Amilcar returned I could see his mood had changed again. He was depressed.

'Those boys,' he said, sucking in air through his teeth to express his exasperation, 'they are too frightened. I told them there was no danger. They would hear the Federals from two miles away. Then they should call me. One shot. One shot and they would retreat.' He went on bemoaning their lack of spirit.

'Maybe we should withdraw a bit,' I suggested. 'Maybe the UNAMO troops are further down the road?'

'No. We will make our stand here.'

He did not want to talk further, I could sense. He picked up the lantern and went to check on the abandoned *matériel*. I pulled some ponchos over me and settled down to sleep.

*

I woke very early. There was a faint light outside, a pale misty grey. Amilcar was nowhere to be seen. I sat up, stiff and sore. I had been badly bitten in the night on my neck and forearm.

Outside it was very still. For the first time I could see the full extent of the disarray of the village: everywhere there were piles of abandoned cardboard boxes and packing-cases. I wondered where Amilcar was, and wandered through the village towards the causeway looking for him. Slowly a pale citron began to infuse the monochrome light around me; there was a low cover of thick cloud and it was cool.

As I drew near the gun pit I saw at once that it was empty. The boys had gone. Propped against the sandbag wall were their new guns, their bandoliers coiled beside them. More tellingly, three track-suit tops were hung over the anti-tank gun's barrel. Team Atomique Boum had finally disbanded.

I folded the track-suit tops and laid them on top of the sandbags. I sat down on one of the gun's tyres and wondered what to do. The gun itself, I thought, my mind wandering, was rather a beautiful object. The long tapered barrel, blistered with dew, looked out of proportion, too long for the compact breech and the neat carriage. There was a booklet encased in a plastic bag hanging from one of the handles on the sight. I tore it open. It was a set of instructions on how to operate the gun – written in French.

I looked down the barrel and the long perspective of the causeway. Banks of mist lay over the marsh. It was all very placid, eerily beautiful. A few birds were beginning to sing. I heard the plangent fluting of a hoopoe.

'They've gone,' Amilcar said.

I turned round. He stood there, slumped yet tense, his jaw muscles working.

'Look.' He pointed at the neatly stacked guns. I think it was only then that the impossibility of his situation – its farcical unreality – struck home. He put his hands on his hips and looked up helplessly at the sky.

'Those boys,' he said, trying to chuckle. 'A great volley-ball player makes a bad soldier. Now I know.' He looked back at the mess in the village. 'Look at this. Terrible.'

I felt cold and shivered. I picked up a track-suit top. 'Can I have this?'

'Take anything. Help yourself. Have an anti-tank gun.'

I pulled on the top. Amilcar was looking incredulously at the instruction booklet for the gun.

'In French . . . can you believe it? How do you think they knew that the one man left to fire it had been to Montpellier University?' He threw the book away. 'How much would a gun like this cost?'

'How would I know?'

'Two hundred thousand dollars? Half a million?'

'What can I tell you? It's brand new. Who knows how much these things cost?'

'Somebody from UNAMO bought this for us in Europe. I wonder what his commission was?'

He levered off the top of one of the flat wooden boxes. Inside, on a polystyrene rack, like wine bottles, were three thin shells with lilac, onion-shaped tops, like domes on a Russian church. He removed one and held it out: it was a rather beautiful object, well designed, like the gun. The lilac shone with a luminescent glow in the yellowy light. Amilcar opened the breech of the gun and offered the onion nose to the opening. It slid in easily. It was far too small. He pulled the shell out.

'How much would one of these cost? Five thousand dollars? Ten?'

I didn't answer him this time. I zipped up my Atomique Boum top. He sat down on the sandbag wall. I felt so sorry for him, in his new uniform – it had acquired a few extra creases but he still looked dapper and neat – with all this redundant sophisticated weaponry. He looked down at the ground without speaking.

The cluster of bites on my neck itched. As I scratched them I realized they were in exactly the same position as Amilcar's curious scar. I thought if we had more time, and the occasion was right, that I would tell him about my port-wine mark, splashed across my skull.

'Hope,' he said suddenly, 'would you help me a little? I need your help. It will save time. Then we'll go back to the airstrip, get you out on a plane tonight. But I just have to do one more thing and if you help me it'll save time.'

'Of course,' I said instantly. 'Glad to.'

I could only manage two land-mines, and even that was an effort. They were heavy, painted black, the size of dinner plates and two inches thick. Amilcar was carrying four and he had a Kalashnikov slung across his back as well.

We walked slowly up the causeway, heading for the middle, stopping occasionally to let me rest. The sun was rising now and the mist was beginning to lift off the marsh. Patches of blue were showing through the thinning clouds.

After about four hundred yards we stopped above a

culvert. Amilcar slid down the sides of the embankment and I passed him the mines one by one, which he then stacked beneath the roadway in the centre of the culvert.

His last contribution to the defence of the heartland, he had told me, was to be the destruction of the causeway. The equipment had been abandoned, the soldiers had fled, but if he could blow a hole in the causeway then he would feel all his efforts had not been in vain. His plan was straightforward: he was going to detonate one of the land-mines by a simple mechanism he had devised. The butt of a Kalashnikov would be balanced above the pressure plate of an activated land-mine, held up by a prop – a two-foot stick. To this stick a long line of string would be attached. When he was far enough away, Amilcar would simply yank on this string, the stick-prop would be removed and the Kalashnikov butt would fall square on the pressure plate. The mine would explode, as would the other five stacked alongside it. The resulting explosion, he assured me, would demolish a considerable section of the causeway. I said it sounded a good plan – a neat bit of improvisation.

So I handed him the last of the land-mines and clambered back up the embankment to the road. I sat down on the verge and waited for Amilcar, taking in the scene around me. It was a fine and clear morning. On the far bank of the marsh some palm trees were reflected perfectly in a reed-free sheet of water. I thought: what an extraordinary and lovely tree the palm is! And I thought now its ubiquity in the tropics often prevents us from appreciating its singular beauty and grace: its slim, curved grey trunk, the delicate frondy splay of its foliage, the fact that no matter how old, or how stunted the tree might be, its essential elegance remained . . .

My stomach rumbled and I felt a sudden nicotine craving seize me. From the culvert I heard the amplified scrape and clunk of heavy metal on rough concrete as Amilcar stacked his land-mines.

I walked to the edge of the embankment and watched as he emerged, stooped, from the culvert, unwinding his ball of string. He backed cautiously up the slope to the road then very delicately straightened the loose, looping curve the string made. He laid the string on the ground and placed a stone on top of it. He removed his spectacles and wiped his sweating face on his jacket sleeve.

'Let's hope the prop doesn't fall too soon,' he said, with a nervous grin.

He stepped down the embankment again to check on a grass stem that was snagging his detonating string. I looked up the causeway road. Carried on the still morning air came the faint noise of an engine. I listened hard. It was an engine. A motor vehicle. I shaded my eyes and peered. Even this early in the morning there was a shimmer of heat haze coming off the road. I saw two vertical black dots ride the wobbling quicksilver of the mirage.

'Amilcar! A truck's coming.'

He scrambled up the embankment.

'Oh no,' he said, his voice full of petulant disappointment. 'Wait a second.'

'Shouldn't we go?' I said, anxiously. But he was already at the culvert's entrance. He went in and emerged moments later with the Kalashnikov.

'Jesus, Amilcar,' I said. 'What're you doing? Let's get out of here.'

'No, I promise you. Just a few shots and they won't

be back 'til tomorrow.' He cocked the gun, awkwardly. 'We'll have plenty of time.'

He waved me away and I crouched down on the embankment behind him. He stood with the gun poised, waiting for the lorry to come closer.

'Nobody wants to get hurt,' he said, snuggling the butt of the gun into his shoulder. 'You watch. I'll fire at them and they'll run away. Then they'll call their mercenaries or their airplanes to come and bomb us. But by then it'll be too late.'

'Don't let them get too close.'

'I want to give them a real fright.'

I could see the lorry clearly now, about a quarter of a mile off. It was opened-topped and looked to be full of men. I saw Amilcar take careful aim and squeeze the trigger. Nothing happened. Safety-catch, I thought. Jesus. He fiddled with the gun and took aim again.

He fired a long burst. Then he fired a quick sequence of short bursts afterwards. The brass cartridges tinkled prettily on the tarmac as the echoes of the shots dispersed across the marsh.

The lorry had stopped abruptly. I heard the sound of confused shouting. Amilcar lay down beside me.

'Watch,' he said.

The lorry began to back away rapidly swerving from side to side. Amilcar took aim and fired again from the prone position. I stuck my fingers in my ears.

In the silence that followed, I heard the frantic tearing of gears as the lorry did a three-point turn. Now the men in the lorry started firing themselves. Far out in the marsh a long spray of bullets churned up water. The lorry finally negotiated its turn, and I heard the engine rev as it accelerated off. There was a manic crackling and popping of gunfire as it retreated, like fat on a skillet. No bullets came near us.

Amilcar stood up and emptied his magazine after them. He let his gun drop and gave a disgusted laugh. The sound of firing diminished.

'Why can't we win this war?' he asked. 'It's so easy.'

I did not hear or see him hit. One of the dozens of aimlessly fired bullets found its target. I was rising to my feet and saw the exit wound form, a sudden spit of blood in the middle of his back, like a fist-sized bolus of phlegm, a tussock of minced flesh suddenly sprouting.

He fell sideways, doubled up, and lay there, one arm weakly paddling like a baby waving.

I scrambled over to him. The fall had knocked his spectacles half off his face. His eyes were tightly closed. His top lip was clamped hard between his teeth. He was making strange, grunting, talking noises in his throat, like a guttural dialect of Chinese.

I took his spectacles off. I felt completely, entirely helpless.

'What should I do, Amilcar?' I said, feebly. 'What should I do?'

I saw his black face lose its sheen, go opaque like drying paint. He opened his eyes and I saw them bulge.

'Don't let them catch you,' he said with a huge effort.

'I'm not talking about me,' I said desperately. 'I'm talking about *you*!'

But he couldn't speak any more. About three minutes later, he died.

I left his body there and strode back to the village. I felt light-headed, absurdly fit, as if I were being blown along by a stiff, following breeze. I forced myself to sit down when I reached the gun pit. I was quivering with huge reserves of energy suddenly unleashed, as if there had been hidden stockpiles of adrenalin in my body, now bequeathed me to do with whatever I wanted. Run twenty miles, demolish the village with my bare hands, chop down a forest of trees.

I sat on the sandbagged wall by the elegant gun for over an hour, debating what to do. Two possible courses of action dominated my thoughts during this period. The first was Amilcar's body: what to do with it? I knew how unhappy he would be to be left out there by the road to bake in the sun. I wondered if I had the strength to dig a grave for him or whether I should simply set him on fire. The second was whether to try and finish what he had accomplished. If I could detonate the mines and blow up the causeway I knew that would have made him happy.

I sat and thought, and in the end could bring myself to do neither. I did the sensible thing.

I made a thorough search through the abandoned stores and weaponry, looking for something white. Eventually I found an empty crate, about twice the size of a tea chest, that was lined with a coarse greyish cream calico. I ripped it away to reveal foil beneath. I could not imagine what the chest had contained.

I went into the bush with a machete and cut two long poles and with my squares of calico fashioned two white flags. I took one to the gun pit and wedged the pole in the sandbags. There was no wind and the flag hung inert. But it was unmistakably a flag of truce, I told myself, quite unambiguously so.

I glanced up the causeway but I was glad to note that

the heat haze made it impossible for me to see Amilcar's body by the roadside. I walked a few paces out towards him but I found I could go no further.

What could I do for him now? I couldn't set him on fire. I had no kerosene or petrol. I couldn't simply set a match to his new uniform and hope that would do the job. Bury him, a voice spoke in my head. Could I take a spade and scrape a grave for him, roll him in and shovel the dirt back on his body? Tip him in the marsh . . .? I turned away, angry at my impotence, frustrated with my lack of ingenuity.

I took my second flag and returned to the centre of the village. I dragged a couple of empty wooden crates into the middle of the road and erected my flag above them. I rigged up a poncho to cast some shade and crawled into one of the crates to wait.

I waited all day. Fatalistically, patiently, deliberately not thinking too far beyond the present moment. I had a clear view down the littered road. The entrance to the causeway was obscured by a bend but I could see the barrel of the gun in the gun pit and the askew pole of my flag of truce.

About mid-afternoon I heard a short burst of firing in the distance and then silence. As the afternoon advanced, a dry breeze sprang up that caused the flag above my head to flap and crack bravely. That made me feel better. I could just see the calico square at the gun pit similarly vigorous. Surely, I reasoned, every army knew the significance of a white flag. I was a prisoner of UNAMO waiting to be rescued.

I saw them coming at dusk, half a dozen figures slipping professionally from house to bush, from door-way to compound wall. I crawled out from my crate and poncho shelter and stood up holding both hands high above my head.

'Help!' I yelled as loudly as I could. 'Help me! I'm a prisoner!'

Silence. I could not see any of them. For a second, I wondered if I had been hallucinating. I called again, my voice cracking into a scream. I turned and seized my flag, waving it to and fro.

'Help me. Help me. I'm a prisoner!'

Then I saw someone move. And another one. I felt a warm flood of relief in my guts as I realized I hadn't been imagining my rescuers. As they scampered closer, still moving from cover to cover, I kept shouting, reassuring them. It's not a trick, I called, there's no one else here. Just me. I'm a prisoner. Help me.

Eventually they emerged from doorways, from behind walls, and walked towards me, guns levelled. There were five of them. The bulk of their packs and webbing made them seem bigger, their helmets round black silhouettes against the dusty amber light of the setting sun. I held my white flag rigid above my head, shoulder muscles aching with the effort.

As they came closer I looked at their faces – dirty, sweaty, bearded, two of them were unmistakably white.

They stared at me, fascinated.

'T'as raison, coco,' one said, in a strong Belgian accent. *'C'est une gonzesse.'*

THREE QUESTIONS

My hair needs cutting . . . The dogs have come back to the beach . . . Water is made from two gases . . . I should buy

344

a new fridge ... nothing in evolutionary thinking can explain consciousness ... Gunther has asked me to visit him in Munich ...

Hope's head is full of such darting, random notions and observations as she sits on her deck with a cold beer and watches the sun set.

She sees her night-watchman arrive and waves to him. He is an old man, greybearded, who guards her house with a flashlight, a bow and three barbed arrows. He hauls out his wooden seat from beneath the deck and sits down to begin his vigil.

She flaps her hands at a whining mosquito and drinks a mouthful of her sour beer. Another subject insinuates its way into her mind. 'There are only three questions ...' Who said that? Some philosopher ... There are three questions, this philosopher said, that every human being everywhere, at any time, of any creed or colour wants the answer to. (Kant? Hope thinks ... Aristotle? Schopenhauer?) Anyway, she remembers the questions now. They are:

What can I know?

What ought I to do?

What may I hope for?

All the world's religions, philosophies, cults and ideologies, this philosopher claimed, have attempted to find the answers to these questions.

When Hope told John about them, he laughed. He said the answers were easy; he could save the philosophers and the suffering mass of humankind a lot of unnecessary grief. He wrote the answers down immediately on a piece of paper.

Hope was irritated by his arrogance. He was reacting as if this were a party trick that he had seen performed before. All the same, she kept the piece of paper he scribbled on. It is creased and soft from being carried

345

*around and handled so often; it feels more like a piece of
fine material or a scrap of soft suede, but you can still
read John's tiny, jagged handwriting. He wrote:*

What can I know? Nothing for sure.

What ought I to do? Try not to hurt anyone.

*What may I hope for? For the best (but it won't make
any difference).*

There, he said, that's that sorted out.

Hope Clearwater stood on the platform at Exeter station
waiting for John to descend from the London train. At
first she could not see him amongst the crowds of
passengers, but eventually she saw him step down from
the first-class carriage at the far end. First class, she
thought, I don't believe it. She went forward to meet
him. He was carrying a heavy case that made him cant
his body over severely to counterbalance it, and its
weight made him walk in a quick, shuffling manner that
under any other circumstances she might have found
amusing. What the hell has he got in there, she thought?

'Books,' he said, answering her unvoiced question.
'Sorry.'

She kissed his face. 'Don't be silly,' she said. 'You
bring what you like.'

He looked pale, and thinner. But not too bad, considering.

On the drive to East Knap he did not have much to
say, passing most of the journey looking out of the
window at the landscape. It was a cold clear day; the
heavy frost from the night before still lay on the ground
and on the hedges. There was no wind and the trees, the
elms and the beeches, stood stark and still.

'God, I love winter,' John said suddenly.

She looked at him. 'So how could you live in California?'

'Exactly,' he said, fiercely. 'Exactly. I wish I had never gone. I wasted so much time.' He shook his head at some memory. 'If only I'd stayed on here, you know ... I wouldn't have got caught up in that game-theory crap.'

'Come on, John. It makes no sense, looking back that way. We can all do that.'

'There's no getting away from it,' he said, his voice full of self-disgust. 'Game theory: a very Californian thing to do.'

There seemed no adequate response to his vehemence, so Hope drove on in silence. Then, after a while, when it was becoming oppressive, she started to list the improvements she had made to the cottage.

'Can we see the sea?' he said, abruptly.

'Well, yes ... Now?'

'Please. If you don't mind.'

She forked right and drove along the deep lanes until she came to a convenient stile.

They climbed over and walked up the slope of the downs through clumps of gorse and whin. Here there was wind, whipping cold off the Channel, and Hope retied her scarf over her ears. They reached the top of the gentle rise and there was the sea, lead-grey and choppy. The weak sun hung low, casting long shadows. They had about another twenty minutes of daylight, she reckoned.

'Aren't you cold, Johnny?'

He had a raincoat on and no scarf. He stared out at the sea, not answering. She looked at his thrusting sharp face, lit by the lemony rays, the keen wind making his eyes water, his hands shoved deep in his pockets.

'God, I've missed this,' he said. 'I've got to live near water. A river or a sea. I have to.'

'You old pseud.'

He turned to look at her, not responding to her joke. 'No, I have to, Hope. It calms me. It's something I feel, very deeply.'

'Come on, let's get back to the car. Bloody freezing.'

'Just another minute or two.'

After a while he said: 'You know that lake you mentioned?'

'Yes.'

'I still can't remember a lake. No memory of it at all.'

'It's still there. I'll show it to you later.'

'Funny, that.' He shook his head. 'You sure I used to know it?'

'You used to say it was your favourite place.'

'Funny, that.'

Hope paced up and down, stamping. Then she hunched her coat over her head as a windbreak and lit a cigarette. John stood quite still, gazing at the water, taking deep breaths, seemingly heedless of the cold.

She went back to the car alone, and switched on the engine, the heater and the radio. He returned ten minutes later, cold radiating from his body like a force field. He was shivering slightly by now, and looked pinched and ill. Hope was too angry to speak, and they drove back to the cottage in silence.

In the cottage she made some tea and ordered herself to be more reasonable and understanding. All her fine resolve disappeared when she emerged from the kitchen to discover John unpacking his suitcase in the sitting-room and stacking the dozens of books he had brought with him on top of hers, overloading the small oak bookcase she had bought, she remembered, from a little shop in West Lulworth. She remembered the name of it, for some reason, as she stood watching him, mugs steaming in her hands. *Antique bric-à-brac*, that was it, *Sam M. Godforth. prop.* A nice oxymoron.

By concentrating on such details she managed to calm down, and accepted John's compliments on her improvements to the cottage with something approaching good grace.

Then she said, more sharply than she had intended: 'Where were you planning to sleep?'

He looked lost for moment, blank. 'Oh God,' he rubbed his forehead. 'I forgot. I hadn't ... I suppose I just assumed we —'

'You can have the bed. I'll have the sofa,' she said, thinking: why am I being so foul? and getting no reply.

'No, no,' he said. 'That's not fair. I'm on the sofa.'

'John. No. please. You're recuperating. I have to get up early. It won't be for long.'

Another shadow crossed his face. He sat down slowly in an armchair.

'How long were you planning to stay?' she asked, in a quieter voice. 'Would you like to stay?' she added.

'I hadn't thought.'

'John —' She caught herself in time. 'We're meant to be separated. We're not married any more. Properly.' She felt almost tearful with frustrated anger. 'It was your idea to split, for Christ's sake.'

He looked desperate, shifting uncomfortably in his seat.

'But that's just it,' he said. 'I made a mistake, a terrible mistake. I don't want ... I don't want us to be separated, Hope. Ever. Ever again,' he went on, before she could interrupt. 'I see now, thanks to my treatment, that it's you I . . .' He lost his way. He emphasized his final words with flat swipes of his hand. 'I should never have broken us up.'

'Let's drop it,' she said, more gently, making an effort. 'There's plenty of time. We can talk about it later.' She closed his almost empty suitcase and picked it up. 'I'll pop this upstairs. Then we'll go to the pub, get something to eat.'

The pub – the Lamb and Flag in Chaldon Keynes – was a mistake, as far as Hope was concerned, and made her feel in even more of a bad mood. The beery atmosphere, the inane chatter, the pinging and bubbling of the gambling games, she found profoundly irksome. She ate half a baked potato filled with creamed tuna and sweetcorn, and drank a mouthful of a glass of tannic red wine that set her teeth immediately on edge, and whose surface was covered with a fine dust of cork fragments.

John seemed to respond to the place and its young, overweight patrons more favourably, consuming three pints of beer and something called a 'Darzet Pastie'. He happily watched two men playing pool for half an hour.

On the drive back he was animated, and talked lucidly about his treatment. He confessed that he did not know if it had actually helped him or not; it was important instead, he said, as a kind of emotional watershed in his life. He would have had to go through the breakdown, depression and recovery anyway, he reasoned, and it would have been, in his words, a rough passage. But because that process was marked by the electric shocks it imposed a time-scale and structure on him. His treatment and recovery had a beginning, middle and end – a strict duration. And that, he decided, was what had been important, and that was how ECT had helped him, no matter what the actual effect the electrical charges had had on his brain cells. He had been through it, and it was now over, and the simple knowledge that there were no more shocks to come gave him the strong sensation of having passed through something. He had navigated his rough passage, and now he was on the other side he was ready to begin again.

He looked over at her and smiled.

'I know I'm better,' he said, 'I know I'm fundamentally all right again because I was able to take the news without flinching. Before the shocks, you see, it would have killed me, I'm sure.'

Hope glanced at him for a second. The night was icy and she was driving with pronounced care. She could practically feel the frost gathering around the car – the heater was on full blast and the windows were fogged with condensation – she felt she was driving through thin solid shards of cold, as if the passage of the car was marked by a cloud, a silver dust of ice particles.

'What news?' she said.

He rubbed his hands together, like a surgeon washing before an operation.

'Do you remember,' he said, 'when you came to see me, just after I'd moved out?'

'A Sunday.'

'Yes. And I said that the work was going well, that I was very close to breaking through? That I had worked out this set?'

'The Clearwater Set.'

His laugh was dry. 'Well, I was beaten to it. Someone got there first.'

He wrote a formula in the condensation of the car window:

$$Z \rightarrow Z^2 + c.$$

'Unreal,' he said. 'Dazzling. But someone else thought it up.'

You know it means nothing to me.'

'It's *so* simple. And that's why it's beautiful. If you knew, if you just knew what you could achieve with that. If you knew what it implied . . .'

$$Z \rightarrow Z^2 + c.$$

She looked at the innocuous figures, bleeding now, mysterious and unknowable. For the first time in ages she felt that old envy of him.

'You see how much better I am,' he laughed, not quite so convincingly. 'I can look at that' – he rubbed it out with a swipe of his fist – 'and not burst into tears.'

FERMAT'S LAST THEOREM II

Outside, I see a herd of cattle on the beach. Thirty big white cows with preposterous horns and humps. Looping pleats of skin, like an old man's wattles, hang at their necks. The herdsman, a tall thin boy from the north, gazes in frank admiration at the ocean. Perhaps this is the first time he has seen it, his whole horizon full of heaving water?

He advances cautiously to the final fizzing ruff of a wave and wets his hand. He tastes it. Spits out salt.

I turn back to my work.

Diligently, ploddingly, with my fat dictionary by my side, I am translating a letter from French into English for Gunther. It is from the manager of an aluminium smelting plant in Morocco.

Something nudges and elbows its way into my mind.

We have been here before, I know, but we might be getting somewhere.

Is Fermat's Last Theorem True? It might be, we decided. Let us say it is true, but incapable of proof. Perhaps there is a small collection of statements which are true, and not solely in the world of mathematics, which are true, but which cannot be proved by any of our recognizable proof procedures? If so, where does that leave us . . .?

I can't prove it, but I know that it is true. There are times when a remark like that appears entirely reasonable to me.

If I say to that boy, the cattle herder, on the beach that the waves on this beach will roll in until the end of time, and he says: prove it – would I be obliged to? Would any efforts I made to come up with an acceptable proof procedure matter, in this particular case?

I think about it and watch the cows sway and shift impatiently. There is nothing to eat on the beach.

It seems to me that there are statements about the world and our lives that have no need of formal proof procedures.

I return to my letter and the price of bauxite.

I used to wonder – occasionally – if I could justifiably describe myself as either an optimist or a pessimist. Whatever response I came up with always depended on my mood. If I was feeling clever, I would consider myself a pessimist, and a proud one at that, no matter how fortunate I had recently been. It was only in my

353

stupid moods that I felt optimistic. The more stupid I was, the more I assumed that events would unfold favourably for me. I now see that there was an error in these neat categorizations: from time to time my cleverness disguised just how stupid I was being.

I think I must have been in one of those phases during the nine days of our capture by Amilcar. I lived in a hazy, thoughtless limbo, existing on blind instinct, trusting to luck, powered by reserves of energy I never knew I possessed. In other words: a classic optimist. When the soldiers surrounded me in that village at the end of the causeway, it all gave way suddenly. I collapsed. I passed out. I had been sitting in the hot sun all day, I had not eaten for twenty-four hours, and I was existing at the screaming pitch of my frazzled, traumatized nerves.

They told me later, the soldiers, that they had almost shot me out of pity. I'm sure they were joking, but from their point of view, they said, all they could see was a filthy dishevelled person waving a flag and screaming what they assumed were insults at them.

The two white men were Belgian mercenaries. They were unusually solicitous because behind them with the main unit of the Federal Army my real saviour was waiting, a man called Mr Doblin, an officious second secretary from the Norwegian consulate (the Norwegians were responsible for the interests of British subjects in the country, there being no British *chargé d'affaires*). Mallabar had helped too. There was a $5000 reward for anyone who rescued us.

Half of this had already been claimed by a lucky staff captain. Ian had evaded his pursuers comparatively easily. He had hidden up for the rest of the night and most of the next day before making his way back to the mission school to discover it had been taken over as a Federal Army battalion HQ.

I learnt all this from Mr Doblin. By the time I had been driven to the nearest airstrip and flown south to the city, Ian was already back at Grosso Arvore, reunited with Roberta. Mr Doblin was in his twenties, possibly younger than me. He was dark and overweight and in an almost continually pent-up mood of exhilaration over his part in our successful rescue. He complimented me on my composure. Mr Vail, he said, had been in very bad shape.

'I think he was absolutely convinced you were dead,' he confided. 'We have to tell him you are safe at once.' I agreed. I left it to Mr Doblin to communicate the good news to Grosso Arvore.

We flew south in a small, high-winged transport plane with fixed, splayed wheels – a Beaver or a Bulldog or some such name – accompanied by eight surly wounded soldiers from the Federal Army who had been unceremoniously loaded on board like so many rolls of carpet. I asked Mr Doblin why they were so fractious and why nobody on board bothered to tend to them.

'They are self-wictims,' he said. 'They all shot themselves,' he told me, in a soft discreet voice, just audible above the noise of the engines. 'They are flying home to their execution.'

In an hour or so the plane banked over the town. I looked out of the window at the clustered spread of tin roofs, like a massive cubist collage, all greys and browns. I watched the ground approach and more details emerge as the plane, following the giant sweep of the river, slowly descended to the airport.

We touched down, and as we taxied we passed the line of Migs parked on their apron. I thought at once of Usman, but I did not experience quite the same jolt of anticipation I expected. I was still tired and numbed by my ordeal, I decided.

We were not dropped at the airport buildings, but taxied round to a wooden hut on the airport perimeter, where the wounded men were delivered over to the airport police. Mr Doblin and I were obliged to tramp back through the afternoon heat to the arrivals hall. It was only when I stepped inside, and saw a kiosk selling beer, soft drinks and magazines, that I realized that I had nothing: no passport, no money, no possessions other than the clothes I was wearing.

Mr Doblin reassured me. A British passport would be provided very shortly. In the meantime he gave me a generous amount of money for which I had to sign an official-looking receipt. He told me a room had been booked at the Airport Hotel and all the necessary authorities had been informed of my rescue. There was talk of some British journalists flying out to interview me, but he doubted they would be issued visas.

'Stay at the hotel for a few days,' he advised kindly. 'Wait for your documentation. Relax, eat, swim, enjoy.' He covered his mouth with a hand and mumbled conspiratorially, 'The British Gowernment will be sent the bill.' He saw me into a taxi and said he would call at the hotel in a couple of days. It was clear to me that he had not had such fun in ages.

Nothing had changed at the hotel. There was no reason on earth why it should have, but I was vaguely disappointed. When you yourself have suffered considerably, it is hard to cope with the rest of the world's indifference to your experience, and upsetting to see how unmarked it is. You cannot understand its relentless preoccupation with the mundane.

I collected the key to my room. I had cleaned myself up a little since my rescue but I needed a bath and some new clothes. But now I wanted to see Usman.

I walked through the hotel gardens, and along the concrete pathways towards his bungalow with a new feeling of benign resignation beginning to suffuse me. Mr Doblin was right: I needed a few days of total, selfish inactivity.

I knocked on Usman's door but there was no reply. I peered through the window and saw his clothes and possessions were still there. Surprises never work for me: the people were never there; the hidden presents were discovered prematurely; the accomplices spoke out of turn; the flowers were delivered to the wrong address. I thought I would leave him a note in any event. 'Guess who?' I would write and leave my room number; that would at least be a low-order surprise.

An obliging chambermaid opened his door for me. I entered. I smelt his smell. The room was dark and I crossed to the desk to switch on the lamp. As I did so I trod on something that gave with a small satisfying crunch – like standing on stubble in a field, or on a walnut shell. I stepped back and trod on something similar. I returned to the door and switched on the ceiling light.

On the floor were half a dozen of Usman's tiny horse-fly aeroplanes. Two had been crushed – pulverized absolutely – by me. The other four lay where they had fallen. I picked one up. The horse-fly was desiccated, a husk, its legs bent, clenched. I picked up the others and laid them carefully on Usman's desk. There was no point in leaving a note.

At the airport I waited in an empty room at the gate-house. There was stricter security than there used to be – no one was allowed near the hangar where the Migs were parked. Something had changed, at any rate.

I waited for nearly an hour, and smoked three cigarettes, before someone arrived. Eventually, an immaculate air force officer came to see me. He had pale brown skin and his eyes were small and deep-set. I told him I was a close friend of Usman Shoukry and I wondered where he was. The officer informed me immediately and matter-of-factly: Usman Shoukry did not return from a mission.

I suppose it was news I was expecting, but, for some reason, I blushed. My eyeballs felt hot in their sockets.

'What happened?'

He shrugged. 'A navaid failure, I believe.'

'Navaid.' I remembered what Usman had told me: your ground crew is your greatest enemy.

'Can I talk to the other pilots?' I asked. I tried to remember their names.

'There are no other pilots.' His face slowly formed an expression of vague disconsolateness, then brightened. 'Can you borrow me a cigarette?'

'Of course.' I handed him the pack, he selected one and passed it back to me. We both lit up. 'Where are the other pilots?' I asked.

'All the other pilots left, after Usman Shoukry never returned.' He looked serious. 'Too many navaid failures, they said.' He spread his hands. 'You see, we have yet to lose an aircraft to enemy fire. And yet we have lost seven, no eight, to navaid failures. And other misfortunes.'

'What do you mean?'

'One aircraft was stolen. Two others were damaged in a parking accident.'

I exhaled and looked around. I was beginning to feel weak again.

'A navaid failure ... Could he have crash-landed somewhere?'

'I suppose so.' He paused and thought. 'In theory.' He picked a shred of tobacco off his tongue and looked unfavourably at the burning tip of his cigarette.

'Is this American?'

'No. Tusker.'

'What's that?'

'It's a local brand. Don't you know it?'

'I only smoke foreign brands ... Do you like it?'

'Yes.'

'My God.'

'Have you any idea where his plane might have come down?'

'No. He was far in the north, on the UNAMO front.'

'Ah.'

'Nobody saw him.' He thought again. 'He may have crash-landed, but we have no aircraft for a search.' He smiled regretfully at me, then, seeing my sad face, said, 'Who can say? Maybe he will make his own way home. One day.'

TWO KINDS OF CATASTROPHE

Catastrophe theory is the one we have been waiting for, the study of abrupt change, the catalogue of discontinuity.

It tells that all the myriad disasters, downfalls, cataclysms and calamities, great and small, from the unbearably tragic to the mildly irritating, derive from seven basic archetypes of catastrophe.

There are seven types of catastrophe. All forms of abrupt, non-continuous change will be covered by one or other of these archetypes. They are known as Fold, Cusp, Swallowtail and Butterfly Catastrophes. There are three varieties of swallowtail, two of butterfly. But the two we are interested in are fold and cusp catastrophes: they are far and away the most common.

Take one easy example of abrupt change in the world – the popping of a balloon. When a balloon bursts there is no way it can be unburst, as it were. The fold catastrophe is like this, conditioned by a single factor. It is the most simple paradigm of change. The balloon bursts, the catastrophe has occurred. There is no going back.

Life is a fold catastrophe, and its single control factor is time. The catastrophe takes place when time stops. In the language of catastrophe theory, our life follows the same mathematical pattern as the inflating and bursting of a balloon. Fold catastrophes cannot be reversed.

Cusp catastrophes are different. In a cusp catastrophe there is always the chance of recovery, a possibility of return to the pre-catastrophic state. Being knocked unconscious would qualify as a cusp catastrophe, so would a nervous breakdown or an epileptic fit, or boiling a kettle of water.

Take a look at anyone's life. Take a look at your own. In the long fold catastrophe that makes up your three score years and ten you will encounter many cusp catastrophes along the way.

Hope slept badly on the sofa. Before dawn she managed an hour or two of sounder sleep, but when she woke she felt unsettled and had a persistent dull ache in the small of her back. She drank strong tea and ate a thick slice of toast and Marmite in the kitchen, trying to stem the sensations of nervy irritability that made her feel oddly tense and jumpy. What was wrong with her? Perhaps it was merely the effects of waking with a sore back after a night of shallow, fitful sleep. Perhaps it was the thin drizzle falling outside that heralded a damp and uncomfortable day in the woods . . . Perhaps it was having her estranged husband at home again, sleeping upstairs in her warm bed.

She drove to Knap House along splashy lanes. The clouds were low, dense and formless, and the light that filtered through them was pale and unflattering. In her rearview mirror her face looked lumpy and bloodless. She parked her car in the courtyard of the stable block and tramped up the wooden steps to the project office.

'You feeling all right?' Munro asked, solicitously. 'Look a bit wan.'

'I didn't sleep very well. I –' she made her tone more brisk. 'I thought you should know that John's here again. Staying with me for a few days.'

'Oh. Good.' Munro's mild polite smile said: how is he?

'He's much better. I thought, you know, if he met up with those estate workers . . .'

'I'll make sure everyone knows.'

'He'll be going for walks, etcetera.'

The office was overheated and overlit. Hope felt a soporific wave wash over her. She wanted to lie down on the wooden floor and sleep.

'Have you thought about the job?' Munro asked, cautiously. 'I mean . . .' He did not elucidate what he meant: it was a coded, timid apology for his presumption in asking.

Hope had in fact hardly considered his offer at all, but she said at once, 'Yes. Yes, I have. I'd like to take it on.'

Munro's glee was touching.

'Wonderful,' he said. 'Well . . . well, that brightens up a dull day.' He went on with his genteel compliments, telling her how pleased he was, but Hope barely listened. Instead, she was asking herself why she had spontaneously committed herself to staying on at Knap right through the next summer. There was only one explanation.

She spent a few hours working doggedly in the sodden wood she was classifying. The rain had thickened and the whole world she moved in seemed a succession of variations on water: earth and water, trees and water, air and water. As the afternoon grew murkier she decided to head for home. She had paperwork to do there. Perhaps she would even have an early night. But then she remembered her bed was occupied.

She parked the car outside the cottage. Light glowed from all the windows and she could hear the noise of music from her gramophone. She walked round to the back door where she stripped off her heavy, wet parka and waterproof trousers and kicked off her rubber boots.

'Hi, I'm back,' she called, as cheerfully as she could manage.

The small kitchen was a shambles. Plates and sauce-pans were stacked in the sink. An open, empty tin of tuna-fish stood on the breadboard beside a crudely cut loaf.

The sitting-room was blurry with cigarette smoke. John sat at the table which was heaped with his books and papers. On one arm of the sofa was a balanced plate with a few shreds of pasta drying on it. A half-empty bottle of red wine stood at John's elbow. He rose to his feet when she came in and crossed the room to kiss her.

'You look freezing,' he said, sweeping a newspaper off an armchair, which he ran up to the fire. She sat down in it obediently, feeling her anger pinch her nostrils.

'Great day,' he said. 'Brilliant.'

'What?'

'Work. Like a house on fire. Glass of wine.'

'I thought you weren't meant to drink when you were taking that stuff. Lithium.'

'Glass or two won't hurt. Mmm?'

'Just a splash.' She took the glass from him.

'Yeah, brilliant,' he said again as if he could hardly believe himself.

'What're you doing?'

'Topology. Mainly. Tiling. Very interesting.'

'What . . . What did you do for lunch?'

'Whipped up my tuna, cheese and spaghetti thing. Finished the lot, I'm afraid. I was starving.'

Hope threw the last log in the basket on the fire. She sipped the wine, distastefully. She was not keen for it – it was the wrong time of day – but she thought it might help to calm her a little. She needed to banish all her selfish, petty irritations – the mess, the food, the coloniza-tion of her space – before she talked to him.

'I spoke to Munro today.'

'Who's he?'

She explained. She explained about the extension to her job, the new work required on the watermeadows and the downland.

'What did you say to him?' John asked.

'I said yes.'

He thought about it for a second, nodding. 'Fine. Good idea. I'd forgotten how much I liked it down here.'

'John, you don't understand!'

'Easy . . . Christ.' He looked hurt.

She sat down. 'You've got to go,' she said simply, flatly. 'You can't stay here.'

He looked at her. Now he had a bright, surprised expression on his face. She noticed that there were small deposits of dried saliva at the corners of his mouth, small sticky drifts at the junction of his lips. Lithium did that, she remembered.

'I'm sorry,' she said.

He spread his arms. 'Look, Hope, I understand,' he began. 'Don't worry. I was just . . .' He turned and gestured at the papers covering his desk. My desk, she corrected herself.

'I'm sorry, Johnny,' she said again. 'There's no point in being dishonest about it.'

'I'll get all this packed away.'

'Christ, there's no hurry. I just had to tell you, that's all. It had to be said. That was the problem. Stay on for a couple of days. Three. Whatever you feel like. We just have to know where we are.'

'I might – if you don't mind. Stay on. Just a day or so. I don't feel quite ready for London.'

'No problem.' She smiled. 'I just couldn't carry on just blandly assuming –'

'No. No, sure. You're right.' He forced a smile. 'I'm bloody sad.' He gave a short, dry laugh. 'But you're right.'

She stood up and came over to him. She put her hand on his shoulder and he leant his head against her forearm for a second or two. She refilled their glasses with wine. She felt a giant relief spread through her.

'Stay on for a couple of days,' she said. 'I'd like that. Take it easy.'

INVARIANTS AND HOMEOMORPHS

After a storm the beach has always changed slightly in some way – the sand washed away here to reveal the rocks beneath, then piled up in a swelling dune four hundred yards away. Once, on what had been a wide flat area, a small lagoon formed for a week or so, about sixty feet long behind a solid sandbar. Then came another high tide with a strong wind and the next morning it was gone. The geography of the beach is always changing, yet it always remains the same.

When I asked John why he had moved from turbulence to topology he told me that it was because he was tired of change, and wanted now to study concepts of permanence. He wanted to look at what remained constant in an object, regardless of the force or scale of its transformation. When something is bent, stretched, or twisted, he said, certain features of it resist deformation. He wanted to investigate these unchanging features. He told me the name that was given to them: topological invariants.

Throw a pebble in a pond and watch the ripples spread. To most people the widening circles would represent change. But to a topologist, John said, a widening circle is a symbol of constancy. A circle is a closed curve; that is its topological invariant, no matter how it grows or shrinks. I want to look at things that endure, he said, even though everything else about them is changing.

The beach endures, I think as I wander along its length, as well as changing all the time. What is its invariant . . .? In the palm groves I see two old women from the village gathering fallen coconuts.

In topology, objects that have the same invariants are regarded as equivalent, no matter how different they may appear when looked at. The crumpled disc of a deflated football has the same invariants as an inflated one, even though they look and perform quite differently. Objects that possess this equivalence are known as homeomorphs.

I stroll up into the palm grove and greet the old women. They return my greeting. Here we are, I think three homeomorphs . . . Yes, it seems to me we share the same invariants. The differences between us are superficial. The women smile modestly at me as I say goodbye and continue on my way, then they stoop and begin to gather their windfalls again.

I sat patiently in my room waiting for reception to call and tell me that Hauser had arrived. I had received a message from Grosso Arvore: Hauser was coming to collect me and drive me back to the camp so that the 'terms of my contract could be discussed'. I was not at all sure what this meant or implied and not very keen, either, to return; but I knew it could not be postponed indefinitely; I had to go back if only to collect my few possessions.

There was a knock at the door. It was one of the assistant managers, a young Ghanaian called Kwame. He informed me that the hotel were clearing out Mr Shoukry's room, and the manager wondered if there was anything I might like to keep as a memento. I was surprised at such thoughtfulness. As we left the room the phone rang: Hauser was waiting in the lobby. He could wait a little longer.

I stood in Usman's sitting-room looking about me, feeling a little uncertain and troubled. Kwame waited discreetly at the door and behind him stood a couple of chambermaids with cardboard boxes and plastic bags.

I went to the desk and opened a drawer. I saw Usman's passport, some documents, some loose change. Nothing for me here. In the bedroom I opened the cupboard. His few clothes hung above four pairs of shoes. I felt strangely panicked. I knew I should take something, that I'd regret it later if I missed this opportunity. But what? I slid the hangers to one side. Did I want that linen jacket? Those ties ...? A sudden sensation of nausea overcame me. The whole idea of a memento – a 'thing' – as substitute for Usman seemed a gross indignity. I pushed another hanger: his official air force uniform, issued to all the pilots, which they never wore. On the shelf above, I saw his peaked cap still in its plastic wrapping and beside it the stiff glossy leather of his belt. The belt? Something useful, at least, that I could wear. I reached up and took it down.

Clipped to the side of the belt was a neat brown holster. The leather was moulded into the shape of a stylized kidney. I unclipped the flap. The holster held his small, compact Italian automatic pistol. I took it out and weighed it in my hand.

I thought, with a sudden wrenching inside me, of Usman, in his swimming-shorts, that day at the airport, showing me his plane so proudly.

His good luck charm, he had said. Why hadn't he taken it with him? I thought, angry now.

My fingers traced his initials on the butt.

I knew at once this was what I wanted to keep. I slid it into my pocket and walked back to the sitting-room. It was a foolish thing to do, I told myself, but I had wanted it, the impulse to take it had been powerful. It was the only object in the entire bungalow that brought an image of Usman Shoukry back to me. But I continued my search of the room, however, for form's sake.

Opening a cupboard in the sitting-room I came across a cardboard box full of the equipment Usman used for the construction of his horse-fly aeroplanes: scalpels and razor blades, a fly-tier's vice, slivers of matchwood and balsa, the almost weightless, transparent tissue paper. That sent me back to the desk again and in a bottom drawer I found a thin file full of delicate drawings of his prototypes. I told Kwame this was what I wanted. As I left the room the chambermaids sidled meekly in.

'You do look well,' Hauser said again. 'No, really well. I mean, you'd never believe . . .'

'I feel fine. I'm well rested. Nothing terribly dramatic happened.'

We had been driving for over an hour. Hauser, to my surprise, had kissed me on both cheeks when we finally met up in the lobby of the hotel. He had looked pleased to see me and was full of compliments. We had conversed carefully at first, diplomatically avoiding contentious subjects, but I could sense the questions massing eagerly in his head. I decided to confront a few of them.

'How's Eugene?' I asked, disingenuously.

'Ah,' Hauser began, his glee almost shamefully evident. He collected himself and made his face solemn. 'Good point. Not very well. No, he hasn't been well. Since you left. We've seen very little of him.' He glanced at me. 'Ginga's been more or less running things. I think Eugene,' he paused, choosing his words, 'has had something of a, a nervous collapse. Nervous exhaustion, Ginga says.'

'Well. That's reasonable, I suppose.'

'What happened?'

'When?'

'That day you left. What went on, Hope? Come on,' he smiled at me. 'You can tell Anton, surely.'

'Well . . . I'm not so sure.'

'Everything's changed. The book's postponed. The feeding area's been closed down. What did you do to him?'

'We had an argument.'

Hauser looked at me sceptically, and saw I was going to say nothing more for a while. He carried on talking.

'Of course the whole place has been in uproar since you were . . . taken. Now that you're safe, and Ian's back, we're almost back to normal. But it's been odd.'

'How's Ian?'

Hauser grimaced sympathetically. 'He's been trying not to show it but I think he was, you know, traumatized. Poor boy.' He glanced at me again. 'I mean compared to you he definitely *is* traumatized.'

369

'Appearances can be misleading.'

Hauser laughed. His laugh was high and staccato. 'No, no, Hope,' he said. 'No, no. You're made of sterner stuff.'

His amusement was annoyingly contagious, and I found myself smiling back at him. Why had I disliked Hauser so, all these months? The tyranny of first impressions, I supposed. But then I thought back to the incident of the half-eaten baby chimp. I should be more cautious.

'Why have they closed the feeding area?' I asked.

'You're kidding?'

'What?'

'They must have told you. The war. The chimpanzee wars they're calling them. The northern chimps – they've been systematically killing the southerners.' He looked for my reaction. 'You do know.'

'I discovered it.'

There was a long pause. Hauser ducked his head, as if apologizing.

'Eugene discovered it,' he said.

'No.'

'That's why the book is being rewritten.'

'I discovered it. That's why I had to leave.'

'Look, we all know it was during those days he was out in the field with you. But,' he paused and then said slowly, 'Eugene was the one who realized what was going on . . .'

'I'd been telling him about it for weeks.'

Hauser frowned. 'That's not the way – how can I tell you? – that events are being presented at the camp.'

I felt a tightening in my head, as if a belt were being cinched around my skull. 'Jesus Christ.'

'I'll be honest. Everyone assumes Eugene had made . . . made some sort of sexual advance to you.'

'For God's sake!'

'We don't know anything. We see you run off. Eugene effectively disappears. Ginga takes control. You know . . .'

'Well, you assumed completely wrong.'

'I'm sorry. I'm pleased to hear it.'

'Ask Ian. He'll tell you. I spotted this weeks ago. Mallabar wouldn't listen.' I looked at Hauser. 'Hasn't Ian said anything?'

'Well, no . . . He's not really been working.'

'Good old Ian.'

I turned on Hauser with some of my old hostility.

'Anyway, you should know, too. Incinerating that baby chimp.'

'Baboon . . . No, Hope, I swear. It *was* a baboon. We were both wrong.'

I looked out of the window at the passing scrubland. A nice irony. A sense of frustration was building inside me that was making my shoulders hunch and my scalp crawl.

'Anyway,' Hauser said, his voice placatory, 'it'll be great to have you back. We've got two new researchers, but we still miss you, Hope. Really.'

The last thing you learn about yourself is your effect. I turned to him. 'Unfortunately I don't think I'll be staying long, somehow.'

It was unsettling to be back at Grosso Arvore: the place appeared to me simultaneously familiar and strange. We arrived at dusk. The blurry glow of the hurricane lamps shone from the canteen. We went straight in to eat, and Hauser introduced me to the two new researchers – young men, Americans, from Stanford University – who were living in my rebuilt tent-hut. I ate my meal quickly and then went to the census hut to pack up my few possessions. There had been no sign of Eugene and Ginga Mallabar, nor of Ian and Roberta Vail.

I sat on my bed in the long gloomy room thinking about the low-key, not to say non-existent, welcome I had received. Only Hauser and Toshiro had seemed pleased to see me. More beds had been moved into the hut since I had last been here, and the framework of a partition had been erected that would eventually divide the room. Good times were returning to Grosso Arvore, that much was clear.

I sat on my bed and allowed my swiftly alternating moods to dominate me, unchecked. I felt by turns apathetic, sullen, hard-done-by, bitter, frustrated, baffled, hurt and, finally, contemptuous and independent. Mallabar, 'nervous exhaustion' or no, was evidently trying to initiate some sort of damage limitation programme, to incorporate my discoveries about the chimpanzees into his *magnum opus* before it was too late. I began to regret my hasty note informing him of my own publishing plans.

There was a quiet knock at my door. Ian Vail, I thought, as I went to answer it, and about time too. But it was Ginga. She embraced me, enquired about my health and state of mind and complimented me on my fresh and calm demeanour.

She was wearing jeans and a dark blue cotton shirt. Her hair was held back from her seamed, sharp face by a velvet band. She looked fresh and calm herself, I thought.

'How's Eugene?' I asked.

She paused before she answered, looking down at the floor.

'He never told me what happened that day,' she said.

'He tried to kill me.' I paused. 'I think.'

Ginga looked away, with an abrupt jerk. She put both hands to her forehead and smoothed it. 'I can't believe that,' she said.

'He went mad, sort of. He hit me. Violently. If I hadn't run away . . .'

Now she was looking fiercely at me again, as if gathering reserves of energy and determination within her. Then she said, in a quiet voice, 'You must understand what this has done to him, Hope, the killings. The attacks, you must try.'

'Look, I *told* him. He didn't want to hear about it. I wasn't trying to . . . outsmart him, or anything.'

'I know, I know. But that didn't make it any less hard on him. And the fact that someone like you – I mean, a new arrival should . . .' She made a flicking gesture with one hand. 'Should turn everything upside down.'

'I suppose . . .' I checked my spontaneous British reasonableness. No lifelines were going to be offered here.

'He's not well,' Ginga went on. 'Very depressed. It's difficult.'

'I'm sorry,' I said. 'Can I see him?'

Ginga looked suddenly ashamed, all her poise and cool capability gone. I had never seen this emotion on her features before; it looked absurd, wholly out of character, like a false moustache or a clown's red nose.

'He won't see you,' she said. 'He refuses.'

'Oh, great . . . So where does that leave me?'

Ginga's composure had returned. 'Well, you understand . . . It's impossible to work on here, my dear.'

I closed my eyes for a second or two, then stood up and wandered round the room, behaving as if I had some choice in the matter, as if this was a decision that had to be mulled over, thought through. Ginga waited with perfect patience.

'You're right,' I said. 'It's impossible. Under the circumstances.'

'I thought you'd agree.'

She took some papers out of her bag and laid them out on the desk.

'It's just a formal letter of release. If you could sign there . . . And I have a cheque,' she tapped an envelope, 'for what is due you for the rest of your contracted period of employment.'

'Very generous of you.'

She responded sharply to my sarcasm. 'This is nothing to do with me, you know, Hope. We're friends, or so I like to think. But that doesn't matter. I have to help Eugene. Grosso Arvore has to keep going. Without him . . . Well, you know how the place works.'

I wondered seriously, for the first time, about the true extent of Mallabar's nervous exhaustion.

I signed. Ginga smiled at me, sadly, I thought.

'There's one more thing,' she said. 'I'm very sorry.'

'What?'

'This is your original contract.' She turned some pages of the document. 'Do you remember this clause?'

I read it. I had to smile. All publications, its gist ran, based on original research carried out at Grosso Arvore, were the copyright of the Grosso Arvore Foundation, unless alternative permission were given. All data gathered was similarly protected and had to be surrendered to the Foundation for its archives on termination of employment.

'No,' I said. 'You can't do this. Forget it.'

'You will get full acknowledgement in the book. Eugene promises. I promise.'

'I don't give a fuck. You can't stop me.'

Ginga rose swiftly to her feet. 'Don't say anything more, my dear. You'll just regret it.' She spoke in her capable, maternal voice. 'I'll see you in the morning before you go. No, please, don't speak. Martim will drive you back to town.' She smiled bravely at me and left.

I went outside and smoked a cigarette. Moths bumped and skittered around the lantern that hung above the census hut's doorway. Three pale, liver-spotted geckoes clung patiently, immobile, to the wooden wall waiting for insects to settle. The air was loud with stridulating crickets and the noise of a laughing argument carried across on the breeze from the kitchen compound.

I felt an associated amusement – an oddly tearful, resigned amusement – shake my body in a weak chuckle. I paced around, smoking my cigarette ruthlessly, like a condemned man about to face a firing squad, wondering aimlessly what to do next, weighing up the few feeble options available to me. In a strange way I felt relieved, as anyone who finally acknowledges defeat does. At least one can stop struggling now, you say to yourself. At least this episode is over and a new one can start.

I sighed, I shook my head, I bayed silently at the stars in the black sky. A phrase came into my head that John had learnt in America: screwed, blued and tattooed. Yes, I thought, that's what's happened to me, I've been screwed, blued and tattooed . . .

Hauser had invited me over for a drink later, if I felt like it. I did, now, and wandered across Main Street towards his bungalow. The starshine threw the fractured shadow of the hagania tree across the dusty road. I was thinking: what should I do? Where shall I go? Who would go with me?

Hauser opened his door, smiling.

'Ah, Hope,' he said. 'Got a surprise for you.'

'No, please,' I said. 'I've had enough surprises for one night.'

I stepped over the threshold. Toshiro stood by the meat-safe opening a bottle of beer. Sitting at the table were Ian and Roberta Vail.

It turned out fine, not bad, considering, not nearly as awkward or tense as I had imagined it might be. We talked for hours about the kidnap, about Amilcar and Atomique Boum, the mission school and the attack. I told them about the last days, about the elegant gun and its too small, lilac shells, of Amilcar's stupid death and the puzzled courtesy of the Belgian mercenaries. And it was a strangely heartening, cheering conversation too, after my depressing encounter with Ginga Mallabar. There was a mild spirit of reunion in that room that night, which was encouraging. Hauser and Toshiro kept supplying us with beer, and the two new researchers – Milton and Brad, I think – were invited over to hear our war stories. Hauser's radio was tuned to a mid-European, short-wave station playing fifties jazz. Roberta smoked two or three of her menthol cigarettes, unreproved by Ian.

Ian himself looked thinner, and it surprised me for a moment to see his face clean-shaven again. He managed to maintain a convincing front of composure and self-confidence but I could sense his unease and insecurity massing edgily beneath it.

He waited until the party broke up, which was after midnight. We all stood outside Hauser's bungalow, chatting, reluctant to have the conviviality disperse abruptly. Seeing Roberta talking vivaciously to Brad or Milton, Ian chose his moment and drew me a few paces to one side.

The lantern-light cast long shadows across his face. I could not see his eyes.

'Listen, Hope,' he said quietly, his voice deep, half-strangled. 'That night, when I ran.'

'Yes.'

'I was trying to divert them. I was trying to lead them away from you. I wasn't –' he cleared his throat. 'You mustn't think I was running away. Leaving you. It was to lure them. Otherwise we'd –'

'I know,' I said simply. 'Don't be stupid. You saved me.'

I could sense rather than see his entire posture relax. This easing – of his soul, I suppose – seemed to emanate from him like a sigh. He was about to say something more when Roberta interrupted him with a called question about some dean or head of department they had known at Stanford. I touched Ian's arm reassuringly and turned away. I said good-night to Hauser and

Toshiro and the others, and walked back across Main Street to the census hut. I had told no one I was leaving the next morning.

As she had promised, Ginga was there to see me go. Alone. She was firm but sweet to me, like a fond but wise headmistress obliged to expel her favourite pupil. Stay in touch ... What will you do ...? Let's meet in London ... We behaved in an exemplary, civilized, adult way. Ginga let her guard drop for a moment and that strange embarrassment reappeared when she hinted that, when Eugene was 'well', perhaps something could be worked out. I did not ask her to specify what that something might be.

She held both my hands, kissed my cheeks and said, with almost Eugene-like sentiment, 'Ah, Hope, Hope,' and then let me go.

I decided to drive and Martim moved across to the passenger seat of the Land Rover. I wanted to experience to the full, and for the last time, that moment when we bumped on to the metalled road south at Sangui. I asked Ginga to make my farewells to the others, started the motor, waved and drove off.

In Sangui I stopped outside João's house. It was shuttered and closed.

'Where is he?' I asked Martim.

'They have moved him, Mam,' Martim said. 'He doesn't work for the project, so he can't live for the house.'

I looked at him uncomprehendingly. 'Where does he live, then?'

Martim led me down a rutted lane to an old mud hut

with a matting compound on the edge of the village. João was there, sitting at the front door with a cloth wrapped around his waist, chewing on a stick of sugar cane. It was oddly upsetting to see him idle, and out of his khaki uniform. His thin chest was covered with a scribble of grey hairs. He looked suddenly ten years older.

But he was pleased to see me and became genuinely angry when I told him I had been sacked also.

'This bad time, Mam,' he said, darkly. 'Very bad time.'

'Yes, but why *you*, João?'

'He say there is no job for me now. Now all the chimps are gone.'

'All?' I was shocked. And ashamed. I realized I had given no thought to my surviving southerners.

'Except Conrad,' he said, then shrugged. 'Maybe.'

He told me that Rita-Mae had gone missing shortly after I had left. At which point Rita-Lu had joined the northern group, now firmly, and apparently permanently, established in the southern core area. João himself had found Clovis's body two days later, minus both legs, he said, and 'very torn'. He had continued to spot Conrad periodically, up to about a week ago. But since Mallabar had sacked him he had not gone into the forest. Alda had left also, to try and find work in the city.

I suddenly knew exactly what I wanted to do. I went back to the Land Rover and told Martim to wait behind in the village for me. I told him only that I was going somewhere with João and would be back in two to three hours. He looked puzzled, but was perfectly happy to oblige. I made him promise not to return to the camp.

João and I then drove to goalpost village. It was just beyond here, João said, that the final sightings of Conrad had been made. He seemed to be lurking around the southernmost slopes of the escarpment, not far from the village. Village boys had caught him once or twice in the maize fields, and had driven him away with stones.

When we reached the village, João still refused to accompany me into the forest. Dr Mallabar had banned him from it, he insisted, and he did not wish to find himself in further trouble. When they built the new research station there might be a job for him there; it was not worth antagonizing the doctor.

So I left him with the Land Rover and trekked off up the slopes of the escarpment to search the areas where Conrad had last been seen.

I walked the bush paths that meandered through the trees above the village looking for suitable chimpanzee food sources. If Conrad was confining himself to this precise area there was a reasonable chance of finding him feeding. It was both pleasing and melancholic to be back in the forest looking for chimps for the last time. It was mid-morning by now and the sun was close to reaching its full strength. The paths were spattered with coins of sunlight and a faint breeze coming up from the valley floor made the dry leaves rattle in the tree-tops and the blonde, bleached grass sway with a parched, rustling sound. The rains were very late this year.

I walked from food source to food source, following João's directions, but with no luck. After an hour and a half of wandering some of my sentimental confidence began to evaporate and I began to rebuke myself for hatching such a preposterous plan. What was I hoping to achieve exactly? What was the purpose of this nostalgic revisiting of the southern area? And if I found Conrad, what then?

Just after noon I stopped walking and sat under a tree to eat the fishpaste sandwiches that the canteen had prepared for me. I debated whether to carry on for another hour or so, or simply make my way back to the Land Rover. This was futile and silly, I thought, this sentimental farewell, this Last Glimpse ...

I was about twenty minutes from the village when I heard the furious screaming of some colobus monkeys not far away. I ran along the path until I saw them, flinging themselves with reckless ease through the branches above and ahead of me. There were a dozen or more chasing a clumsily brachiating chimpanzee, which was hooting and yelping in fear and panic.

Conrad thumped heavily to the ground in a flurry of torn leaves, and bounded off through the undergrowth. The monkeys gave up their pursuit and returned to whatever fruit tree they had been feeding in. I followed Conrad as best I could.

I found him minutes later sitting in the lower branches of a tree scanning a small valley that lay below. He was thin and wasted-looking, and he had a red, glistening sore on one thigh, like a shiny tin badge. He looked round nervously as I approached, and I at once sank to my haunches and pretended to scrabble for seeds in the dust and dead leaves around me. I looked up fleetingly from time to time to meet Conrad's fixed and disconcerting human gaze. His brown eyes never wavered from me. I saw also that he had two scabbed-over cuts on his forehead and muzzle.

Finally he ceased to be alarmed by my presence and resumed his scrutiny of the valley.

The valley was small, cut by a stream which trickled sluggishly through livid green grass on the valley floor. At one stage the stream ran over a sharp, grey, inclined wedge of rock and fell a few feet into a shallow, pebbly pool with a noisy patter that I could hear even from my position high on the valley side.

I saw that Conrad was gazing at a clump of mesquinho bushes that grew around the pool. The mesquinho was a tall, dense bush with small, sharp leaves with a silvery underside like an olive tree. Their fruit was out, loose bunches of button-sized, black seeds which, when cracked, yielded a fuzzy salty-sweet kernel. I had eaten mesquinho fruits before. They split neatly when squeezed between thumb and forefinger. You sucked the paste off the kernel to reveal a shiny brown pip. They were good to eat when you were thirsty, some chemical in them stimulated your saliva glands.

Hungry Conrad stared at the black bunches and wondered if it was safe to go down. He watched on for half an hour before he decided to do so, picking his way cautiously, and in some discomfort, down the valley side and wading across the stream to the bushes. I watched him for a while as he ate rapidly and intently, cramming bunches of the black seeds into his mouth and chewing them up, husk and all.

I never heard anything, and neither did he, because of the patter of water flowing off the wedge-shaped rock. By the time he looked up – prompted by other noises intruding into the slap and plash of the waterfall – the other chimps were all around him.

FINESSE

John Clearwater told me that in the seventeenth century, when the calculus was first being developed, there was a protracted debate over the rigour of some of the proofs. There were gaps, the stricter mathematicians said, sums didn't quite add up, there were little inconsistencies in the definitions of certain terms. There was no refuting their arguments but, whatever their validity, there was also no denying that the calculus, all the same, was working. The results it provided were accurate and useful.

Blaise Pascal (1623–62) defended these minor inaccuracies, these nuances and ambiguities in the calculus. The formal demands of logic, he said, cannot always have the last word. If the calculus worked, but failed to measure up to the most rigorous definitions of proof, then in the end that didn't matter. The basic idea was sound. It seemed right, even if it could not be fully or pedantically justified.

On this sort of occasion, Pascal said, your intuition rates higher than rigorous proof. Rely on your heart to tell you if this is the right mathematical step to take. In cases like these the correct mental attitude to apply to the task in hand was one of 'finesse' rather than 'logic', finesse being employed here in its original sense, meaning 'delicacy of discrimination'.

I go about my business. I live in my little house on the beach. I think about what has happened to me and what I have done and wonder if I have reacted and behaved correctly. I don't know. Yet. Perhaps this is an area where I should employ Blaise Pascal's 'finesse'. I like the idea of finessing my way to a correct answer, rather than relying on the power of logical argument. Perhaps I shall finesse my way through the rest of my life?

Hope left early the next morning, once again without waking John. She went directly to Bowling Green Wood and measured coppice stools all forenoon. She considered going home at lunchtime, but decided against it. There should be a decent interval of a few hours, she felt, before they saw each other again.

They had talked until late, sensibly, with no rancour or upset on either side. John had seemed calm and resigned, not depressed and lost as she had feared. They had made all the usual promises about future friendship and contact, and had reluctantly conceded that there was nothing either of them could reasonably do that would rescue their marriage. Neither of them, they averred, had a moment's regret about the time they had spent together. And they both recognized, sadly, that to try and patch it up, to limp along in a mutually hurtful and unsatisfactory way, would be wrong, a grave error.

As she worked, Hope thought about their discussion. In herself, she felt an enormous relief, coupled with a vague dissatisfaction. It was odd, was it not, she thought, how sometimes rational and tolerant attitudes left you curiously bereft? Reasonable behaviour was the last thing you wanted. You felt as if the resolution of human problems demanded passion and brute unreason, some spitting and shouting. This absence of recrimination, of accusation and counter-accusation, the lack of long-term unspoken resentments and grudges suddenly unearthed and exposed in the heat of argument, disturbed her. Neither she nor John was that type of person so why were they being so serene and worldly-wise . . .? Because of John and his illness, she supposed. But what about him? Didn't he want to shout filthy names at her? Demean and debase her for the sake of his own wounded self-esteem? That would have been more natural, she thought, than all this low-voiced, sad sagacity.

There had been only one occasion when she had been angered. Out of the blue, he had asked her if she were having an affair. 'Is there someone else? There is, I know. Who is he? You can tell me, don't worry, I'll understand.' She stopped him from talking on in this vein by the uncompromising vehemence of her denial. She was thinking, all the time: you're a fine one to talk. And he seemed to accept her word, as suddenly as he had brought the matter up he let it drop. But perhaps she should invent a lover, she wondered? Just to make it messier, more *real* ... Perhaps she should say she was having an affair with Graham Munro, literally for the sake of argument (the notion was otherwise unimaginable, not to say hilarious, as far as she was concerned) but at least it might provoke a fur-flying spat: they could spill some bile and purge themselves of their adult rationality.

She thought on through the afternoon as she searched the underwood for flowers and grass species, taking samples here and there for confirmation and checking later. At least it wasn't raining, she thought, as she stood bareheaded in the pewtery afternoon light, beneath the stripped trees, scraping the dirt from under her fingernails with the point of her penknife.

She felt unduly tired, she realized. John's simple presence these last two days had made her ill at ease and tense. For a moment she wondered if she had the temperament for living with another man – any man, she added cynically – if she was in fact 'the marrying kind' ... But then she remembered that indeed she was:

that for a while her life with John Clearwater had been as perfect as she could ever have wished. It made her feel sad, then, and she felt a curious respect for John's restraint and tormented dignity. He had his own problems, John, that she could not share, and that she did not really understand. She resolved, as she walked home, that her mood that evening would be a fond one and charitable.

The cottage was empty when she returned, although lights and heaters throughout it were on. Her fondness and charity shrivelled and died. There was a note on the table. 'Gone for a stroll. Back for tea. J.' She changed out of her clothes, tidied up the sitting-room and kitchen, and put the kettle on the Raeburn to boil. She sat down to wait for his return.

She had no idea why the question should have arisen in her mind, but it did so with a force and conviction that were irresistible. She went outside, through the back door and down the tussocky strip of grass and beds of wind-lashed roses that was the cottage garden. There was a small green wooden shed at its foot containing a cobwebbed lawnmower and a pile of split logs. A few gardening implements hung from big rusty nails. She opened the door. The spade had gone from its place on the wall.

She stood and swore for a minute, rigid with disappointed anger. *Stupid fucking idiot. Stupid mad fucking crazy nutter bastard.* And so on. No, she couldn't be bothered with this all over again. No, she couldn't tolerate this any more. The sooner he was gone the better.

She knew where to find him.

Still trembling, positively vibrating with her anger at

him, she collected her torch from the cottage and drove down to the lake by the ruins of the old manor house. She parked at the end of the ride and walked quickly through the beech wood to the yew trees. It was almost dark and growing colder by the minute. She rounded the opaque mass of the yews to find the lake stretching ahead of her like dirty chrome. The setting of the sun was marked by a mean stripe of sulphurous yellow-grey on the horizon. The colours of the trees and bushes had virtually gone and the grassy meadows sloping down to the water were full of shadows.

She could not see him. She listened. Nothing. The wind. A wood pigeon. The filthy call of some rooks. She shouted his name several times. No reply. She played the torch-beam aimlessly about looking for any signs of his digging, but saw nothing. She shouldn't have driven down here, she now realized; he would have walked home through Blacknoll Farm and, in any case, the darkness would have brought him home soon enough. She turned and headed back towards her car.

About fifty yards beyond the yew trees, on the verge of the ride, her foot kicked the abandoned spade. Her torch-beam illuminated a few square feet of turf that had been removed, and the small hole that had been dug.

She stood, breathless, and looked around her. Her ears were filled with the noise of the ornamental falls of the stream that fed the lake, and the rush of water through the green frondy pools, flowing around the carefully positioned rocks of the overgrown grottoes and bowers.

Hope walked through the beech trees towards the stream. Pathways and steps ran beside it, mossy and worn away. This had been designed as a complementary walk to the ride, another more intimate scenic descent to the lake. At the larger pools with the more picturesque falls, carved stone benches had been placed for those who wished to pause awhile to indulge in some tailored reverie. On one of these stone benches Hope found John's wallet and a small notebook.

'John!' she shouted, vainly. 'Johnny ... Johnny it's me!'

There was no answer.

She made herself shine her torch into the pool beneath her. It was a shallow saucer, lined with stone and about twenty feet across. The waterfall that fed it was twelve feet high, but so bearded with moss and weed that the water oozed and dripped rather than fell. Black alder and willow overhung the hollow in which the pool was set, overgrown and unmanaged, a dense arbour run wild, screening the sky and cutting out whatever ambient light there was. It was dark and still, and there was a curious moist fungoid smell in the air, like a damp cellar.

The light from her torch bounced off the water surface, making it opaque and shiny. She stepped carefully down some stone treads to the pool's edge and shone the beam obliquely.

John was lying, face down, in about three or four feet of water, fully clothed, in the attitude of a shallow dive, his heels floating higher than his head. His hands appeared to be folded across his chest. The posture was stiff and unnatural: he looked like a public statue that had been toppled forward off its plinth.

Setting her torch down so that its beam shone across the pool, Hope waded in, barely registering the cold as the water flowed over the tops of her rubber boots. By the time she reached John, she was thigh-deep. She took hold of an ankle with both hands and tugged. She realized, with a small sob of grief, that his face was dragging along the pool bottom. He felt unnaturally heavy.

She reached below the surface and with enormous difficulty turned him over. He had none of that near-weightlessness, that easy, oiled manoeuvrability, that bodies supported in water normally possess. She saw why. The blunt snout of a thick fragment of paving stone – a stair tread, part of a bench? – stuck out between his tweed lapels. His jacket was buttoned tightly – three buttons – across it, and both his hands were thrust inside, double Napoleon, hugging the heavy rectangle of rock to his chest and belly.

With thick icy fingers she freed his hands and managed to unbutton the jacket. The stone rolled slowly off him, and John's wide-eyed, bloodless, utterly calm face, buoyant now, rose easily through the three feet of green water, his stiff frizzy hair – for once in his life – swaying free and fluid, until his features broke the surface and bobbed and settled there, deaf and indifferent to the shrill, ragged misery of her scream.

THE LANGUID FIRE

Every day we inhale and exhale four thousand gallons of air. How many inhalations did it take for John to fill his lungs with icy water? Two? Three?

Four thousand gallons of air a day. How we need that gas! To feed our blood, to help us burn, fuel for the languid fire that warms us inside . . . It is the coldness of

389

the dead that is so unnerving. And that perfect stillness,
too. The actor feigning death on the stage cannot fully
disguise the minute rise and fall of his chest and stomach,
cannot wholly control every minuscule twitch and shudder
of his hundreds of muscles. He is not still. The systems
inside him pump and sift, decompose and consume. But
the absolute stillness of the dead is manifestly non-human.
The inert, inanimate body is a thing – all that motion has
stopped for ever. The human being has become a roll of
carpet, a sack of potatoes, a log of wood.

I started yelling and shouting crazily as I slithered down
the valley side towards them, but the chimpanzees
appeared not to hear me, or pay any attention. In any
event, the noise they were making themselves was enormous, and Conrad was screaming viciously in pain and
terror. I could see Darius beating his head remorselessly
with both fists, as Sebastian and Pulul held him down.

I ran across the valley floor towards the mesquinho
bushes, shouting constantly, one hand searching in my
shoulder bag for Usman's gun.

There were eight adult males attacking Conrad, each
one many times stronger than a strong man. As I waded
through the livid green grass at the stream's edge the
thought of what might happen if they turned on me
made me stop with a lurch of horrible fear. For a
second I didn't move. Then I heard Conrad's screams
reach a new intensity, before suddenly cutting off.

They were all on the other side of the stream from
me, thrashing around the mesquinho bushes, leaping on
Conrad's body in their mad excitement. I fired the gun
in the air and they whirled round, chattering and screech-

ing. Darius ripped a branch off a mesquinho bush and beat the ground with it. Americo and Pulul dashed across the stream towards me, displaying, howling, their yellow teeth bared. Darius reared back on his legs, fur bristling, arms held wide. The noise was grotesque, like a metallic tearing sound, reverberating everywhere, raw and coarse.

'*GO AWAY!*' I screamed at them, levelling the gun. '*RUN AWAY! RUN AWAY!*' But what was a gun to them, *Homo troglodytes*? And what was I? Just another strange, bipedal ape, displaying, noisy, threatening.

Two others crossed the stream. Pulul rushed a few paces at me, stopped and retreated. Darius screamed, frenziedly tearing branches of the mesquinho bushes. I saw Americo lift a stone from the stream bed and lob it clumsily in my direction. Pulul was leaping up and down, thumping the ground with his hands about twelve feet to my left. Gaspar was inching forward on my right. My eyes flicked to the mesquinho bushes, wondering if there was any sign of Conrad.

Then Pulul charged me.

My first shot caught him in the chest, high on one side, and knocked him spinning off his feet. Then Darius leapt across the stream and galloped towards me. I shot him full in the face when he was about six feet away. I saw shards of his disintegrating skull fly up into the air like spun coins. I turned and fired at Sebastian and Gaspar as they fled, but I missed. Then they were all gone, bounding away out of the valley, screaming in panic.

Then it was silent again. There were no bird calls, just the sound of water pattering off the rock.

Pulul was still alive. I walked carefully over to him,

watching a leg twitch and move irregularly. He was turned away from me and I could see that the exit wound had left a hole in his back the size of my fist. I fired into his head from a range of two feet.

Darius lay on his back, his arms spread like a sunbather. The top of his head, from his eye sockets upward, had either disappeared or had been reduced to a long clotted fringe of expressed flesh and bone.

I waded across the stream to look for Conrad. I found him twisted and bloody under the mesquinho bushes. His right hand had been torn off at the wrist, and he waved the stump at me in parody aggression. His face was red and pulpy, minced by Darius's fists and nails. But his brown eyes looked at me as directly as ever. Accusing? Pleading? Hostile? Baffled?

I crouched round behind him, so he couldn't see me, and fired once into the top of his head from six inches away.

I sat down on a rock for a while. When I stopped shivering I wet my face in the stream. Then I filled a pocket with mesquinho nuts, skirted the bodies of Darius and Pulul and walked back to the village where João was waiting patiently for me.

I felt much better. I was glad I had killed Darius and Pulul. I was glad I had been there to end Conrad's suffering. I recovered my nerve and calm quickly. I knew my conscience would never be troubled, because I had done the right thing, for once.

The chimpanzee wars were over.

EPILOGUE

I look out on the beach. A heavy shower of rain has just passed over. In the sun the warm teak planks of my deck steam visibly, as if a vat were bubbling beneath them. Out at sea the sky is filled with the soft baggy furniture of clouds – the dented bean-bags and winded sofas, the exploding kapok cushions. The wind hurries them away, and leaves the beach to everyone and me, washed and smooth.

My house, you will have guessed a while ago, was Usman's. His legacy to me. I spent most of my severance pay from Grosso Arvore renovating it and moved in as soon as the roof was on. I had his fine drawings of his horse-fly aeroplanes framed and they hang now on my sitting-room wall above my bookcases. Usman with his vivid dreams of flight . . .

And they were dreams. I bought a book (I don't know why – because I missed him, I suppose), a history of the exploration of outer space. On reflection, I should not have been that surprised, but I have to tell you it came as something of a shock to learn that there were no Egyptian astronauts. Not one. There were Vietnamese, Indian, Syrian, Mexican and Saudi Arabian, but not a single Egyptian. But Usman's lie does not really bother me: the dream enchanted for a moment, which gives it a kind of validity, I would have thought.

Usman has been much in my mind, recently. A week ago, the newspapers were full of a bizarre story. In a Latin American country an insurance claim was filed for a Mig 15 Fagot that had crashed on take-off. When the loss adjusters examined the wreckage it was discovered – from serial numbers on certain components – that this very jet had crashed before, here, in this country, a year previously, victim of a navaid failure while returning from a raid on FIDE positions in the central highlands. The plane had been lost without trace.

It has since transpired that, of the eight Migs lost to navaid failures, the wreckage of only three was ever located. There has been a hum of scandal in the air; the noise is all sour accusation. A former minister of defence has been forced to resign over his business connections with a Middle East arms dealer. Nothing can be proved, but there is a powerful suspicion that, while the war was at its height, these jets were being systematically stolen by their pilots, flown to a foreign country, repainted and covertly sold.

Of course, I realize there were some genuine navaid failures, some genuine crashes, so who can say? Who can be sure of anything? But I have my own strong intuitions, and a curious feeling that one day the former owner of this beach house may pass by to check on the renovations.

And, strangely enough, everywhere I go now, I think I see him. There are many Syrians and Lebanese here, and my glance is always lighting on bearded or moustachioed men (somehow I imagine he would grow a beard . . .).

It reminds me of that time before I met John Clearwater, when my life was gravid with the anticipation of our encounter; the air thickened with the imminence of that meeting.

I step out on to the deck and squint out to sea, over the refulgent ocean, the sun warm on my face.

John Clearwater.

I had hoped there would be a message in the notebook he left on that stone bench, but there was nothing, apart from some scrawled, runic equations. So I am left with my imagination, and I imagine that he did everything spontaneously, in a matter of seconds. He started to dig and, suddenly, could not tolerate what the future held for him and walked to the pond. It is the future that bears down on the suicide – all that time, waiting.

John selected his slab of stone, eased it out of its mossy socket, hugged it to him and waded out to the centre of the pond and fell forward. One deep, open-mouthed breath would be enough. What cannot be avoided, must be welcomed, as Amilcar had told me.

I look at my watch. I have an appointment with Ginga in an hour. I still work for the project, you might be surprised to learn. I meet people off planes, organize transport and supplies in town for the two research stations. It was Ginga's idea: now they were twice as large, the project needed a contact here, an administrator. They pay me reasonably well; there is no shortage of funds since the book was published. *Primate: the society of a great ape*. Look it up, check it out. Read the large footnote on page 74. 'We acknowledge here the invaluable work of Dr Hope Clearwater . . .'

I have not been back to Grosso Arvore – Ginga thinks it prudent to stay away – but I have seen Eugene Mallabar three times, briefly. He greets me fondly, but with a distant pomposity – a false avuncular charm. 'My dear Hope...', 'Ah, Hope, bless you ..' He spends more time in America these days, lecturing. Ginga and Hauser run the research stations on a day-to-day basis. Nothing has ever been said about that time in the forest. And no one, as far as I know, ever found the bodies of Pulul, Darius and Conrad.

I walk down the steps on to the beach. The heavy rain has levelled the ridges and obliterated the footprints. The sand is dimpled like a golf ball, firm and damp.

What now? What next? All these questions. All these doubts. So few certainties. But then I have taken new comfort and refuge in the doctrine that advises one not to seek tranquillity in certainty, but in permanently suspended judgement.

I walk along the beach enjoying my indecision, my moral limbo. But it never lasts for long. The beach endures, the waves roll in.

Two dogs appear from the treeline and sniff at the tidewrack. My beefy Syrian neighbour jogs down from his beach house in a pair of indigo swimming-trunks. He waves cheerfully at me. 'The sea is always fresher after rain,' he shouts, and sashays confidently into the surf. I wave back. A boy watches three goats graze in the palm groves. A crab sidles into its hole. Someone laughs raucously in the village. The webbed shadow of the volley-ball net is sharp on the smooth sand. I examine these documents of the real carefully, these days. The unexamined life is not worth living.

READ MORE IN PENGUIN

In every corner of the world, on every subject under the sun, Penguin represents quality and variety – the very best in publishing today.

For complete information about books available from Penguin – including Puffins, Penguin Classics and Arkana – and how to order them, write to us at the appropriate address below. Please note that for copyright reasons the selection of books varies from country to country.

In the United Kingdom: Please write to *Dept. JC, Penguin Books Ltd, FREEPOST, West Drayton, Middlesex UB7 0BR*

If you have any difficulty in obtaining a title, please send your order with the correct money, plus ten per cent for postage and packaging, to *PO Box No. 11, West Drayton, Middlesex UB7 0BR*

In the United States: Please write to *Penguin USA Inc., 375 Hudson Street, New York, NY 10014*

In Canada: Please write to *Penguin Books Canada Ltd, 10 Alcorn Avenue, Suite 300, Toronto, Ontario M4V 3B2*

In Australia: Please write to *Penguin Books Australia Ltd, 487 Maroondah Highway, Ringwood, Victoria 3134*

In New Zealand: Please write to *Penguin Books (NZ) Ltd,182–190 Wairau Road, Private Bag, Takapuna, Auckland 9*

In India: Please write to *Penguin Books India Pvt Ltd, 706 Eros Apartments, 56 Nehru Place, New Delhi 110 019*

In the Netherlands: Please write to *Penguin Books Netherlands B.V., Keizersgracht 231 NL-1016 DV Amsterdam*

In Germany: Please write to *Penguin Books Deutschland GmbH, Friedrichstrasse 10–12, W-6000 Frankfurt/Main 1*

In Spain: Please write to *Penguin Books S. A., C. San Bernardo 117–6 E-28015 Madrid*

In Italy: Please write to *Penguin Italia s.r.l., Via Felice Casati 20, I-20124 Milano*

In France: Please write to *Penguin France S. A., 17 rue Lejeune, F-31000 Toulouse*

In Japan: Please write to *Penguin Books Japan, Ishikiribashi Building, 2-5-4, Suido, Bunkyo-ku, Tokyo 112*

In Greece: Please write to *Penguin Hellas Ltd, Dimocritou 3, GR-106 71 Athens*

In South Africa: Please write to *Longman Penguin Southern Africa (Pty) Ltd, Private Bag X08, Bertsham 2013*

READ MORE IN PENGUIN

A CHOICE OF BESTSELLERS

Paradise News   David Lodge

'Lodge could never be solemn and the book crackles with good jokes . . . leaves you with a mild and thoughtful glow of happiness' – *Sunday Telegraph*. 'Amusing, accessible, intelligent . . . the story rolls, the sparks fly' – *Financial Times*

Scoundrel   Bernard Cornwell

Five million dollars in gold will buy fifty-three Stinger missiles, which may be for the IRA but might have more to do with Iraq's invasion of Kuwait. Or that kind of money will buy retirement for the man hired to sail it from Morocco to Miami – if, that is, he can outwit the IRA, CIA, British Intelligence, infamous Palestinian terrorist il Hayaween, and the ghost of his lost love Roisin.

Devices and Desires   P. D. James

'Like the wind-lashed Norfolk headland buffeted by the sea, which is so tangily evoked, *Devices and Desires* always has an intensely bracing chill to its atmosphere' – Peter Kemp in the *Sunday Times*

Doctor Criminale   Malcolm Bradbury

'The best novel so far about post-modernism. With grace and wit its author deconstructs fifty years of European thought and history' – *Observer*. 'A playful, smart and entertaining work of art with deadly serious underpinnings' – *The New York Times Book Review*

The Burden of Proof   Scott Turow

'Rarely has a plot as political, as sexual, as criminal, as moral, so lip-smackingly thickened . . . A wonderful read from tight start to taut end' – *Mail on Sunday*. 'Expert and excellent . . . a new sort of novel – a detective story full of people on the make, on the break or settling for second best: [a] riveting tale' – *Evening Standard*

READ MORE IN PENGUIN

A CHOICE OF BESTSELLERS

Brightness Falls Jay McInerney

'The story of a disintegrating marriage set in New York in the frenzied few months leading up to the Wall Street crash of 1987. It is his biggest, most ambitious novel yet – a sort of *Bonfire of the Vanities* with the added advantage of believable, likeable characters' – Lynn Barber in the *Independent on Sunday*

Chicago Loop Paul Theroux

'Like *Doctor Slaughter*, this novel watches a character blunder to disaster through emotionless, anonymous sex . . . [a] fast-paced horror-excursion into what Theroux once called "subterranean gothic"' – *Sunday Times*

The Russian Girl Kingsley Amis

'Dazzling skill with dialogue and . . . no less dazzling ability to conjure up minor characters – policemen, academics, businessmen, Russian émigrés – who, for all their hilarious oddity, somehow remain believable' – *Evening Standard*

Dunster John Mortimer

'Masterly . . . Part thriller, part observer of current mores, realistic yet full of ambiguities, Dunster raises every kind of question, moral and psychological, while spinning along at a cracking pace' – *Financial Times*

Rum Punch Elmore Leonard

For bail bondsman Max Cherry, control is slipping away fast. His ex just moved in with some Cuban artist, the mob is into his business, and he's broken the golden rule: never fall in love with a client . . . 'A brilliant and subversive book' – A. Alvarez in the *Sunday Telegraph*

BY THE SAME AUTHOR

A Good Man in Africa

'After Evelyn Waugh came Kingsley Amis; after Amis, Tom Sharpe; after Sharpe, William Boyd' – *Yorkshire Post*

Morgan Leafy isn't overburdened with worldly success. Actually he is refreshingly free from it. But then, as a representative of Her Britannic Majesty in tropical Kinjanja, it was not exactly oiling his way up the ladder to hunt down the improbably pointed breasts of his boss's daughter. Nor was it very constructive of him to get involved in wholesale bribery with sensitive local politicians . . .

'Wickedly funny' – *The Times*

Winner of a 1981 Whitbread Literary Award

Winner of the 1982 Somerset Maugham Award

A Good Man in Africa is also available in Penguin Audiobooks, read by Timothy Spall.

An Ice-Cream War

As millions are slaughtered on the Western Front, a ridiculous and little remarked-on campaign is being waged in East Africa – a war that continued after the Armistice because no one told them to stop.

Primarily a gripping story of the men and women swept up by the passions of love and battle, William Boyd's magnificently entertaining novel also elicits the cruel futility and tragedy of it all.

'A towering achievement' – John Carey, Chairman of the Booker Prize Judges 1982

'Quite outstanding' – *Sunday Times*

'If you can imagine John Buchan or Rider Haggard rewritten by Evelyn Waugh then you have something of the flavour of this book . . . Very funny' – Robert Nye in the *Guardian*

BY THE SAME AUTHOR

The New Confessions

The New Confessions is the outrageous, extraordinary, hilarious and heartbreaking autobiography of John James Todd, a Scotsman born in 1899 and one of the great self-appointed (and failed) geniuses of the twentieth century.

'An often magnificent feat of story-telling and panoramic reconstruction ... John James Todd's reminiscences carry us through the ups and downs of a long and lively career that begins in genteel Edinburgh, devastatingly detours out to the Western Front, forks off after a period of cosy family life in London, to the electric excitements of the Berlin film-world of the Twenties, then moves to Hollywood to ordeal by McCarthyism and eventually escape to Europe' – *Observer*

School Ties

Public School – bizarre hothouse? Hell on earth? The time of your life? At the most formative and turbulent time of their lives, five per cent of our male adolescents go into exile, locked into the cold, badly equipped edifices of the single-sex boarding school.

William Boyd's wonderfully comic and darkly questioning screenplays, *Good and Bad at Games* and *Dutch Girls* (both televised), recreate with painful intimacy the farce and bravado, the rigid codes and the sometimes absurdly tragic pretensions of that most extraordinary of forcing grounds.

Stars and Bars

Sent south to the sunbelt by his art-dealer firm on a delicate mission to persuade millionaire Loomis Gage to part with his priceless collection of Impressionists, Henderson encounters increasingly comic, grotesque and deeply embarrassing failures in his ability to 'relate' ...

'Boyd can turn a predictable joke to gold' – *Sunday Telegraph*

'Speed, skill and fun ... the intricacies of the slithering plot leave you weak with suspense and laughter' – *Listener*

BY THE SAME AUTHOR

The Blue Afternoon

His new bestseller

Winner of the 1993 *Sunday Express* Book of the Year Award

'William Boyd has always, and justifiably, been described as a great storyteller ... here he creates a world both elegiac and hopeful, and achingly memorable' – Nigella Lawson in *The Times*

Los Angeles, 1936, Kay Fischer, a young, independent and ambitious architect, is shadowed by Salvador Carriscant, a compelling and enigmatic stranger who claims to be her father. Within weeks of their first meeting, Kay will join him for an extraordinary journey into the old man's past, initially in search of a murderer, but finally in celebration of a glorious, undying love.

'The finest storyteller of his generation. I would rate this book as the best, and the least cynical, of Boyd's novels, apart from *The New Confessions*. And I am sure that I could not say more in its praise' – David Holloway in the *Daily Telegraph*

The Blue Afternoon is also available in Penguin Audiobooks, read by Kate Harper.

On the Yankee Station

Adolescent sex in a Scottish boys' public school, oddballs on the seedy side of America, murder in a quiet Devon cottage ... Comical, ironical or lacerating wit is the keynote of these stories, which include two early adventures from the career of Morgan Leafy, glorious anti-hero of William Boyd's prize-winning novel, *A Good Man in Africa*.

'Mr Boyd is set fair for a dazzling career' – *Spectator*

'His writing, with nods in the direction of Borges and Nabokov, combines violence, comedy and experiment ... a publisher's dream' – *Time Out*

'He takes on depressing netherworlds like glitterless Los Angeles. He tells of failures, obsessions, hopeless loves ... and he's funny, witty and wise' – *Company*